# HAVEN

## JOHN PEYTON COOKE

**THE MYSTERIOUS PRESS**

Published by Warner Books

A Time Warner Company

Mysterious Press books are published by Warner Books, Inc.,
1271 Avenue of the Americas, New York, NY 10020.

A Time Warner Company

The Mysterious Press name and logo are registered trademarks of Warner Books, Inc.

Printed in the United States of America

First printing: August 1996

10 9 8 7 6 5 4 3 2 1

Library of Congress Cataloging-in-Publication Data

Cooke, John Peyton
    Haven / John Peyton Cooke.
       p.   cm.
    ISBN 0-89296-610-6
    I. Title.
    PS3553.O5565H38   1996
    813'.54—dc20                                          96-13688
                                                             CIP

This book is for
*Keng*


*Dear camerado! I confess I have urged you onward*
  *with me, and still urge you, without the least*
  *idea what is our destination,*
*Or whether we shall be victorious, or utterly quell'd*
  *and defeated.*

—WALT WHITMAN

# HAVEN

# I
# Harbinger

# Chapter 1

"We've been put in a bit of a spot," Tim Vandam said over the telephone. "Had what you might call a priority request. From Idaho. They're in with us, too, you know. They don't have a medical college of their own, and they've been having a devil of a time filling rural spots, so naturally they turn to us. Haven, it's called—a very small town somewhere up in the mountains. They had two doctors till some years back when one passed on, and they've had to make do since then with just the one, and now *he's* retiring. They're in a bloody hurry, I'm sorry to say. Sorry for you *and* for us. Rather unusual, I must admit."

"But I'm supposed to go to Colville. I thought it was all set." Cecilia had been looking forward to Colville: five years at an economically depressed reservation in eastern Washington where she could really do some good. She had been to Colville already, met some of the people, even looked at some houses. It wasn't going to be easy, but she was certain it would have its rewards.

"So did I, and believe me, I don't like it any more than you do. But the game has changed, and you seem the one best suited to the Haven post, quite frankly. They're on a much faster track. They'd like you to go out next week—that is, if it's not too much trouble—"

"For an interview?"

"No, no need for that. They trust our judgment on you, as well they should. They want you to go on out there and start work so the old boy can retire."

"Come on, Tim." She laughed uneasily. "A week's much too soon. Mike hasn't even given notice yet at the paper—"

"Cecilia, please—"

"I thought we had another month. Can't their doctor wait a little longer?"

"That's not our decision to make," Vandam said shortly. "Of course, I wish they'd called us sooner, but . . ." He trailed off, as if hoping Cecilia would jump in and save him, but she simply hung there on the line until he picked up his script. "I think this is a good move for you, actually. Though you can still say no."

"No," she said.

Vandam chuckled, as if she had been making a joke. "Better hear what they're offering first. They're prepared to give you half again the salary as Colville, as well as the complete use of a much larger home, *rent-free*, during your commitment. You'll make out much better, especially when you consider—and you'll pardon me, please, for sticking in my nose where it truly doesn't belong—but you'll no longer be able to count on your husband's income after the move."

Cecilia sighed. Of course he was right; they were hardly in a position to be choosy. "Okay. Let me talk it over with Mike first."

"Fair enough, Cecilia, fair enough." Vandam sounded relieved. "Call me when you've reached a decision. Sorry again to be ringing so late."

"I'll call in the morning and let you know, Tim."

"You can ring me tonight, if you like. I mean, I'll be up—not waiting for your call, really, just busy with other things—bits and pieces, you know—so you wouldn't be bothering me in the slightest if you should happen to—"

"All right, Tim. Bye."

Cecilia hung up and simply sat there for a minute, wondering why Tim Vandam had sounded nervous.

She crawled out of bed and into her bathrobe and went off to look for Mike, whom she found standing before the refrigerator in complete undress, drinking whole milk from the lip of the carton, the refrigerator light warming his skin against the shadows and gloomy blues of their apartment.

"You've got a milk mustache," Cecilia said.

"Only kind I can grow," Mike said, which was true. His facial hair grew only on his upper lip and on the point of his chin, and it took him only a few seconds every morning to shave them. Once, not long after they had started living together, Cecilia had innocently asked him to grow them out, but he had protested he would look like Charlie Chan or Fu Manchu or Emperor Ming of the planet Mongo. She had wanted to tell him she thought it would look cute but held her tongue for fear he would think her racist. She wondered if, in a kind of reverse way, she was. She had never been attracted to white guys. Throughout high school and college, she had only dated black men, Latinos, Native Americans, and, at last, Mike.

He closed the door of the fridge, set down the carton, and held her close, mashing the soft terry cloth against her breasts, clutching the small of her back. "Who was that on the phone?"

"Tim Vandam."

"Oh." Nuzzling her cheek.

"They've changed my assignment. Colville's out."

"Too bad." Whispering in her ear, his teeth scraping her lobe. "Can they do that?"

"I guess so. I signed my life away when I joined up. Now they're sending us to some little Podunk town in Idaho."

"Mmm. Sun Valley? Ski country?"

"Haven."

"Heaven?"

"Haven. I don't know where it is."

"Oh, well." Rolling his eyes and planting a milky kiss on her forehead. "How could it be more Podunk than Colville? And what do I care? I'll be with you."

"You're a smoothie, Mike."

"You think so?" Untying her robe and pushing it gently back over her shoulders and onto the floor, splaying it out like a throw rug, lying down upon it, smiling up an invitation, grabbing her wrist and pulling her down on top of him, closing his eyes, parting his lips.

Cecilia straddled his hard muscles and leaned over to kiss him. He knit his fingers through her hair and held her fast. The milk on his lips was warm and sweet.

She had neglected to tell him they would be moving in a week rather than a month and that he would have to give his notice tomorrow. She didn't want to ruin the moment. It would have to wait because now he could not, and for that matter, neither could she.

"Ha-ven," Mike sang, softly. "I'm in Ha-ven—"

"Shh." Cecilia pressed her fingers against his lips. "We're not there yet."

# Chapter 2

Mike was transcribing pertinent quotes from his tape of last night's city council meeting when Tawanda Neebli came up to his desk and stretched his headphones apart.

"Emergency staff meeting in the chief's office," she shouted.

"What meeting?"

"Come on, don't keep everybody waiting."

Grumbling, Mike shut off his tape recorder and followed.

The *Post-Intelligencer* city editor's office was an old-fashioned windowed enclosure—not a padded cubicle like Mike's—and for once the slats of his venetian blinds were closed. Mike finally caught on that this wasn't a meeting at all.

Tawanda fell back, letting him open the door.

"Surprise!" shouted the reporters crammed inside.

The lights were off, the office illuminated only by the candles on the cake.

"Oh, Jesus," Mike said, and felt himself blushing.

"Got you," Tawanda said. "Blow them out. I'm starving."

"You thought we'd let you get away with turning in your

last story and ducking out?" said Alex Kondrashin, the city editor.

Mike leaned over and blew out the candles, making a wish that the move would go off without a hitch. The movers were some outfit he had never heard of, courtesy of Tim Vandam and the Rural Physicians Program. He would rather have rented a U-Haul and done it himself.

There was a smattering of applause, and Tawanda turned on the lights.

"Here," she said, handing Mike a plastic knife.

"Thanks a lot."

"I want a piece with a flower," said Janine Thomas.

"You got it."

The cake was glazed in mocha brown and decorated with two oblong lumps that were apparently supposed to be potatoes—though they had smiley faces on them—with pale potato flowers and green twisting vines that spelled out GOOD LUCK, SPUD!

"I thought it said stud," Mike said.

"Well, that goes without saying," said Tawanda.

"Our last chance to rib you," said Ken Boman. "Still don't know why you'd want to move to Idaho."

"It wasn't exactly up to me," Mike said, serving up gooey slices. He had suffered enough jokes this week; anonymous potatoes had been left on his desk and in his drawers. "It won't be that bad. It's up in the mountains."

"What are you going to do with all that free time?" Alex asked. When Mike had broken the news to him, he had scowled and told him he should think about his own career first, not his wife's. He thought Mike was making a big mistake. Mostly, he was sore about losing a good reporter he had been grooming since Mike was an intern. Today was the first time all week Mike had seen Alex smile.

"I don't know—write a novel, probably," Mike said.

"About us, I bet," Janine said.

"Don't flatter yourself," Tawanda said, mouth full of cake.

"Well, I was thinking of writing a murder mystery in which this cigar-smoking city editor is pushed out the window by a disgruntled employee. He leaves behind a suicide note, so the cops think he killed himself. But his star reporter looks at the note and sees that he misused 'comprise'—so the reporter figures someone was holding a gun to the editor's head."

"If you write about us," Alex said, "I will come to Idaho and personally kill you."

"Just kidding. I'm thinking of something more ambitious."

"Open your gift," Tawanda said, nudging him.

He held up the wrapped package—obviously a book.

"Some inspiration for you," Ken said.

He had barely torn the edge of the wrapping paper when Tawanda said, "It's a first edition."

"Maxine Hong Kingston! *Tripmaster Monkey*." He had a trade paperback he had read twice but had never seen it in hardcover before. He held it up proudly. "My favorite novel."

"We know," Janine said, rolling her eyes.

"Thanks, guys."

"We thought you'd like to bring a little bit of culture with you to the backwoods," Tawanda said. "All they read there is Louis L'Amour and Rush Limbaugh."

Alex popped open a bottle of champagne and poured it into plastic cups that were passed around.

"Speech!" Janine said.

"I'm going to miss you guys," Mike said. "I don't know what else to say. Alex, can you hold my job for me? I'll be back in five years."

"If we're still here." Alex crossed his fingers nervously.

*    *    *

9

After the party, Tawanda took Mike back to her desk.

"I've got something else for you," she said.

She handed him a file folder. He opened it up and fanned through the pages. It was filled with various articles under Tawanda's byline.

"Oh, thanks. Your string book."

"No, stupid, look closer."

The clippings spanned the last two years, and he quickly realized they were Tawanda's series on right-wing hate groups of the Northwest. One of the articles had won an award from a local chapter of the Anti-Defamation League. It represented her best work, but Mike had read them all before.

"Thanks," he said. "Why are you giving me this?"

"I just want you to be careful. Idaho is full of nuts."

"I'm sure that's just a small minority."

"I don't know. . . . You remember those threats I got when these pieces ran. I'm not sure I ever want to go back there."

"But these groups are all up north, right? In the panhandle?"

"Yeah, around Coeur d'Alene. Gorgeous place, but those people kind of ruin it. The Aryan Nation Church is up there. I interviewed one of their leaders on his front porch. He was nice enough, but when I got back to my car, all the tires were slashed. They didn't make it easy."

"That's nowhere near where I'm going. Haven's down south."

"I'm just saying you should watch out. Lots of fringy folk all over—Mormons, John Birchers, and worse."

Mike leafed through the pages, noting the names of the groups: the Idaho Militia, the Knights of the Ku Klux Klan, the Mountain Church, the National Alliance, the Posse Comitatus, the Socialist Nationalist Aryan People's Party, the White American Bastion, the White American Resistance, the White

Student Union. As Tawanda's pieces pointed out, northwestern white supremacists had been implicated in nearly twenty murders since 1980, the victims usually Jews, blacks, or homosexuals. Right here in Seattle they had bombed a gay disco, killing and injuring several patrons. They had gone on record as saying that they wanted the states of Washington, Oregon, and Idaho all to themselves as a whites-only "Aryan nation." They were preparing for a "coming racial war" and called themselves not racists but racialists. Some young skinheads lived in the cities, but most white supremacists were older, with families, and tended to gather together in rural areas where they could thrive, openly march in Nazi uniforms, carry weird flags, wear swastikas on their sleeves.

"You don't think I'll really run into any trouble, do you?"

"I'm just saying keep your eyes open. Not likely to be a lot of other Chinese where you're going."

"I've got a right to go wherever I want."

"Huh." Tawanda snorted. "America's the home of slavery and Jim Crow. Whites were burning crosses in Dubuque, Iowa, just a couple of years ago. Even if there's only one nut in Haven, you'd be wise to watch your back."

"Okay," he said. "I will. I promise."

"Forewarned is forearmed. I'd say good luck, but you've always been one lucky son of a bitch. You'd probably have my job before long if you stuck around here."

"In that case, you should say good riddance."

"Don't tempt me."

"God, I hate mushy good-byes."

# Chapter 3

They had been on the road since before dawn but still had forty miles to go before they slept. They stopped in Elliott, a small town made up of a sad handful of clapboard shops and homes planted at the edge of the Salmon National Forest. They pulled up to the pump island at Ernie's Self-Serve Gas & Fly Store, above the steep gorge where the Little Lost River commingled with the Salmon—also known to the locals as the River of No Return. The air was cool and still, the first stars gleaming.

Cecilia got out and stretched her limbs and filled up the gas tank for what would be their final leg, while Mike grabbed his tool kit and went to take a look at the engine. As they had driven higher up into the Sawtooths, the car had been losing power. It was Mike's baby, a '76 Chevy Camaro Rally Sport with a 350 V-8 and dual glasspack exhausts, and it was a good car, but the carburetor was adjusted for sea level, and they were higher than eight thousand feet. The speedometer had begun falling around Castle Peak as they drove on under a gray, anvil-shaped cumulonimbus that rained cold layers onto their windshield and challenged their defroster. Half an hour later, with bright sun and a rainbow over Greylock Mountain, they were able to roll their windows back down, but by then Mike was having to floor the accelerator just to get up to forty, and even retirees in their Winnebagos were passing them. The highway had been carved out above the swath of the Salmon, whose dull roar followed them all the way to the service station at Elliott. By then they were within an hour of Haven.

An old man with a fragile underbite and a few days' growth of peppery beard stood on the porch of Ernie's Self-Serve Gas & Fly Store, watching Cecilia and grinning. He acknowledged her with a lift of his fly- and lure-covered canvas hat and popped open a sixteen-ounce can of Coors, spraying a burst of foam onto his fishing vest and all down his hands.

"Goddammit," he muttered, shaking his fingers.

Cecilia replaced the gas cap in its hidey-hole behind the license plate and hung the nozzle back up on the pump and asked Mike if he wanted anything from inside.

"Just some flies." He remained bent over the black engine, his work gloves already greasy. The sunlight was nearly all gone; if it took him any longer Cecilia would have to assist him with a flashlight. He grunted as he turned the wrench. Metal clanged dully. "And some worms," he added.

"Be careful what you wish for," Cecilia said, and went inside to pay. The tattered screen door banged shut behind her like a teacher's ruler against a desk, and a jolt shot up her spine. The old man was now standing behind the cash register and reeking of beer, listening to a thundering preacher on the radio who may as well have been speaking a foreign language as far as Cecilia was concerned. She had stopped going to church shortly after the death of her mother.

*"Ask yourselves if you are prepared. . . ."*

"How-do," the old man said.

"Hi," Cecilia said.

Outside, the fluorescent lights flickered to life against the twilit sky. Mike, under the shadow of the hood, remained visible only from his running shoes to his glutes, his faded blue jeans snug around his muscular thighs.

"Pump number two?" the old man said as if he had all the time in the world. "That'll be twenty-five."

Cecilia handed him a crisp twenty and ten. He examined them front and back and held them up to the light, squinting.

*"The Lord is coming, my friends, make no mistake. . . ."*

Outside, Mike stood upright and slammed down the hood, fully visible now in the stark lights. A smear of black engine grease graced his cheek like war paint. He got back inside the car and it rumbled pleasantly to life, with none of the sputtering, coughing, or hesitation that had been plaguing it.

"That your car?" The old man was staring out at Mike.

"That's us." No one else had pulled up to the station. No other pump was in use. "There a problem?"

"Nope."

"Then could I have my change, please?"

He handed her five filthy singles, his jaw grimly set.

*"And He will reign for a thousand years. . . ."*

"That's the Haven turnoff up there, isn't it?" Cecilia pointed along US 93 to an unmarked T intersection that lay ahead in the shadows near the bridge over the Little Lost.

"Haven?" He snapped her a suspicious glance. "You goin' up there with your boyfriend?" His fingers darted back and forth, from her to Mike and back.

"Husband," Cecilia said.

The old man shook his head, *tsk*ing, and said, "Let me show you somethin'." He unbuttoned his work shirt and pulled down his right sleeve to display a flabby bicep etched with a blue bulldog over the initials USMC. "You ever heard of Guadalcanal, missy? My buddies and me in that jungle . . . we were

14

mowed down like jackrabbits." His voice became sandpaper, and his thin lips quivered as he tried to hold back the water from his eyes. "That was the last time I ever saw anybody looked like your husband, up close and personal. Japanese soldier, he was. Younger than me—seventeen, maybe. I'll never forget that face. Looked me straight in the eye, he did, just before I run him through."

Cecilia felt her throat constrict. All she could think to say was that Mike wasn't Japanese, but she said nothing.

"He got me in the foot. I buried it on that island."

"I . . . I'm sorry." She started to go.

The old man spat a gob of chewing tobacco into an empty coffee can by the register with a *ping*. "Ain't no one like him in Haven."

"Excuse me?"

"*His millennium is at hand, fellow Americans. Ask yourselves if you are prepared to face His judgment. . . .*"

"Good luck to you, missy," the old man said. He turned up the volume on his radio.

Cecilia left without another word. The breeze caught the screen door and kept it from closing. The sky was darker, and already she could make out more stars than one could ever see in Seattle. A chill wind sprang up.

"*Up from the grave He arose,*" sang the preacher's choir over the radio. Cecilia cringed; that had been one of the hymns sung at her mother's funeral. She was eight years old, towered over by her brothers and all the grown-ups, and her eyes were too tearful for her to follow along in the hymnal—she thought they were singing "*Up from the gravy, a rose.*" It boomed out in her father's basso voice, sounding absurd and unholy. And all through the service, as she stared up at her mother's pallid face in profile in the casket, she saw in her mind's eye a single long-stemmed red rose rising of its own accord from a dish of gray Thanksgiving gravy.

She clutched the goose bumps on her bare shoulders and chafed them briskly. Mike swung open her door, and she fell into the warm bucket seat that had been her home all day.

"What took you so long?" His face glowed comfortingly in the dome light.

Cecilia gave him a resounding kiss on the lips and felt the scratch of light stubble on his chin.

"Mmm," he said as they broke. "What's that for?"

"Nothing. The car sounds perfect. You're a genius."

"Super genius," he corrected. He looked over his shoulder as he backed out. "Like Wile E. Coyote."

Mike turned on his headlights and pulled out onto US 93. Cecilia pointed out the Haven turnoff ahead in the darkness. With a glance out the back window, she saw that the old man was staring out at them now from his porch and opening another Coors.

# Chapter 4

The Haven Road was a steep, wending way—corkscrew bends and blind curves without benefit of guardrails, above the blackened ravine of the Little Lost, below the shadowed Lemhis. Cecilia and Mike rounded a bend that arced downhill for a stretch, and their headlight beams reached a shower trickling over a pile of rock. At runoff it probably raged as the great falls of the Little Lost, but these were the last, brittle days of summer and the river more of a creek.

Sleep, sleep, Cecilia thought. She could not sleep in the Camaro, had to become prone, still. Her muscles were fatigued from doing nothing, her eyes weary of scenery.

She opened them to find Smokey the Bear illuminated by their headlights, announcing WELCOME TO THE SALMON NATIONAL FOREST—FIRE HAZARD IS: *EXTREMELY HIGH*—ONLY *YOU* CAN PREVENT FOREST FIRES! Throughout the Northwest this year the reservoirs were low, the pines a tinderbox. Cecilia found this worrisome: If a forest fire were to kick up and spread along these foothills, the people of Haven would be trapped unless any helicopters could get through. The map, at least, showed this to be the only route in or out by car.

They were nearing the town when Mike nudged her. "Look, there."

She had to crane her neck to see the immense house standing alone atop the cliff. Its silhouette revealed a gloomy Gothic façade of peaked roofs, gables, overhanging eaves, narrow chimneys, warmly lighted windows—no more could be discerned before the house vanished in the embrace of the forest and the night.

"Spooky," Cecilia said.

"I thought this was Hemingway country, not Walter Scott." Mike had often said that as a child, books had been his entire world and the public library his second home. As a teen, he had volunteered there and was later paid to shelve books, a job he stayed with until he left Laramie altogether. But whenever he went back to see his family, he always paid a call on "the ladies at the library" (he had been the only guy) and they were always delighted to see him.

"*Son of Frankenstein*," Cecilia said. With her father always working and her mother gone and her brothers all wrapped up in themselves, she had raised herself on old movies, the more the merrier after the advent of the VCR. "Anyway, it's only Hemingway country because it's where he blew his brains out."

"Jeremy thinks Hemingway was gay," Mike said.

"Jeremy thinks everyone is gay."

The Camaro's glasspacks rumbled softly as they crossed the narrow concrete bridge over the river and entered the village. A sign declared HAVEN—POP. 918—ELEV. 9,281. The next sign was diamond-shaped, rusted out, pumped so full of buckshot that it was barely readable.

"Dead end," Cecilia made out.

"We must have come to the right place."

Haven lay before them in a dark box canyon, encircled and protected by mountains looming black now under the stars. Tall wooden pole lamps lit up the businesses along Center Street, which snaked its way up the farthest hill to end in a cul-de-sac. There, a tall, whitewashed church stood bathed in spotlights, surrounded by a cemetery. Stark lights of windows sparsely dotted the hillsides. Pickups and station wagons were parked along the streets, but no people were out or about. Tuesday night in Haven, and only 8:45. Perhaps this was their dinner hour. Cecilia half-expected to see a tumbleweed come blowing along in a cloud of dust down Center Street, or Clint Eastwood on a horse.

"It's totally dead," she said.

"Duh," said Mike.

Out the rear window, Cecilia saw the mansion again. Its dark front looked out over Haven, met by a long, winding private road. The huge house at one end of town and the church at the other anchored the valley like the twin towers of a suspension bridge. But church, house, and hills were all dwarfed by the close alpine peaks, which seemed ready to fall and crush everything in a flash.

"Do we know where we're going?" Mike asked, slowing.

Cecilia pulled out the Haven map, hand-drawn in smudged pencil, that had been sent to her anonymously in the mail along with the house keys, and flicked on the dome light. "Stuart Lane. Follow Center a ways. I'll look for it."

They drove past a grocery, a gas station, a bait-and-tackle shop, a gun shop, the post office, the ancient Olbrich Music Hall, and the town square at the Prospect County Courthouse, a Victorian sandstone monstrosity with crumbling cupola. The Haven Clinic, soon to be Cecilia's, was also along Center, a squat, aluminum-sided box at the intersection with Stuart Lane.

"That's our street," Cecilia said, and Mike, yawning, made the turn. *He's driving in his sleep*, she thought, and kept her eye out for number 326. Porch lights were off, so the numerals on the old homes were not always easy to discern. Three blocks up she found it, windows completely dark, back of a neatly trimmed lawn with a flagstone path that led up to the veranda.

"I hope it's haunted," Mike said, pulling up slowly, the Michelin radials softly crunching gravel.

"Don't give it any ideas," Cecilia said.

They got out and walked up the garden path. She placed it in the mid-1870s for its machined scrollwork and other Victoriana. A roomy porch wrapped around the front, balustrades and other trim all done in white, the thin wood-slat siding a fresh canary yellow, but in the gloom of night the pale shades appeared almost ashen. The porch swing was rocking slowly and creaking in the breeze. The steep roof was coupled against an octagonal gable, and the wood shingles looked new. Stained glass had been set along the upper quarter of the front bay window, glistening in the moonlight like blackberry jam.

Cecilia saw a gray face in the window. Then the curtain fell back and it was gone.

"Mike!"

He put his arm around her shoulders. "What?"

"There. I saw something."

"Don't joke. Come on, hon, I'll show you. Got the keys."

He led her up the porch steps. Cecilia felt idiotic—a dumb blonde in a horror movie needing steady reassurance from her football-player boyfriend—who in two beats would be lunched by a chain saw–wielding psycho.

Mike was relishing his role as protector. While he was trying to fit the right key into the right lock, she slowly reached on either side and poked him just under the ribs. He gave a start and shrieked, falsetto, almost womanly.

Cecilia laughed. "Sorry," she said, and hoped he wasn't angry.

Mike sighed heavily and stared her down. She placed a hand on the deep cleft between his pectorals and felt his heart thumping rapidly. She really had given him a fright.

"Let's go in," she said guiltily.

They swung the door silently open and stepped into the foyer, but it was too dark for them to see. Cecilia fumbled for the lights but could find no switch.

"What's that?" Mike whispered, digging his fingers into her wrist. "There's someone here."

"Won't work."

Cecilia was not easily frightened. But as her eyes adjusted she made out, against the walls of the parlor, shapes that looked faintly human, with luminous eyes like those of a cat hiding under a bed.

"Mike." She grabbed his hand.

The lights came on, and a dozen smiling people all at once yelled, "Surprise!" and blew loudly on noisemakers. A banner hanging swaybacked from the ceiling greeted them imperfectly:

WELCOME DR. AND MR. MACK

The room fell silent again in expectation.

A tawny-haired blue-eyed young man in a beige sheriff's uniform stepped forward, his cowboy boots falling heavily on the parquet floor. He held out his hand to Cecilia, looked her straight in the eyes, and said, "I'd like to be the first to welcome you and your husband to Haven, Dr. Mak."

The sheriff bowed deeply and planted a chaste kiss on her fingertips.

Mike cleared his throat unambiguously.

# Chapter 5

"Sheriff Franklin Tyler." His smile was broad, toothy, dimpled—an innocuous attempt at charm that was all lost on Cecilia. "Everyone calls me Frank."

His uniform was well tailored, pressed, and creased, and he filled it well. His boots were of polished brown leather. His utility belt carried a heavy-duty flashlight, portable radio, handcuffs, pepper mace, expandable baton, and a nine-millimeter semiautomatic pistol with a checkered black plastic grip. An additional, gold-buckled strap stretched diagonally across his chest and under the right epaulet. A hand mike hung loosely from the left epaulet, emitting quiet static. Over the left shirt pocket were pinned a gold nameplate and a gold five-pointed star, in the center of which was a black-enameled American eagle clutching olive branch and arrows, its breast emblazoned with the gold initials P.C.S.D. These initials were also patent in gold block letters pinned along the point of either shirt collar, the black eagle again on tiepin and cuff links.

"You don't have to call me doctor, either," Cecilia said with a nervous chuckle, duly intimidated by the regalia. Tyler's oddly formal kiss had already put her off, and she was sure Mike was even more irked. "It's just Cecilia."

Tyler led them into the parlor, bowlegged and tall as if he had just dismounted a horse. *All he needs now*, Cecilia thought, *is a pair of gold spurs*.

"I'm Mike," Mike said. He and Tyler exchanged a firm handshake and sized each other up like a pair of cocks ready to go at it. "Oh, by the way," Mike added, "your banner's misspelled. It's M-A-K."

"I know," Tyler said with a wink. "None of the gals let me have a peek at it till it was too late, or I would have had it fixed." He cast a cold eye over his shoulder, and an elderly woman's smile collapsed.

The parlor was more than roomy enough for those who had come to greet them, but the wallpaper was too dark and made the room feel close. A small chandelier tinkled in the draft. The oil paintings on the walls were curiously gray, bland, and naturalistic—family groupings of stout men, demure wives, and studious children. They could have been Norman Rockwells but for the absence of *life* in any of the figures. They were, frankly, depressing; had she anything to put in their place, she would take them down. But it was better, she supposed, to have something. In a perfect world, her walls would be filled with bright Matisses and Chagalls.

"We're the Welcome Wagon!" A short, white-haired woman of at least eighty thrust herself forward and held out her hand, as bony and wrinkly as a chicken's foot. Her dentures gleamed wetly. "I'm Lizzie Polk! Pleased to meet you! As acting chairwoman of the Welcoming Subcommittee, Haven Society Women's Auxiliary, I'd like to give the both of you a big fat *welcome to Haven!*"

This was met by polite applause.

In the middle of the Persian rug sat a child's shiny red

wagon stocked with goods—breakfast cereal, biscuit mix, milk, jellies, cheese, sausage, beer, dish soap, shampoo—all bundled up in pink cellophane with a big red ribbon.

"With our compliments and our blessing!" Lizzie said, shaking Mike's hand and staring beamishly into his face for far too long. Mike couldn't help but smile.

"You shouldn't have," Cecilia said, and felt her face grow warm. "Thanks a lot, everybody." She was moved, but all she really wanted was to lie down and get some sleep.

"There's punch and *horse doovers* in *your* kitchen!" Lizzie said, patting Cecilia's shoulder. She dragged over a tall, cadaverous man and said, "By the way, this is my husband, Ralph!"

"Honored, Dr. Mak," Ralph said in a harsh, strained voice like steel scraping concrete. Cecilia had heard such voices before during her residency at Seattle's University Medical Center: Ralph Polk had obviously undergone some kind of major throat surgery—most likely for the removal of a squamous cell carcinoma of the larynx, which had probably been brought on by years of alcohol and tobacco use—and the surgery had removed or damaged most of his vocal cords. Any scars were hidden behind his high collar and bolo tie. He was lucky, though, still to have any kind of a speaking voice at all without the assistance of an electronic squawk box.

"Nice to meet you, Mr. Polk," Cecilia said sincerely.

"Ralph's not on the committee—or in the Women's Auxiliary, are you, Ralph?" Lizzie said, interrupting whatever Ralph had been opening his mouth to say. Everything Lizzie said was a kind of shout, and Cecilia noticed she was wearing discreet hearing aids in each ear. "Us gals brought along our *worse halves* for the party!"

Ralph Polk seemed to give up hope of getting in a word with Cecilia, turning now to Mike and eking out, "Mike Mak—isn't that some kind of Indian tribe?"

"No," Mike said, laughing easily. Cecilia could tell he was beginning to relax. "You're thinking of the Micmacs."

"You're not a Micmac, are you?" Ralph said warily.

"No, actually I'm Chinese."

"From China?"

"Oh, no. I grew up in Wyoming."

"Wyoming!" Lizzie squealed, grasping Mike's arm with her sharp-nailed fingers. "You mean we were neighbors! Oh, that is so thrilling! Who would have thunk it! This country really is such a *melting pot*, isn't it, Ralph! I mean, we're all of us immigrants, now, aren't we?" Lizzie looked around the room.

"Lizzie," Sheriff Tyler cautioned.

"Well, aren't we?" Lizzie was undeterred. "Well, except for the Micmacs, of course! That's what America's all about, isn't it! A haven for the cast-outs! A home for the homeless! A refuge for the vast unwashed!"

"Lizzie, please." Tyler placed his hand on her low, fragile-looking shoulder. "Mike might think you're being too personal."

"Me?" Lizzie looked aghast, embarrassed. "I'm sorry."

"Oh, no," Mike said, touching her hand. "Not at all."

Tyler's hand fell away from Lizzie's shoulder, and she quickly recovered herself. "I'd like to introduce the rest of the committee! This is Peg Harrison, our postmistress, who also did our wonderful banner!"

"Sorry about your name," said Peg, a plump, rosy-cheeked, elderly cherub. She threw a nervous glance Tyler's way, still feeling his chastisement. Her eyes were small black buttons. "Forgive me."

"It's all right," Cecilia assured her.

"This is Marge and Dave Clinton, a couple of our local entrepreneurs," Lizzie said, though she didn't say what of.

"Your reputation precedes you, Cecilia," said Marge serenely,

25

her voice deep and resonant, postmenopausal. She had tight skin and bottled strawberry blond hair; Dave had gray follicles creeping in, with hen's feet at his eyes and a rough-hewn jaw. Both were sixtysomething and in rugged good health.

"We could use some new blood around here," said Dave; then, to Mike, shaking his hand and patting him chummily on the back, "Mike, my boy, you like to go fishing?"

"Sure," Mike said, blinking, trying to stay awake.

Dave Clinton stared at him even longer than Lizzie had done, with what Cecilia hoped was not a pederastic grin. Jeremy had once apprised her and Mike of the fact that older gay men who were attracted to boyish Asian guys were known as rice queens. But Mike was hardly boyish, and no doubt Dave Clinton was trying a bit too hard to be friendly, simply to show that he wasn't racist.

Cecilia became suddenly eager to escape the crush. Guests were filing into the kitchen and coming back with food on paper plates, cups red with punch.

A bald old man pushed his way up, forgoing Lizzie's introduction, and announced himself: "Clark Jackson, ma'am." It was hard to meet his myopic stare; one eyeball was dull and still—made of glass, Cecilia realized—possibly a war wound, since he was at least in his seventies and old enough to have fought in Europe or the Pacific. His flannel shirt of red-and-black plaid seemed too heavy for late summer. "So you're a doctor, huh?"

"I sure hope so."

Jackson allowed his one good eye to examine her up and down, as if she didn't look like any doctor *he* had ever seen. He was probably recalling his last prostate exam and wondering exactly how he was ever going to tolerate a woman palpating his innards.

26

"This is my grandson, Lewis," Jackson said, shoving the boy in front of her as if to get the introductions over with.

Cute, she thought. Lewis and Clark. She wondered if the boy's father was Clark Junior or Lewis Senior.

"Hi." Lewis Jackson was shy, seventeen, and lanky, a tawny blond like Tyler, dressed in a knockoff uniform—beige pressed pants, button-up shirt, dark brown cowboy boots and belt— except Lewis wore a billowy brown bandanna around his neck instead of a tie, threaded in front through a golden clasp like a Boy Scout neckerchief.

"Nice to meet you." Cecilia offered an encouraging smile, conscious of being perceived by him as just another adult, wishing for some way to bridge the gap. "Spiffy—are you a scout?"

"Junior Posse," Lewis mumbled, staring at her from under thick eyelashes. He plucked at his shirtsleeves as if he were itching to take it off. "We don't wear these all the time or any-thing, we just had our meeting down at the music hall."

"Where are your parents?"

"They're dead," Lewis said flatly.

"I'm sorry." Cecilia touched his hand. "I lost my mother when I was very young. I know. It's hard."

"It's okay, really," Lewis said, as if she needn't bother.

How could it possibly be okay?

"Lewis lives with Dottie and me," Clark Jackson said.

"Dottie Jackson's the real chairwoman of our Welcoming Subcommittee!" Lizzie said jarringly. "But she couldn't make it tonight, so I'm acting in her stead! This is Joe Doyle and his lovely wife, Vicky!"

"How do you do," said the pink-faced Joe Doyle, putting a barbecued miniature wiener in his porcine mouth. His toupee did not quite match the highlights of his actual hair, and he wore a dark business suit and long red-striped tie, exuding the slippery goodwill of a used-car salesman or a politician. "I'm the county coroner." He smacked his lips and licked his fingers. "We'll be seeing a lot of each other."

Cecilia was aghast at his choice of words, given the advanced age of some within earshot. But perhaps she was being overly sensitive.

Vicky Doyle's hair had a Marilyn Quayle flip, her olive summer dress a Peter Pan collar. "Joe only does that part time, though, don't you, Joe," she said. "He also runs our funeral home. Give her your card, honey."

Cecilia found it hard to believe the town had elected an undertaker as their coroner. She took the proffered business card and said, "Um, thank you."

Prompted by their questions, Mike was regaling the citizens with tales of what it had been like as a city reporter at the *Post-Intelligencer*. What he did not say was that by following Cecilia out here and giving up his job, he was making an enormous sacrifice—the kind husbands normally expected of their wives. Cecilia was privately terrified that he might wind up resenting her for it.

"Mike," she interrupted, "I'll go get you some punch." He didn't seem to hear her, caught up as he was in his new fame. She was happy for him, though, and relieved to find the Havenites so open and friendly; she and Mike had expected more of what she had encountered at Ernie's Self-Serve Gas & Fly Store.

The kitchen was roomy and clean, with plenty of counter space and cupboards as well as modern, new appliances—not that Cecilia would use them much. Mike was the better cook, and he actually enjoyed it. In their small one-bedroom apartment in Seattle, they had always traded off dinner chores—at least when their schedules overlapped to allow them to eat together—but whenever her turn came up, they would end up eating out, ordering in, or simply nuking some frozen dinners in the mike.

"You must hate us, Dr. Mak," said a woman by the sink. She was no older than Cecilia, with long brown hair tied back in a ponytail, face suntanned, her figure swallowed up by a loose cotton work shirt, baggy blue jeans, and pointy-toed boots.

"Excuse me?" Cecilia said. She had never hated anyone in her life, not even her father.

"Taking over your house like this. It *is* your house now, after all. I told Frank a surprise party was a bad idea, but he can be a stubborn cuss."

"Oh, no, I think it's sweet."

"Really? Good. I'm Bonnie Gillette. I sent you the map and the keys. I'm sorry, I'd written up a note to throw in with it and somehow I mislaid it. I run a diner, the Raven's Roost, up on Green Hill, near the church. Come on up sometime for a meal on me." Bonnie stared up at the ceiling. "I do love this old house. Such a shame . . . Now, don't you worry about cleaning up the mess. I volunteered to take care of it."

"Thanks." Cecilia certainly wasn't going to.

"Sometimes, Doc, I think Frank thinks I'm his slave."

"It's Cecilia, please. Anything but Doc!"

"Cecilia it is." Bonnie stepped up and, to Cecilia's surprise, hugged her like a long-lost sister.

Cecilia was happy that not all of Haven's women were as old as Lizzie Polk or as old-fashioned as Vicky Doyle. She would need friends here, and Bonnie struck her as an independent woman in a classically western, outdoorsy fashion.

"Trouble on the road?" Bonnie asked.

"No," Cecilia said. "Why do you ask?"

"We were expecting you a little sooner. No matter."

"Just some car trouble," she said, "but Mike fixed it."

"Oh, where is your husband?"

"He's out there. I came to get him some punch."

"I'll bring it to him, Cecilia. You take a breather. You look bushed."

"Thanks, I think I will." She sat in the breakfast nook.

Bonnie ladled out three cups of punch from the crystal bowl on the bar, giving one to Cecilia and holding the other two. "Have some weenies," she said, and handed Cecilia a paper plate of franks stabbed through with toothpicks. "I'll be back," she added, and went out through the swinging saloon doors into the parlor.

The punch tasted tartly of artificial strawberry, with a loud belt of strawberry schnapps. But the franks were surprisingly good, redolent of garlic; she loaded more onto her soggy plate, along with some German potato salad and raw carrots and celery.

Frank Tyler came in abruptly through the swinging doors. "Thought I might find you here."

"Somebody spiked the punch," Cecilia said.

"I did," he confessed. "When Bon's back was turned."

"You must like schnapps, then." She was thinking, *He looks much too young to be a county sheriff. Not my type, anyway.*

"Don't you?"

"It's okay," she said. "I guess it reminds me of those secret drinking parties back in high school. It was always a choice between schnapps, Black Velvet, or Everclear."

"You were a bad girl?"

"I wouldn't say I was bad," Cecilia said. "Just a rebel."

"Say, Jim Hamilton wanted me to tell you he's sorry he couldn't make it," Tyler said briskly. "He and Susan are too busy, what with the move and all. But he's looking forward to showing you his setup tomorrow. Come on." He held out his arm for her. "Your husband was wondering where you were."

"I told him where I was." Cecilia pretended not to notice

Tyler's arm gesture and instead placed both hands under her sagging plate.

"Okay, I'll just tell him you're in here chomping on weenies." Tyler shrugged, looking self-satisfied, and went on out through the swinging doors.

Cecilia followed him out into the parlor in her own time, once the doors had settled down.

"Bonnie was telling me about the house," Mike said, his face ruddy from punch. "Built by some eccentric madam."

"Have a weenie," Cecilia said, popping one into his mouth. She put her arm tightly around his waist. She was beginning to feel cranky and wanted more than ever simply to go to bed. Tyler was snooping around in the shadows of the room around the side of the fireplace.

"Maddie Gahagan," Bonnie said, "back in Haven's boom years. It wasn't a whorehouse, but it was built from her brothel earnings. About eighteen seventy-five, I think."

Cecilia was pleased that the original occupant had been the town's most liberated woman, of sorts.

"It's eclectic," Bonnie said, smiling and making direct eye contact with Cecilia. "Reflects her personality. You'll see. The upstairs bathroom was built for two. The tub and shower are separate, and it's got a vanity on one wall and another big mirror over the pedestal sink, so the woman could preen as long as she liked while her man was busy shaving."

Cecilia could hardly imagine wanting to "preen" all day before her own reflection. She supposed Maddie Gahagan hadn't been that liberated after all.

"Show her the fireplace!" Lizzie Polk shouted with the indecorous timing of a mad parrot.

Bonnie pointed out the glazed tiles along the sides and underneath the mantel. "Some builder must have had a big as-

31

sortment of these. You were supposed to pick one style, but apparently Maddie liked them all. There's an Egyptian scene with the Sphinx, and the Notre Dame Cathedral, and a little Dutch girl, a couple of angels, an American farm scene, George Washington, old San Francisco. . . ."

"The Hintons loved this old house!" said Lizzie.

"Lizzie, let's not—" Tyler said, cutting himself off.

Lizzie put cupped fingers up to her mouth and said, softly, "Sorry, Frank. I did it again."

"What?" Mike asked, as though he had missed something. "Who are the Hintons?"

"They used to live here, but they moved away," Bonnie said, as if it were a matter of no importance.

"Don't you think it's late, Lizzie?" Tyler said, looking at his gold watch. "Maybe it's time you got Ralph on home."

"Well . . . all right, Frank." Lizzie grabbed her husband's arm. Her hands were shaking. "Let's go, Ralph! Bedtime!"

Cecilia whispered into Mike's ear, "Who does he think he is?"

Mike shrugged.

"Did you see the sunroom?" Bonnie asked brightly.

"Mike, you go." Cecilia nudged him. He looked askance at her: *You want me to?* She nodded, and he followed Bonnie alone to the other side of the fireplace, to a room filled with tall ferns.

Tyler rolled his eyes as if he were sharing a confidence with Cecilia. "Lizzie likes to wax nostalgic. I didn't want her boring you with old tales of old people who you wouldn't care one whit about. Anyway, it's almost time to round everybody up. You've put up with us long enough. And it *is* past Ralph's bedtime."

Cecilia decided Sheriff Tyler was something of a bully, but what was she going to do, take him aside and scold him?

Mike popped his head out from the sunroom and said, "It's beautiful, Cee. Come take a look."

"Excuse me," she said.

"Ma'am," said Tyler, sidestepping out of her way.

Cecilia brushed ticklish fern fronds from her face as she stepped into the sunroom. She found Bonnie and Mike sitting around a small pool that had two goldfish swimming around in circles. A trickle of water spilled over a pile of smooth stones, reminding her of the dried-up waterfall she and Mike had glimpsed on their way up the Haven Road. The sunroom was enclosed in glass and surrounded by the night. All Cecilia could make out in the narrow panes were their own faces reflected. She hooded her eyes up against the cool glass and saw the monstrously huge house on the hill.

"Who lives up in that mansion?" Cecilia asked.

"Up on Olbrich Hill? Oh, that's the Tyler place," Bonnie said, as if they should know this already.

"He lives there all by himself?"

"Nearly. Used to be old Doc Tyler—Frank's grandfather—lived there with the rest of his clan, but now he's dead, and most of the rest are either dead or moved away. All that's left is Frank and the Widow Tyler."

"His mother?"

"Grandmother."

"Oh." Cecilia had never known her own grandparents and decided not to pry any further. She would learn all about Haven in due course, not that she imagined there was so much to know aside from the idlest gossip.

"Before Doc Tyler came to Haven and bought the place, it belonged to some descendant of our founder, Henry Jameson Olbrich," Bonnie said, as if this should impress her. "I think it was built on the spot where the original Olbrich House burned down. You might say the Tylers inherited the Olbrichs' mantle along with the property. But you folks must be about ready for sleep. I'm boring you."

"Oh, no, not at all," Cecilia protested.

"The Widow owns this place, too. She was gracious enough to let the town borrow it so they could let you use it. Though we all hope you'll decide to stay forever."

Cecilia certainly did not.

"Is she here, the Widow? I'd like to thank her."

"Oh, no. She hardly ever sets foot outside the old house."

Back in the parlor, Cecilia and Mike stood by the door to thank everybody as they filed out. Peg Harrison could not stop giggling (the schnapps, Cecilia thought). Dave Clinton reminded Mike to get his fishing pole unpacked and rigged up. Lewis Jackson looked up at Mike with wide eyes and a broad grin, fascinated. Clark Jackson hustled his grandson out the door hurriedly and didn't bother to shake either Mike's or Cecilia's hand or even to say good-bye.

"We got to go home and put our little Tommy and Jeffrey and Kathy and Becky and Joe Junior to bed," said Joe Doyle. "Come on, Vicky."

Vicky trailed behind him like an obedient dog. "Bye, now."

Tyler was the last to leave. "I'd better go check in at the station," he said, "see what Herb's gotten himself into."

"I wouldn't worry," Bonnie said. "I don't think he'd try to take a piss on his own without your approval."

Tyler blew air out his nose like a bull ready to charge. "A pleasure, as always, Bon. Cecilia, Mike, sleep tight, don't let the bedbugs bite." His eyes lingered on Cecilia, the corner of his mouth twitched, and then he was out the door, cowboy hat on his head, hitching up his utility belt and whistling tunelessly down the flagstone path.

Bonnie closed the door firmly, looking relieved that he was gone. "I'll have this place cleaned up in a jiffy."

"Cee and I'll take care of the Welcome Wagon," Mike said.

Together they wheeled it into the kitchen, and Cecilia discovered that her back was dreadfully sore. They broke open the cellophane and found places for things while Bonnie stood at the sink doing dishes. Mike pulled out the beer and looked at it queerly.

"Haven Bräu?" he said dubiously.

"Oh, that's from the Clintons," Bonnie said. "They've set themselves up a microbrewery, with a beer garden in the summer. They've just started bottling it for local distribution. It's selling pretty well up in Salmon. Pretty good Bavarian-style lager. They made a dark, too, though I can't drink the stuff. Dave's the brewmaster, so if you like it, let him know, he'll be tickled to death."

"I will."

"You got movers coming?"

"Tomorrow, supposedly," Cecilia said.

"You all set for furniture? Because the Widow asked me to tell you she's got a lot of extra pieces in storage, and you can have your pick. She had some brought in already, plus the artwork, and if you don't like anything and want it moved away, just let me know. I'm kind of acting as her agent. There's no such thing as real estate in Haven. The Widow pretty much owns everything."

"Thank her for us. It's very generous of her."

"Oh, it's her pleasure, believe me."

Cecilia found herself eager to meet their benefactor.

"You lived in Seattle all your life?" Bonnie asked.

"As far back as I can remember," Cecilia said.

"Where are you from, Mike?"

"Laramie, Wyoming," Mike said.

"Oh, Laramie? I think I drove through there once on I-80."

"My dad's a professor there at the university. Entomology."

"Oh, really. How'd you and Cecilia meet?"

"I went out to Seattle for school. I could have gone to the University of Wyoming, but I'd already spent my whole life there, and I kind of wanted to get away from my family."

"I don't know why," Cecilia said. "His family's wonderful."

"Well, you didn't have to live with them," Mike said. "Anyway, if I'd stayed in Laramie, I'd still be living at home and I never would have met Cee." He gave her a proprietary kiss on the cheek.

"How about you, Bonnie?" Cecilia asked. "Have you lived here all your life?"

"Born and bred," Bonnie said. "I love it here. Salmon fishing, backpacking, river rafting. I've got the Raven's Roost and no man to boss me around. I'd say I'm pretty content."

"Don't tell me ravens really roost up there," Cecilia said.

"Ravens, crows, all kinds."

"Cecilia was attacked when she was a child," Mike said.

"By a bird?" Bonnie was incredulous.

"I guess so," Cecilia said, feeling suddenly woozy (the schnapps again). "I was very young. I hardly remember a thing about it. But I still hate black birds. You don't have a pet raven around your place or anything, do you?"

"No," Bonnie said, amused. "I used to have one on my sign—a painted one. People thought it was morbid. Joe Doyle liked it, at least. Anyway, the sign blew away one day. Maybe somebody stole it. The new sign has no bird, so you're safe."

"You must think I'm hopelessly neurotic, even superstitious. I know that's not very becoming in a doctor."

"No, no, not at all," Bonnie said. "I almost drowned in the Salmon River when I was a girl. Frank's father pulled me out, and I was all right, but to this day I can barely dog-paddle.

Whenever I'm in the water, my heart beats a mile a minute and I feel like I can't breathe."

"I thought you said you liked river rafting," Mike said.

"Sure, but I stay on the raft."

"I keep my eyes peeled for black birds," Cecilia said, knowing it sounded ridiculous. "Ever since I was a little girl, I've dreamed that someday it was going to come back."

"Come on, Mike," Bonnie said. "What's your neurosis?"

Mike shook his head. "Oh, I'm a calm, level-headed guy, perfectly well adjusted. Just ask Cee."

Cecilia looked at him. Of course he had his own neuroses, but she wasn't about to say so. For one, he thought people treated him unfairly because of his race, which was sometimes true but not always. On occasion, this ballooned into full-scale paranoia, but he would be embarrassed if Cecilia were to tell Bonnie he sometimes thought everyone was out to get him.

"Well, Maks," Bonnie said, throwing in the towel. "I'd say that just about does it."

By the time Bonnie left, it was after eleven, but it felt like the wee small hours of the morning. Cecilia and Mike finally had the place all to themselves. The master bedroom upstairs had already been furnished with an ample four-poster bed, tall antique wardrobe, table, and mirror. Mike lay down on the comforter and pulled Cecilia down alongside him.

"Whew!" he said, and they both began laughing.

"I'm exhausted," Cecilia said.

"How do you like our sheriff?" Mike asked, twirling his fingers in her hair.

"I think he's in love with himself."

"Male chauvinist pig?" Mike wondered.

"That's no longer PC."

"Well, he *is* a *pig*. You know, as in fuzz? Or do PC people not say 'pig' for 'cop' anymore, either?"

"'Cop' is pejorative, too. They just want to be called police officers."

"*He* just wants to be called Frank."

"He's rich," Cecilia said. "I wonder why he'd want to be sheriff."

"I don't know, and I don't care. We need to get some sleep. *You* have to get up in the morning."

"Bonnie's sweet, don't you think?"

"Whatever." Mike stretched, yawning like a lion. "I feel grungy. Let's go wash it off before we hit the hay, what do you say?"

"Mmm, I say yes."

Cecilia pulled Mike's shirt off over his head. He was musky from the day-long trip. Mike's fingers nimbly found the buttons of her jeans. The rest of the clothes were removed quickly, and they went down the hall to the huge bathroom-built-for-two and stepped into the hot spray of the shower.

"I feel possessed by Maddie Gahagan," Cecilia said in her best Blanche DuBois as they embraced under the hot spray. The water spilled over Mike's hard muscles and down her milky-white breasts.

"The spirit is willing?" Mike touched his forehead against hers and clutched at her back.

"I'll say." She wrapped herself around him and grabbed onto his glutes as he inched his way lovingly in.

# Chapter 6

"All I wish for," said Dr. Hamilton, pausing to draw from his pipe, "is that Susan and I should live five more years, to witness the birth of the new millennium. Then the Lord may do with us as He pleases."

Cecilia thought that if there was a God, He or She would find this presumptuous. Hamilton's flesh was wrinkled and crisp and leathery, his jowls droopy, hair hennaed and combed thinly over a liver-spotted pate. He looked to Cecilia like the world's oldest and largest living turkey, and she doubted he had five months in him, let alone five years.

"When I was your age, Dr. Mak," he continued in his tobacco-seasoned voice, enunciating each word as if he remained under the spell of a diction coach, "I had scant hope of living long enough to see the turn of the century, but now I believe that it is indeed possible, if not likely."

"I'm sure you will," Cecilia said.

Hamilton had removed most of his things from the office, but he was leaving the desk, the pine bookcases, the dusty medical texts. Behind him, filling the broad picture window, stood sturdy Flatiron, tallest of the Lemhis, its sunny summit troughed by glaciers.

Cecilia glanced down at the milk crate she had brought along, filled with items she would be putting up once Hamilton was gone. On top were three framed photos of Mike, hinged together and coated with a thin layer of dust: one a formal studio portrait; one of Mike lying with her in a park; and a more personal shot from their honeymoon three months ago, of Mike sitting on a rock somewhere along the Big Sur coast in a navy bikini swimsuit, flexing his arms and showing off his body, his taut abdominals dusted with flecks of sand.

"So much of it is a matter of breeding, you know," Hamilton went on. "Simple genetics . . . and I come from unusually *robust* genes. My parents and grandparents lived well into their eighties, and my family has no history of heart trouble, Alzheimer's disease, or any such defect. Though you may think I'm pushing my luck with this pipe." He stuck it in his mouth and puffed, as if to provoke her.

Cecilia's first order of business would be to fumigate; the room reeked. The yellowed walls might have passed for clean if he had not already removed his diplomas, leaving behind neat rectangles of white. She would have enjoyed sneaking a peek at where he might have earned his degree (and when—the 1930s?) but did not want to embarrass him now by inquiring.

"So why would you want to leave Haven?"

"Because I am *retiring*, Dr. Mak." His eyes grew watery, as if he was undone by the sight of her—perhaps sentimental about the passing of the caduceus, unless it was simply the smoke. He spoke like a pedant but showed such grandfatherly affection that she could hardly take offense.

"But Haven is so beautiful." She and Mike would be here into the new millennium, she realized, now that Hamilton had pointed it out, and she wanted to know if there was a catch.

"San Carlos de Bariloche is even more lovely, my dear," he said.

She tried not to let it show that she was annoyed by the "my dear" or that she had no idea where or what San Carlos de Bariloche was. She could not help but feel that she was being tested.

"Susan and I used to vacation there," Hamilton explained, "when Dr. Tyler was still among us to fill in. I haven't left Haven since *he* left *us*. Even if I could find a temp physician I could trust, actually employing one would be expensive, and there are too many old folks—if you will pardon my political ineptitude—too many of *us* old folks here who are dependent on a doctor's care." He withdrew pink silk from his shirt pocket and dabbed at his bloodshot eyes. Cecilia saw that it wasn't a handkerchief at all but a large pair of women's panties—his wife's, she assumed. Hamilton didn't seem to notice, then absently stuffed it back in his pocket and said, "You appreciate, then, what you are taking on, Dr. Mak?"

"Of course," said Cecilia, slightly resentful.

"You will have Janice Fremont, but then a nurse is hardly a surrogate for a good family physician. I have taken care of these people—my friends—for so long, I would never be able to stop if I did not get out of town altogether. I am afraid you would find me a terrible nuisance."

"Oh, I doubt that—"

"And Susan and I would rather spend what time we have left in the Argentine, where no one will bother us."

"Argentina?" Cecilia could not conceal her surprise; older Americans retired to Arizona or Florida, not Argentina.

Hamilton's eyes gleamed; he seemed pleased somehow with her reaction and continued, smugly, "A very civilized, a very *European* country. Bariloche is a village much like Haven, high in the Andes. The altitude and the climate agree with us, and we have already made many friends there over the years."

"But your friends here—"

"Are also my patients, and always will be. Believe me, Dr. Mak, you will be *ecstatic* that I am gone."

"You've only stayed on because the program failed to find anyone to replace you, is that it?" Cecilia said. Tim Vandam had hinted that they had had some difficulty finding someone quite to Hamilton's liking, but as far as Cecilia was concerned, the precise reason why her assignment had been changed from Colville, Washington, to Haven, Idaho, remained obscure.

"Failed is precisely the word!" Hamilton tapped out his ashes, rapping the bowl repeatedly against the ebony ashtray as if it were a gavel. "They kept sending us these Arabs and Indians—from *India!*—and the interviews did not go well. They barely spoke intelligible English! If our people were not so set in their ways, so accustomed to doctors like Tyler and myself, perhaps I might have risked it. But as it was I had to turn them away. It was fortuitous, shall we say, that we managed to find you."

"Thank you," Cecilia said, though it was a dubious compliment. Hamilton meant they were lucky to get their hands on a blond-haired, blue-eyed Caucasian (even if she was a woman) who happened to have needed help paying for her education. Vandam had signed her up with the RPP when she was still premed, still Cecilia Jones, before she had ever laid eyes on cute Michael Mak or made any other future plans. She had had no control over where they might ultimately send her, but she could never have paid for med school otherwise. Her father had set aside money for her brothers to attend college, but not for her; it was not a woman's place to have a professional career that would interfere with her natural duties.

"No, Doctor, I must thank you." Hamilton's eyes grew teary

again. Deftly he refilled his pipe. "Susan and I can finally make our move south."

"*Way* south," Cecilia said, attempting levity, but Hamilton's face remained as stern as Mount Rushmore.

"Too many things have gone so wrong with this country, my dear!" He relit his pipe, speaking out of the side of his mouth. "I would rather retire to a place where a man can feel that his house is not a cage or that he will be attacked by a gang of human vermin if he sets foot outside of it!"

Cecilia was alarmed at the venom in his voice, and she said, "I wouldn't have thought there was so much crime here."

"Oh, no, very little. Young Tyler and Herb Monroe see to that. I'm afraid I've been rambling on about what I read in the newspapers. The loss of order, too many illegitimate welfare babies, illegal aliens flooding in demanding free health care, the spread of AIDS and perversion, the teaching of false history—multiculturalism indeed!—the lack of any kind of a real education. I ask you, where are we ever to find the leaders of tomorrow?"

Cecilia held her tongue against Hamilton's rant.

"Thank God Haven is what it is! We could teach the rest of the country a thing or two! You and your husband might be wise to consider staying here to raise your family."

"I won't be having any children."

"Not having any?"

"Not while I'm here, I mean," Cecilia amended. "We're putting that off for a few years, at least." There was little chance, anyway, that she and Mike would stay beyond her initial commitment, and then Haven would have to go through the physician-search process all over again. In five years' time, Cecilia and Mike would probably return to Seattle, where she would join a group practice or an HMO, and he would try to return to the *Post-Intelligencer* (unless he had managed to become a world-famous novelist)—but only after Cecilia's career was well established might she take time off to have a kid. That was years off—maybe eight or ten. Mike had made it no secret that he wanted a child, and Cecilia was fairly certain she did, too. They both agreed they had plenty of time.

"Yes, of course," Hamilton said. "I hadn't considered that. If you were to have a child, where would Haven be?" He slapped his thigh and stood up. "Well, shall we go and make the rounds? I would like to introduce you to at least those patients you'll be seeing most often."

"You don't mind if I leave my crate?"

"Be my guest. It's your office now." Hamilton came slowly around from behind his desk and looked down at it.

"Odds and ends," Cecilia said, as if in apology.

Hamilton reached down and picked up the photos, frowning slightly and squinting. "Who, might I ask, is this?"

"That's Mike." Cecilia rose, grabbing her bag. She felt embarrassed that she had included the fleshy photo of him in his brief swim trunks, but it was too late now.

Hamilton's face had grown cold, a clump of hair fallen across his brow. His face darted from one photo to another. If Mike had been a doctor and had applied to the position, he would never have stood a chance.

"What is he . . . Korean?"

"Chinese," Cecilia said, and quickly amended, "American. Second generation. Born in Laramie."

"Wyoming?"

"That's right."

"Huh."

"We met during school." She hated herself for defending her choice of husband—hated Hamilton for making her feel as if she had to. She had been through enough of this with her father, far too often.

"Indeed."

"You'd like him," she insisted, though she hardly cared if he did. Hamilton would soon be off tangoing with his wife in the Andes and would never have the distinct pleasure of getting to know Mike.

"I see." Though the pictures had lain open before, he now closed them firmly and set them back down atop the crate. His jaundiced smile came back on, and he opened the door, gesturing with a slight bow for Cecilia to precede him. "Shall we?"

"After you." Cecilia stood back, smiling, arms folded. As Hamilton had said, it was her office now. And with all his talk of the millennium, he should be the first to realize that the age of chivalry was history.

# Chapter 7

Hamilton simply stood there, and they remained at loggerheads like the northgoing Zax and the southgoing Zax until Nurse Fremont appeared from down the hall. Her gaze was fixed on the documents in her hands, but once she set foot on Hamilton's carpet in her small white tennis shoes, she looked up and found herself caught in the middle.

"Oh!" Fremont said. Her gray-streaked hair was pulled back from her forehead, eyebrows unnaturally arched. She was not far from retirement herself, no younger than sixty. "You startled me! Meeting over?"

"We were on our way out." Hamilton was short.

"Dr. Mak, I've got some forms here that'll need your signature," Fremont said, ignoring Hamilton. "Want me to put them on your desk?"

"Yes," Cecilia said. "Thank you."

"Jim," Fremont said, and handed Hamilton a pink message slip. "Susan called. She said it was urgent."

Hamilton crumpled the message in his palm and swore

under his breath—not *goddammit* or *son of a bitch*, but a low, guttural sound Cecilia could not make out.

"If you will excuse me," he said, his smile painful now, and ushered Fremont and Cecilia out. The textured glass rattled as he shut the door. The gold letters spelled out JAMES K. HAMILTON, M.D. Cecilia scratched at the H with her fingernail and a gold flake came off. Fremont caught her at it and cracked a sly, knowing smile.

"Come on," Fremont whispered. "He'll want his privacy."

Cecilia followed her down the hallway, past the elaborately equipped examination rooms—they seemed to have everything short of computed tomographic scanners and magnetic resonance imagers. One room seemed to be reserved solely for obstetric and gynecologic needs and had just about every machine one could possibly want for the maintenance of a woman's health. During the grand tour, when Cecilia had asked how the Haven Clinic could have afforded all of this, Hamilton had offered a cagey response: "Medicare loves us."

"How long have you worked with him?" Cecilia asked at the reception desk, out in the waiting room. From down the hall, she could hear Hamilton raising his voice to his wife, but the sound was muffled, the words unintelligible. She wondered if it was even English.

Fremont searched the ceiling tiles for an answer. "Thirty-five years? Thirty-six? Heck, I don't know."

"You must be sorry to see him go."

"Oh, he's a *wonderful* man." Fremont lowered herself sidesaddle into the chair, grabbed a pen, fiddled with some papers. Hamilton's virtues were left unextolled.

Cecilia felt awkward, half Fremont's age and now her boss. The first thing the nurse had said to her was, "It's Janice, *not* Jan," though Cecilia had as yet called her neither.

"You'll tell him I'm outside?"

Fremont, scribbling with a pen, said, "Mmm-hmm."

Cecilia put on her sunglasses and opened the door, wondering exactly what Hamilton had been yelling to his wife. *Oh, mind your own business*, she told herself. Hamilton and his wife were probably brushing up on their Spanish, was all, in preparation for the big move south—*way* south.

Cecilia stepped out of the clinic and into the glorious view of the Rockies. The thrust-up peaks here in Idaho were different from the symmetrical volcanoes she had grown up with in Washington—perhaps more dramatic but not *alive* like Mount Rainier or Mount Saint Helens, whose gritty ash she had tasted after the first, massive eruption, when she was fourteen. It had been the final week of the eighth grade, and her father tried to keep her indoors. Defiantly, she had spent many hours out of the house. She was seeing Eddie Morales—another act of defiance, though luckily for Eddie, her father never knew—Eddie, with his beautiful caramel skin and feeble attempt at a mustache. They smoked pot together in alleys behind buildings, made out in his bedroom while his mother was at work, and nearly had sex twice. But once school was over, Eddie and his family moved down to El Paso, and Cecilia never saw him again. But she emerged unscathed and was left with nothing but good memories of him who had treated her so sweetly, and of the fine soot that had fallen in layers over everything and made everyone else so angry.

Cecilia's father had hated the ash; mixed with rain, it had corroded the finish of his BMW. But he would have been far more upset had he ever learned of Eddie Morales. He had once told Cecilia that he had known only one Mexican in his life who had *not* been a lazy bum: This had been a fellow named Pablo who had operated a tamale cart on the street, saved up all his money, and eventually bought a house. "But it was easy for him," he said—Cecilia could still remember distinctly his exact words and the manner of casual authority with which he had spoken them—"because aside from alcohol, Pablo didn't really have anything to spend his money on, because, you know, Mexicans will eat cats, dogs, anything." In his own inimitable fashion, he was apparently trying to instill in his daughter the value of saving, if not the supremacy of the free-market economy, capitalism, and the American way of life. All she ever gleaned from this, however, was that he was a bigot.

Even if he had set aside money for Cecilia's college education, it would have seemed somehow tainted, and in a way she was glad she had been forced to find her own way. Indirectly, she supposed, that was how she had ended up in Haven—which was fine with her, though she still felt guilty about dragging Mike along, interrupting his career.

"I'm sorry about that," Hamilton said from behind her.

Cecilia turned with a start.

"The wife," he added, blowing a smoke ring.

"Oh, that's all right. I was soaking up the view."

"Yes, Flatiron." Hamilton pointed with the tip of his pipe, as if he thought she was too stupid to make it out for herself.

Cecilia decided he was right on one point, at least. If he were to stay on, she would find him a terrible nuisance.

# Chapter 8

They were bouncing along on rutted Lee Circle on the east side of town, Hamilton behind the wheel of the Haven Clinic "ambulance," a ten-year-old, full-sized Blazer 4X4 that sat high off the ground on huge, knobby tires and was fitted out with basic lifesaving equipment and a collapsible gurney—better suited for mere transportation than for the dispensation of acute medical care. Hamilton said he mostly used it for "getting around the county." In back of the clinic was a huge snowplow attachment that Cecilia was going to have to bribe Mike into helping her install before winter, or she would be snowbound and unable to reach her patients.

"I'm sorry I was unable to attend your welcoming last night," Hamilton said. "Susan and I were busy with some last-minute packing."

The Blazer's interior was pungent from years of pipe smoke. Cecilia became the victim of serial sneeze. She was going to have to buy a pine-tree air-freshener to hang from the rearview mirror, like all the cars had in *Repo Man*. But she doubted if one lone pine would do the trick. She hoped at least that Hamilton had never smoked with a patient in back.

"Jim, what can you tell me about Lewis Jackson's grandmother?" Cecilia asked. "Dottie, is it?"

"What about her?"

"I thought she was ill."

"Who told you that?"

"Lizzie Polk." She wondered why he should care. "At least she gave me that impression. She didn't exactly say so. Dottie couldn't make it to the welcoming party even though she was chair of the subcommittee, so I figured she must be sick. Her husband was there—"

"Dottie is as right as rain," Hamilton said, booming with stubborn conviction, "and she does not like people going up and bothering her, so I think you and I will just take a pass on that idea for this afternoon, Doctor."

If she doesn't like people bothering her, why would she want to chair the Welcoming Subcommittee? Cecilia wanted to ask. But it would not help to push the issue. Once Hamilton was gone, she would be free to bother anyone she liked, including Dottie and the Widow Tyler. She was not afraid of committing a social faux pas during the daily exercise of her doctorly duties.

"The movers left this morning," Hamilton said, back to his subject. "Susan and I will be driving down to Idaho Falls tomorrow to turn in our Mercedes at the dealership and pick up our puddle-jumper to Salt Lake City. From there, we will be flying quite comfortably, first class, to Buenos Aires in a new Seven-seventy-seven. Terribly exciting."

"What about all your things?"

"Oh, they'll be flying along as cargo in the hold." Hamilton paused a moment, puffing and thinking. "I am worried, though, about our cats, Martin and Eva. I wish the poor creatures could sit in my lap, but they are required to ride down below, and I have heard too many horror stories of what can happen to pets in transit." At this he shuddered theatrically. "Should a weather restriction come up, the airline will not even allow Martin and Eva on our flight. I have made suitable arrangements with a vet in Idaho Falls to take care of them should it prove necessary, and then they can follow when the weather is right. But I will be very anxious until I see that they have arrived safe and sound."

"I'm sure they'll be fine." Cecilia was touched by Hamilton's concern. She had observed that men her father's age and older showed their softer side only with excruciating difficulty. A chink had fallen from Hamilton's hard-bitten exterior, and Cecilia's estimation of him had risen a notch.

"Eh, you and Mike have no pets?"

"We've never had the time."

"Perhaps, now that you are here and your husband is no longer working . . . a dog or a cat can be very good company. Back in Haven's gold-rush days, in the eighteen seventies, cats were a genuine commodity, selling for fifteen, twenty dollars a head—which was quite a lot back then! Everything was inflated because of the gold. Miners would make small fortunes and then spend it all right here or else gamble it away. Oh well, easy come, easy go."

Hamilton made it sound as if he had been there. Some men spoke with such strong conviction, they could be talking of Napoleon and come across as if they had known him personally. Cecilia's father was like that—always the expert, always there with the "right" answer on every subject under the sun. Having grown up and discovered that he was not always right—in fact, he seldom was—she had learned to distrust any man who spoke with such an intense belief in his own words. She liked a man who could be wrong and admit it with grace, which was one reason she would never let go of Mike or allow anyone else to take him from her.

Cecilia lumbered into the driveway behind the wheel of the ambulance. At the end of their rounds, Hamilton had handed over the keys and said, "She's all yours." Cecilia was not so sure that the ambulance wasn't a he; it certainly smelled like one.

On her way home, she had realized that practically every other house in Haven stood vacant, abandoned. Old paint was peeling away, windows shattered, lawns overgrown with weeds, sunflowers, dandelions. A few of the very oldest were leaning on weathered timbers, roofs bowed in and ready to collapse in the next heavy snow. The still-inhabited ones stood straight and well maintained, with recent paint or aluminum siding and neat lawns of Kentucky bluegrass. Each had a four-wheel-drive truck parked in the drive: a Ford, Chevy, Jeep, or Dodge Ram. Havenites bought American and were looking for utility rather than status—no Nissans, Isuzus, or Range Rovers here.

Mike waved at Cecilia from the porch swing as she stepped on the ratchety emergency brake and leaped down from the high cab. He was in his workout duds—a pair of cotton fleece shorts, low-slung tank top, and sneakers—and drinking a bottle of Haven Bräu. She came up the steps and sat down with him. He threw his arm around her shoulders.

"Aren't you chilly?" she said. Though the sun had been out all day, the wind off the mountains had an arctic bite.

"I'm hot," Mike said.

"You're not sick—" Her hand sprang toward his forehead.

He grabbed her wrist. "No, Ma, I've been unpacking."

"They came already?"

"Came and went, like that. It's not as if we had a lot of stuff. You want one of these beers?" He tried to get up, but she grabbed the waistband of his shorts and yanked him back down. He could have kept going, but he would have been de-pantsed, and Haven was not ready to see Mike in his jockstrap.

"I'll get it myself," Cecilia said. "You relax. You've probably been working a lot harder than me."

"Suit yourself. That's some macho rig you've got there, Cee."

"Yeah, isn't it?" She stood up, and the swing rocked back lopsidedly. "How's the beer?"

"Pretty good," Mike judged, which meant it was great. He was never one to give too strong a compliment. "Pretty authentic tasting for an American brew."

"So tell Dave Clinton."

"I already did. He called a little while ago to invite me fishing on Tuesday."

"Are you going to?"

"Hell yes."

"Watch out, Mike. He looks like a rice queen." It came out sounding bitchy, and she regretted having opened her mouth.

Mike frowned, looking doubtful. "Speaking of which, Jeremy called to see how we're making out."

Cecilia swore under her breath, sorry she had missed him. She would have to call him back. "How is he?"

"Same old Jeremy. He and Tom were thinking of taking a road trip out here before winter hits. I said they could stay as long as they liked."

Cecilia kissed him, intending a mere peck, but Mike put his hands in her hair and held her fast, poking his tongue inside. It turned her on, but she hastily broke; they were out-of-doors and in full view of the street, and she disliked such public displays of affection. Anyway, she wanted her Haven Bräu. Mike smiled up at her, though, contented, just having his fun.

"I'll be back," Cecilia said, dropping her voice, trying for Arnold Schwarzenegger.

As she opened the screen door and was about to go in, she noticed young Lewis Jackson standing stock-still in the middle of the dusty lane in jeans, T-shirt, and a light windbreaker. He was watching them, his face impassive, the wind buffeting his hair and grabbing at his jacket. Cecilia waved, and he waved back for a moment with an awkward smile before moving on, hanging his head down and kicking rocks along his path.

Poor kid, Cecilia thought. His grandparents are too old, his parents are gone, and he's doomed to grow up in this one-horse town. She thought too late of inviting him in. She could have scared up some iced tea or lemonade. He and Mike could have played some Super Nintendo. She had to try to see Lewis's grandmother, find out what was going on. She had a strange feeling that something was amiss.

Her father would call it women's intuition, but she was certain that nothing in nature could be so sexist. Mike had it stronger than she did, and she could attest to the fact that he wasn't a girl. Her father had used the word *girl* on her brothers as a way of demeaning them if they failed to perform. "You throw like a girl," he would say, or "Come on, girls, put some muscle into it!" He had got what he wanted, of course—her brothers had turned out just like him. They had even joined their father's lodge, and they went bowling together and out as a bunch to see the Mariners. They actually enjoyed being around him, for Christ's sake.

Growing up, Cecilia had wondered if she were an alien from Outer Space who had fallen to Earth by accident and into this strange family. It was hard for her to believe she had any of her father's genes. Her memories of her mother were vague, but she was sure she took more after her. This would mean that her mother must have had a rebellious side, and Cecilia wondered how her father might have put up with that—if he had. It was a not-so-funny joke between Cecilia and Mike that her father was like Archie Bunker, only without the cuddly side. Edith Bunker might have sometimes stood up to Archie, but Cecilia could hardly imagine her father exhibiting the same physical restraint in his response. She couldn't remember him ever laying a hand on her, but she had witnessed him knocking her brothers around often enough. "He'll never think of you as anything but his little *goil*," Mike had said once, and he was right. Her father had never approved of her having a career; she would have thought he would be proud of her becoming a doctor, but if he was he had done nothing to show it. He still believed she should be a wife and stay home and raise a large family, but he had never conceived that she would marry someone like Mike, and now he didn't want her bearing any "mixed" children. "Think of what they'll go through," he had said. "Growing up mongrels." She had hung up on that conversation.

It was hard for Cecilia to imagine he even loved her, though she supposed he did. As far back as she could remember, they had been conducting a cold war. She was happy now to be at some distance from him—*a safe distance*. Now why did she think that?

"Get me another beer, Edith," Mike said, and belched.

"How did you—"

"What?"

"Nothing," Cecilia said, sighed, and went inside.

Cecilia dialed from the master bedroom but only managed to reach Jeremy Horowitz and Tom Parker's answering machine.

"Hello. This is the party to whom you are speaking. We can't come to the phone right now. Tom's all tied up, and I'm not kidding. Leave a message after the muffled scream. *Ciao*."

"Jeremy, it's Cecilia. Pick up the phone."

She heard the fumbling noise of the receiver being lifted. "Well, hello, dammit," came Jeremy's voice.

"I knew you were just screening."

"I was hovering over the thing like a vulture. You could probably hear me breathing. I was expecting my mother, and I just don't want to talk to her today."

"You want your mother to hear that message?"

"Oh, she'll get all kinds of strange and wonderful ideas."

"Jeremy, that's cruel."

"I'll never make her happy. I'm gay and I married a goy, and he's not a doctor, but a chiropractor. Somewhere there's a nice Jewish girl crying her eyes out. Anyway, Tom's too WASPisher for Ma. We went home for the High Holies and he was so good to her I can't tell you. She thinks he's too blond, 'like a Hitler Youth,' she says. But he did a little number on her back and she stopped complaining. I keep telling her, I could do a lot worse. You wouldn't remember Allal?"

"The Algerian?" Cecilia said. "Of course, I was there when you guys met, at that dance. What a cutie."

"Yeah, well, he left me for that ROTC guy. Anyway, my ma would've had an aneurysm if I'd brought him home for Yom Kippur, so I guess it was a good thing. She would have found a way to get us out of the house so she could check his suitcase for explosives. To her, Arab means terrorist, just like gay means AIDS. God forbid she should meet a gay Arab."

Cecilia thought Jeremy was too hard on his mother, but it had always been so, ever since they were in grade school. Jeremy had once said that his mother and Cecilia's father were a lot alike; to Cecilia, Mrs. Horowitz left a much sweeter impression. "Listen, you didn't have to live with her," was Jeremy's retort, and she supposed that was true, except Jeremy didn't have to live with her father, either, and even Jeremy agreed her father was an asshole.

"Mike said you called," Cecilia said. "What's up?"

"Oh, just checking up on you, like Dr. Bellows. I'm sorry. They've been showing *I Dream of Jeannie* on Nick at Nite, and it made me think of you."

They used to go over to each other's houses every day after school and watch reruns of *Big Valley*, *Star Trek*, *The Brady Bunch*, and *Jeannie*; Jeremy had always told her she looked like Barbara Eden, which she certainly did not. But even as kids, they found it inexplicable that a NASA psychiatrist would invite himself to sleep over at one of his astronauts' homes on such a frequent basis and on such short notice, and still never quite realize that tongue-tied Tony Nelson was keeping his lover in a bottle. When they grew older and Jeremy came out of the closet, he laid on her his theory that *Jeannie*, *Bewitched*, and *My Favorite Martian* were nothing more than thinly disguised metaphors for pre-Stonewall gay relationships, the "husband" having to keep the genie/witch/ Martian tightly under wraps or else risk the ruin of his career or being carted off to a mental institution. There was something to this, yet Cecilia thought he was stretching it when he tried to make a similar case for the Japanese POW that the *McHale's Navy* crew kept out of sight of ol' Leadbottom "so they could use him as their personal houseboy and sex slave." And when Jeremy started talking about *Alf*, Cecilia covered her ears and said she didn't want to hear about it.

"Haven's beautiful," Cecilia said, "and the people are lovely, a lot nicer than we expected. I think we're going to like it here."

"I'll be the judge of that," Jeremy said in his haughty Dr. Bellows. "Tom and I are going to come out and see for ourselves. The Mikester said it was okay."

"Of course it is. We've got tons of space. Really, you should see this place. It was built by an actual Old West madam."

"Like Miss Kitty?"

"Miss Kitty wasn't a madam!"

"Oh, yeah?"

"Well, you should see it. We've got a sunroom and a gold-fish pond. Just give us a week or two to get more settled in. How about the first week of October?"

"Delightful. I'll square dates with Tom and see when he can squeeze in a vacation. It sounds like there's something fishy going on over there." Dr. Bellows again.

"Only in the fish pond. We'll be looking forward to seeing you guys. Stay as long as you like, and bring your camera. You'll think you've died and gone to Switzerland."

"*This* I've *got* to see."

"Stop that."

"Stop what?"

"Stop being Dr. Bellows. You're driving me crazy."

"Crazy? Hmm, perhaps we should schedule an appointment."

"That's it, Jeremy, I'm hanging up. It's been real."

"Sure, Cecilia. I've got to run, anyway. I'll let you know when we're coming. Love to Mike. Kiss-kiss."

She pressed disconnect and was surprised to find that her eyes had teared up. All while they were growing up, she had got the impression that Mrs. Horowitz wouldn't have minded one bit if Jeremy had ended up marrying her, even if she was a shiksa. At least she'd become a doctor. Mrs. Horowitz was proud of her, which was more than she could say for her father. Funny, but until this moment, Cecilia had never realized what a mother figure Mrs. Horowitz had been to her all this time.

Mike came in, put his arm around her, and said, "Hey, what's wrong?"

"Nothing," Cecilia said.

"It's not nothing, now what is it?"

"I think I miss my mom."

"It's okay," he said, squeezing her tight, kissing her cheek. "It's okay. I'm here."

# Chapter 9

Their booth at the Raven's Roost had a good, lofty view of the town, from high up on Green Hill. A Wednesday night, and the place was packed, large families squeezed into the circular corner booths, elderly single men parked on the vinyl stools along the lunch counter and flirting with the waitresses, who were both gray-haired and in their fifties and looked like sisters. Bonnie herself seemed to do a bit of everything, from clearing dishes to taking orders to bringing out food. Her menu offered such fare as Flatiron Flapjacks, Roost Goose, Buffaloed Stew, Little Lost Salmon Steaks, and Spaghetti with Mooseballs.

"I bet they've got a lot of angry moose roaming around," Mike said dryly.

Mike had unpacked some of their kitchen already, but neither of them exactly felt like cooking, so at twilight they had donned leather jackets against the wind and headed up to the Roost, which sat catercorner from the Old Haven Church and the cemetery. The prices were so cheap, Cecilia was surprised

Bonnie could stay in business; then again, she had a loyal clientele and little competition.

"Evening, Maks." Bonnie was standing over Mike, her ballpoint pen clicked and licked and ready against the order pad. "How's the move coming along?"

"We're getting there," Mike said. "You look busy."

"Yeah, it's a good night. So what's it going to be?"

"I'll have the salmon steak," Cecilia said.

"Spoken like a true northwesterner." Bonnie gave her a wink and scribbled the order. "How's about you, Mike?"

"These mooseballs, they aren't—"

"Just ground moose meat. *Not* fried testicles."

Mike's face turned red. "I'll have the Buffaloed Stew."

"Good choice," Bonnie said, and touched his shoulder. "My own recipe. Popular around here. Everyone wants to eat buffalo since they saw *Dances with Wolves*."

Mike's stew came with a huge hunk of cornbread and several pats of butter. Cecilia's salmon steak had been broiled in a lemony marinade and topped with ground hazelnuts; she had had it prepared this way before, but never this good.

By the time they were halfway through dinner, most of the customers had cleared out. It was seven forty-five. Bonnie was untying her apron, unpinning her hair and letting it fall down her back. Nice hair, Cecilia thought.

"Where's everybody going?" she asked.

"Oh, it's the Haven Society," Bonnie said. "Just some stuffy old founder's club. Usually pretty dull. We meet Wednesday nights at eight down at the music hall. Tonight we're having a little bon voyage thingie for the Hamiltons. They're leaving tomorrow. Guess you knew that."

"You're not closing, are you?"

"Oh, no! Sadie and Millie can run the place all right, and the cooks are still here. Don't you two worry about a thing. Take your time, relax, enjoy yourselves. Have some dessert. I've got to go. I'm the secretary, and I've got to read back the minutes."

"We'll be back," Mike said, swallowing a bite of cornbread. "Excellent food."

"Thank *you*. Coming from the Maks, that means something."

Bonnie headed down Center Street to the Olbrich Music Hall. From their high vantage point, Cecilia and Mike could see her in the streetlight joining the large crowd in front. They all filed in promptly before the Old Haven Church could finish ringing out eight bells. The street became deserted.

"You want dessert?" Mike asked.

They had a choice of pies, ice cream, and a beautiful Black Forest torte layered with raspberry Bavarian cream. Mike opted for apple pie *à la mode*, but Cecilia could not resist the torte. Her slice was much too much to eat, but she ate it anyway, promising herself she would work it off once Mike got their home-gym equipment unpacked.

They were the last customers to leave. Sadie and Millie had been turning chairs over onto tables and mopping the floor, and the cooks were cleaning up the kitchen and listening to country music over the radio. Cecilia paid their bill in cash and left a good-sized tip.

"Come on back!" said either Sadie or Millie.

The door banged shut behind them.

"As if we had anywhere else to eat," Mike said once they were safely away.

The wind had grown stronger. Cecilia zipped up her jacket. A block down the hill, she looked over her shoulder and saw that the lights in the dining area were already turned off. One of the waitresses was locking the front doors.

"Is everybody in this Haven Society?" Mike asked.

"I have no idea," Cecilia said. "But I wish someone had told me. I made my good-byes already with Jim Hamilton, but I've never even met his wife, and neither of them have met you, and I wouldn't mind joining the party. But it doesn't look like we're invited, does it?"

"Let's go take a peek anyway." Mike never liked to be excluded from anything. Neither did Cecilia, but she was less aggressive about actually doing anything about it. Shortly after they had started living together, her father kept promising to come over to meet Mike and then never showed up; after a few weeks of this, Mike took it upon himself to show up on her father's doorstep one Saturday afternoon, unannounced and by himself, bearing a six-pack of Olympia. Cecilia's father had grumpily complained of having weekend projects to take care of and no time for chitchat and hadn't even invited him inside.

The Olbrich Music Hall, down in the bowl of the valley, was old and housed in brick, but its name had nothing to do with this. It rose up a good four stories tall, its façade minimally decorated. The granite cornerstone spoke volumes:

IN LOVING MEMORY OF MY WIFE

SALLY ANN OLBRICH

THIS BUILDING IS HEREBY DEDICATED

JULY 4, 1876, A.D.

HENRY JAMESON OLBRICH, BUILDER

"The founder's club meets in the founder's shrine to his dead wife," Mike said, stroking the stubble on his chin. "Velly intelesting, numba-one son."

Two beige-uniformed men were standing guard on the steps at the front entrance, arms folded across their chests, looking down at Cecilia and Mike.

"I'll do the talking," Cecilia whispered. If Mike felt slighted, he might go off half-cocked, and these guys didn't look like they wanted to be anybody's friend.

They wore dark, broad-brimmed cowboy hats that cast their eyes and half their faces in shadow, their square jaws thrusting out into the light from the street lamps. The first was easily six-two, the other as much as six-four; cowboy boots added a couple of inches in both cases. Their uniforms were the same as what Lewis Jackson had been wearing at the welcoming gala, similar to Sheriff Tyler's but with brown bandanna and golden clasp instead of a necktie, and no sidearms or other police gear.

"May we go in?" Cecilia asked the first guard.

"Sorry, ma'am." He held out his beefy arm. "Only members of the Haven Society allowed inside."

"My name's Cecilia Mak. I'm the new doctor. And this is my husband, Mike. I'm sure they'll let us in. I'm taking over the clinic from Jim Hamilton, and—"

"No one is allowed in unless they're a member," he said firmly. "Are you or your husband members?"

"No, but—"

"They're conducting a private meeting, ma'am."

The second guard came over to join his buddy. They were both in their midtwenties and built like Frigidaires, their shirt buttons straining to keep their muscles in check.

"Problem?" asked the second guard, balling his hands into fists and resting them on his hips.

"You guys must be in the Junior Posse."

The guards nudged each other, mouths breaking into white-enameled grins so bright Cecilia couldn't make out the spaces between their teeth.

"Ma'am," the first one said, "I aged out of the Junior Posse when I was eighteen. I'm twenty-four, my brother's twenty-six. Who told you about the Junior Posse, anyway?"

Cecilia decided not to tell them. She assumed these guys,

having aged out, were now in the regular, plain ol' Posse. If these were the kind of guys who were in it, no wonder Lewis Jackson had looked so uncomfortable in his uniform. She exchanged a look with Mike.

The second guard suggested, "Why don't you go on home now?"

"You're sure there's no chance you could let us in?" said Cecilia. "I'd really like to say good-bye—"

"We're just following orders," the second guard said, throwing up his hands as if it were beyond his control. "Sorry."

"That's all right," Cecilia said. "I didn't realize."

"I guess you didn't," said the first guard.

"I'd like your names," Mike said.

"You *what?*"

"Your names," Mike repeated testily. "We gave you ours. You say you can't let us in, but all we have is your word. I'd like your names so I can say who my wife and I have had the pleasure of speaking with when I bring this up with someone in the Haven Society, which I *will* do."

"I'm Jason Marsh," said the first one, coming toward them step by step, "and that's my brother Ted." He thumbed over his shoulder.

"Jason and Ted Marsh," Mike repeated.

"For all the good it'll do you," said Jason.

Mike and Cecilia backed down, keeping a safe distance in case Jason or Ted suddenly felt like flattening Mike's nose. "I guess I'll have to try my luck. You guys have a good evening."

Jason stopped, and Ted hovered back a few steps above, smiling condescendingly.

"Good night," Cecilia said.

"Take care, ma'am," said Jason. "You and your nice husband have yourselves a *safe* walk home, you hear?"

She heard, all right; she heard loud and clear.

*     *     *

"Fucking Hans and Franz," Mike muttered when they were a safe distance away. "This is bullshit."

"I know, Mike, I know. Let's just go home, okay?"

On their way back up Center Street, Cecilia kept looking back over her shoulder, but no one was following them. The streets were dead. Everyone, she imagined, was inside the music hall, at the meeting or bon voyage party or whatever the hell was really going on.

Everyone in all of Haven, apparently, except them.

# Chapter 10

It was after work the following Tuesday that Cecilia found the cats.

She parked the ambulance in the drive, behind the Camaro, and thought at first that Mike might be back from fishing. Then she recalled that he and Dave Clinton had gone together in Dave's red Ford Bronco. It had been early morning, and she had been barely awake. She had watched them from the bathroom window just before stepping into her shower. Now it was after six, the sun gone behind the westerly peaks, the valley in shadow, but there was still a good hour and a half before the fall of night. She didn't expect to see Mike home until it got dark.

"Mike?" she called as she entered the house. No answer came. The only sounds were the wind rustling the curtains and the low hum of the refrigerator kicking in.

Mike's note lay undisturbed on the breakfast-nook table where she had found it on coming downstairs after her shower. She had left it there before heading off to work, not wanting to throw it away for whatever reason.

Cecilia opened the refrigerator door and stared at the meager contents before grabbing a Haven Bräu for herself. Dave's product had a no-screw top, so she grabbed the bottle opener magnet from the freezer door and popped it off, producing a pleasant beer hiss and a ghostly wisp of mist. She blew it off, making an owlish hoot.

She settled into the sofa in the box-piled parlor, staring at the cold fireplace, exhausted. The windows were open, curtains billowing. The room was too chilly by half. She could not rest until she closed all the windows. She got back up, taking her beer with her, and headed upstairs.

She locked the windows tight in the bathroom and the small front bedroom where Mike was going to set up his writing space. The movers had put his computer desk against the far window, but his computer, printer, and fax machine remained sealed shut in their boxes.

At the master bedroom, she found herself setting down her beer and lying on the bed before getting to the windows. It had been a long day. She hoped Mike would be coming home with some trout. She would even clean them, as long as he would cook. Her eyelids fell.

Her day had started with routine appointments: end-of-summer colds, a child with an ear infection, a logger with a badly sprained ankle. Before lunch, she had been called down to the school, where some third-grade boys had gotten into a fight at recess. She made repairs and took the two worst cases down to the clinic for stitches. The aggressor had been Joe Doyle's eldest boy, Joe Junior, a tubby kid who acted as if his dad were mayor of New York. His scrawny victim, Timmy Pons, had received a solid kick in the shin with the rough leather sole of Joe Junior's boot, but in the melee Timmy had managed to zonk Joe Junior on the forehead with the metal point of his umbrella. Joe Junior's cut had gushed, and when Cecilia arrived he looked like a war casualty. She cleaned them up and put on bandages and loaded them into the ambulance, where she had to tell them to "knock it off" when they began slapping each other en route. Janice Fremont looked as if she had seen them before for similar offenses. When they were fixed up, Fremont volunteered to drop them back off at the school. Cecilia let her.

After lunch, Cecilia made house calls to the homes of elderly, unhealthy patients. They were retired, overweight, and sedentary. They suffered from arthritis, osteoporosis, angina, clogged arteries, chronic airway obstruction, and a host of gastrointestinal complaints; some had adult-onset diabetes, Alzheimer's, or were in remission from cancer. One woman of eighty-one was still recovering from a total hip replacement from two months ago. Cecilia did not try to assume Hamilton's manner, which had been pleasant and folksy but at times supercilious. She had observed that his approach was old-fashioned; he had spent all of his time fixing problems, none trying to prevent them. Cecilia was already pushing more vigorous exercise and a healthier, low-fat, low-cholesterol diet. The seniors took a genuine interest, acting as if they had never heard of such things. Perhaps they listened to Cecilia because of her youth and good health. Hamilton, with his pipe-smoking, had been not much of an example to anyone about anything.

During a lull between calls, Cecilia drove down to the end of Davis Lane, on the fringes of Haven, to see if she could meet Dottie Jackson. Some people were simply stubborn when it came to medical care and would rather wait for a problem to fix itself than go see a doctor. Perhaps Hamilton was sympathetic, but Cecilia considered it incumbent on her to look in on anyone she suspected might be ailing.

The Jackson place, a low-slung ranch-style house with pastel green aluminum siding, announced itself with a barking of dogs. A pair of big, well-muscled rottweilers bared their slobbery teeth and smashed repeatedly up against the chain-link fencing on the shady side of the house like great white sharks trying to break through an observer's underwater cage to get at the meat. It was a tall fence; the dogs could not get out without someone opening the gate. The garage door was open, the garage filled with tools and junk. Front and back lawns were an automobile graveyard, with the rusting carcasses of a forty-year-old Ford pickup, a Volkswagen Beetle of unknown vintage, a '59 Mercury station wagon, a '70 Olds Cutlass, a '74 Dodge Dart, and '81 Pontiac Phoenix, and a boxy white sedan that Cecilia first took to be an old Mercedes but which turned out to be one of the last of the Studebakers, its hood ornament a stylized S in a circle rather than the Mercedes triad. Some were up on blocks, and they all had cracked windows, missing wheels, deflated tires, fender dents, bullet holes, and other signs of disuse.

Trying to ignore the dogs, Cecilia went up the path and knocked on the door. She received no answer. If anyone was inside calling, unable to come to the door, Cecilia would never hear it for the incessant barking and snarling. She went to the nearest window, cupped her hands against the dusty surface, and peered into the living room. The TV set was off, no lamps on, the only signs of life three mangy cats asleep on the sofa. She tried knocking loudly for several more minutes, then gave up altogether and went back to her truck. If Dottie was home and truly didn't want to be bothered, she had succeeded. Cecilia was determined to try again another day.

She returned to the clinic to dictate some reports and catch up on paperwork, wanting not to let it stack up. She saw six more patients before closing up shop.

Cecilia forced her eyes open. She was about to fall asleep there on the bed. She sat up on the comforter and finished her beer. The room had grown colder. Then she remembered why

71

she had gone there in the first place and got back up to close the windows. As she turned the lock-latch on the last frame, something caught her eye down below in the grass, in the backyard, near the base of a blue spruce, half-hidden by the low-hanging boughs. It appeared to be a dead animal. All she could make out was grayish fur and a ringed tail. Perhaps it was a raccoon. It might not be dead at all but in need of a vet.

She hurried downstairs and out the back door to find out. The freezing wind drew goose bumps on her flesh. She armed herself with a small dead tree branch in case the animal tried to make a move at her.

As she neared the spruce, she realized that this was not a raccoon at all but two dead cats. One was a gray tabby with a black-ringed tail, the other a large, black tom. She prodded them gently with her stick, but they were stiff as boards, their coats matted with dirt and spruce needles, smelling foul and buzzing with horseflies. Purplish blood had congealed and caked around their mouths. Their heads lay askew at impossible backward angles; without examining any closer, she would guess that they had been strangled.

Someone had dumped them here, side by side, in the shadow of the spruce, perhaps as much as a few days ago, right in her and Mike's backyard.

Cecilia dropped the stick on the ground and dashed back inside. She called the sheriff's department, and the secretary told her that yes, the sheriff was in his office and would she please hold for just one moment. While she was waiting for Tyler to pick up the line, she stared out the front window and wished that Dave Clinton would pull up *right now* and drop Mike off safe and sound, smiling and waving and bearing a stringful of beautiful brookies.

"Yello," said the voice, "this is Frank Tyler."

"Frank," she said, "it's Cecilia Mak."

"Hi, Cee!" Tyler might have heard Mike doing that at the welcoming, but only Mike called her Cee, and she didn't like Tyler or anyone else picking up on it.

"Frank," she said, "can you come on out here?"

"Why, sure. Is it an emergency?"

"I don't know, Frank. I'd rather show you. I think someone's trying to scare Mike and me."

"Trying?" Tyler said, and chuckled sympathetically.

"It's Martin and Eva, all right," Tyler said, prodding them with the toe of his boot. "They went missing during Hamilton's going-away shindig last week, when we were all down at the music hall. I told Jim it was the Argentinian jitters. Animals pick up on stuff, you know, like they've got radar. They didn't want to go into those goddamned travel crates and spend a whole day flying down to South America. So they skittered off—at least, that's what I figured, that's what I told Jim. I said, Jim, they'll come on back in some kind of rattletrap condition, and I'll stick them in a box, poke a few holes in top, and FedEx them to you. He didn't think it was funny, and he isn't going to be too happy about this, either, no way, no sir, not one damned bit."

"Poor things," Cecilia said, hardly able to look. She shooed away an aggressive green fly that tried to bite her on the forearm. "Who do you know would do such a thing?"

Herb Monroe, Tyler's deputy, snapped flash pictures with his Polaroid. He was not much older than Lewis Jackson— maybe nineteen—and his face was pockmarked and riddled with pimples. Jason or Ted Marsh from the Posse, whatever that was, would have made more impressive deputies, but they probably would have failed the exam. At least Herb Monroe didn't look stupid. He was slighter of build, but he was also carrying a nine-millimeter semiautomatic of the same make as Tyler's; he didn't need muscle.

"Did anyone hold a grudge against Jim Hamilton?" Cecilia asked.

Tyler shook his head, turned up his lip, and looked over at Monroe, who returned his befuddlement. "Not that I am aware of, no. He was more well-to-do than most, but that's never been the cause of any tension around here."

"So you don't have any idea who might have done this?"

"Haven't a clue, yet." Tyler sighed heavily, closed his notepad, looked around at the sky. They were losing their light. Monroe finished his pictures and other evidence collection and with gloved hands began bagging up the cats.

"I don't like the fact they were dumped on our lawn, Frank. You think there's anything to it?"

"You mean, because of you and Mike?"

"You said it, not me."

Tyler cocked his head back. "Naw, I doubt it."

Cecilia told him about Jason and Ted Marsh and the refused entrée into the Haven Society meeting. "That was when the cats disappeared, wasn't it? How long did that party last?"

"A couple of hours," Tyler said, not following her.

"Couldn't they have left—or only one of them—and gone and taken Martin and Eva?"

"Who do you mean, Jason and Ted?"

"Why not?"

"And *strangled* them?" Tyler shook his head, smiling almost to himself. "To get at you and Mike? That really doesn't make any sense now, does it? Sounds a little far-fetched."

"Not to me it doesn't. They acted like a couple of brutes. What in the world is this Posse, anyway?"

Herb Monroe disappeared around the side of the house carrying two large garbage bags with Martin and Eva inside.

"I'm sorry, Cee, I was watching Herb. What did you say?"

"Cee!" All of a sudden, Mike came running up from around the side of the house and into the backyard, short of breath. "What's going on? What happened? Are you all right?"

"I'm fine. A little shook up." She would hate to imagine what Mike must have thought, arriving at the end of his fishing trip to find two Prospect County Sheriff's Department Blazers out front, red and blue lights swirling, radios squawking.

Mike gave her a big bear hug. His fishing vest exuded the strong and somehow pleasant smell of fish-for-dinner.

"It's Martin and Eva," she said. "I found them over there under our blue spruce. Someone strangled them."

"Jesus Christ!" Mike looked around, as if expecting to see a couple of human corpses lying naked in the brush. Cecilia realized she had never said a word to him about Hamilton's cats. She had had no reason to.

"*Who are Martin and Eva?*" he asked.

# Chapter 11

A few days later, Cecilia awoke to the cawing of a crow outside their bedroom window. Her heart skipped a beat, and her eyes snapped open, as if she had been roused from the finale of a nightmare. The curtains remained drawn, framed in a bluish aura of dawn light, and although she could not see the bird, it appeared in her mind: a large crow, perhaps a raven, dripping with glossy, blue-black feathers, staring at her with an obsidian eye. If she were to lift the curtains, it would be there perched on a stalwart pine branch, waiting. In her dream-weariness, she imagined that the crow had been biding its time since she was a little girl, to finish the job it had begun. She remembered only vaguely the attack that had left her so bruised and bloodied, until her father had come and saved her. Distant though that memory remained, the image of the bird—spread wings, sharp beak, gripping talons—had never left.

With a fluttering of feathers, the crow cawed again, and the subtle light and shadows on the curtain shifted.

"Mike?" she whispered.

She lay splayed across the bed, her head on his pillow, her

own clamped between her thighs, but Mike was nowhere to be seen. She sat up rubbing her face, wondering where he had gone. It was early yet and hardly his custom to be up. She would have expected him to sleep through her alarm and for her instead to desert him.

"Mike?" she called.

She could smell his gentle scent on their sheets, could see the unbalanced lay of the bedcovers on this side, *his* side—evidence that he had yanked them over toward him again during the night. She had probably lain there snuggled up against his bulk, her arm resting on his smooth, hairless chest, and when he had awakened he had managed to sneak out from under without disturbing her, placing her pillow where it was to try to fool her into thinking it was him.

It had worked.

"Mike?"

She looked over at the alarm clock on the night table. It read 5:59, then switched to 6:00 and began its rhythmic beep. She groaned loudly and reached over to silence it. She smelled something burning and wondered if the house was on fire.

"*Mike!*"

"Good morning," he said, standing in the doorway.

Cecilia placed a hand on her breast. "You scared me."

Mike, naked except for his boxer shorts, was carrying a four-legged tray one-handed on the pads of five fingers, a trick he had learned in his waiter days, around the time they had met. Geoffrey's Bistro—that was the name of the place—miles away now, five years ago.

Breakfast smells wafted into the room, and Mike said, "Just what the doctor ordered."

"Oh, that's cute," Cecilia said. "Corny, but cute."

"That's me, horny but cute." He smiled as he stood there showing off his body; he wanted Cecilia's mouth to water for more than just his cooking. He planted the tray across her lap: two eggs sunny-side up, three crisp strips of bacon, a toasted buttered English muffin, a handful of green grapes, a glass of orange juice, a cup of light coffee, tiny salt and pepper shakers, and wild violets in a six-ounce bottle of bubbling Perrier.

"Wow," Cecilia said.

"That's all you can say? *Wow?*"

"Sorry, just woke up. It looks wonderful."

"Thanks. Here's to the head honcho."

"Only honcho," Cecilia corrected. She snapped an end of bacon into her mouth. "I can't tell if you love me or if you're trying to kill me."

"Everything in moderation, right?" Mike sat down on the other side of the bed and crossed his legs lotus-style. The fly on his boxers parted teasingly. He plucked a grape and popped it into Cecilia's mouth.

"You are *not* going to feed me," she protested.

He unfurled the paper napkin, draped it across her, and planted fork and knife in her fists. "Go on," he said, elbows on knees, head in his hands. "I'll sit and watch."

"You like to watch?"

"Mmm, yes." Mike raised his eyebrows lasciviously.

"You are cute." Cecilia dug into the eggs.

"Horny, too, don't forget that."

"I wish my father could see you like this."

"Like what?"

"Half-naked."

"I beg your pardon."

"He sees what he wants to see. He probably thinks of you as mild-tempered, effeminate."

"Like our waiters at Siam Gardens," Mike said—their favorite Thai restaurant back in Seattle, the thought of which made Cecilia homesick.

"My father has never had a bite of Thai food."

"Hi," Mike said in an affected, high-pitched voice smooth as honey. He pursed his lips and batted his thick eyelashes. "I'll be your waiter. My name is Lemongrass."

"He'd kill you if he heard you talking like that. Bad enough I didn't marry a white boy. If he ever thought you were gay—"

"Hasn't he ever seen any Bruce Lee movies? Or Toshiro Mifune, even? *The Seven Samurai?*"

"I don't think he's even seen *The King and I*. He likes John Wayne Westerns where they kill all the Indians."

"You want him to see how macho I am?" Mike deepened his voice to a gruff basso, puffed out his chest, bulged his biceps, flexed his pecs alternately so that they seemed to shift from one side to the other—a dubious display of machismo that always made Cecilia laugh.

"Doesn't it excite you to think of me fixing your food this morning all naked and sweaty?" Mike asked.

"Gross," Cecilia said.

The phone rang.

"Gross but cute. That's why you love me." Mike kissed her squarely on the lips. "Go ahead, eat. I'll get it."

He reached across to grab the phone, and as he did, she caught a whiff of him that aroused her. But she had a sinking feeling this call was going to get her out of bed.

"Hello? Sure, she's right here." Mike tried to hand Cecilia the phone, but she waved him off, in the middle of a bite of English muffin. *Who is it?* she mouthed. Mike covered the receiver and whispered, "Sheriff Friendly."

She glared at him, took the phone, and asked, "Yes?"

"Cecilia? Frank Tyler," said the voice, sounding too cheerful for this or any hour. "Herb Monroe just called in a shooting victim north of here—"

"Christ," Cecilia said, and tucked the phone between shoul-

79

der and chin, moving the breakfast tray aside and wriggling off the bed.

Mike cocked his head to listen as he drew open the curtains, letting in the soft light and the broad vista of mountains and evergreens. The crow, screaming, flew from its perch and cast a fleeting shadow across the window. The bough swayed gently up and down. Needles fell from the air.

"Looks like a hunting accident," said Tyler. "Some fellow with a shotgun wound to the abdomen. Herb doesn't even know who he is."

"I'll get my ambulance." Cecilia was already stepping into the jeans Mike had so eagerly ripped off her last night. Mike was pulling on his sweatpants, paying close attention to her end of the conversation.

"You'd better follow my truck," said Tyler, "or you're liable to get lost. It's up in the forest."

"I'll be there in less than a minute, Frank."

"In front of the courthouse."

"Right." She hung up.

"I'll drive you," Mike said, pulling his sweatshirt down over his head and slipping into a pair of running shoes.

"You don't have to." Mike was not her ambulance driver; she didn't have one. She was to do it herself, as Hamilton had done before her. She wondered how he had managed to do much of anything at his age. Haven should have gotten rid of him years ago. Not that they had had much of a choice.

"I want to," Mike insisted, grabbing the ambulance keys from off the dresser. "What is it?"

"Shotgun wound, sounds like he won't make it." Cecilia threw on her sneakers and a University of Washington–Seattle tee, downed her coffee, grabbed her black leather doctor's bag and Mike's sinewy arm, gave him a smart peck on the lips, and said, "Come on, hon, let's go."

*　　*　　*

They met Sheriff Tyler on Center Street in front of the sandstone courthouse. He was smoking a cigarette outside his truck, a full-sized, four-wheel-drive Blazer on whose doors, mudflaps, and spare-tire slipcover were emblazoned the five-pointed gold star with the black-enameled eagle and the P.C.S.D. Its roof was bedecked with a gaudy array of horns, warning lights, and a rotatable search, and it stood so high off the ground that its axles and undercarriage were visible, the housings so caked with mud they resembled wasps' nests. As Mike pulled the Blazer up sharply behind him, Tyler grinned back over his shoulder, tipped his hat, waved for them to follow, and vaulted himself into his cab.

Tyler drove off at a high speed—it was early yet, and no Havenites were about—and led them out of town and over the bridge, going fast even after they had turned off the main road, onto an unmarked winding jeep trail that was barely wide enough for one vehicle. Cecilia hoped no one was coming in the other direction, or she would have multiple victims to tend to on this lovely September morning.

If she were ever to face a real crisis up here—a person with severe trauma or extensive burns or in desperate need of emergency surgery—she would have to call the Medflight helicopter in from Boise and hope they could come. The closest hospital that she could reasonably reach by ambulance was the Pocatello Regional Medical Center, about a three-hour drive as long as the weather cooperated and she didn't get stuck behind too many logging trucks. The few routes out of the mountains were all two-lane and too narrow, with tricky curves.

Tyler pulled off the road and into a grassy clearing. He parked alongside Herb Monroe's own Blazer and an old, beat-up International Harvester pickup that had the large, bloody carcass of a four-point buck in its bed. An NRA bumper sticker on the pickup said THEY CAN HAVE MY GUN WHEN THEY PRY IT FROM MY COLD DEAD FINGERS. Tyler got out and ran into the forest to join his deputy and the two hunters who were standing over a dark heap on the ground.

Mike backed up the ambulance next to the pickup. He helped Cecilia unload the gurney, and together they carried it through the trees. The carpet of pine needles was damp from a light rain that had come during the night. The trees had grown too close together, their only live branches high overhead, battling for sunlight. Cecilia and Mike had to duck under some dead trees, smooth and gray and stripped of their bark, that had fallen between their neighbors.

"I thought he was a deer, ma'am," said the younger of the two hunters. It was Lewis Jackson, standing alongside his grandfather, Clark. Both wore fluorescent orange vests and carried shotguns, double barrels dangling toward the ground. They wore nearly identical red baseball caps that advertised BLACK & DECKER CHAIN SAWS. Clark Jackson's was greasy, Lewis's cleaner and newer.

"Shut up." Jackson thwacked his grandson smartly on the back of his head.

"Is he still breathing?" Cecilia asked, before she and Mike could set the gurney down.

"No, ma'am," Lewis said. "I think he's dead."

"You let her be the judge of that, Lewis," Jackson snapped.

Blood and entrails had erupted from the victim's abdominal cavity, darkly staining his camouflage fatigues, combat boots, and a nearby duffel full of gear. His face was pale, eyes wide and glassy. A broad ribbon of blood marked his cheek and dripped down off his ear onto the damp forest floor. A stinkbug crawled onto his forehead; Mike reached down and flicked it off.

"Christ," Cecilia muttered, kneeling. She hastily put on latex gloves and felt for a pulse, but the body was cold and lifeless. He had probably been dead since Herb Monroe had called it in. But the damage was so extensive that it would not ultimately have mattered. No need for any heroics today, no emergency trip to the clinic or to Pocatello.

"He's dead," Cecilia said. She wished she might have been able to try to do something.

"Dr. Mak," said Sheriff Tyler, and she thought he was going to say he was sorry, but he was all smiles. "You've met Herb Monroe."

"Ma'am," said Deputy Monroe with a tip of his hat.

Cecilia held her tongue; now was not the time for introductions. A man had just died of a horrible accident, and Tyler was trying to maintain social graces. The gore around her she had been trained to withstand as best she could, but Tyler's cavalier attitude made her ill.

"What time was the shooting?" she asked.

Lewis opened his mouth to speak, but his grandfather snapped out his hand and said, "I reckon a quarter of six, ma'am." Jackson's good eye darted from one side to the other, the glass one staring off into the distance, ghostly and dead.

"We were yonder about thirty yards," Lewis said, his voice quavering. "I . . . I heard a rustling over here and turned my gun. I had it in my sights. I thought it was a deer. And it made a quick, darting movement. And—"

"For Christ's sake, Lewis!" said Jackson. "The little lady doesn't care about that. She's just the damn doctor!"

"None of you know the victim?" Cecilia asked.

"Never seen him before in my life, ma'am," Jackson said.

"Me neither," Lewis said, shaking his head sadly.

"Don't recognize him, myself," Deputy Monroe said, then turned to Tyler. "I don't think he's from around here, do you, Frank?"

"Outsider," Tyler pronounced, prodding the body with the

toe of his boot as he had done with Martin and Eva. He reached down, pat-searched the victim's blood- and piss-soaked pants, and removed a wallet from a zippered pocket on the thigh. "New York State photo DL. That's him, all right. Wouldn't you say, Herb?"

Monroe glanced at the driver's license and nodded.

"Raphael Abramowitz," Tyler said, sounding out each sylla-ble. "Of Brooklyn, New York. Isn't that strange?"

"What's so strange about it?" Mike blurted.

Tyler gave Mike a sharp, smoldering look. "I only think it's strange that he should be out here hunting in Idaho when he lives in New York."

"Maybe it's an old driver's license," Mike said. "He could have just moved here, like us."

"I would have known about it," Tyler said. "No, he doesn't live around here, that's for sure."

"Why is that?" Mike said.

"I know just about everybody in the whole county, and I know who's dead, who's dying, who's moving in, and who's moving out. And I know for a fact that Mr. Abramowitz does not live around Haven. It hasn't got a damned thing to do with anything else."

"He doesn't live anywhere anymore," Cecilia said levelly. She wanted to quell this burgeoning male rivalry. Mike and the sheriff could argue some other day. And if there were to be any lingering questions about the Abramowitz case, they would be Tyler's to solve. At the very least, there ought to be an inquest, but that was up to Joe Doyle and the DA's office to decide and had nothing to do with her. Hunting accidents were routine enough, but she wondered if any trigger-happy hunter was ever fully prosecuted, even for manslaughter. The rest of Abramowitz's story, if there even was one, would come out in due course. Once the coroner got here, her part in it would be mercifully over.

"Herb." Tyler snapped his fingers. "Try to raise Joe Doyle on your radio and tell him to get his carcass out of bed, will you? And bring back your Polaroid so we can wrap up the scene."

"Yes sir." Monroe shuffled off to his truck.

"Mike, I'm going to need to clean up here," Cecilia said. Her hands were sticky and noxious with blood. "Would you mind going and getting my kit? It's in the back of the truck."

"Sure, Cee." Mike went to retrieve it.

"Touchy, isn't he?" Tyler cocked his head in Mike's direction. Cecilia said nothing.

"I didn't mean anything." Tyler's smile turned from death's-head to senior prom. He removed his cowboy hat, revealing his hair mashed into the shape of the brim. He wiped the sweat from his brow with his shirtsleeve. A shaft of sunlight broke through the trees and struck his eyes.

"Mike's a very nice guy," Cecilia said. "If the two of you just try to get to know each other, I don't think you'll have any trouble at all."

"Cecilia," Tyler said, "I sincerely hope we won't have a stitch of trouble, but if we do, I hope you and I can still be friends."

Cecilia turned her gaze back toward the body. Tyler excused himself, and he and Monroe began snapping photos and collecting evidence. The Jacksons stood opposite and quietly kept their distance.

Mike returned with Cecilia's kit. She disposed of the gloves and disinfected her hands. They wandered a short distance away, safely out of the others' earshot.

"What do you make of it?" she asked.

Mike dropped his voice to a wry whisper. "Tyler should bust the Jacksons for one thing at least."

"Besides killing a person?"

"He won't do anything about that, trust me." Mike shook his head cynically. "They're his buddies. Look at him. He's already decided it's an accident."

"And you don't think it is?"

"I don't know, Cee," Mike said, toying with the stubble on the point of his chin. "I'd like to know what the Jacksons were doing out here in the first place. Deer season doesn't start for another week."

"Are you sure?"

"Positive."

"How would you know?"

"When Dave Clinton and I went fishing, he said he had to renew his hunting license so he could go out next week for the start of deer season. He invited me along, but I told him no thanks. I never was a hunter."

Cecilia glanced over at the Jacksons. Lewis was staring uneasily at the body, his face withdrawn and blank. Clark Jackson's good eye caught Cecilia staring, and he spat a thick, brown stream of chewing tobacco onto the forest floor, as if in some kind of challenge. He shifted his weight from one foot to the other, looking around at the tree trunks, the entire time exchanging not a single word with his grandson.

As Cecilia waited for Tyler and Monroe to finish their work, a long black Cadillac hearse pulled up and parked alongside the ambulance. A white vinyl magnetic sign on the driver's door announced DOYLE FUNERAL HOME and gave the phone number. Joe and Vicky got out looking suitably sober.

"That was fast," Mike said. "How long since Monroe went to his radio—five minutes, ten?"

"It's not far from town." Cecilia gave the Doyles the benefit of a doubt. "They were probably already awake."

"I still say it was fast."

The Doyles came slowly toward them bearing their own

gurney, on the top of which was laid out a black vinyl body bag, its silvery zipper glinting as it picked up shafts of sunlight.

"Just what exactly are you saying?"

"I don't know, Cee," Mike said with a crooked half-smile, as if whatever he had been thinking seemed ludicrous to him now. "Naw, it's nothing. I'll tell you later. Here they come."

# Chapter 12

Mike spent the rest of the morning setting up his computer and trying to arrange an office for himself in one of the smaller upstairs bedrooms. The movers had put his desk next to the south-facing window, but the splendid view of the mountains would be too distracting, so he moved it to the opposite wall. After a long search downstairs for the right box, he unpacked his reference books and shelved them along the hutch above the monitor. Along the other half he placed books of inspiration, including oral histories by Studs Terkel; essay collections by Gore Vidal, Gary Wills, and Noam Chomsky; volumes of Emerson, Thoreau, and Whitman; and the copy of *Tripmaster Monkey* his colleagues had given him.

Mike had yearned to be a reporter ever since he was nine, when his mother took him to the Wyo Theater to see *All the President's Men*. Though his parents tried to teach him what they could about their family's heritage and culture, they had grown somewhat apart from it themselves, and they knew only a handful of other ethnic Chinese in Laramie, so it was not like it would have been if he had grown up in an American Chinatown in New York City, San Francisco, or even Seattle. The only other Chinese kids he knew were sons and daughters of other professors, and he had never particularly gotten along with any of them, anyway. His mother always wanted him growing up one-hundred-percent American, and Laramie was not a bad place for that. So, in that bicentennial year, she had taken little Michael to see *All the President's Men* in the hopes that it would teach him a useful civics lesson about Richard Nixon and Watergate.

Instead, Mike came away captivated by the glamour of investigative journalism. The movie led him to the book, and he came to idolize Woodward and Bernstein (whom he imagined as Redford and Hoffman). He edited his high-school newspaper and never thought of pursuing anything else as a career. After college, he interned at the *Post-Intelligencer*, then landed a job there and found that not every reporter was given the opportunity to do time-consuming, in-depth, world-shattering investigations. After a few years, he considered himself damned lucky to have worked his way up from features to a position as a city-government reporter, which mainly entailed covering meetings and the arcana of local-election politics. When he had the time, he would pore carefully over the minutiae of urban redevelopment grants and subway-construction contracts, searching for any hint of scandal, but he was never able to sniff out anything untoward; the city was clean—clean and boring.

He was by nature a conspiracy buff, and he dreamed of a job around Washington, D.C., where all the conspirators lived. He subscribed to his own theories: JFK had been killed by the South Vietnamese in retaliation for Diem and Nhu, and the CIA had covered it up in the broader interests of prosecuting the war in Vietnam and making the world safe for democracy; the CIA had dosed Edmund Muskie's coffee with LSD in the 1972 New Hampshire primary to make it appear as if he were having a nervous breakdown, thus causing him to drop out, George McGovern to be nominated, and Nixon to win his cakewalk; William Casey had stolen Jimmy Carter's debate notebooks so his boss Ronald Reagan would know what was up Mr. Peanut's sleeve; a Republican conspiracy had planted Donna Rice in Gary Hart's bedroom and on board the *Monkey Business* in a particularly hardball form of entrapment; Reagan had been firmly at the helm of the good ship Iran-Contra, and CIA director Casey's "brain tumor" had been an all-too-convenient way of keeping the old spook from testifying. Patness was the hallmark of every good conspiracy.

As an undergrad, Mike was elated when the Iran-Contra scandal broke. He skipped classes to watch the hearings on CNN. Even Watergate had only historical relevance, but here was a scandal with even broader Constitutional issues at stake, and it was part of his own generation's history. With it came disillusionment about the power of the press, or the lack thereof. Reporters had done excellent work uncovering the myriad details—the Eugene Hasenfus connection, the secret bank accounts, the transfers of money, the shipments of arms, the return shipments of drugs into America, the hostage deals, the involvement of Ollie North and CIA officials and the vice-president—to no avail. George Bush became president. Ollie North became a hero and nearly a U.S. senator. No one in America understood what had happened or even gave a goddamn.

Mike might have made investigative reporter at the *Post-Intelligencer* in a few years if it weren't for the move to Haven—which he was happy to make, because he loved Cecilia and would do anything for her. He had known of her commitment to the Rural Physicians Program since their earliest days together, and it was partly this altruistic side of her that he had been so taken with. Perhaps she could have found some other way of financing her education and paying it back, but this route had spoken to her heart, to the very reasons she wanted to be a doctor in the first place. The nation had a shortage of rural doctors, and Cecilia wanted to help stop the gap. She also believed in the ideal of the old-fashioned, caring, all-knowing family practitioner; one of her great heroes was the late physician and man of letters William Carlos Williams, whose poems and stories she frequently read for their keen insight. Before meeting Cecilia, Mike had considered women of his generation flighty and trivial, unserious about anything but themselves and certainly incompatible with him. He considered himself lucky to have found her.

They lived together for four years before tying the knot. They had never wanted to marry for any religious reason, since neither of them was any kind of believer. Mike's parents back in Laramie adored Cecilia and had remained nonjudgmental (or at least politely reticent) about their living arrangements. Cecilia's father, of course, was dead-set against her being with Mike at all. Cecilia's relationship with her father had always been strained, but it had taken a turn for the worse ever since she had met Mike. She put up a good front that it didn't matter, but Mike was sure that deep down, she longed to have a normal, healthy, happy relationship with him. Mike felt guilty about being the cause of the problem. But now, at least, Cecilia had some living space.

The move would be good for her, and Mike understood this. Rather than start on the bottom of the totem pole at a small practice or as part of a large, impersonal HMO, she was being given the chance to do the kind of doctoring she believed in. She would make house calls, make her own diagnoses without having to consult a thousand others, treat her own patients according to her own program, get to know them not just as their doctor but as their friend. Even if she and Mike were to stay only for the five years, she would be bringing these experiences back with her to the city. It would enrich her future life as a doctor.

Mike was proud of her and was rather proud of himself for not minding putting on hold his dream of becoming the next Woodward-and-Bernstein. He had always wanted to write a novel, and he believed he could do it; this was the perfect opportunity. Journalism was a more practical career, but in Haven it would be impossible. He could try to do some freelance work long-distance, perhaps magazine articles, but he had tried in the past to secure such assignments with no luck, and he did not want to sit around and be a househusband. He had to do something to occupy his time. He planned to write, spend time with his wife if she could ever find any for him, and do more fishing.

Cecilia was going to be too busy today even to come home for lunch. They had come back together after the shooting victim, and Mike had nuked the cold breakfast for her and fixed himself some oatmeal. She had hurried off to the clinic, where she would spend her morning with her scheduled appointments. The rest of the day, she was going to have to "assist" Joe Doyle with the autopsy down at the morgue, though in reality, she had told him, it would be the other way around. Mike had no idea when she would be coming home.

He missed her today more than ever. He needed to get his office set up and get going on his writing or he would end up in a funk, wandering around the house looking for things to fix, turning on the TV and watching *Geraldo*.

This morning he had been keeping busy, distracting himself from the more disturbing thoughts that had lodged in his brain. He had decided from the way that Clark and Lewis Jackson had been acting that Clark, not Lewis, had been the shooter. He doubted it was an accident. He had said nothing yet to Cecilia because he did not want to influence her autopsy observations. Clark Jackson had stumbled across a Jew in his forest and shot him dead; could he be some kind of white supremacist, a member of one of the groups Tawanda Neebli had warned him about?

For part of the morning, Mike had searched through still-packed boxes for Tawanda Neebli's articles on hate groups in the Northwest, but he had no luck turning them up. He put in a call to Tawanda's desk, but she was out and he had to leave a message on her voice mail.

The NRA bumper sticker on Clark Jackson's pickup, of course, only indicated that Jackson was an avid sportsman, and it didn't necessarily mean that he was any more right-wing than Ronald Reagan or Charlton Heston, or Bill Clinton for that matter. If Clark Jackson belonged to one of these organized hate groups, Mike might never find out. But a little sniffing around town might turn up something, he thought.

Mike finally shut off his computer and decided to go out for a nice afternoon walk around Haven. Like the bear who went over the mountain, he was going to see what he could see.

Low-flying cumulus drifted over the town, pushed eastward by a biting wind off the mountains. The sky was deep and clear, the afternoon sun out in force, but still the air was brisk. Mike donned his black leather bomber jacket, which was plenty warm, and stepped into his deep motorcycle boots rather than his sneakers. The rain that had come during the night had left patches of mud all around the town.

Mike walked up Green Hill to the church and wandered into the lush, overgrown cemetery lawn. He walked among the rows and scanned the names on the gravestones: Walter and Emma Gillette, Zebulon and Alice Marsh, Hattie McKinley, Mary Downey. A simple marker of pink granite stood at the

head of the side-by-side plots of what had to have been Lewis
Jackson's parents:

MERIWETHER LEWIS JACKSON
BORN MAY 5, 1951—DIED DECEMBER 21, 1992

KATHERINE LEE JACKSON
BORN OCTOBER 29, 1953—DIED DECEMBER 21, 1992

There were no flowers at the grave, no sign whatsoever that
anyone had paid them any recent attention. Mike wondered,
morbidly, how exactly they had come to die together, and at
such a relatively young age. It had been at about the time of
the winter solstice, the shortest day of the year. Had it been an
auto accident in the snow? A suicide pact? Murder? Meteor?

The view from on high, of Haven at midday, was grand. The
town's vertical location had been dictated by the mining activ-
ity that had brought the first nonnative peoples into the territory in the 1870s. Mike wondered where one might find the
actual site of the Olbrich Lode Mine; no modern map that he
had seen revealed its location. The hills blocked the view of
some parts of town, and the old mine, if it still stood, was
probably farther up along the Little Lost River. The higher wa-
ters disappeared up into the foothills below Flatiron. The
clouds seemed to be skimming the top of the peak, an easy two
thousand feet above the town.

While Mike was wandering the cemetery, he looked for a
grave marker that might bear the name Hinton, but he found
none.

Coming down, he noticed the Reverend Andrew Cleveland
crouched on his knees, fitting plastic tack-on letters onto the
black sign in front of the Old Haven Church. Mike stood there

in silence and waited until he was finished. The Reverend Mr. Cleveland closed and locked the glass, sealing up his message:

CALL TO WORSHIP

SUNDAY, SEPTEMBER 25

8:00, 9:30, 11:00 A.M.

THE REV. ANDREW CLEVELAND

"THE NEW MILLENNIUM"

"What's that about, Reverend?" Mike asked.

"What's what about?"

"The new millennium."

"Oh, that. Come and find out." Cleveland stood, dusted off his knees, shook Mike's hand. His thin hair was blowing in all directions. His glasses had thick, black frames of a style Mike had only seen on the liner notes of some of his mother's old LPs, in photos of Dimitri Shostakovich. "Nice to make your acquaintance, Mr. Mak. Mike, is it? I had the pleasure of meeting your wife yesterday. A kind and generous woman, I should think. I've got this back, you see. She showed me a few exercises, and already I feel like a new man."

"Born again?" Mike smiled to show he was kidding.

"We're not Southern Baptists up here, Mr. Mak!" Cleveland said in mock horror, though he did not divulge what precisely they were, and Mike was not going to ask. "But I must admit, I do feel as if your wife 'laid hands' on me. She's a healer."

"That's her job."

"She's good at it. What's her trick?"

"Her professors would probably condemn her if they knew this, but she's picked up a few pointers from our friend Tom, who's a chiropractor."

"I won't tell if you won't." Cleveland winked cheekily.

"Medicine's kind of a religion," Mike ventured, "and chiropractors are still considered heretics. But Cecilia's from a different generation, and she doesn't buy into a lot of the conventional wisdom. She goes to see Tom regularly. Or she did, before we moved."

"Yes, well." Cleveland was facing into the sun, squinting. His hair was blowing into his eyes. "Very clever of her."

Cleveland seemed friendly enough, and Mike wondered if he could safely ask him what had happened to Lewis Jackson's parents. But he didn't know what he might be getting himself into and didn't want to appear too nosy.

"Out for a walk, then, are you?" asked Cleveland.

"Yes," Mike said. "Such a nice, sunny day."

"A little too blustery for me. But I suppose one should take advantage of it while one can. There won't be too many more days like this. Winter comes early to Haven, you know."

"So I've been told."

"We already had our first frost the week before you and your wife arrived. This is a snatch of Indian summer. But don't count on it lasting very long. Winter lasts from October through at least May. We've had blizzards that dumped three, four feet of snow in a day, and when it does that, the Haven Road can be blocked for days at a time until the state plows bother to come up this way. You'd better keep yourselves a well-stocked pantry, unless you prefer eating every night at the Raven's Roost."

"You heard about the hunting accident." Mike wanted to gauge the reverend's response.

"The . . . uh, New Yorker?" Cleveland said, almost shouting now over the howl of the wind. He shook his head sadly. "Tragic. A tragic thing. Well, if you'll excuse me, Mike, I think the Good Lord's trying to tell me to hightail it back inside!"

*Whatever,* Mike thought.

Cleveland hurried back up the steps of the church, holding onto his hair as if it were a hat about to be blown off.

Mike walked a block down to the Raven's Roost to have some lunch and see if the locals were talking any about the incident. Escaping from the wind, he pulled the door shut and sat down along the lunch counter, combing his fingers through his hair to get it back off his face. Vince Gill was on the jukebox.

"Howdy, Mike!" said Bonnie, finishing ringing someone up at the register. Sadie and Millie were working the tables.

"Hi, Bonnie," Mike said, removing his sunglasses. "What's good today?"

"You still haven't tried my Spaghetti with Mooseballs," she said, clearing some dirty dishes from the counter.

"Well, if you insist."

Bonnie scribbled down the order and clipped it on the revolving rack, which spun around wobbly until the cook in back snatched it up.

"You were out there this morning, weren't you?" she asked.

"Uh, yeah, Bonnie, I was," Mike said.

"Awful ting," said an elderly man sitting two stools away, with bushy white eyebrows and a wine-red nose. He corrected his diction angrily, talking down into his soupspoon: "Thing. An awful *thing*."

"Yeah," Mike remarked, "it was pretty awful."

"Does anyone know anything about this man?" Bonnie asked.

"I don't know any more than you do," Mike said.

"A city boy, he *vass*," said the red-nosed old man. "*Was*."

Bonnie smiled nervously. "Eat your soup," she told him.

The man seemed to be trying to mask some kind of a European accent. Mike wouldn't venture to guess where the man was from. He had once flown on a plane next to a talkative woman whose accent made him think she was Russian or at least Slavic. When at last he had asked if she was from Eastern Europe, she had told him she was from Sicily, though she had been in America for the last forty years. She had admitted her English still wasn't very good, and asked him to tell her what was meant by this word *flotation* that had been staring her in the face all these miles.

"We haven't met," Mike said, reaching out his hand to the old man. "Mike Mak, from Seattle. My wife's the new doctor."

"I know who you are," the man said, in a perfectly plain American voice—though Mike noted how carefully he was now enunciating each word. Cecilia had mentioned that Hamilton spoke similarly, as if he were trying to maintain correct speech and pronunciation at all times. "My name is Hank Harrison. You've already met my wife."

"I don't think so."

"Peg o' My Heart. Our postmistress."

"Oh, sure."

"Hank comes here every day," Bonnie said. "Regular."

"I guess news travels fast around here," Mike said to Harrison. "What did you hear about the shooting?"

"I heard tell it was the Jackson boy," Harrison said grimly, any hint of an accent all worked out of his system. "Don't know when to hold his fire. They was hunting out of season, too, but they already took their buck down to George's Meats, I hear. You know, Mike, Clark Jackson showing his grandson how to hunt is like the blind leading the blind. Clark can't shoot, and that boy can't learn a damned thing, according to what I hear from down at the school. So this Jewish boy walks into the forest—God knows why—and gets himself shot at by a couple of nimrods. New York City. Ain't you from there?"

"No," Mike said. "Seattle. Grew up in Wyoming."

"He wasn't wearing any bright clothing, was he?" asked Harrison rhetorically, as if the victim had been at fault, too.

"No, but then, as you said, it's not even deer season."

"True enough," Harrison said, and closed one eye to make his final point. "So what was that feller doing in our forest, then, if it wasn't the season yet? Answer me that!"

"You got me."

"Haven't you ever heard of camping, Hank?" Bonnie said. "People from the big cities camp too, you know." She gave Mike a wink and set his Spaghetti with Mooseballs down before him, a large oval platter abundantly piled with firm pasta and a tomato sauce that smelled pleasantly gamy. "Here you are."

"Tell you one thing, though, Mike Mak, just between us men." Harrison leaned over and spoke into Mike's ear, his breath smelling strongly of whiskey and decay. "That little piss-ant Lewis Jackson's in for one whale of an ass-whupping!" Harrison stood and laid some bills aimlessly down atop the counter. As he left the diner, he laughed heartily and deeply, phlegm rattling his throat. The door was caught by the wind but drifted shut of its own accord.

"That Hank's a character," Bonnie said. "How's the chow?"

"Wonderful." Mike loaded up his fork.

"You don't feel so sorry for the moose now, do you?"

Mike didn't say anything; his mouth was full.

"You and me should go for a hike one of these days," Bonnie said. "Up along the Little Lost."

"Is that where the mine is?"

"Sure, I could take you on up there. Shaft's all flooded now, of course, but there's still a lot to see."

"Sounds great, Bonnie. I'd love to."

"Maybe next week?" she suggested. "Some day when you've

99

got nothing better to do. The girls can always take over here if I want to take a day off for myself."

"Next week sounds fine, if the weather's still good."

"Great. I'll give you a call." She excused herself to go ring up some customers and help clear tables.

The hike sounded fun, but already he was suspicious of her motives; she probably just wanted to get into his pants.

Mike walked off his mooseballs along the winding path of Center Street, deeper into the heart of Haven, and stopped at the corner of Stuart Lane to check in at the clinic. Janice Fremont was sitting at the reception desk, her eyes rolled up in her head, showing the whites. She was zoning out.

"Hi, Jan," Mike said, to irk her.

"It's Janice." Fremont's eyes snapped back into place. "Your wife isn't here. She's down at the courthouse."

"They've started already?"

"I suppose they have."

"Awful thing," Mike prompted, since it seemed to be what everybody was saying. He hoped Fremont might have an opinion she wished to offer about the strange Jewish man who had wandered into their forest and got himself shot.

Her smile simply grew thinner, her hands clasping more tightly upon the desktop. "I'll tell her you stopped by."

"You do that," he said. "See you later, Janice."

Near the edge of town, Mike turned onto Davis Lane, a dirt road that took him up and around one of the smaller hills, past more of Haven's abandoned homes and the odd one that was still inhabited. One of the sheriff's department Blazers came down the road toward him, kicking up a pale cloud of dust. The sun glared blindingly off the windshield, but as the truck passed the reflection vanished and Mike was able to make out

Frank Tyler behind the wheel in mirrored sunglasses, smiling and waving at him. Tyler could only have been coming from the Jackson place, because it was all that was left, and Davis, like most of Haven's streets, was a dead end.

Mike didn't mind being seen. If Tyler or anyone else cared, he was out for an exploratory walk, and it was a free country.

# Chapter 13

The Prospect County Morgue, in the basement of the courthouse, was a dank and musty place, and Cecilia was none too
happy to be there. She had had to reschedule her afternoon appointments and had been unable to tell Mike, realistically,
what time she would be home for dinner. She was angry at the
absent Dr. Hamilton for having neglected to tell her that "as-
sisting" Joe Doyle would be part of her job—it had *not* been in
her job description. She doubted if his oversight could be at-
tributed to senility or Alzheimer's disease; as he had been so
proud to point out, his family had never suffered from "any
such defect."

The morgue consisted of an unmanned security desk, a simple laboratory, the autopsy room, and the morgue room itself,
each chamber covered floor to ceiling in white porcelain tiles.
The autopsy room, though it mimicked the sterility of a hospital OR with its stainless-steel tables and sinks, had an unmistakable air of corruption. The light fixture above the tables was
simply two bright incandescent low-wattage bulbs in a rusty
metal flange that might once have been chromium-plated; now

it looked as if it belonged in a pool hall. The bulbs themselves
were coated with dust, flecked with dead bugs, and gave off a
sickly, yellow-tinged light. The musty odor in all the rooms
came from mildew that Cecilia found growing along the grout.
She wondered if mushrooms grew under the table.

"When was the last time anyone cleaned this place?" Cecilia
asked. She had not wanted to bring it up while they were conducting the gruesome business, but now they were essentially
finished.

Joe Doyle, spectacles resting on the tip of his nose, his white
lab coat darkly stained, was leaning over the corpse and replacing Abramowitz's internal organs, each in its own separate Zip-
loc plastic bag.

"Shh!" he said, lost in concentration.

"The janitors come down here," Frank Tyler said. He was
leaning against the morgue-room door, thumbs hooked into
his utility belt, one boot planted against the wall, toothpick
bobbing up and down at the corner of his mouth. "But we've
had some burst pipes upstairs, and these rooms seem to have
borne the brunt of the leaks. I'll have the super have maintenance come back down and do a thorough scrubbing."

It sounded for some reason like a clever lie. Cecilia suspected
that neither Doyle nor Tyler had ever given much thought to
keeping the morgue tidy—nor had Hamilton, who must have
been down here as often. If Cecilia was going to be a part of this
team, the place had better be made sterile and adequate venti-
lation installed. She would see that Tyler followed through on
his promises.

"You should get a health inspector down here, Frank."

"Okay."

Idaho, it had turned out (to her misfortune), still relied on
the antiquated coroner system rather than a certified medical
examiner. Here, as in ten other states, county coroners were

merely elected officials who were not required to have any medical training or even a basic knowledge of forensic pathology, even though they were ultimately responsible for determining the cause of death in any case under their purview. The assistance of an MD was not required but was certainly desirable, since it helped establish medicolegal credibility, but most physicians, Cecilia included, did not have the training required of a true ME. Hamilton and the dead Dr. Tyler had provided such assistance for the better part of half a century to whichever local politician might have managed to buy the coroner's seat. Now it was Cecilia's turn. She felt out of her element.

There was still some laboratory analysis to be performed, and Doyle would have to write up his report. He was sewing back up the large Y-shaped incision that ran from either shoulder down to the pubic region. It was cruel and unusual: The damage inflicted by Lewis Jackson's shotgun paled in comparison with the defilement of a thorough medicolegal autopsy. After all this work, the examination of internal organs, the taking of tissue samples, the reading of fluid pressures, Doyle was likely to reach the conclusion that the cause of death had been a shotgun wound to the abdomen and corresponding loss of blood—not much more than what Tyler had told Cecilia over the phone early this morning before either of them had even seen the body.

Cecilia's own observations were that Raphael Abramowitz had been suffering from no underlying disease and that, pending lab results, there were no obvious cofactors that might have contributed to his death. She was no pathologist and was incapable of performing any of the fancy investigative footwork seen on *Quincy, M.E.* She hoped that in her official comments made during the procedure—which Doyle had recorded on the microcassette he was using for his own contemporaneous dictation—she had not missed anything. She had tried to be thorough; it was too late now for doubts.

Tyler helped Doyle replace the body in the vinyl bag and zipped it back up, ready for Doyle to remove it to his funeral home. Vicky Doyle, Cecilia had learned, was the cosmetic specialist of the family business. She wondered if Joe Junior and the other kids pitched in as well.

"Well, if you two'll excuse me," Doyle said after he was finished scrubbing his arms. "I'm going upstairs to my office for a little while to use the phone. I've got to see if I can track down the next of kin."

Doyle left the room and went out to the creaky old elevator. Cecilia hoped the Abramowitzes weren't Orthodox, because she had an inkling they had specific procedures for the preparation of corpses, most of which Doyle had probably already violated before even bothering to call them.

"I saw your husband this afternoon," Tyler said.

Cecilia was washing down the table. "What about?"

"No, I didn't talk to him, I just saw him. Just after lunch, before I came down here." Tyler was standing a few feet back, arms folded, keeping his distance from the mess and not offering to help clean up. She wished he would go away. She wanted to be done with this and go home. "I was coming down from the Jackson place, and I saw Mike walking up Davis Lane in the opposite direction. The only house out that far is the Jacksons', so I reckon that's where he was headed."

"I went out there yesterday to see if I could meet Dottie." Cecilia put some muscle into her scrubbing. Doyle had left his tools in the sink; did he expect her to clean them? "She didn't come to the welcoming. I've been wondering if she's sick."

"Beats me," Tyler said, taking his toothpick out of his mouth and looking at it as if it had let him down.

"You said you were out there today."

"I had a few questions for them. Clark wasn't there, just little Lewis. I didn't see any sign of Dottie, but that's not unusual. She doesn't like visitors."

"Then why does she chair the Welcoming Committee, if she's so antisocial?"

"I don't know. Guess you'd have to ask her. I wouldn't say she's antisocial. Maybe she talked to Mike when he went out there. I can't think of what he might have been doing, though. If he tells you what he was up to, will you let me in on it?"

"He was probably just out for a walk, taking a look around."

"He was a reporter in Seattle, wasn't he?"

"Yep." She was running short on patience.

"Tell him he should be more careful. I've known the Jacksons' dogs to sometimes get loose when strangers come walking up to the house. They usually just chase folks away, but you know, with those jaws, they could easily bite right through a man's leg, down to the bone."

"I'll tell him," Cecilia said. Tyler was trying to scare her, to make her worry about Mike so that she would be upset at Mike when she got home. She *was* worried now, and she *was* upset, but she was damned if she would let Tyler manipulate her.

"You just be sure to tell your husband that until I've finished my investigation and written my report, he shouldn't be going around and asking Lewis Jackson or Clark Jackson or anyone else any questions about it."

"I doubt that's what he was doing," Cecilia said, and tried to come up with something convincing. "I'd told him about the old cars they've got. Mike's a car nut, and I'm sure he just went out there to have a look. I specifically mentioned the old Studebaker, which is a pretty rare model. Mike's not here to do any snooping around on anybody. He's going to write a novel."

*Stop it*, she thought. *Don't protest too much.*

"How come you know about rare models of Studebakers?" Tyler asked, a mischievous grin on his face.

"When you grow up with four older brothers, you pick up a lot of boy stuff."

"Oh, is that why you're so . . ." He was at a loss.

"So what, Frank?" She stopped scrubbing.

"You've really got it together, Cecilia. You've got your career going, you've got your education, you can do whatever the hell you want. I mean, if things didn't work out with you and Mike, you could go it alone."

"Why wouldn't things work out—" she began, but Tyler didn't stop for her. His voice only grew louder.

"He'd probably be worse off than you. You're probably laughing at me because I find this so strange, but you've got to realize, we don't have a lot of women like you around here. My grandma does all right, but that's only because she's loaded, and anyway, she spent most of her life married to my grandpa, hanging around in his shadow. Not exactly liberated. But I guess rich women have always had it made. Bonnie can take care of herself, too, but she's not going anywhere, if you know what I mean."

"No, I don't."

"You, you're different—you've got some kind of a future. I bet you're some kind of feminist, and I just want you to know I don't have anything against it. I listen to Rush Limbaugh when I'm driving around in my truck, and he's always talking about 'feminazis'—now, I've never met a whole lot of feminists, but I still don't think that's fair."

"To women, or to Nazis?" Cecilia asked.

"Now, see?" He laughed uncomfortably, his face growing flushed. "Here I'm opening up to you, Cecilia, sharing my thoughts and trying to be friendly, and you come back at me with a zinger. You're not intimidated by me, are you?"

"Should I be?"

Tyler shrugged. "Most people are. It's like I'm not a real person just because I'm the sheriff. They expect me to have all the answers. I've got plenty, but I've been known to be wrong."

"Anything ever happen between you and Bonnie?"

"What's she been telling you?"

"Nothing. It was just a guess."

"She's like you, see. She's never been impressed by this badge and this uniform. She doesn't like anyone telling her what to do, and I guess that's what turned me on. But once we started seeing each other, it got goddamned frustrating. We just weren't meant to be together, I'm sure of that. That's who I'm looking for, that one perfect woman that I was meant to be with from the start. I sure haven't found her in Haven, and I don't know when I'm going to meet her, because I'm pretty much stuck here, least for now. But when I meet her, I'll know. Grandma's not going to be around forever, and then I'll be living up there all alone in that empty old house. I want to have a beautiful wife and about seven little blond rugrats to fill up the place."

"They have to be blond?"

"Oh, I'm just saying that. When I think of the perfect kid, I always picture little blond cuties like the *Full House* girls."

"You want a house full of girls?"

"Nothing wrong with girls. Without girls there'd be no boys."

"And vice versa."

"Well, sure," Tyler said, "but you know what I mean."

"Not really."

Doyle came back into the room, his face a river of sweat. "Sorry to leave you with all this scrubbing, Cecilia," he said. "I didn't mean to. I'll take over. You can go, if you like."

"Did you reach the Abramowitzes?" Cecilia didn't care a whit about the scrubbing.

"Yes, I did. They were pretty shook up. They want me to arrange for the casket to be shipped back to New York. They didn't see any reason to come all the way out to Idaho. He's going to be buried in their family plot at some cemetery in Queens."

"That's it? Did they say what he was doing out here?"

"I didn't ask. I was just fulfilling my duties as coroner, and then offering my assistance as funeral director. If Frank wants to ask them any questions, that's up to him."

"Is there going to be an inquest?"

"Haven't decided," Doyle said. "Depends on what Frank digs up, I suppose. But I think we already know all we'll ever know. It's my opinion it was just a tragic hunting accident, that's all, and I don't see any point in making a federal case of it."

# Chapter 14

Mike noted the automobile graveyard, just as Cecilia had described it, but saw no sign of the old International Harvester pickup Clark Jackson had taken out hunting. The Jacksons' rottweilers made a big stink as he came walking up the path, snarling and barking with doggie bravado. Their chain-link fence rattled as they tried to break through.

Mike chuckled, continuing toward the front door. No one had come out to see what all the commotion was about, and he figured no one was home, unless the reclusive Dottie Jackson was hiding within. Hank Harrison had said Clark was down at the meat shop. Lewis was probably at school.

The rottweilers were frantic, clambering over one another with their big feet. Before Mike had time to believe what he was seeing, one of them had climbed onto the back of the other and was vaulting himself up over the top of the six-foot fencing. The dog fell gracefully to the ground and came running through the thistle and scrub, straight at Mike.

Mike turned and ran. He could never outrun the dog; it was built like Carl Lewis, and it looked hungry. Rottweilers were often trained to kill; in Seattle, some drug dealers paid as much as $10,000 for a suitably deadly attack dog. Mike could only hope this wasn't one of those. He doubted if his leather jacket or motorcycle boots would be much protection.

The closest car was the '59 Mercury. It still had all its doors, and its windows were cracked into spiderwebs but still intact. He tried the door latch, but it held fast, either locked or rusted shut. He turned to find the dog lunging the last several yards, baring its teeth, homing in for the kill.

Mike threw his arms up over his face, expecting the full force of the dog's body against him. Nothing happened.

Lowering his arms, he found the dog crouching a few inches away, emitting a steady, low growl, holding its tail still.

Lewis Jackson was standing on the front steps, a silver dog whistle shining in his lips. "Come on, Jasper," he called. "Here, boy."

Reluctantly, the dog backed off, keeping his eyes fixed on Mike. Then he turned and ran back to Lewis, who grabbed him by the collar, led him to the fence, opened the gate, and nudged him back inside. Both dogs paced around their pen, calmer than before but anxious for more action. To them, this was fun.

"Sorry about that," Lewis said.

Mike's heart was beating about twice its normal rate, and he was trying to catch his breath. He still wasn't used to the alpine altitude. Looking down, he was relieved to find that he had not peed his pants. He followed the path up to meet Lewis.

"I'm all right," Mike said, but his hands were shaking.

"I bet you're looking for Gramps."

"Doesn't look like he's here."

"Naw, he's down at George's Meats with our buck."

Lewis shoved his hands in his front pockets, his shoulders slumped forward. Mike noticed how long his eyelashes were, which lent his eyes a feminine aspect. Poor guy; he probably had to live this down every day at school.

Mike could sympathize. Growing up in Laramie, where 95 percent of the kids were white, his race was not the only hurdle he'd had to overcome; being Asian, he had been perceived by some of the white boys as being somehow less than a complete man. He had smoother skin and exotic-looking eyes. His body was built differently, with short legs and a long torso, and during high school he had been skinny and slight. The Mexican kids and the Shoshoni kids didn't seem to have this problem of being perceived as effeminate. Mike had been cowed by it and had had a very unhappy time during high school. He had wanted to escape from Laramie, and college had provided him with a suitable excuse, though his parents had expected him to enroll at the University of Wyoming and continue living at home. Once he was out on his own, living at the dorms at the University of Washington–Seattle, he had taken up weightlifting in his free time at the student gym, started subscribing to *Muscle & Fitness*, and spent the next several years turning his high-school frustrations into sculpted muscle mass. Perhaps he had been insecure before, but now he was happy with his muscular frame, and he'd found a better wife than any of those rednecks back in Laramie could ever hope for.

"You want to come in?" Lewis asked.

"I don't want to bother you."

"Come on." Lewis motioned him inside. "I'll give you something to drink."

"Okay," Mike said, and went on into the living room.

The house had the dry, stale odor of sun-warmed dust. Three cats lay sleeping on the sofa. The TV was on and turned to *Another World*. Haven had no cable TV; Mike didn't think he would miss it much. He had noticed a few homes with satellite dishes, but the Jackson place had nothing. There were no decorations on the walls, no books or bookshelves, only overstuffed furniture, end tables, lamps, and a stained carpet. The air had a uriny smell to it, and Mike wondered if it came from the cats or from something else—Lewis's grandmother, perhaps? He wondered how well the cats got along with the dogs, but then the rottweilers were probably not allowed inside.

"Have a seat." Lewis continued on toward the kitchen. "I'm going to have a pop. You want a beer?"

"Sure, whatever you got."

He took off his jacket and sat in the middle of the sofa, in between the cats. The white tee he was wearing was a size too small; he saw no point in developing his muscles if he was going to wear baggy clothes that wouldn't show them off. He reached out to stroke the cats, and they responded with lazy flips of their tails. Lewis came back with a sweaty bottle of Haven Bräu.

"Thanks," Mike said.

Just as Lewis was sitting down in the La-Z-Boy recliner with his Diet Pepsi, a high-pitched wailing sound came from a back room, echoing throughout the house.

"Just a minute," Lewis said. He set his soda down on a crocheted coaster and disappeared down the hall.

Mike craned his neck but could see nothing. He heard Lewis's voice and that of an older person of indeterminate sex, but the sound was muffled and Mike had no idea what they were saying. A door was shut firmly, and Lewis reappeared.

"Sorry," he said with a nervous smile. He sat and looked at the TV screen. "What did I miss?"

"Hmm?"

"My soap."

"Oh, I don't know." Mike had paid no attention to it.

"Normally I have to set up the VCR and watch it when I come home from school."

"Who's that back there?"

"Oh," Lewis said, as if surprised Mike had noticed. "That was Gran."

"Is she all right?"

"She's resting."

The plastic faces of the actors on the TV stared at each other as the cameras dollied in for tight close-ups before cutting away to a cheerful commercial about vaginal yeast infections.

"How are you feeling?" Mike asked. He had no idea how he would react himself to shooting a man accidentally. The kid seemed all right, if a little jumpy. He probably hadn't been the one to shoot Abramowitz and had no genuine guilt to dredge up, unless he simply had no feelings. Mike still believed that Clark Jackson had actually been the one to pull the trigger, and they were fudging the truth for whatever reason.

"I'm fine," Lewis said, sighing. "Gran can be pretty demanding."

"No, I mean about this morning. The accident."

"I'm trying not to think about it. Sheriff was here a few minutes ago with some questions, but it's all right, it was an accident, and he knows that. I took a nap a while ago, and I'm doing much better. Thanks for asking."

None of this exactly rang true, any more than did Lewis's feeble delivery this morning of the events of the shooting, recounted as if they were something his grandfather had prepared hastily and put in his mouth.

"I'm glad to hear you're okay," Mike said. "That's really why I came up here, to see how you were doing."

"That's nice of you." Lewis lost interest in the TV. He turned to look at Mike, his eyes drifting across Mike's arms and legs. "You lift weights?"

"Yeah." Mike didn't mind the change of subject; he was not about to sit here and grill Lewis all day, any more than he would ask him what ever happened to his parents. "I used to go to a gym in Seattle. Cecilia and I bought a home gym before moving out here, but I haven't set it up yet. Do you work out?"

"Not really," Lewis said, sneaking a peek at Mike's biceps. He blushed, then seemed self-conscious about his blushing and frowned miserably. "We've got some weights in the backstage area at the old music hall, for the guys in the Posse and us in the Junior Posse. They're always trying to get me to use them more, but I feel embarrassed in front of everybody."

"You get along with other guys your age?" Mike asked.

"They kind of pick on me."

*I bet they do*, Mike thought. Lewis probably thought his glances at Mike's muscles were surreptitious.

"Want another beer?" Lewis asked.

"Are you trying to get me drunk?"

Lewis turned red in the face again, and Mike wondered how much he knew about himself. If he was gay, he would have a hell of a life if he never got a chance to leave Haven.

"No, Mike, I just thought you'd like another."

"I've got to go," Mike said, standing up. "Cecilia must be wondering what happened to me."

"I thought she was at the courthouse helping with the autopsy."

Mike stared. "How do you know?"

"Sheriff said so. Why don't you stay a bit longer?"

"I guess I can." Mike sat back down, jarring the cats. "Don't you have school today?"

"Oh, I had a prearranged absence so I could go hunting."

There was another wailing moan from the back bedroom. Mike imagined that Dottie was a bedridden invalid, and he got the impression Lewis was taking care of her when his grandfather wasn't around—quite a burden to put on a teenage boy who had already lost his parents.

From looking around the living room, certainly there was nothing to indicate that Clark Jackson was any kind of a white supremacist—no red flags with swastikas, no portraits of Hitler, no Confederate flags or white Klan robes lying around ready to be laundered. Mike wondered now just what he had expected to find. He could hardly go rifling through their closets or snooping around their basement.

He wanted to keep an eye on Lewis, however, and see what more he could learn in the future.

"You know, Lewis."

"Yes?"

"When Cecilia and I get our gym equipment set up, would you like to come over and try it out? You might find you enjoy it without all those other Posse bullies watching you all the time."

"Sure, Mike," Lewis said, eyes agleam. "I'd love to."

# Chapter 15

Day settled into night, and by the time Cecilia got home, she was dog tired. She parked her doctor's bag inside the foyer and drifted into Mike's waiting, welcoming hug. From his torn T-shirt wafted the acidic smell of old book dust mingled with his sweat. He had moved a heavy bookcase into place along the parlor wall and had been in the process of lining its dark shelves with some of the books they had never had room for.

She felt another stab of guilt, for having removed Mike from his Seattle haunts. One of his great pastimes was browsing in bookstores, but here in Haven he would have to settle for the revolving paperback rack down at Whitman's Drugs, with its romance novels, Westerns, and joke books for the toilet.

"How did it go?" he asked, kissing her.

"Fine," she said. "Just fine."

"You smell nice." Crinkling his nose in disgust.

"Carbolic soap."

"Oh." Clearing his throat. "Anything suspicious?"

Cecilia sighed, freeing herself. "Joe says it was just a bad accident, and he doesn't plan on holding an inquest unless Frank says it's necessary."

"In a shooting death?"

"Who am I to argue? There was nothing I could do."

"What about all that stuff in his duffel?"

"Mike, I don't know anything about it." She sighed. "Frank took it as evidence, and it wasn't relevant to us. We collected some blood spatter before he took it, that was all."

"What about the family? Did you contact them?"

"Joe Doyle did. It was his responsibility."

"What did they say?"

"Nothing, as far as I know. They discussed what he should do with the body, not much else, according to him."

"What about what Abramowitz was doing here? They say anything about that?"

"Mike, why the—"

"Camping, hunting, anything?"

"I don't know, I didn't talk to them." She was losing patience. *I didn't expect the Spanish Inquisition.* She wanted to forget about Raphael Abramowitz for a while, but Mike wouldn't let go. "Can we talk about it later?"

"Sure," Mike said, picking up on her touchy mood. "Sit down, relax. Want some dinner? A Haven Bräu?"

"Ugh. I don't feel much like putting anything in my stomach. I'm going to go take a shower and then drench myself in that perfume I never use. The stuff Jeremy gave me."

"Oh, yeah." Mike snapped his fingers, trying to remember.

"Elizabeth Taylor's White Diamonds."

"*'Not so fast!'*" he quoted from the TV commercial.

Cecilia was thankful for the relief. She dragged herself upstairs, stepped into the shower, and scrubbed herself raw with pumice and deodorant soap until her nose was no longer offended by the various morgue smells. After drying off, she decided she was clean enough and could forgo the perfume. Mike would be grateful. She stared at herself in quintuplicate in Maddie Gahagan's elaborate vanity mirror: dark bags under her eyes, cheeks a fresh pink from her rough scrubbing. She wrapped a towel around her hair, pulled on her terry-cloth bathrobe, and went back downstairs to join Mike. She found him sitting in the kitchen at the breakfast nook, a glass of ice water at the ready for her. She needed it.

"Thanks."

"Has Tyler come up with anything on Martin and Eva?"

"No," she said. "They were 'strangled by person or persons unknown.' They weren't killed where we found them but somewhere else, then dumped. He's told us to keep him apprised if anything similar happens."

"I hope nothing similar happens." Mike held her hand.

"Don't worry about it."

"What do you know about Clark Jackson?"

"Nothing, really."

"I've got this funny idea that he's the one who shot Abramowitz."

"Not Lewis?"

"Not Lewis."

"Wait, how could it be Clark? No depth perception."

"So what's he doing out there carrying a shotgun in the first place?" Mike was crunching noisily on an ice cube, a nasty habit of his. Cecilia's teeth were sensitive to cold, and she cringed thinking about it. "He hunts anyway. No wonder they were ahead of the season—Fish and Game probably won't give him a license, so what does he care, he just goes out there early. He doesn't want his glass eye to get in the way of his fun, probably takes aim at whatever's moving. This time it got him in trouble, so he's making Lewis cover for him."

"You're probably right."

"Of course I am," he said lightly. He swirled his glass of ice and let another cube slide onto his tongue.

"No wonder poor Lewis looked so uncomfortable this morning."

"Yeah, poor Lewis. Old grandpa's making him take the heat. I want to know more about Clark, but I don't know where to start. We don't know much about Abramowitz, either, except he's from Brooklyn and presumably Jewish. If it wasn't an accident—"

"Mike, we don't know that it wasn't."

"If it was intentional, if it was homicide, then my guess is it was a hate crime."

"Is that why you went out there today?"

Mike looked surprised. "How did you—"

"Frank saw you. He thought you were going out there to snoop around. He told me to warn you about their dogs."

"Yeah. Fun-loving Jasper tried to kill me."

"Are you all right?"

"Missed me by *that much*. Lewis came out and called him off. You know what he was watching inside? *Another World*."

"We should introduce him to Jeremy," Cecilia said.

"Anyway, I didn't make it past the living room, but I didn't see any proof that Clark Jackson is a militia nut or anything."

"What did you expect, a Nazi flag?"

"Well, yeah."

"If they just stumbled onto Abramowitz in the forest, how could they even have known he was Jewish?"

"How do we know they didn't know him? All we have is their word."

"Just be sure you know what you're doing before you go stirring up any trouble. Maybe there's nothing to it."

"I know. That's why I was thinking of contacting Abramowitz's family myself and—"

"Mike, please . . ."

"I know, Cee. They haven't even had time to mourn. I don't want to start raising their suspicions when I don't know anything myself. I'll wait at least until I can see Tyler's report. It'll be public record."

"Mike, don't take this the wrong way, but don't you think you're looking for a good story where there's probably nothing?"

"Maybe," he said. "Maybe not."

"It all sounds a little paranoid."

"If Tyler can come up with a plausible explanation, I'll put the whole thing to rest."

"Well, let's put it to rest for tonight, at least."

"Okay. But there's one more thing. When I was over at the Jackson place, Dottie Jackson kept moaning from the back room. It sounded to me like she's bedridden, and it looked like Lewis is having to take care of her. She didn't sound comfortable."

"I'd better find a way to see her. Maybe Lizzie Polk can come with me and make the introduction. Don't laugh. I'm serious."

"No, that's a good idea. And if you see any Nazi banners in Dottie's bedroom, you'll let me know?" Mike stood up, arms loaded with dirty dishes from the dinner he'd eaten alone.

"Ha, ha," Cecilia said, and gave him a kiss. He kissed her back without dropping a dish. Sometimes it was nice being married to a former waiter.

Cecilia lay on her side of the bed, arms folded under her breasts, eyes wide open and staring at the ceiling. Mike had rolled onto his side, away from her, and had been sleeping deeply since at least twelve-thirty, which was when she had realized that their bed chat had turned into her own running monologue. She envied Mike his way of dropping off; her own rest never came so readily. The alarm clock now read 3:23. She promised herself this was the last time she would look at it. Tomorrow was Thursday—or today was—and she had all those rescheduled appointments to make up. She had to sleep.

*Raphael Abramowitz of Brooklyn, New York. Outsider. You've met Herb Monroe. . . .*

She turned over on her side. They had left the window open a crack for some fresh air, but it had since grown too cold. She did not want to get out of bed to grab extra cover or close the window, so she huddled closer to Mike for warmth. The curtain breathed in and out with the wind. An owl hooted. Mike, still asleep, rolled over and draped an arm around her. With this added comfort she might at last sleep.

She turned again, and her eye began to follow the flowery pattern of the wallpaper. In the near-darkness it appeared blue-gray, though by day it was goldenrod. Yellow wallpaper, like that in the old Charlotte Perkins Gilman story. She had read it years ago in one of her undergrad Women's Studies courses, but it had never left her: a woman gone mad, shut up in an attic room, the intricate wallpaper reflecting what was going on in her mind. The professor had tried to make some correlation between the wallpaper's design and fractals and chaos theory, which Cecilia had thought a lot of academic nonsense, a professor grasping for tenure. She found the pattern here in their bedroom endlessly fascinating, and exploring it beat counting sheep. She wondered if the Widow Tyler had selected it or if it had been here before. It certainly was not from Maddie Gahagan's day. She would have to remember to ask Bonnie what ever happened to the Hintons.

The owl hooted once more, as if asking her if she was still awake, but Cecilia had rolled again into a comfortable position, and her eyes had drifted shut.

\*     \*     \*

*"Fe, fi, fo, fum!" her father shouts. He has become a giant towering above her. She only comes up to his knee, but of course, she's on the floor. "What do you think you're doing?"*

*The big black bird had been at the bottom of a bottomless bag, and Cecilia has taken it out and is playing with it. It's been posing for her, stretching out its wings, opening its beak as if to speak, scratching at the linoleum with its talons, winking at her, rubbing the dark grease from its feathers and onto her pale, virgin flesh.*

*"Nevermore," says the bird, looking up at her father, and snickers like a hyena.*

*"Put that down!" her father says, grabbing her arm.*

*"Ow!" Cecilia says, dropping the bird onto the floor. "Daddy, that hurts!"*

*The black bird rolls around on its back, screaming and crying, its legs broken, blood oozing out of its beak in a perfect circle on the linoleum.*

*"This is going to hurt even worse!" His mouth spreads into a grin as he raises his hand miles above his head, a vile cobra head coiled and ready to strike. . . .*

The phone was ringing.

Cecilia snapped awake, sweating, her heart pounding. Mike had rolled over away from her and was still sound asleep. She took a deep breath and hurried to answer the bedside phone, not wanting it to awaken him. It was almost surely for her. This was what was meant by being always on call, twenty-four hours a day, seven days a week. She wondered if someone had died. Ralph Polk? Dottie Jackson?

"Hello?" she said, breathing heavily.

No one was there.

"Hello?" she said again. "Hello, who's there?"

Only static.

"Who is this? Do you need help?"

Cecilia stayed on the line for a few more seconds, then felt like a fool and hung up as if the receiver had become a hot rock. If it was a bad connection or if somebody needed her, they would call back. But it was probably a wrong number or a crank call.

Still, she could not get her heart to calm down. She whispered Mike's name, but he didn't stir. She changed her mind and decided not to wake him. Wrong numbers happened all the time; it was nothing to worry about. It could even be the phone company checking the lines. That had happened to her before, back in Seattle; an operator had called again a few minutes later to apologize for the inconvenience.

She went downstairs to fetch a glass of water. When she returned to the bedroom, she shut the window tight, and the billowing curtains relaxed against the sill. She grabbed an extra blanket from the closet, draped it over Mike and her own side of the bed, and tucked it in hastily. Against her better judgment, she glanced at the clock: 4:57.

Whatever sleep she may have had, it had not been restful. She had been having a nightmare, though she could no longer recall what it was about. It was probably just as well. The autopsy had been one of the grislier sights she had ever seen, and she would hate to know what kind of visions it might have spawned.

She thought of Frank Tyler standing against the filthy wall, thumbs hitched in his pockets, toothpick bobbing, as casual and relaxed as if he were watching his laundry tumbling in a dryer.

*I only think it's strange that he should be out here hunting in Idaho when he lives in New York.*

Back in bed, warmer now, Cecilia lay with arms folded under her breasts, eyes wide open and staring at the ceiling.

\*     \*     \*

The phone rang, jolting her awake again just as she was drifting off. She picked it up on the first ring.

"Hello?" she asked. "Who's there?"

"*Traitor*," said a man's voice, and the line went dead.

"Hmm?" Mike said, struggling awake. "Who is it?"

A series of clicks, then the dial tone.

"What's the matter?" He touched her hand.

"Nothing. A crank call, that's all. Sorry it woke you."

# Chapter 16

Upriver they climbed, following a moist, earthen path through the woods along the banks of the Little Lost. Enough of the smooth boulders of the riverbed were exposed that they could cross it without getting wet. The water was clear and pure, and Mike took several handfuls of it into his mouth along the way. Brook and rainbow trout were hanging out, swishing their tails lazily, facing the current. Along the southern bank, the forest blanketed a hill that obscured what would have been a view of Haven. Amid the evergreens grew clumps of aspens now turned a crisp, pale gold. To the north, the pines rose another thousand feet up Flatiron to the tree line. Above that, the mountain was barren, slate-gray rock, a fresh dusting of snow at the peak.

It was noon, with a smattering of clouds. The wind was a steady, brisk nudge of cool. Frost had been settling on the ground every night since Mike and Cecilia had moved in, but it was gone by midmorning once the sun broke over the Lemhis. Winter was perched, waiting for its moment.

"How many more days like this?" Mike asked.

"Not a lot," Bonnie said. "They say there's a front moving in tonight, probably give us some flurries. Once that hits, we're talking arctic air pretty much till next Memorial Day, and lots and lots of snow. Hope you and Cecilia can handle it. You'll get cabin fever right about January. Snow won't let up till May."

Bonnie was leading the way in a pair of hiking boots, faded blue jeans, a canvas day pack, and a black felt cowboy hat banded around with the dried and pressed hide of a western diamondback whose head she claimed to have blown off at a range of six feet with a sawed-off .30-30 Winchester right in her backyard. Mike liked the hat but doubted the tale, which fell into the "big and tall" category along with Paul Bunyan and his ox. Rattlers were never to be found at such elevations; Bonnie had probably purchased the hat with the skin already on. Mike had lived the better part of his life near the Rockies and knew better. In fact, he had admired similar hats at a western outfitter in Laramie the last time he and Cecilia had visited. It made him wonder if Bonnie thought he was a dupe.

"You people don't get like the Donner party, do you?" Mike was breathing heavily, not yet reacclimated to high altitudes after ten years around Puget Sound. Bonnie had no such trouble and was maintaining a good pace. They had not yet reached their destination, the Olbrich Lode Mine, but already he was looking forward to the trek back down.

"You never know," Bonnie said. "Maybe that wasn't moose meat in your Spaghetti and Mooseballs."

"I don't suppose that's why all those houses are sitting empty."

"Sure, every winter we round up everybody for a big barbecue."

"Like 'The Lottery,'" Mike suggested.

"Something like that. We draw lots. Loser gets the spit.

Everybody else gets a piece. You know how it is in these small towns. Full of crazy people who'd just as soon eat you."

"Bonnie, you're freaking me out."

"Seriously, Mike, you can get pretty stir-crazy up here, like that guy in *The Shining*."

"Don't tell me you need a Sno-Cat."

"No, but you and Cecilia'd better get that plow on that ambulance before you get caught unawares. Lots of us with trucks have plows and winches."

"Wenches?"

Bonnie sighed. "I don't know how Cecilia puts up with you. I can help you with the plow if you need it. You've probably never done it before."

"Oh, I bet I can figure it out."

"You might at that. But you'll probably wrassle with it longer than you have to unless you call me first."

"Okay, I promise."

"Once we get over this crest here there's something I've been wanting to show you."

"Rattlesnake pit?"

"No," she said, her tone noting his sarcasm. "The old Chinese cemetery."

"Yeah," Mike said. "Right."


"Aren't the aspens lovely!" shouted Lizzie Polk, sitting high in the passenger seat of the ambulance, staring out the window. A rut in Davis Lane jostled her almost off, and she clutched the dashboard. Her feet did not quite touch the floor. "Oof! Going to peak just in time for Jubilee Days, don't you think?"

Cecilia was not taken with aspens the way most people were. The golden leaves amid the evergreen forest reminded her of nothing so much as a lush lawn gone patchy from a dog's pee. They seemed sinister—every grove an organism unto itself,

128

each tree sharing the same DNA, new ones growing from feeler roots like strawberries or pod people, a community of tree clones. They would insinuate themselves, crowd out the pines, and take over, like a weed or a retrovirus.

"Don't you think?"

"Hmm?" Cecilia said. "I'm sorry, Lizzie, I was zoning out. What were you saying? Jubilee Days?"

"It's the Haven celebration! The big annual festival! Aren't you and Mike coming? But of course you are! You can't miss it, anyhow! It'll be all up and down the street!"

"When?"

"You mean no one's told you?"

"No."

"Well, that *is* a shame! But then, I guess your not being in the society . . ." Lizzie caught herself before continuing her thought. "Why, of course, how silly. . . . Anyhow, it's all next week! We've been preparing for months! Us gals've got a sewing circle going for flags and pennants! I suppose they didn't want you feeling obligated to do a blessed thing, seeing that you're new and still settling into the old Hinton place! It's not like you've got any free time! Couldn't rightly ask you to do your doctoring by day and then come on down and join us for some stitching! Though I guess you probably do enough stitching in your what-do-you-call-it, your practice?"

"Sure, sometimes," Cecilia said. "Lizzie, is there any reason we shouldn't be going out to look in on Dottie?"

Lizzie turned and looked at her. "No, why should there be?"

"I thought she didn't like to be bothered."

"Who told you that? Oh, I'll bet it was Frank!"

Cecilia thought a moment. It had been Frank, the second time; the first had been Jim Hamilton.

"Frank is such a nice boy! Too bad you're already married!

You two would make the cutest couple! Birds of a feather! Not that I have a *thing* against Mike, you understand, but—"

"But what?"

They came upon the automobile graveyard. The two rottweilers circled their pen and began to bark loudly.

"I just don't understand Chinese people! Well, here we are! Why don't you just pull on up the drive there so I don't have so far to walk! Looks like Clark's gone! That's good!"

"What do you mean, Lizzie? About Chinese people? What don't you understand?" Cecilia parked in the empty driveway and shut off the engine.

"Oh, how they live, the things they eat!" Lizzie opened her door to get out.

"Wait," Cecilia said, but Lizzie was already climbing out with astonishing agility. Cecilia grabbed her doctor's bag and followed Lizzie up the path. "I do appreciate this, Lizzie, on such short notice—"

"Pshaw! Don't mention it!"

The dogs rushed their gate, and the chain-link fencing rattled. One of the dogs tried digging a hole underneath.

"I'll ring first," Lizzie said, pressing the doorbell.

Cats meowed from inside. No one came to the door.

"What do you mean, how they live, how they eat?" Cecilia asked. "Are you talking about the Communists?"

"Don't they all live the same way?"

"Mike's not Chinese Chinese, you know." Cecilia liked Lizzie and was hoping to reach her somehow, or at least to dig enough to find what it was she thought she knew about the Chinese that she didn't understand.

"Dottie!" Lizzie called, knocking on the door. "It's me, Lizzie! I'm here with Dr. Mak! You know, the woman doctor!"

There was no response.

"I thought you liked Mike," Cecilia said.

130

"Why, of course I do! I wasn't talking about him, anyhow! He's different! You said yourself he's not Chinese Chinese! Hell, he's from Montana, isn't he?"

"Wyoming."

"That's what I said, Wyoming! Dottie, are you in there?" Lizzie tried the doorknob, and the door came open. "Why don't we just go on in? I'm sure she won't mind!"

"Mrs. Jackson?" Cecilia called.

A cat came up and brushed itself against her leg.

"Dottie? It's Lizzie, hon!"

The smell was just as Mike had described, dusty and uriny.

"Where are you, dearie?"

Lizzie headed down the hall and motioned for Cecilia to follow. She knocked on the door to the back bedroom, but no sound came from within. She smiled nervously at Cecilia.

Cecilia took a deep breath and grabbed the doorknob, and together they went in.

Mike had thought she was kidding. But there it was, a hundred yards before the ruins of the Olbrich Lode Mine, an entire hillside terraced top to bottom and planted with stout markers. Though the stones were weathered, blackened, and covered with lichens, the Chinese decorations and symbols had been carved deep and could still be made out.

Unfortunately, Mike failed to recognize most of the characters. He could speak passable Cantonese, but his knowledge of written Chinese was sketchy; his father had taught him much, but after going off to college and being overwhelmed with other studies, he had lost most of it. He had always known he would someday regret it, but he hadn't expected that day to come for at least another twenty years.

"Jesus." Mike began climbing the hill, passing between the rows. Some plots had been taken over by juniper bushes and small pines. Some of the headstones had been tipped over, either by vandals or by persistent roots.

"What do they say?" Bonnie asked, coming up behind.

"I don't know. Just that there's a lot of dead Chinese here." He reached out and touched the edges of several stones as he went up toward the green, grassy hilltop.

"They were miners."

"I guessed that."

"There was a cave-in."

"All of them at once? There must be hundreds."

"Over a thousand. I counted them once, but I forget."

"There were that many Chinese in Haven?"

"More. It's said there were three thousand at one point."

"Three thousand?"

"I know it's hard to believe, but Haven had a population of fifty-five hundred at the peak of the gold rush. Most of them were miners working for Olbrich, and more than half of those were Chinese."

"Jesus Christ. What year was this?"

"Well, the cave-in was eighteen seventy-six. There was never a Chinese cemetery until after the accident. Usually, when a Chinese worker died, the others would ship the body back to his family in China."

"Why weren't these shipped back?"

"Too many, I guess. Or it was just too much trouble. Not enough Chinese left to handle the chore, and I reckon no one else was going to do it. After that, the Chinese in Haven pretty much died out. I mean, most of them eventually packed up and went back home. Olbrich couldn't find any more Chinese workers and had to hire settlers to replace them. Of course, he had to pay them more money."

"That was because of the Exclusion Act," Mike said.

"Excuse me?"

"Congress passed it in eighteen eighty-two to keep the Chinese out and send back all the rest they could find. It was renewed over and over again and wasn't repealed until nineteen forty-three. The western railroads were practically built by Chinese labor. I knew about the Chinese miners in California, but I never realized any had made their way up here."

"Oh, sure. Haven had its own Chinatown, just across the river from the town proper. They had their own shops and saloons, joss houses, opium dens, brothels. There was a fair number of Chinese women here, too—some of them wives, some of them whores. Maddie Gahagan wouldn't let a Chinaman have one of her girls, no matter how much money he had."

"I bet the white guys didn't mind going to the Chinese girls," Mike said. "Are any of those buildings left?"

Bonnie shook her head. "If there were, I would have shown you before I lugged you on up here. There's some cement blocks—I think they were the foundation for the Chinese bank. Nothing left standing, though. You might find chunks of leaded glass, old rusted barrel rings, some nails. A lot of old junk."

"Hard to imagine," Mike said, squatting before one of the stones and caressing its rough surface, "coming all the way across the ocean to America, seeking your fortune, ending up in the mountains of Idaho mining gold for some robber baron, then getting killed in a horrible accident. Their families back in China probably never knew what happened to them. I bet no one outside of Haven even knows they're here."

"You must be the first Chinese man to come back here in all that time."

She was probably right, though it seemed a great burden. If he believed in such things as the spirit world, he would have to think that the ghosts of these men were calling out to him to remember them to their homeland. But he would be of no

133

help. He was an American, not a Chinese, and he was no kind of a believer in anything. China as they had known it wasn't really there anymore, either. The sight of this hill, however, was extraordinary. He would have to tell his dad about it. Perhaps there was a magazine piece in this. He would have to do some digging and see what more he could learn.

"You must know a lot of Haven's history."

"Certain things," she said. "I've always been interested in this place especially. I thought maybe you could help me with it, tell me what some of these stones say. I've been coming up here since I was a little girl, but I've never even known any of their names."

"Do their names really matter?"

"There's supposed to be someone here named Hong Wah something. I don't know, I guess it's not that important."

"I'll be happy to help with what I can, but it won't amount to much. I'd have to spend some time with it, maybe some other day when we have nothing else to do. You were taking me up to the mine?"

"I still am."

"Well?"

"Got to stop for lunch first." Bonnie shrugged off her day pack. "We've got cold fried chicken, three-bean salad, and a couple of thick slices of rhubarb pie. How's that?"

"Sounds pretty good."

Mike sat and looked out over the lush hill, surprised at feeling so melancholy. He had never before felt much of a connection to Chinese from China, but this was somehow different. All these men had traveled all this distance to get paid half a white man's wage for what was nonstop, backbreaking work, only to be trapped in an unstable tunnel at the moment of explosion or collapse, crushed beneath tons of Flatiron rock. He wondered if any of these grave markers were carved from the stones that had come crumbling down on their heads. The owner of the mine, Olbrich, had apparently managed to replace them easily enough; no one had missed them.

"Mike?"

"Huh? Sorry, Bonnie, I was off somewhere. What is it?"

"I've got a loaded question for you."

"Shoot."

"Are you a breast man or a thigh man?"

"Wing," he said. "If you've got any."

Dottie lay sleeping in the middle of a twin-size bed, flat on her back, her mouth half open. She breathed in with a wheeze and out with a whistle, and the action seemed to take a lot out of her. Her hair was wiry and entangled like an S.O.S. pad; no one had brushed it for her in some time.

It was a small bedroom, a child's bedroom, into which she had apparently been moved to keep her out of sight. The window curtains were shut, the air awash in putridity.

"What's the smell?" Lizzie whispered.

"Lizzie, help me pull these covers down, will you?"

It was then they saw the stains.

"Oh!" Lizzie said.

Some were of blood, but others were a sickly yellow color from matter that had oozed out of her bedsores. Purplish blotches showed where blood had pooled in her peripheral tissues. Her right calf had an abscess that had grown infected and showed signs of becoming gangrenous.

Dottie was bedridden, all right, but she was not receiving proper medical attention. No one had turned her. No one had made any attempt at physical therapy that might have improved her circulation and prevented the blood pooling. The abscess had probably formed as a complication of arteriosclerosis, yet no one had monitored her condition or sought any qualified medical help. Jim Hamilton had claimed she was "right as rain"—Cecilia wondered when he had looked in on her last. Whether he had seen her and done nothing or simply not been to see her for a while, it amounted to the same thing: neglect. Clark and Lewis Jackson, likewise, had no excuse for not getting Dottie to a hospital.

"Lizzie, would you wake her up, please? Gently."

Lizzie laid a hand alongside Dottie's cheek. "Dottie, honey? Wake up, dear. It's Lizzie. I'm here with Dr. Mak."

Dottie's eyes opened slightly. "*Was? Herr Doktor? Ich dachte er fortging.*" Her eyes grew immediately wider, and she shook her head as if trying to refuse the doctor's presence. She had not yet seen Cecilia.

"*Nein, nein! Eine Frau!*" Lizzie said. "*Doktor Mak. Sie ist gekommen dir helfen!*"

Cecilia stepped closer. "Let me take your temperature."

Dottie merely stared at her.

"*Die ist ein Doktor?*"

"Does she understand me?" Cecilia asked.

"Probably not."

"Tell her I'm going to take her temperature and her blood pressure and tend to her bedsores. Then we'll be taking her in the ambulance to the medical center at Pocatello."

"You're going to what?"

"Pocatello?" Dottie, though weary, seemed in great distress. "*Nein, nein. Ich will nicht gehen!*"

"I'm going to help you," Cecilia said, raising her voice. "Lizzie, tell her I'm going to help her."

"I already did! Oh, dear, Clark isn't going to like this a bit!"

"What Clark wants doesn't make any difference." Gently, Cecilia poked a digital thermometer into Dottie's mouth. She grabbed the blood-pressure cuff from her bag and strapped it around Dottie's left arm. She put on her stethoscope and began taking a reading.

"Someone's coming!" Lizzie said, clutching her hearing aid as if a loud noise had jolted her. Cecilia, listening to Dottie's blood flow, had heard nothing.

Just then, Frank Tyler came into the room, his service weapon drawn and at the ready. When he saw Cecilia and Lizzie, he reholstered his weapon and looked greatly relieved.

"What's going on here?" he demanded.

Cecilia ignored him; she had a patient to take care of. Lizzie took timid steps away from Tyler, back against the far wall of the bedroom.

"Frank, why, we were just—"

Cecilia unstrapped the cuff and removed the beeping thermometer from Dottie's mouth. She was running a fever of 102°F. "Frank, you're here just in time."

"What the hell are you talking about?" He was shouting. Dottie winced noticeably. "You and Lizzie tripped Clark's silent alarm. It rang off at the station, and I came flying out here expecting burglars. God knows what would have happened to Dottie if someone had broken in here. Lizzie, you should know better."

"Sorry, Frank, I was only—"

"Save it, Lizzie." Tyler lifted a hand to silence her. "You should have called me first before you came out here, and I could have come in with you. Clark's doing business down at Salmon all day. You know, you don't just go wandering into someone else's home, Lizzie. I could have come into this room and shot you before I knew who you were."

"I'm sorry, F-Frank, honest." Lizzie attempted a smile, but it soon withered. Tyler was unmoved.

"No you're not, Lizzie," Cecilia said. "Frank, if it's anyone's fault, it's mine for asking Lizzie to take me out here, so you can blame me if you want, but to be quite honest, I don't give a damn. Right now I need you to help me get Dottie loaded up in the ambulance so I can drive her down to Pocatello."

"Now, hold on a minute . . ." Tyler began.

Cecilia cut him off. "Lizzie, you stay here with Dottie for a minute while Frank and I go get the gurney." She threw him a glance as if daring him to refuse her.

Tyler's nostrils flared as he took in the smell. He looked down on Dottie's filthy bed in disgust.

"Unless Frank has any problem with that."

Tyler shook his head.

"I did the right thing coming out here, Frank. But now I need your help, and I don't want any argument. Is that okay?"

Tyler nodded.

"Come on, then, give me a hand."

Cecilia and Tyler headed down the hall and into the living room. Cecilia could hear Lizzie speaking comfortingly to Dottie in German; she wondered if it was what Jim Hamilton had been using on the phone with his wife that day at the clinic. She hadn't given it a second thought while she was in Dottie's bedroom. She had treated patients before in Seattle who spoke no English, and as long as there was a friend or family member present who could help her communicate, everything was fine. Lizzie had been there and could obviously speak German well, but until now, Cecilia hadn't drawn any conclusions about it. Dottie, at least, must have been a German immigrant, and Lizzie might have been one, too. Though in Lizzie's case, she had done a masterful job of shedding the accent.

"*Alles wird fein sein, Dottie! Cecilia Mak ist ein guter Doktor. Ja, ja! Ein guter Doktor!*"

Mike had expected a hole in the side of the mountain, weathered support beams framing the void, perhaps some rails leading over the lip and down. But Olbrich's operation had been on a much grander scale. The most visible marker of the mine's location was a mammoth slope of rust-orange ore pilings that had been dumped down the side of the mountain more than a century ago. At its base, the waste ore was bordered by a still, stagnant pond of sulfur-colored rainwater that had collected in a depression where no grass or trees grew. Mining engineers in the nineteenth century hadn't had to obtain any environmental impact statements, or consult with any bureaus of land management, or fight lawsuits from any Sierra Club, or listen to Woodsy the Owl.

The Olbrich Lode Mine had once been made up of five large wooden structures with peaked roofs, along with a brick smokestack towering over them all. Half of the topmost bricks had crumbled away, and now the smokestack looked more like the tower of a medieval castle whose archers' nest had met a clean blow from a cannonball.

The huge main building still stood and would have been easy to spot from a distance even without the mountain of waste ore. It resembled a giant, decrepit barn with a giant chicken coop on top. Its plank siding was bowed in upon its sturdier frame like the flaky skin of a mummy stretched taut around a petrified skull. Its geometry seemed all wrong, like a skewed expressionistic set from a German silent film, as if none of the angles quite added up to the whole, as though if you turned away for a second and looked back again it would seem somehow changed. The letters that had been painted in a gentle arc across the front of the building were almost completely faded, but Mike could still make them out: H. J. OLBRICH GEM & MINERAL CO. The entryway beneath seemed near-triangular, but as Mike grew closer and faced it head-on, he saw how one-half of the door frame had collapsed outward and sagged to one side to create the illusion. Fresher planks had been nailed across the opening in a Saint Andrew's cross, a neatly hand-lettered sign tacked in the middle:

ATTENTION!

PRIVATE PROPERTY

TRESPASSERS WILL BE SHOT

ON SIGHT—BY OWNER

YOU HAVE BEEN WARNED

"Who's the owner?" Mike asked. Bonnie hesitated, so he added, "Don't tell me. The Widow Tyler."

"That's right."

"Where's the shaft?"

"Inside," she said. "I'll show you."

"No one's going to shoot us, are they?"

"No, of course not. I'm the Widow's right hand, and I don't think she'd ever want to lop it off. Come on."

Swiftly, she ducked under the cross and stepped inside. It was light within because plenty of planks had fallen away and the sun was shining in.

"It doesn't look safe," Mike said.

"It's not dangerous. I've been in plenty of times."

"I don't know, Bonnie."

"I thought this was what you came to see."

The wind picked up, whistling through the gaps in the building. Boards creaked like the hull of a tempest-tossed ship. Mike could imagine the whole damned thing falling down around them—one more name added to the Chinese cemetery.

"Fraidy cat," Bonnie said.

Mike hadn't heard that since the third grade, and it annoyed him. "All right, I'm coming." He ducked under.

"Didn't mean to shame you," she said.

"You sure did."

The space within was vast. It must have once housed the machinery of the mine's operations, but no railcars or tools or conveyer belts remained. Second and third levels of flooring had collapsed halfway, staircases fallen aside. Some rusted chains and pulleys still hung from the rafters, way out of reach, and the ground was littered with scraps of wood, metal, and pipe.

"Watch out for rusty nails," Bonnie said.

She led the way toward the back, where Mike was met with the sight he had anticipated—a shaftway dug into the mountain, framed by beams that looked as flimsy as the plank siding.

"Want a peek?"

"Just for a moment."

Bonnie got out her flashlight, a long, sturdy Maglite like police officers used, and turned its beam deep into the tunnel.

"Follow me." Her voice echoed off the walls.

Mike ducked his head under the low beam. The ground sloped downward rapidly and was gritty beneath his feet. If railcars had once taken men down into the shaft, the rails had long since been taken up and sold for scrap.

"Hold onto my hand," Bonnie said, and reached behind her.

Mike gave her his hand, if only to have some connection to the light source. She kept it steady, trained ahead. The tunnel curved gradually, removing them completely from any sunlight that had filtered in through the building.

"Whoa! Stop!" Bonnie said.

Mike ran into her. His feet kicked some small rocks that went skittering forward and *blooped* into some water.

"See? Flooded."

Bonnie shined her light on the surface. The water stretched off into the distance, black and deep like a tar pit. The roof of the shaft sloped sharply down to meet the pool at its far end.

"If something were to happen to you down here, nobody

would know about it," Bonnie said, and turned off the flash-light.

"Lizzie, can you come along with us to Pocatello?" Cecilia asked.

"Oh, no, I couldn't!"

Tyler had volunteered to drive the ambulance so Cecilia could tend to Dottie in the back, but there was room for Lizzie, and Cecilia felt she needed her along.

"Does Dottie know any English at all?"

"Well, no, not well. She had a lot of trouble with it."

"Then I need you."

"But Ralph! I can't leave him for so long, honestly! I have to get back, I'm late already! I'm very sorry!"

Cecilia hadn't thought of that. Of course Lizzie couldn't come. But the drive to Pocatello would be at least three hours long, and if they needed to communicate with Dottie . . .

"Frank can talk to her," Lizzie whispered.

"Excuse me?" The rottweilers had been barking in their pen, and Cecilia wasn't sure she had heard right.

Tyler had gone back inside the Jackson place to use the phone. He was calling the school to talk to Lewis and let him know what was going on and where they were taking his grandmother. Clark was still in Salmon and unreachable.

"He speaks German," Lizzie said. "He may not want to fess up to it. He can talk to Dottie if need be."

"Did you come here from Germany?" Cecilia asked frankly.

"Yes, yes." Lizzie continued to keep her voice down. "We were refugees after the war. Not Frank, of course, but his grandfather was."

"When did you come here?"

"Oh, the fifties." Lizzie was vague. "We were escaping the iron curtain. I was from Leipzig, and well, you know all about it, I'm sure. There were a lot of us, not just here in Haven. My picture was in *Life* magazine. Hush! Frank's coming!" She clutched her hearing aid. "I sure do hope Dottie's going to be all right! She's one of my truest friends! Please, Doctor, take good care of her!"

Tyler appeared in the front door.

"I will," Cecilia said warmly. "Thank you, Lizzie."

Lizzie clutched Cecilia's hand in both of hers and shook it once, firmly. Tears welled up in her eyes.

"Lizzie, you going to be all right?" Tyler asked, coming up and patting her on the back.

"Yes, Frank, fine," she said, not looking at him.

"Cecilia, let's go. I'll get you there in record time."

"Did you talk to Lewis?"

"I told him. Lizzie, you can talk to Lewis when he gets out of school, can't you?"

"I sure will, Frank!"

"And Clark, when he gets back?"

"I promise, Frank!"

Tyler hopped up into the cab, revved the engine, turned on the red flashing lights. Cecilia said good-bye to Lizzie and climbed into the back of the ambulance.

They headed through the automobile graveyard and back down Davis Lane. As they left the village limit and were cruising along the Haven Road, Cecilia noted the huge Tyler house atop its hill, and not long after spotted the turnoff they had taken into the forest to find Raphael Abramowitz's body. The dirt road disappeared up into the hills, but she imagined it headed up into the woods on the far end of the hill, not far from the mansion.

"Hey!" Mike shouted. He couldn't see a thing in the darkness. His voice echoed sharply off the walls of the tunnel. *Hey, hey,*

*hey* . . . "What are you doing?" *What are you doing, are you doing, you doing* . . .

"Mike." *Mike, Mike* . . .

Bonnie's hand came up and felt his chest.

He batted it away. "Bonnie, stop." *Stop, stop* . . .

"Mike, I want you." *Want you, you, you* . . .

She backed him against the stone wall. His head struck a rock. She had undone two buttons of his shirt before he could stop her. He felt her breath on his skin. Her hand went inside, feeling his smooth pectorals. He pushed her away gently, but she wouldn't stay back. She wrapped her arms around him.

"Give me the flashlight."

"It's on the ground somewhere."

"Let me go." He struggled out of her clutch.

"Don't you want me?"

"No." He wrenched himself out of her arms.

"Come on, Mike, just give in."

"Bonnie, let's go back outside."

"Let's stay."

Mike felt his way along the wall, but his foot stepped into six inches of water. He had gone the wrong way. Bonnie was right behind him. He pushed around her and tried to head back out of the tunnel.

"Mike!" *Mike, Mike, Mike* . . .

He stepped on the flashlight, which rolled out from under him, and he fell forward, his hands breaking his fall and getting cut on some rocks. He was facedown in the dirt. "Shit."

"Mike, are you all right?"

"Fine," he said, getting up and dusting off. "Stay away."

"Come on, Mike, nobody will know."

"I'm married."

She laughed.

He reached down for the flashlight but couldn't find it.

"Are you looking for this?" Bonnie flicked the switch, and the flashlight came back on. She was pointing it toward the ceiling, holding it down at her navel. She had taken off her day pack and her shirt. The light accentuated the curves of her breasts but cast hollow shadows across her face.

"Put your shirt on, for Christ's sake."

"Here," she said. "I'll give you the flashlight."

She came forward. Mike stepped back, hesitant.

"I'm not going to bite you."

She held it out to him, and he snatched it from her and immediately shined the light up the way they had come, as if he wanted to make sure the opening was still there.

Bonnie seized the moment of his distraction to unbuckle his belt and unbutton the fly of his jeans.

"Cut it out!" *Cut it out, it out, it out* . . .

She pushed him backward, and he struck the wall again, rubbed the back of his head. His fingers came back graced with a trickle of blood.

Bonnie yanked his jeans down over his hips. His knees came up reflexively and struck her in the chest. She fell back onto the ground.

"Mike, that hurt!" *Hurt, hurt* . . .

Mike hiked his jeans back up and headed back, up the tunnel.

"Don't leave me here!" she called.

Once he rounded a bend and saw a hint of sunlight, he tossed the flashlight on the ground, leaving it on with the beam aimed down into the tunnel, as a beacon Bonnie could follow to get out.

He could hardly believe this had happened. He had had a glimmer of a notion that Bonnie might be interested in him, but nothing like this. In Haven the sex life of the young single woman was probably dull, and ever since she had broken up with Frank Tyler, she had been lacking something. It still gave her no right to rip his clothes off and try to reach into his pants.

"Mike!" she called after him.

He heard her running, saw the bouncing beam of the flashlight along the walls. He picked up his pace, wanting to keep a certain distance.

Back in the main building, he negotiated his way through the piles of rubble and out the skewed entryway, ducking under the cross of boards and into the glaring late-afternoon sun. He shaded his eyes, and on doing so saw one of the sheriff's department Blazers sitting high on its tires right outside.

"What the hell?" said Herb Monroe, removing his sunglasses. He was wearing full uniform and cowboy hat. His right hand hovered for a moment near the gun on his belt, then relaxed at his side. Behind him, at the rear of the truck, was Joe Doyle in a pair of grubby work jeans and a plaid hunting jacket. He appeared to be throwing his weight behind a large object, shoving it back into the truck. He slammed the back door shut solid.

"What's he doing here?" Doyle asked.

"I don't know. What are you doing here, Mike?"

"Bonnie and I—"

"Bonnie and you?" Deputy Monroe smirked, staring down at Mike's crotch.

Though he had pulled his pants up, the fly was still completely undone, the belt unbuckled, his boxer shorts showing. Mike felt his face flush warmly and quickly fixed up his pants.

Bonnie came out from under the cross.

"Herb!"

"Bonnie."

Bonnie had put her shirt back on, at least, but it was untucked and hanging loose. Both she and Mike were covered in dust. Mike tried to redo the top buttons of his shirt, but they were no longer there. He hadn't realized she had ripped them off.

"Herb, it's not how it looks," Bonnie said.

"I believe you," Monroe replied with a curt laugh.

Doyle joined them, out of breath from whatever labors he had been engaged in. "What the hell is this? No one's supposed to be up here, Bonnie, you know that."

"Don't tell anybody, please, Joe," she said.

"Looks to me like you folks were trespassing," Monroe said.

"You're not going to shoot us, are you?" Mike asked.

"Naw." The deputy made it sound as if, hell, he had decided to give them a break. "The Widow's sign's just to scare people. We all know Bonnie ain't scared of nothing or nobody."

"Shut up, Herb."

"That's right, Bonnie, shut up. You'd like me to shut up, wouldn't you, before I go blabbing on about you. You wouldn't want me telling Mike any stories."

"Herb, stop it."

"Leave it," Doyle said. "We've got things to do. Just let them go."

"We came up here on a hike," Mike said. "And that's all."

"Uh huh," Monroe said. "Go on, the both of you. Get out of here, get back to town."

"Are you going to make a report?" Bonnie asked.

"Well, now, Bon, that depends." Monroe grinned at her like the Big Bad Wolf. "Give me a call later, and we'll discuss it, in private."

Bonnie stiffened, her face turned to stone.

"Let's go, Herb," Doyle said. He was in an awful hurry.

"All right, you two, go on. Get out of here before I fine you for trespassing. And I mean it."

"What's in the truck, guys?" Mike asked.

"Nothing. What makes you think there is something?"

"No reason." Mike shrugged. "I guess I was just wondering why you and the coroner would want to come all the way up here on such a nice day to this secluded spot, why Doyle was acting like we'd caught you two in the middle of doing something dirty."

"What the hell?" Doyle blustered, stepping forward.

"Easy, hoss." Monroe held him back. "We've got things to do, remember?"

"Have a nice day." Mike would have liked to walk past the truck and try to catch a glimpse of what lay inside, but Monroe and Doyle were standing between him and it, and it was unlikely they would allow him near. He did not want to provoke any further discussion.

Mike and Bonnie walked down the hill to their trail along the Little Lost, maintaining a distance at first. After about a mile, out of sight of the old mine, they drifted back together.

"I'm sorry," Bonnie said.

Mike said nothing.

"I said I'm sorry."

"It doesn't help."

"It's all a misunderstanding, Mike. I'm so embarrassed. You've been so friendly to me since you came, and I guess I misinterpreted that as more than friendship. I thought you were attracted to me."

"Bonnie, stop."

"No, Mike, listen to me. I really think you're special. Not too many people in Haven could see you the way I do. I think you and Cecilia make a wonderful couple, and now that I know how you feel, I wouldn't want to come between you."

"Uh, thanks."

"Can we be friends?"

"I'll think on it."

"Please, Mike? I feel like such an idiot. Honest, I didn't plan any of this. I only wanted to show you the cemetery and the mine. Once we were down in there, all alone, this feeling just swept over me, and I couldn't help myself."

"It's okay, Bonnie, relax."

They walked along together for a while in silence.

"I'm sorry if I hurt you," she said. "I'd hate to think what Joe and Herb are thinking."

"Are they going to spread it around?"

"I don't know. Possibly."

"Jesus—if Cecilia hears about it—that's the last thing I need."

"Mike, if anything gets stirred up, I promise you I'll speak with her myself and tell her nothing happened."

"I don't think that will help."

"Then I'll tell her I made a pass at you and that you rejected me. Do you think she'd believe me?"

Mike nodded firmly. "Yes, I think she probably would. But I don't want to think about it. And I don't want to talk about it anymore, either."

"Please don't hate me."

"I don't hate you," Mike said. "I'm glad you showed me the cemetery. Let's forget about the mine. It's history."

Cecilia and Tyler stayed with Dottie in the emergency department at the Pocatello Regional Medical Center while she was examined. Tyler went to the pay phone in the lounge several times in an attempt to reach Clark Jackson. He reported no success—nobody seemed to know where Clark was or what he was up to.

The ER physician agreed with Cecilia that Dottie's right lower leg was gangrenous and would have to be amputated above the knee as soon as possible. Despite her infections and fever, Dottie appeared lucid and cogent, and through a translator she gave her consent for the operation. The physician had her admitted to the hospital.

Tyler suggested it was time they headed back. "I can't afford to be gone this long from Haven," he said, looking anxiously at his watch. "Neither can you, I reckon."

"You reckon right. Mike's going to kill me."

"You hungry? I know a diner—not as good as Bon's, but that'd be asking a lot."

"I thought you were in a hurry to get back."

"Got to eat. I don't know about you, but I don't much care for pulling up at a drive-through. I don't trust these fast-food joints, anyway."

"Because of the chemicals and preservatives?"

"Naw, life's full of chemicals. What gets me is all these chains are coming out of New York. You got all these rich fat cats sitting around in their hundredth-floor offices in their foreign-made suits, scheming up ways they can screw us. You think they eat any of that crap themselves? When a McDonald's bigwig sits down to a power lunch with his advertisers, you think he's going to treat them to a Big Mac, fries, and a Coke, or a giant porterhouse steak and a half-dozen other courses and a big jug of wine?"

"So where's this diner?"

"Now this is what I call food." Tyler spoke with his mouth full. He had ordered not a porterhouse but a nice juicy rib eye cooked rare. The red liquid was pooling around the plate, commingling with the melted butter that oozed from his steaming baked potato.

Cecilia had ordered the fried shrimp platter, and she was pleasantly surprised that the shrimp were truly jumbo. She had to hand it to Tyler; he knew how to pick a diner.

"I'm sorry about how I acted earlier," Tyler said. "You did the right thing, Cecilia. I had no idea Dottie was in such bad shape. I'm sure Jim Hamilton didn't know, either."

"Why are you so sure?"

"Because if he'd known, he would have done something. He's a great man, really loves kids. He's my godfather, as a matter of fact. He and my granddad worked together all their lives."

"Your grandfather was the other doctor in Haven."

"That's right. I'm his namesake. He was Franklin Tyler the first. I'm the third. I thought he'd never die."

Tyler spoke with an awkward emotion; Cecilia was unable to determine whether it was relief that his grandfather was gone or awed disbelief that he was actually mortal.

"You loved your grandfather?"

"Of course."

"I never knew any of my grandparents."

"I'm sorry to hear that."

"What about Franklin Tyler the Second?"

"My father? He's dead. I don't like to talk about it."

"I can't wait to meet your grandmother."

"You'll meet her. She wants to meet you, but she's just not ready."

"So she came over from Germany with your grandfather?"

Tyler looked up from his plate, his cheek bulging with a bite of meat he had just put in his mouth. "Excuse me?"

"That's what I was told," Cecilia said, deciding it might not be best to reveal who had told her, "that Dr. Tyler was among the group of émigrés who had come out to Idaho after the war, in the fifties, to escape Stalinism in East Germany."

"That's right," Tyler said. "Who told you? Lizzie?"

"I don't remember who it was or when it came up. So it's true, then?"

"Sure. A few of the old folks came from Germany."

151

"Dottie, obviously. What about Clark?"

"What about him? What does it matter? They're all American citizens."

"Why did they get rid of their German names?"

"I don't know," Tyler said, growing increasingly testy. "They don't much like to talk about these things."

"Your names are all American patriots and presidents."

"I don't know why they did that. . . . Look, Cecilia, they were all looking for a home, for a fresh start. Most of them found it. Lizzie probably told you how her picture was in *Life*."

"Yeah, she—" Cecilia stopped herself, but it was too late. She had given Lizzie away. She changed the subject. "So what do you know about Clark?"

"What do you want to know?"

"How he lost his eye. Was it in the war?"

"Yeah. He was in the German army."

"Was he a Nazi?"

"No, he wasn't a Nazi, Jesus. Clark was just a plain German soldier, and most of them weren't Nazis, case you didn't know. He got his eye shot out by a partisan somewhere in Belorussia."

Cecilia wondered what happened to the partisan.

"Anyway, if he had been a Nazi, he never would have been allowed into the United States, would he?"

It was late in the evening when they got back. Herb Monroe's truck was parked in front of the Jackson place with its red and blue lights swirling, alongside the one Tyler had left behind. The Doyle Funeral Home hearse was there, too, with its back door swung wide open. Vicky Doyle stood nearby, sobbing, while Doyle and Monroe removed the gurney from the back of the hearse.

"Oh, no," Cecilia said. "Is it Clark?"

Tyler's face looked grim.

As he was parking the ambulance, Cecilia saw Clark standing in the doorway of his home, looking fine. She got out before Tyler had shut off the engine.

A white, blood-stained sheet was draped over a small heap on the ground, too small to be a person, and of an odd shape.

"Go ahead," said Monroe.

Cecilia lifted the sheet to find the bodies of the Jacksons' two rottweilers, each riddled with bullet holes.

"Who did this?" Tyler asked, coming up behind her.

"I did," Monroe said. "But it was too late to save her."

"Who?"

"Lizzie." Monroe motioned toward the larger body, also draped in a blood-stained sheet, that lay closer to the dog pen.

"No!" Cecilia said.

"She was coming up the walk, on her way to see Clark, apparently. Somehow the dogs got out and attacked."

Cecilia went over to lift up the sheet.

"I wouldn't do that—" Monroe cautioned.

She knew it might be gruesome, but she could not help herself. Blood filled deep gouges in Lizzie's flesh. The dogs had eaten half of her face away.

"Jesus." Cecilia shut her eyes and dropped the sheet.

Vicky Doyle came up and put an arm around her. "Cecilia, I'm so sorry."

Cecilia glanced up and met Clark Jackson's gaze. "Where were you when this happened?"

"In the basement," he said. His one good eye darted back and forth disconcertingly. It was amazing how a one-time employee of the Wehrmacht had managed to get rid of any accent and transform himself into an all-American good ol' boy. "Now you can answer me something, missy."

"Yes?"

"Just what in hell have you done with my wife?"

# II
## Jubilee Days

# Chapter 17

By the day Lizzie Polk was to be buried, the ground was stiff and had to be broken with pickaxes. For days, the snow came down fine and dry and crystalline, unsuitable for packing snowballs or building snow people. The wind swirling off the Lemhis blew it into drifts that shifted from one spot to another and back again, leaving patches of black ice. Drivers along the Haven Road battled snow-sprites that skimmed across the asphalt, trying to lure them into the rock wall or over the edge, into the ravine.

Cecilia stood in snow up to her ankles. There atop Green Hill the wind had polished the snow into an icy crust, and wherever she stepped it caved in beneath her. Her legs were freezing; she could hardly recall the last time she had worn a dress and hose. Mike, at her side, looked dapper in his black suit and greatcoat. He had pulled his hair back and tied it into a discreet ponytail behind his coat collar to prevent it from blowing in all directions. Neither of them had been to a funeral since Mike's grandmother died two years ago. Before that, Cecilia had not been to one since her mother's.

"When are she and Frank going to get here?" whispered Bonnie Gillette behind them. "They expect us to freeze to death?"

"Shh!" someone said from among the crowd of faces, most of them elderly and pale as the snow. The mourners were gathered around the newly dug hole and the black aluminum coffin.

Cecilia had assisted Joe Doyle with the postmortem; what the dogs had done to Lizzie was almost more than she could bear. According to Clark Jackson, Lizzie had come walking up the path while he and Lewis were in their basement workshop refinishing a chair. They heard the commotion of the dogs escaping their pen and rushed upstairs to see. The animals had knocked Lizzie flat on her back, and they had been tearing at her flesh. Lewis looked for his dog whistle, but it was nowhere to be found. Clark tried verbal commands to call off the dogs. Lewis was afraid to use a shotgun because he was a poor shot. He rang the sheriff's number, and Herb Monroe came out with his rifle and shot the dogs, but by then it was too late. Lizzie had died of blood loss and cardiac arrest. A freshly baked crumb cake, still warm, lay splattered with blood but otherwise intact on the ground beside her; the dogs had ignored it altogether. None of the evidence that Cecilia had seen refuted Jackson's story.

The Reverend Mr. Cleveland stood at the head of the open grave, robes billowing up, prayer book at the ready. The crowd had been standing a quarter of an hour awaiting the arrival of the Widow.

The black Mercedes 500SEL sedan drove up and parked in the cul-de-sac before the Old Haven Church. Frank Tyler got out and opened the door for his grandmother, whose black-gloved hand took hold of his. Tyler escorted her up the cemetery path. She was dressed all in black from her shoes to her pillbox hat, and she wore a full black veil that wholly obscured her face. She carried a modest bouquet of wild violets. Tyler was wearing his uniform, cowboy hat, and a bulky sheepskin coat. The circle parted to allow them in, and the Tylers took their places to the right of the reverend. Ralph Polk stood at Cleveland's left, propped up by Joe Doyle alongside Vicky and their children. Joe Junior was cleaning wax from his ear with a pinky finger.

The Widow gave a nod, and the crowd inched forward slightly.

"In the midst of life we are in death. . . ." Cleveland recited. The wind snapped his robes as if they were the flags over the courthouse.

The friends of Lizzie Polk sniffled and sobbed quietly. Peg Harrison's button eyes were transfixed upon the coffin lid. The wind had burned her cheeks and the bulb of her nose a deep rose color. Her husband, Hank, stood beside her, glancing covertly at his watch. Clark and Lewis Jackson were not present; they were in Pocatello at Dottie's bedside, fearful that her recovery from the leg amputation might not go well.

"Earth to earth, ashes to ashes, dust to dust; in sure and certain hope of the Resurrection unto eternal life . . ."

Jason and Ted Marsh and two other men lowered the coffin gently into its home. The Widow daintily disengaged herself from Tyler's arm and knelt gracefully at the edge to toss in her violets. She grabbed a clump of loosened earth and, rising to her feet, crushed it theatrically between her fingers. The dirt and pebbles skittered across the polished coffin lid. Jason and Ted grabbed spades and began shoveling in the dirt.

"Good-bye, Elizabeth," the Widow whispered.

Mike squeezed Cecilia's hand. She was grateful for the touch. Since the accident, he had been so understanding of the guilt she felt. If she had had the guts to go into the Jackson place on her own, she would never have asked Lizzie to get involved, and Lizzie would never have felt the need to go talk to Clark that evening, and this would never have happened. Mike had pointed out to Cecilia that the dogs had been an accident waiting to happen—they had nearly happened to him—and he reminded her that she *had* tried going out there on her own, with no luck. He was almost able to convince her that it was not her fault.

Peg Harrison, her lips sputtering, took a timid step toward the grave and began to sing. From the astonished look on everyone's faces, it came unexpectedly. Peg's voice, halting at first, soon blossomed into a rich soprano, singing words in German to a melody at once loving and forlorn:

> *"Und morgen wird die Sonne wieder scheinen,*
> *und auf dem Wege, den ich gehen werde,*
> *wird uns, die Glücklichen, sei wieder einen*
> *inmitten dieser sonnenatmenden Erde. . . ."*

She faltered, unable to continue, and sobbed in full operatic voice, her whole body shaking, her hand clenched in a fist and covering her face. The sobbing diminished, and she fell back into her more typical shyness, blushing as if she had been found out at a masquerade ball. She looked anxiously at the Widow's veil and at Tyler's reproving look. Hank Harrison threw his arm around her and took her back into the crowd— like a hook reaching out from the wings to remove a burlesque comic who was bombing badly. The difference was, Peg had sung extraordinarily well, and even though Cecilia hadn't understood a word, the sincerity had come through.

Every other face looked horribly aghast. Dave Clinton was shaking his head at Marge. Peg had broken some unwritten law and somehow shamed them.

When Cecilia turned to look at the Widow, she felt that the

Widow was staring at her. If the mourners had been embarrassed, it could only have been because Peg's emotions had come forth in front of the newcomers. The Widow appeared to be gauging Cecilia's reaction.

She felt hot and prickly under her heavy wool coat.

The Widow turned on her heels, and Frank Tyler escorted her back down the path to her sedan. The crowd did not disperse until the car backed out and disappeared down the hill.

"She's not coming to the wake?"

"Frank's taking her home," Bonnie said. "He'll be back."

Cecilia didn't care about Tyler, but she was desperate to meet the Widow. If it could not happen today, she would have to arrange it soon. It was her duty to check on an elderly patient—especially a reclusive one. She would not make the same mistake she had made with Dottie Jackson.

"They're Germans," Mike said. They were together in the upstairs bathroom, getting out of their funeral clothes. Mike, at the pedestal sink, pulled off his black tie and draped it over the shaving mirror's arm, unbuttoned his tight shirt collar, shucked his slacks down to his ankles, and stepped out of them to stand there in shirttails and boxers. "Didn't I tell you about Hank Harrison, when I met him at the Raven's Roost? I'm sure it was a German accent he was masking. And his wife, what was that!"

"Peg." Cecilia was still depressed after the service and the wake. She had never gotten to know Lizzie well but missed her terribly. She wasn't in the mood for a lot of talk.

"Yeah, Peg. Didn't you say you thought Jim Hamilton spoke like he'd taken diction lessons?"

"That's what it sounded like." Cecilia stared at herself in the vanity mirror, brushing the wind-blown tangles out of her hair.

Mike placed his hands on her shoulders and began massaging the kinks out of her neck.

"That feels good." Cecilia fell into it. Mike undid the top buttons of her shirt and pulled it down over her shoulders so his hands could work her flesh. "Harder."

"They didn't want us to know. Did you see the looks on their faces when Peg started up?"

"I think it's why they tried to keep me away from Dottie, too. She only speaks German."

"You never told me that." Mike's hands stopped.

"Don't get upset. I meant to. When I got back I had to deal with Lizzie, and it just slipped my mind. Mike, I'm sorry."

"Are you saying there was a plot to keep you from her?"

"It was Hamilton who wouldn't let me. He got very touchy."

"Hamilton—see? And he went down to Argentina."

"So?"

"He's an old man. If he's a German, he could have been a Nazi."

"Mike, the Nazis went to South America because they couldn't go anyplace else. If Hamilton's a Nazi, why would he live all his life in Idaho and then suddenly flee to Argentina?"

"Beats me. Who said he was fleeing?"

"There's plenty of Germans in Argentina who aren't Nazis. How many Chinese outside of China are Communists?"

"That's beside the point."

"No, that is the point. My dad thinks all Asians are Communists—even the Japanese."

"Your dad's an asshole."

"Mike, I don't want to argue."

"Are we arguing?" Mike smiled.

"No, but we're about to." Cecilia gave him a warning look.

"Sorry. I guess only you have the right to call your dad an asshole. But how do you know they're *not* Nazis?"

"All of Haven's Germans?"

"How many can there be?"

Cecilia shook her head. "It's impossible. They would never have been let into the country."

"What about Wernher von Braun?"

"He was a rocket scientist. That's different."

"Come on, there were plenty of Nazis who came to America."

"Name one."

"Trust me, Cee. I read about it. The FBI let them in."

"Sure. And the CIA slipped Edmund Muskie a mickey. You're a guy, so I shouldn't be questioning anything you say."

"Cee—"

"I suppose I shouldn't ask what you and Bonnie were doing at the mine when Herb Monroe and Joe Doyle caught you."

Mike stared. "Caught me? They didn't catch me at anything."

"Your pants were down."

Mike shut his eyes, wincing. "Where did you hear this?"

"Joe Doyle told me, while we were working on Lizzie."

"Bonnie attacked me. I had to fight her off, honest."

"I don't want to hear the rest, Mike."

"Nothing happened, for Christ's sake!"

"I don't want to hear it."

Just then the oval window of the bathroom exploded, and shards of glass came flying across the room. Mike threw himself over Cecilia, knocking her off the chair and onto the floor. The five-paned vanity mirror shattered an instant later, sending bits of mirrored glass into their hair and across their backs. With a *thunk*, a large and heavy brick came tumbling off the vanity table and onto the floor, missing them by inches. Freezing wind gusted into the room.

"Jesus! Mike!"

"Cee, you all right?"

"I guess so."

"Careful." He helped her up. He had a few superficial cuts; blood dripped down his face.

Bits of broken glass were all over the floor, on the vanity table, in the tub. The mirror over the pedestal sink was still intact. Cecilia stepped gingerly over to it and looked at herself—a few cuts to the forehead, bits of glass stuck in her hair. She opened the medicine chest and found the tweezers.

Mike went over and peered out the window. The wind whipped his hair and made his eyes squint.

"Nobody out there," he said.

"They had time to run away."

"Is there a note?" He tiptoed around the glass to the brick, picked it up, turned it over, found nothing.

"There doesn't have to be any note," she said. "We're supposed to know what it means. Put it down. We should leave everything like it is for Frank Tyler to look at."

"Hell of a lot of good that's going to do, calling him."

Mike helped Cecilia out into the hall. They went to the bedroom and helped each other pluck the slivers of glass from their skin. Mike's exposed legs had been cut in several places. Cecilia found it warmly intimate to be plucking minuscule glass fragments from his flesh, dabbing at the blood with cotton balls and rubbing alcohol.

"Mike, I'm sorry."

"Honey, you have nothing to be sorry about."

"I'm sorry for not trusting you."

"That's okay. I'm sorry it happened. I like Bonnie, but only as a friend. She apologized. She was very embarrassed. She thought she had been picking up signals from me. Ow! Honey, that hurts!"

"Sorry. Hold still." She was trying to pull a long sliver from

164

his scalp, but the angle was wrong. She tried it another way, and it slid right out, dripping blood.

"You're right, of course. We'd better call Tyler."

Cecilia was holding the receiver and punching out the number before she remembered something else she had neglected to tell Mike. She depressed the hook and held it down, hesitating. She hoped he wouldn't be too angry at her for holding it back.

"What is it?" Mike asked.

"Do you remember the phone ringing a few times early in the morning, about a week ago?"

"No."

"First time he called, it was almost five."

"Who?"

"I don't know who. There was nobody there. Second time he called—"

"How do you know it was a he?"

"He spoke."

"What did he say?"

"Just one word, '*Traitor.*' Then he hung up."

"Why didn't you tell me? This is serious."

"I didn't want to worry you."

"Cee, you know what he meant, don't you?"

"I know, I assume he meant that I'm a traitor to my race. I just wanted to ignore it, hope it would go away, I guess. I'm sorry I didn't tell you."

"Here." Mike lifted her fingers off the hook, restoring the dial tone. "Call up Sheriff Andy."

"You think it's the same person? The cats, the phone calls, the brick?" Cecilia punched the number again.

"It's the same message. Somebody wants us out of here. They may not be Nazis, but they—"

"Hello?" came Tyler's voice.

Cecilia cupped the receiver and said, "Shh!" to Mike.

165

"Hello?" Tyler said, hesitating. "Bon, is that you?"

"Frank, it's Cecilia Mak. Hi. Mike and I have a problem here. Somebody threw a brick through our window."

"A brick? Son of a bitch."

"It could have killed us."

"Goddamned fools," he muttered. "You all right, Cee?"

"We're okay. Shaken."

"I'll be right there. You two stay put, hear?"

# Chapter 18

Sheriff Tyler took Polaroid photos of their cuts and abrasions, of the brick, of the broken window, of the bits of glass scattered over the breadth of the bathroom. He scribbled copious notes on a steno pad, leaf after olive-colored leaf, writing in a stormy, exuberant script with a gold-plated fountain pen and flowing India ink. Cecilia looked over his shoulder while he was crouched on the floor but could not read a word of it. It was worse than doctors' handwriting; she was fairly certain, however, that it was *not* German.

Tyler crunched glass beneath his boot heel, crossing the room to peer out the window. Cecilia, in leather-soled house slippers, followed to see what he was looking at. The window faced onto the snowy front lawn, alternately bathed in the red and blue light from Tyler's Blazer. Snow and ice crystals carried by the wind cast a misty aura over the scene. Mike was down there, looking like a cat burglar in his black leather jacket and ski cap, coming back up the hill armed with Tyler's flashlight, shining it in a broad swath across the snow.

"Any luck?" Tyler called.

"Nothing," Mike shouted back. "There were some tracks, but now they've all blown away. I think he parked down the road a bit, just out of sight, walked back down there, and drove off."

"Okay, thanks." Tyler turned away from the window. "You got some cardboard you can stuff this hole with tonight?"

"Plenty of moving boxes we could cannibalize."

"I'll send Jason Marsh over in the morning to fix the glass."

"How can you be sure he's not the one who broke it?"

"Listen to me, I know better. It's not Jason—or Ted."

"Who were you talking about, then, on the phone?"

"Hm?" They went together out into the hallway. Tyler closed the door behind.

"You called them goddamned fools." Cecilia chafed her arms to warm them up.

"The Marshes?"

"No, you just said, 'Goddamned fools.' I don't know, it sounded to me like you had an idea who might have done this."

"Sorry." A sigh of regret. "I must have just meant that who-ever'd done this must have been some kind of darned fool."

"You said *fools*."

"It only takes one man to lob a brick."

"Or woman."

Half of Tyler's face rose in a smile. "Cecilia, listen, if I knew who he, she, or it was, I'd have Herb Monroe out at their house right now to haul them in for criminal damage."

"Really." She raised an eyebrow at him.

"Hell, it's my Gran's property. You think we want people coming over and busting the place up?" He swung the lid of his steno pad shut and shoved it in the waist of his trousers, be-hind his utility belt. "Anyway, someone comes along and throws a brick within inches of your pretty little head, I'm going to get mad. That's why I said they were fools."

"But who are *they?*"

"That's what I'm going to find out, so help me."

"Promise?"

"Cross my heart, hope to die, stick a needle in my eye."

"See anything?" Cecilia asked, helping Mike off with his coat.

"The Jacksons came back tonight," Mike said. He shook the snow out of his ski cap.

"Do you think it was them?"

"Clark, maybe."

"Why not Lewis?"

"I don't know. Just a feeling. I don't think he's got it in him to hurt anybody."

"Because he called the dog off you?"

"Maybe." He sat down and began untying his boots. "Where's Sheriff Frankenberry?"

"Huh? Oh, upstairs, collecting the brick and the glass."

"What did he say?"

"He says it wasn't Jason or Ted Marsh."

"How would he know that?"

"Beats me."

"Did you tell him about the phone calls?"

"Yes. He asked if I had any enemies."

"Well, do you?"

"No."

"What about your dad?"

"Mike, he's not my enemy. Anyway, it wasn't his voice, and it didn't sound like long-distance."

"Long-distance doesn't sound like long-distance anymore," Mike said. "Fiber optics. I bet it was your dad."

"It was *not* my dad. Frank's going to have a trace rigged on our line."

"That's nice." The sarcasm was thick. "Frank is so nice."

169

"What's eating you, Mike? Why do you have to be so weird about him all the time? He's only trying to help." Cecilia held her tongue, almost forgetting Tyler was right upstairs.

"Look, are we going to have another argument?"

"Who's arguing?"

"I thought we had everything settled. I want to go to bed."

"We have to plug the window," she said. "I'm freezing."

Headlights swept across the bay window as a car pulled up into the driveway. The engine purred, then died. The head-lights went off.

"Looks like you've got company." Tyler's boots trod heavily down the stairs. In his arms were a couple of brown paper bags from the Haven Food Mart sealed with tape labeled EVIDENCE.

The doorbell rang. Cecilia went and opened the door.

"We're here!" said Jeremy Horowitz.

"Where's dinner?" Tom said, standing behind him with the suitcases. "Only kidding."

"Oh, my God, Jeremy!" Cecilia kissed him and kissed Tom and ushered them inside. "Come in! Tom, Jesus fucking Christ!"

"Ooh, what happened to your face?" Jeremy said.

"I got cut."

"I can see that. The Mikester!" Jeremy gave Mike a bear hug and a peck on the cheek. "Shit, you're like ice. Is that rouge on your face?"

"Windburn," Mike said. "I just came in from the cold."

"Spying, were you?" Tom asked.

"Something like that."

"You're cut, too." Jeremy folded his arms admonishingly. "Were you guys fighting with razor blades again?"

"We'll tell you later," Mike said.

Cecilia grabbed the bags from Tom, gave him a kiss, and

closed the door. "You guys are going to kill us, but we forgot all about you. Things have been a little harried."

"Howdy." Tyler was on the last step of the stairs, loaded down with evidence.

"Howdy, yourself," Jeremy said, looking askance. He turned to Mike: "You didn't tell us you had a chauffeur."

"I'm the sheriff," Tyler said stiffly. He set his bags on the floor and shook Jeremy's hand, then Tom's. "Frank Tyler."

"Ouch," Jeremy said, his fingers crumbling.

"Tom Parker," Tom said. "And my partner, Jeremy."

"Your what?" Tyler asked.

"Tom's a chiropractor," Cecilia said. "Jeremy's a freelance photographer. They've been together . . . how long now?"

"Three years," Jeremy said, "depending on where you want to start counting."

"Oh." Tyler wiped his palm on his trouser leg; Cecilia wondered if he was afraid of catching AIDS from shaking a gay man's hand. "How long you guys staying?"

"A week, maybe?" Jeremy said, eyeing Cecilia inquiringly. "If they can stand us that long."

"You didn't come for Jubilee Days, did you?"

"Jubilee Days? Sounds wonderful," Jeremy said.

"Just a coincidence, Frank," said Cecilia.

"Well, it might not be the kind of fun you're used to," Tyler said. "Long as you're here, you might as well join in."

Cecilia didn't quite catch what Tyler meant by any of this, but then she had no idea what the Jubilee Days were.

Tyler donned his sheepskin coat and cowboy hat and grabbed up his evidence bags. "Well, I've got to get these logged in down at the station. Pleasure meeting you, Tom, Jerry."

"Jerry's a mouse," Jeremy said. It wasn't the first time someone had made this mistake. "It's Jeremy. Jeremy Horowitz."

Tyler's eyes snapped up. "Like the . . . er, pianist."

"You got it."

"Oh, Cecilia, by the way. Joe Doyle's going down to Pocatello tomorrow to pick up Dottie's body, but Vicky's busy with the women's auxiliary, so he wanted me to ask if you'd like to go down with him and lend a hand."

"Dottie didn't make it?"

"Afraid not."

"Dammit, Frank, why didn't you tell me?"

"Forgot."

"When did you find out?"

"Oh, about an hour before you called. Clark came by to see me once he got back into town. I never seen a man cry like that. He kept saying he should have got help for Dottie. The doctors told him if he'd got her into the hospital and on an IV a little sooner, she wouldn't have had to lose her leg."

"They're probably right."

"Clark was a logger all his life, doesn't know any better. It's hard to blame him."

"I've never considered ignorance much of an excuse for anything. You can't tell me he's never heard of infection."

"So you want to go with Joe?"

"He doesn't need me, Frank. He's just loading her up in his hearse. I've got appointments tomorrow, and as you can see, we've got company. Tell him I'm sorry, I'll pass."

"Okey-doke. You all sleep tight, now. Don't let the bedbugs bite. And don't you and Mike forget to plug that hole."

Cecilia closed the door, turned the lock, threw the bolt, hooked the chain. "Whew!"

"Don't tell me, he's a Jew-baiting homophobe," Jeremy said.

Cecilia looked from Jeremy to Tom with a sheepish smile.

"Well . . ." Mike said, stroking his chin.

"And what's this about plugging a hole?" Jeremy said impishly.

"Sit down," said Cecilia, and moved him and Tom into the parlor, where they sat on the overstuffed sofa and chairs the Widow Tyler had loaned them.

Jeremy regarded the bland domestic scene in the painting over the fireplace and said, "Nice."

"Can I get you guys some Haven Bräu?" Mike asked.

"Whoo-zi-what?" Tom said.

"Four Haven Bräus, coming up." Mike went into the kitchen.

"You guys feel like staying up?" Cecilia asked.

"You mean a slumber party?" Jeremy perked up.

"I'm bushed." Tom rubbed his eyes. "All that driving."

"Oh, you loved it," Jeremy said. "He almost drove us off the road on the way up here. Way down into a canyon. I slept most of the way. So what's the plan?"

Mike came back in with the open beers clutched against his chest. "No plan. Cee and I just have a lot to tell you."

"Is it cold in here, or is it just me?"

"That's the hole that needs plugging," Cecilia said. "Upstairs. Someone sent a brick through it."

"Oh, shit." Jeremy straightened up, suitably serious.

"Oh, yeah," Mike said, handing him his beer.

Jeremy examined the label. "You cross the KKK?"

"No. Cee, do you want to tell them?"

"You tell them. It's your theory. I'll sit back and watch their faces."

"It's just a theory, you guys."

"We're all ears," Tom said. "Hey, this is good beer."

"Should be," Mike said. "It's made by real Germans."

"Hm?"

"Just bear with me."

"Are you guys all right?" Tom asked.

"Yeah, luckily. The bathroom light was the only one on, so it gave him a target. I'm assuming he meant to hurt us."

"He who?" Jeremy said.

"There's an old man here named Clark Jackson. Don't let the name fool you. He's really a German who immigrated with a bunch of others in the fifties. Cecilia found out he fought in the Wehrmacht."

"You mean for Hitler?" Jeremy said. "He's a Nazi?"

"That's what we're wondering—"

"And you think he threw the brick? Through a second-floor window? That's pretty good for an old man."

"An old man with one eye," Cecilia put in. "He has a glass eye in the other."

"Like Columbo," Jeremy said.

"I didn't see him," Mike said. "I'm not even saying it had to be him. What I'm saying is, he's not the only one. There's something about this town. We were warned about it in a way, when we stopped at the gas station in Elliott. This old man there told Cecilia the last time he'd met an Asian man was when he bayonetted a Japanese solidier on Guadalcanal. Now, maybe this old man's full of shit. Maybe he thinks he killed Japs on Guadalcanal. Maybe he actually spent the whole war polishing radios at Fort Bliss. I don't know."

"He seemed real surprised that I was taking an Asian person up into Haven," Cecilia said.

"When we got here, everybody was all smiles—all friendly and cloying and asking about Seattle, saying how happy they were to have us."

"So?" Jeremy shrugged.

"They were too nice," Mike said. "Look, people are racist all over. Back in Laramie, there wasn't a day in my life I didn't get a funny look from a cashier at the grocery store or a policeman or

even my high-school teachers. I remember my art teacher—
how he used to help all the other kids. He left me alone to do
my own thing, never bothered to come over and check me out.
And I was always called names by the other kids. I thought it
would be different in Seattle, but in some ways it was even
worse. Here it all seems hidden beneath the surface, like they
made a decision not to let it show."

"So what's the problem?" Tom asked. "If they're going out of
their way to welcome you—"

"That's not what they're up to," Mike argued. "They're trying to trick me—trick *us*."

"I don't follow you."

"I've wondered if they might not be some kind of millennial
cult. The reverend gave a sermon on 'The New Millennium,'
and I wanted to know what that was all about, but I forgot to
go."

"It *is* almost the millennium," Tom offered, "and whoever
wins the presidential election is going to be sitting on the big
throne when the numbers all turn to zero. It's on a lot of people's minds. I don't see anything strange about it."

"I don't really think it's a cult," Mike said. "I think some of
them are Nazis."

Tom laughed. "Nazis! Here?"

"Listen to me. The old people who came over from Germany
say they were refugees from East Germany, which is probably
true. If they are Nazis, they would have had even more reason
to get away from the Stalinists. They changed their names
when they got here. Don't ask me how they got in. I'm sure
there were ways. Wasn't there some kind of underground railroad?"

"You mean, via the Vatican?" Jeremy said. "Yeah, there were
quite a few priests who helped Nazis obtain false documents

and visas to emigrate to South America. But I doubt if any could have got into North America."

"Of course they could have. Lots of them made it in. I swear I read something about it. And one of these Haven families—the Tylers—had a lot of money."

"Why would they come to Idaho, of all places?" Tom asked.

"That I don't know—except that this particular location is so isolated, maybe they thought they would never be found out. And the mountains probably reminded them of Bavaria. And, you guys, this Dr. Hamilton is eighty-some-odd years old. I never met him, but Cee says he talked like he was masking an accent. She heard him speaking German over the phone to his wife."

"I know German, and I'm not a Nazi," Tom said.

"That's just what Cee keeps pointing out. But the whole reason she and I are here in the first place is because this Dr. Hamilton just retired to a small town high up in the Andes—in Argentina." Mike paused for effect.

"So what you're implying," Jeremy said in mock seriousness, folding his hands together, "is this Dr. Who-ski's gone off to share an Andean hunting lodge with Martin Bormann and Eva Braun?"

Mike glowered at him.

"Why do those names sound familiar?" Cecilia said.

"Martin Bormann and Eva Braun?" Jeremy was incredulous.

"No, I know who they were, it's just that—"

"They were the last to see Hitler alive, before Eva Braun became Eva Hitler and the newlyweds shared some honeymoon bullets—supposedly. Bormann was supposedly killed while trying to escape Germany, but nobody believes that anymore. There's ample proof he made it to South America along with Mengele. And if he didn't die, it's doubtful that the Hitlers killed themselves."

"I'm not talking about Hitler," Mike said. "I'm talking about Hamilton. Cee was wondering why, after living all these years in Idaho, he would suddenly want to 'flee' to Argentina. What if he was about to be found out?"

"By whom?" Jeremy asked.

"I don't know—Sam Donaldson or somebody. It doesn't matter. He left in a kind of hurry. That's why Cee and I had to come here right away. We were all set to go to Colville in about a month's time, and then out of the blue Cee's recruiter calls with an offer she can't refuse. I had to give the newspaper a one-week notice. And it's all because of Hamilton."

"Martin and Eva!" Cecilia said. "Jesus Christ! Those were the names of Hamilton's cats!"

"See? Now we're onto something," Mike said. "That can't be a coincidence, can it?"

Jeremy began laughing. "You guys are pulling my wang, aren't you? You expect me to believe some ex-German doctor named his cats after Martin Bormann and Eva Braun?"

"Maybe your Dr. Hamilton is really Hitler." Tom smirked.

"That would make him over a hundred years old," said Mike, taking Tom perfectly seriously. "And I doubt he would have gone unrecognized in Idaho all this time. He certainly wouldn't have gone unrecognized by Cecilia. But the thing with the cats is, somebody strangled them and left them in our backyard just after Hamilton had already left for South America. It was right before Raphael Abramowitz was shot."

"Wait, wait, cut," Jeremy said, making a time-out gesture with his hands. "Who's Raphael Abramowitz?"

"We don't know," Cecilia said. "He was in the forest and was accidentally shot by a couple of hunters."

"By Clark Jackson, hunting out of season," Mike added. "His grandson Lewis was with him, but I don't think he had anything to do with it. And I don't think it was an accident. Let me draw you guys a map."

Mike sat down at the coffee table and grabbed a pad of yellow Post-it notes and a ballpoint pen.

"This is the road up into the woods. This $X$ is where Abramowitz was shot. Now, when you're in the forest, it's impossible to see from this vantage point, but the Tyler mansion is just top of this ridge, here—no more than a couple hundred yards away. Abramowitz was practically in their backyard."

"I didn't know that," Cecilia said. "You think he was looking for the Tyler place?"

"No. On the far side of the hill, there's another house. You can't see it from town like you can the Tyler mansion." He drew its location on the map, showing it to be equidistant from the place where Abramowitz fell.

"Who lives there?" Cecilia asked.

"Nobody now. The Hamiltons used to. I think Abramowitz was onto Hamilton."

"How do you mean, onto him? To do what?"

"To capture him, hurt him, I don't know," Mike said.

"Why?"

"Revenge, if Hamilton was a Nazi. We don't know anything about Abramowitz, but he was dressed in combat fatigues and had an army-style duffel bag. I bet he was carrying weapons."

"What are you suggesting, Mike?" said Jeremy. "That he was from the Jewish Defense League?"

"Something like that."

"You think he was Nazi-hunting? In Idaho?"

"Hamilton was already gone," Cecilia pointed out.

"Of course—because he was tipped off—and how was Abramowitz to know Hamilton had left, or where he might have gone? So Clark Jackson goes out into the woods to kill him, and it all gets swept under the rug."

"Are you serious?" Jeremy looked to Cecilia.

Cecilia looked to Mike.

"You are, aren't you?" Jeremy said.

"I told you," Mike said, "it's just a theory."

"Just what are these Nazis supposed to be up to?" said Jeremy. "They got Hitler's brain on ice, or what?"

"Look, Hamilton had an associate—another doctor, a Dr. Tyler—who's now dead. The Tylers are the ones with the money. The grandson is the nice sheriff you just met. It's down to just him and his grandmother—the dead doctor's wife. The Widow Tyler owns the whole town—owns this house, in fact, and most of the furniture. She never shows herself. We saw her once, at a funeral. She rode up in the back of her black Mercedes—"

"Ooh, that clinches it." Jeremy rolled his eyes. "Definitely a Nazi."

"She won't show her face, always wears a veil."

"She was in mourning," Cecilia said.

"But what's she trying to hide?"

"Maybe *she's* Eva Braun," Jeremy said.

Tom laughed, scratching his head.

"You guys aren't taking me seriously."

"Do you really expect us to? Mike, if you're really worried about it, call the FBI or the Simon Wiesenthal Center and let them investigate. If it turns out your Widow Tyler was the Butcher of Bialystok, they can extradite her to Poland—where she'll probably be made a martyr."

"You and Tom had better keep your eyes open while you're here. It's probably all over town by now that our visitors are gay, and as dim as Sheriff Tyler is, he's already picked up on the fact that Jeremy's a Jew."

"So? They're going to haul us off to a concentration camp?

We're here to relax and see you guys. No one's going to do anything to us."

"I've got to tell you, a lot of weird things have been going on around here. Let's say for the sake of argument that they are Nazis. We don't know how big the group was that came over, but it's my impression it was fairly small. Haven's got a thousand people, and they can't all be Nazis. But a lot of the more powerful people were from this group. There's the Widow, her dead husband, Hamilton, a few others. There's a group that meets once a week called the Haven Society, and the Widow's the head of that. There's a suspicious group of men called the Posse, which they try to pass off as a social club."

"I think you guys are thinking too hard about all this," Jeremy said. "I'm not trying to psychoanalyze you or anything, but don't you think maybe you just have the jitters—you know, moving to a new place, feeling uncomfortable, maybe having a chip on your shoulder because of being a mixed-race couple? You guys have got something to prove, and the townspeople don't react the way you think they should, so you start dreaming up this fantasy that they're Nazis."

"Jeremy, we're not paranoid," said Mike. "This is real."

"There were a lot of German immigrants to America after the war," Jeremy said. "Are you going to tell me they were all Nazis or that we should be afraid of them? And most of them came to the West because it was where the opportunities were."

"Does Haven look like the land of opportunity to you?" Mike asked. "The place is dead. There's some logging, but the mills are shut down. They have to truck the logs hundreds of miles away. Most people in Haven are retired or unemployed."

"Maybe it wasn't like that in the fifties," Jeremy said.

"What about the harassing phone calls?" Mike said. "The brick? The cats?"

"I think both of you are jumping to conclusions."

"Okay, Jer, have it your way," Mike said. "I'm tired and want to go to bed. Cee's got to go to work in the morning. But I'm warning you two to be careful. There's been too many so-called accidents around here. I don't want anything to happen to you."

"I got you," Jeremy said. "If it'll make you and Cecilia any happier, Tom and I will just assume your neighbors are all looking at us like we've got pink triangles stitched to our lapels. And a yellow star for me, too. I'm twice blessed."

# Chapter 19

Cecilia was sitting in the breakfast nook eating a bowl of Grape-Nuts with skim milk when someone rapped on the back door. She had left Mike upstairs asleep in bed, and she had heard not a peep from Tom and Jeremy in the guest room. They had all been up until 3:00 A.M., and she had only had four hours' sleep. She had showered in the downstairs bathroom, crouched under a shower head that had been installed at a height suitable for a midget.

She looked out the kitchen-door window. It was Jason Marsh. She undid the lock and opened the door. "Hi, Jason."

"Morning, Doc." Jason tipped his cowboy hat at her. His lips smacked as he chewed his tobacco. His breath came out as mist and smelled worse than cigarette smoke.

"It's Cecilia," she said automatically, "not Doc."

"Yes, ma'am."

*Ma'am* was hardly preferable—she was only a few years older than he was. "Do you want to come in?"

He shook his head. "Naw, I just wanted to tell you I'll be starting with the phone line, then I'll go to work on the window once it warms up a bit. Sun's supposed to be out today, maybe even melt some of this stuff."

"Would you like to come in for some coffee?"

"No, thanks." He hefted his big red plastic Rubbermaid toolbox, rattling the contents. "I'd better get started."

"I just brewed a fresh pot."

"This isn't any of that women's flavored shit, is it?"

"Plain old MJB from the Food Mart."

"I guess I could take a cup."

Holding the door open for him, she looked out into the backyard, to the blue spruce where she had found Hamilton's cats.

"Have a seat," she said. He handed her his down ski jacket. "Milk or sugar?"

"Black," he said curtly, as if she were insulting his manhood. "You got somewhere I can spit?"

She handed him the empty MJB can.


"So tell me about the Posse." She sat down with their cups.

"Strong stuff." He gave her an approving grin. "The Posse? Aw, hell, people have been trying to make something out of the Posse for years. It's nothing like you might think."

"Just what do you think I think?"

"You might think we're working for the sheriff, but we're not, not really. We're not lawmen. It's just a lodge, that's all, like your Masons or your Elks."

"Fred Flintstone's Buffalo Lodge," she put in.

"You got it. Secret handshakes and shit."

"So you just bowl and watch stag films?"

"Well, there ain't no bowling alley in Haven, case you hadn't noticed. You got to go all the way back to the old mining days, see. There was a lot more people in Haven back then, more than five thousand. A lot of them worked up at the mine for old Olbrich, but there was a lot of them with their own placer claims along the Little Lost, too, bringing in a nugget here, a nugget there. Most of them were men, and they were pretty rowdy."

"I heard about half were Chinese," Cecilia said.

"That didn't last long." Jason snorted. "It was a real Old West kind of place. A big shortage of lawmen. Gambling, prostitution. When you got a lot of money changing hands like that, you get a lot of killing. There was only one full-time lawman, but he needed help every now and then rounding up desperados, so he'd deputize able male bodies."

"You're talking about a real posse."

"Sure as shit. You think this was only in the movies?"

"Doesn't sound much like the Masons to me."

"Naw, you're getting it all wrong," Jason said. "What we call the Posse grew out of that old tradition, but it's really just a social club, like I said. We've got ourselves a gym down at the music hall, we go on rafting trips, fishing together—"

"Watch *Naughty Nurses*?" Cecilia's father and brothers belonged to a lodge back in Seattle, and she had no idea what they did together. They could be smoking pot or having gay orgies for all she knew. She had always found the secrecy and male exclusivity of such organizations comical in the extreme, and she was even more baffled by women who fought to join them.

"It's a big part of Haven life, at least for us guys. We start them young in the Junior Posse—something like your Boy Scouts or your Demolay—you know, to keep the kids out of trouble. When they turn eighteen, we initiate them into the bona fide Posse—if they want to join. We do most of the good work that gets done around here. My brother Ted and I are in the volunteer fire unit. All the other firemen are members, too."

"Frank does call on you sometimes."

"Oh, sure, security details, shit like that."

"Why would he be worried about security at a meeting of the Haven Society?"

"They've always relied on us to act as door monitors."

"Door monitors?"

"That's right. They're just a private, exclusive club, like a country club, only there's no clubhouse and no golf course. You never saw anyone hire private security in Seattle?"

"How many men are in the Posse?"

"I don't know, a lot."

"What about the Haven Society?"

"Now, that's men and women, but again, I couldn't tell. All I know is, there are *some* who have turned down their invitation."

"How old is Lewis Jackson? You going to graduate him soon?"

"Well, Lewis is seventeen, so it wouldn't be for another year, but I'm not sure that puppy's going to make the grade. He'd be kind of useless in the Posse. Not good for much."

"Why not?"

"He's a wuss." He downed the last of his coffee. "I'd better get to work. After I'm done here, I'm supposed to go on up to the church, see if I can patch up the reverend's roof. He's been running around all night placing pails in the pews."

"I should go on to work, myself."

"Thanks for the coffee, ma'am." Jason grabbed his toolbox.

She let him out and saw that he had placed a tall ladder against the back of the house. She followed him outside to get a closer look. The ladder went up to the second floor, in between the windows of the master bedroom and the guest room, where the phone line went into the house. She was concerned that he might wake up Mike. Then she wondered why he had to touch the phone lines at all.

"Don't you have a switch you can throw or something?"

"Huh?" Jason said, grabbing a handful of tools out of his box and starting up the ladder.

"You're setting up a trace, right?"

"That's right. Look, we don't got a lot of sophisticated equipment up here. Phone company can't just 'throw' some 'switch.' It's a pretty simple operation, but I still got to go into your line to rig the traceback."

"You don't work for the phone company."

"No, ma'am. You think they want to pay one of their men a whole day's pay to come all the way up here?"

"They give you the authority to mess with the line?"

"Lady, I'm not 'messing' with no line."

That cut her—first *ma'am*, now *lady*.

"Sheriff Tyler gives me the authority," Jason added, now at the top of the ladder and opening up the wire's insulation with snub-nosed pliers. "You want a trace, I'm giving you a trace."

"No need to get defensive," she said.

"It's the Widow's house. Sheriff asked me to do the job. That enough authority for you?"

"I suppose. Jason?"

"Yeah?" He had the pliers in his mouth.

"Try not to wake my husband. We've got guests, too. I want them all to be able to sleep in, all right?"

"You let your husband sleep in every day? Sorry, none of my business." Jason craned his neck and took another step up the ladder. "I don't see him. He must be up."

"Jason, get down." She was pissed that he would go looking into their windows.

Jason looked to the other side, into the guest-room window.

"Hey!" Cecilia said. "Get down!"

"Will you lookee there!"

"Jason, stop. Come down right now."

He retreated down one rung, shaking his head. "Sorry, I didn't mean to look. I never seen three guys in bed before."

"Three?"

"Looks like they're going at it," Jason said, snickering.

Cecilia was halfway up the stairs before she realized she had been tricked. Of course she wasn't going to find Mike in bed with Tom and Jeremy. Jason had wanted to get rid of her for some reason. She opened the door to the master bedroom and found Mike in bed, alone, sleeping soundly.

"Mike," she said.

"Hmm?" he said.

She went over and rapped her knuckles on the window. Jason was talking into an orange handset attached to the exposed wires with small alligator clips. He looked up and waved at her.

She pulled the shade down and closed the curtains.

"Mike." She sat down on the bed and stroked his hair.

"What time is it?" His eyes remained peacefully shut.

"Never mind." She spoke softly. "Jason Marsh is here fixing a phone trace."

Mike opened his eyes. "Why'd you close the curtains?"

"He was looking in at you." She decided not to tell him what Jason had told her, or he might go running outside and knock him off the ladder. Even Mike was not immune to the call of machismo.

"Twisted."

"I'm late for work. Jason's going to be here a while, fixing the bathroom window. Maybe you ought to get up and keep an eye on him."

"Will do," he said without enthusiasm.

"Bye." She kissed him.

"Mmm. Bye."

She went into the hall and knocked on the guest-room door, softly. Then a little louder. "Guys?"

"*Entrez,*" said Jeremy.

She popped her head in. Tom was snoring, and Jeremy was propped up against the pillows reading a Clive Barker novel.

"Sorry," she whispered, going over to the window. Jason was still out there, hooking the handset back on his belt and climbing down the ladder. She drew the curtains shut. "Our repairman was looking in your window."

"A peeper," Jeremy whispered back. "I know, Cee-Cee, I heard all. I wonder about your repairman."

"You wonder about everybody."

"Seriously, daydreaming about three guys in a sandwich."

"He was trying to get me into the house."

"Oh, really?"

"Look, be careful today. Remember this isn't Seattle. The natives may be hostile."

"You mean I can't wear my tutu?"

Cecilia laughed nervously. "I'm sorry. I'm not trying to insult you. Just keep your eyes open. Tell Tom."

"Oh, I think he's listening. He's playing possum."

"Am not," Tom said, his voice muffled by the pillow.

"If you need me, you can call me at the clinic. The number's by the kitchen phone. Sorry I have to work."

"That's okay. We've got the Mikester all to ourselves."

"Jeremy, don't scare her," Tom said. "She's paranoid enough as it is."

Three guys in a sandwich or no, Cecilia was beginning to feel like the butt of a joke. She tried to let it slide off. "Tomorrow's Saturday. We can spend the whole weekend together."

"Yeah," Jeremy said. "Jubilee Days. I can't wait."

"See you later." Cecilia closed the door on her way out.

She went downstairs to the kitchen and looked out the back window. Jason was wandering around the perimeter of the spruce tree, looking at the ground where Martin and Eva had been found, tapping the snowy ground with the toe of his boot.

# Chapter 20

Janice Fremont was in a foul mood when Cecilia got in. Patients had been in the waiting room for an hour thumbing through dated issues of *Field & Stream*, *Wyoming Wildlife*, and *Ranger Rick*, coughing and sniffling. Fremont followed Cecilia into the back office and continued talking while Cecilia hung up her winter coat and got into her doctor's coat.

"I put Bonnie Gillette in the ob-gyn room," Fremont said. "I'd have a look at her first if I was you."

"I wasn't expecting her. Is it an emergency?"

"Could be. She was waiting at the door when I opened up. Abdominal pain. I promised her you'd examine her right away, and that was almost an hour ago."

Cecilia ignored the lecture; she knew very well she was late. "Fever?"

"A hundred-and-two." Fremont handed Cecilia a clipboard with Bonnie's current stats.

"These are just today's. Where's Bonnie's file?"

"Couldn't find it." Fremont was looking at the carpet.

Cecilia looked up from the data sheet. "Find it."

"Yes, Doctor." Fremont turned back down the hall.

Cecilia entered the ob-gyn room. Bonnie lay on the examination table clad only in a turquoise medical gown. Her skin was pale, forehead beaded with sweat.

"You didn't have to change," Cecilia said. "Are you warm enough?"

"I'm more comfortable now that I'm out of my jeans."

"I'm sorry I kept you waiting. How are you feeling?"

"Not so good." Bonnie's attempt at a smile turned into a wince. "Oh! There it is again. Shit."

"In the abdomen?"

"Uh-huh. Real bad."

"A sharp pain or a dull ache?"

"Sharp as all hell. I think my appendix is about to bust."

"When did the pain start?"

"Late last night, early this morning. It started off as a stomachache. I threw up a couple times. I went to bed, got the chills, finally went to sleep. The pain woke me up this morning around seven."

"Was it still in the stomach?"

"No, by then it had traveled down to my groin. I figured it wasn't just a flu bug, so I thought I'd better get on down here and have you check it out. Doesn't it sound like appendicitis to you?"

"Mind if I take a look first?" Cecilia lifted Bonnie's gown and saw a long, well-healed surgical scar extending down the lower half of her belly. "How did you get this?"

"Operation. It doesn't have anything to do with this."

"Not a cesarean."

"No, I've never been pregnant. Hamilton gave me a vaginal hysterectomy."

"Why?"

"Cervical dysplasia."

There was no point in pressing her further about it. Once Fremont located Bonnie's file, Cecilia could find out from Hamilton's notes anything she needed to know. The subject must be upsetting for Bonnie, and at the moment Cecilia didn't want her patient any more excited than she was already. Bonnie was probably right that the long-ago operation had nothing to do with the current problem. Cecilia would have time to look into it.

"How does this feel?" Cecilia pressed down firmly on Bonnie's stomach.

"It's okay."

"A little tender?"

"Yeah, a little. That's where the pain was last night."

"Have you had any cramping?"

"Sometimes. Spasms and things."

"All right." Cecilia proceeded down Bonnie's abdomen, pressing and asking her how it felt. If it was appendicitis, she would know when she located the right spot.

"Ow!"

"Right here?" Cecilia kept her two fingers depressed on Bonnie's right lower quadrant, about midway between the rim of the pelvis and her genitalia.

"Yes, yes, that hurts! Jesus!"

Cecilia lifted her fingers to assess rebound pain. "Does that hurt?"

"Yes."

"And this?"

Using only one finger, Cecilia pressed in the same spot.

Bonnie drew breath through her teeth. "Yes, there."

"And when I lift it up?"

"Yeah, that hurts, too."

Cecilia palpated the surrounding area. Although Bonnie's

entire right lower quadrant was rather tender, it was only that one spot that elicited such a strong reaction.

"I'm not convinced you have appendicitis," Cecilia said. "Not yet, anyway."

"What if it bursts while you're trying to decide?"

"Relax. If it is, it's in an early stage, which means you're not anywhere close to rupture. Your symptoms are certainly typical of acute appendicitis, but I couldn't possibly rely on them for a definitive diagnosis. The pain's in the right spot, but I don't think it's great enough."

"Not great enough? It's excruciating!"

"Believe me, Bonnie, I've witnessed a lot of cases of acute appendicitis, and your condition seems mild in comparison. You probably do have some form of bacterial infection. We'll have to send some blood work overnight to our lab, take a day."

"What if I don't have a day?"

"Please, Bonnie, calm down. You're going to be fine, honest. We're not finished here. I'll need to do a more thorough examination."

Cecilia certainly did not want to suggest to Bonnie the many varieties of illness that mimicked appendicitis. The hysterectomy ruled out ectopic pregnancy, ovarian cyst, or pelvic inflammatory disease, but she could still have acute gastroenteritis or a mucosal ulceration with bacterial infestation or any number of other afflictions.

"You're sure it's not going to bust on me?"

"Nothing's going to bust. If I can confirm appendicitis, we'll take you down to Pocatello. If I can't, the choice may be up to you. We could still take you down and have you admitted at the medical center for observation. Or you could go home, rest, and see how your symptoms progress. They may resolve on their own. If they grow worse, call me, and we'll get you admitted down at Pocatello."

"I'd miss Jubilee Days."

"Bonnie, I promise I'll take care of you. I'll be back in a few minutes. I'd like to have a closer look at your file, and then I'll come back and have a second look at you. All right?"

"Okay, Cecilia," Bonnie said. "Thanks. Really, I mean it. I'm sorry about all those ugly rumors going around town. There's nothing to them. I hope you know that."

"Now's not the time for this. It's water under the bridge as far as I'm concerned. We'll both get over it. Right now I want to make sure you get well. Be back as soon as I can."

When Cecilia returned to her office, a file folder lay in the seat of her chair. A pink Post-it note had been slapped across it with the notation *Bonnie G.'s file*. The tab was blank; no wonder Fremont had had trouble finding it. The file folder had been creased squarely at the bottom and showed no sign of use. Even before opening it, she thought it seemed terribly thin for a patient who had been born and lived all her thirty-odd years right here in Haven. She was ready to buzz Fremont and ask if this was all there was to the file, but she decided she had better open it up first before she stuck her foot in her mouth.

The most recent pages were at the front, the oldest at the back. Jim Hamilton's vain scribblings were cryptic in the extreme—worse than the average doctor's handwriting—and although Cecilia considered herself adept at translating, she found this slow going. The last time Bonnie had seen Hamilton was in March, when she had been ill with a cough, diagnosed with a mild case of bronchitis, and given a two-week prescription of erythromycin. Cecilia paged through other visits, all of which were standard: stitches for a cut received in the kitchen at the Raven's Roost, yearly physical exams, a sprained ankle received in a softball game, a tetanus booster shot administered, a pregnancy test that came back negative.

There was no record of any hysterectomy.

"Janice," she said over the intercom. "About Bonnie's file. Did you give me the complete file, or is this just part?"

"I believe that's it," Fremont's voice came back. "That's all I could find."

"Okay, Janice, thanks."

At the back of Bonnie's file was a photostat of her birth certificate. According to it, she was born in the town of Haven, the county of Prospect, the state of Idaho, on April 5, 1967—which made her a month younger than Cecilia and a couple months older than Mike. Father's name was given as Walter Wilson Gillette, Jr., color or race "White," age thirty-five, birthplace Idaho, occupation Newspaper Editor. Mother's maiden name was Emma Zander, color or race "White," age thirty-two, birthplace Idaho. The certificate did not ask for the mother's occupation. Her signature was written in a scrabbled hand. The attendant at birth was Franklin W. Tyler, M.D., Haven, Idaho, signing with an illegible flourish.

Fremont buzzed Cecilia back.

"Yes?" Cecilia used the speaker. She guessed Fremont had not managed to turn up the rest of the file.

"Your husband's on the line. Shall I put him through?"

"Please."

The phone line clicked as Fremont transferred the call—or were the clicks from a phone tap?

"Cee? You there?"

"I'm here," she said. "What's up?"

"Nothing much. Jason's working on the window. I'm fixing Tom and Jeremy some breakfast. They're in the shower."

"Downstairs, I hope."

"No, Cee, they're upstairs freezing while Jason's looking in on them. I was thinking—"

"Yes?"

"Maybe I can shanghai Tom and Jeremy down to the clinic so they can help me put the plow on the ambulance."

"Sounds fine, except I might need the ambulance today."

"What's come up?"

Cecilia had trapped herself. She shouldn't discuss Bonnie's possible condition with anyone, and she didn't even want to mention Bonnie's name to Mike, though part of her was itching to tell him about the pages apparently missing from the file.

"It may be nothing," she said, though she thought there was still a good chance she would be taking Bonnie to Pocatello today if only to be on the safe side. This was the day Joe Doyle was going to Pocatello, too, to pick up Dottie Jackson's body. She wondered why Sheriff Tyler had made a point of suggesting she go along with Doyle, when even he knew that her assistance in transporting the body was unnecessary.

"Cee? You still there?" Mike asked.

"Sorry, Mike, I was thinking about my case. You know, you guys better skip the plow for today. Anyway, I don't want Tom and Jeremy to think we've been waiting for them to visit so we could put them to work."

"I'm sure they wouldn't mind."

"I might need the truck, that's all," Cecilia said.

"Okay." He sounded disappointed. He had been trying to do her a favor, and she didn't want it.

"You guys have fun today, but don't let them get into trouble. And keep your eyes open."

"For what?"

"I don't know. Look, Mike, I've really got to go. I've got a tricky case and a full waiting room."

"Okay, hon. Bye."

*Damn*, she thought, hanging up. She couldn't help but feel

that she had let him down, that she had acted ungratefully. It was going to gnaw at her all day.

She called Fremont into her office.

"Janice, shut the door," she said.

"Yes?"

"Where are the records of Bonnie's hysterectomy?"

"Pardon me?" Fremont batted her eyes.

"Not only that, but it looks like there's a lot else missing. I'd say what I've got is less than half."

"Well, there may be another file. . . ."

"You've worked here thirty-five years, Janice. I'd imagine you're fairly familiar with your own filing system. I would guess that you could pluck Bonnie's or anyone else's file out of the cabinet with your eyes closed."

"I'm an RN, Dr. Mak, not a secretary."

"This is a new file folder, isn't it?" Cecilia thrust it out toward her.

Fremont looked at it blankly. "I noticed that myself. That's why I couldn't find it. There wasn't any label, and it was misfiled. I had to look through the whole set of cabinets. It turned up in the *T*'s."

"In the *T*'s. Why would it be there?"

"I haven't the foggiest."

"What about the missing pages?"

"I don't know anything about any missing pages."

"Look at it. Does it look complete to you?"

Fremont gave it a cursory thumb-through. "To the best of my recollection, yes."

"Come on, Janice. You helped Dr. Tyler deliver Bonnie. You've kept her file since she was a baby, am I right?"

"Yes." Fremont's eyes welled up and she dropped her gaze, seemingly unable to look Cecilia in the eye.

Cecilia felt bad about browbeating her, but right now all

that mattered was Bonnie's health, and she could not be fully informed without the complete records. She could grill Bonnie further about her medical history, but people's own memories of such things were never as good as the attending physician's records. She needed the missing paperwork.

"If I can tell pages are missing, you ought to be able to tell me what's written on them."

"Excuse me, Doctor, if I seem out of line," Fremont began, "but I will warrant to you that to the best of my knowledge, nothing could possibly be missing from Bonnie's file. If Jim Hamilton is guilty of keeping sketchy records, so be it. That has nothing to do with me."

"Did Hamilton keep bad records?"

"Well, yes."

"Why?"

"He kept it all up in his head. I don't imagine he ever thought there'd come a day when he wouldn't be our physician."

"What about Dr. Tyler? Are you going to tell me he kept as poor records as Hamilton?"

"They were, how do you say . . ." Fremont searched for her words. "Birds of a feather."

"They were a lot alike?"

"Yes, their methods." Fremont seemed almost to smile.

"How long did they know each other?"

"They worked in tandem their whole professional career."

"In tandem? Did they go to school together?"

"Yes, I believe so."

"Where did they get their degrees?"

"Oh, I'm afraid I don't know."

This was such an obvious lie, Cecilia gave up. She was beginning to wonder why Hamilton had made sure to remove his diplomas before she ever came to meet him. If he truly was

198

among the group of German immigrants, he had most likely attended medical school there, as well.

"Do you think maybe Jim Hamilton removed some of these pages himself before he left?"

"That's absurd. Whyever would he do that?"

"You tell me. Did he have something to hide?"

"Such as?"

"Malpractice."

"Now you're insulting me."

"No, I'm not. If Hamilton asked you to assist him in an operation, you wouldn't have had any authority to question the procedure or his methods. I'm not accusing you of any wrongdoing, I'm just trying to come up with a reason why he might have wanted to get rid of some records. Did he perform the operation himself?"

"Bonnie's hysterectomy? Yes, with my assistance."

"He didn't take her to Pocatello, or to Boise, even?"

"No, he was a perfectly confident surgeon."

"This wasn't too long ago, then? Dr. Tyler had already passed away?"

"Yes, that's correct. I believe it was two years ago."

"How extensive was the operation?"

"A radical hysterectomy."

Cecilia felt a pain in her own belly at the thought. She had to be careful with Fremont; she was letting her emotions rule the interrogation. "What was the reason for it?"

"Cervical dysplasia."

"Any evidence of malignancy?"

"None that I'm aware of."

"Did he consider cryotherapy?"

"I don't think it will do any good now to second-guess the doctor's course of action," Fremont said with condescension.

"Bonnie's life couldn't have been in any immediate danger. Did he seek consultation with an ob-gyn specialist?"

"Jim Hamilton *was* an ob-gyn specialist. He was also quite a handy surgeon. I daresay we will miss his talents around here."

Cecilia tried to ignore the slam. She may have had it coming. It was certainly possible that Hamilton had chosen the correct course, that Bonnie's cervical dysplasia had been so chronic or severe that it seemed likely to lead to future malignancy. Perhaps a biopsy had even come back positive and Hamilton had withheld that from Bonnie so as not to alarm her further. Cecilia may have grilled Fremont unnecessarily, and she may have just received her due. On the other hand, no records existed to back up Fremont's claims. It amounted to hearsay.

"Janice, I'm sorry. Please try to understand that it's not much help to me if Hamilton sometimes kept shoddy records. If I said anything personally hurtful, I apologize."

"Not necessary," Fremont said. "You had a right to be concerned. I'm glad to see you're so thorough. I'm sorry I couldn't be of more help to you. Will that be all?"

Cecilia dismissed her and gave herself a moment alone. She would need to examine Bonnie much more closely before she could reach a decision about her case. No definitive test for appendicitis existed; blood work could show an elevated leukocyte count that would agree with such a diagnosis—absence of such a result would almost certainly rule it out—but elevated leukocytes could also mean a number of other things. One out of ten appendectomies performed were unnecessary, and any surgical procedure always posed a risk, no matter how routine. The prevalence of malpractice litigation made any physician cautious about simply going in and removing an appendix without first confirming the diagnosis to the best of his or her ability.

Before going back in to see Bonnie, Cecilia decided that no matter what, she would take Bonnie to the Pocatello Regional Medical Center and have her admitted for observation. After Lizzie Polk and Dottie Jackson, she could never bear the guilt if something were to go wrong with Bonnie.

"Sorry about the delay," Cecilia said, entering the room.

"That's okay," Bonnie said sleepily. "I was resting."

"Let me take your temperature."

"Janice already took it. I've got a fever of a hundred and two," she said.

"I know, but that was over an hour ago. Open wide."

Bonnie closed her lips around the digital thermometer. In the meantime, Cecilia took a reading of her pulse. It was steady and regular at seventy beats per minute.

The thermometer beeped, and Cecilia withdrew it. It read 98.9°F—not on the dot, but well within normal range.

"You're normal," Cecilia said.

"That's impossible! I feel the same."

"Well, it doesn't rule anything out. Sometimes appendicitis doesn't even present with fever."

Cecilia went again through the palpation of Bonnie's abdomen to see if the pain had grown any stronger. She found that when she pressed the spot she had pressed before, Bonnie failed to react at all.

"Do you feel any pain here?" Cecilia kept her fingers pressed down.

"Tender," Bonnie said.

Cecilia pressed deeper, enough to make any normal person feel pain, and received only a slightly stronger response. When she lifted her fingers, there was no noticeable rebound pain.

She picked a new spot about three inches away from the original source of pain.

"Ow!" Bonnie said. "It still hurts."

If it were truly appendicitis, the sharp pain would have been so well localized that it most likely would not have moved three inches. Bonnie's pain still was not great enough, either.

"Bonnie, tell you what," Cecilia began, though she wasn't sure how she was going to present her case. "Would you mind staying here today so I could continue observing you? Or you could even go on home, and I could check in on you later. I don't think you're in any immediate danger."

"I'd rather you take me to Pocatello," Bonnie said. "I'm getting worried."

"Okay," Cecilia said, resigned. In this case, what the patient chose was most important. If Cecilia were to assert to Bonnie that she did not have appendicitis, she would be acting as stubborn and haughty as Jim Hamilton, and it would do nothing for Bonnie's peace of mind. "We'll get you to Pocatello and have you admitted. I can do a few more tests here first. I'll examine your pelvis, and then we can try the ultrasound and see if anything comes up, all right?"

She returned to her office and sat down to think. She did not want to leave Haven today, not when it seemed the world was conspiring to make her go. She picked up Bonnie's file again and brooded over the pages.

As she read Hamilton's notes more closely, she saw that in some cases the writing at the end of one page did not continue onto the back or onto the next, and she could find no page anywhere that picked up the dangling thoughts. She had difficulty making out a scribbled comment that barely fit at the bottom of the page of Bonnie's last recorded gynecological exam, from over two years ago. At first it seemed to read *Morken for Hisch.*, which made no sense. She wondered if the *Morken* was some German verb. She looked for it in her German-English dictionary, but it did not exist, at least in this reference. As she continued staring at it, she realized she was mistaken. It was not *Morken* but *Marker*. The only medically relevant meaning she could think of had to do with genetics—a genetic marker. And *Hisch.* was obviously an abbreviation—did he mean *Hirsch.?*

Cecilia went to her medical dictionary to look it up. She found something: Hirschsprung's disease, or congenital megacolon, a potentially lethal birth defect. Given the right genetic testing—only available through an expensive outside laboratory—it was certainly conceivable that Bonnie could have been found to bear a genetic marker for Hirschsprung's disease.

All of this was leading somewhere, but somehow it didn't quite add up. Perhaps Bonnie's family had a history of the disease, but why would Hamilton go to all the trouble and expense of having her genetically tested?

Cecilia looked at the notation again, and it all came clear. Hamilton hadn't written *Marker for Hisch.* at all. He had written *Marker for H.'s ch.* Cecilia knew exactly what this meant: a marker for Huntington's disease, or Huntington's chorea.

Cervical dysplasia was only the excuse Hamilton had given for Bonnie's hysterectomy. Technically, it had not been a hysterectomy at all. It had been a sterilization.

# Chapter 21

"Joe?"

"Speaking."

"Cecilia Mak."

"Oh, hi! Say, I was just heading out. Frank told me you can't come with me. I understand. You've got your appointments. I'm sure you're much too busy."

"That's just it. I've got a special case."

"Listen, I'll manage somehow."

"But you're still going, Joe, aren't you?"

"Sure, weather's perfect, and I can't delay this, anyhow. I'm chairman of the Jubilee Days festivities tomorrow, and Dottie's funeral is set for Sunday. Busy weekend."

"You still got room for one more to Pocatello?"

"You've changed your mind?"

"Not exactly. It's Bonnie Gillette."

"Oh?"

"She's not feeling well. She thinks she has appendicitis, but I'm not so sure. I told her she could let me keep an eye on her here, but she'd rather go to Pocatello and get admitted at the medical center. It's probably best, but since it's not really an emergency, I can't break all my other appointments to take her down. Since you're going that way yourself—"

"I'm not sure if I'll have the time, Cecilia—"

"It won't take up any more of your time. If you can just get Bonnie to the medical center, she can admit herself and take care of everything. I'll be in touch with her doctors by phone."

"She can't . . . she . . . she'll miss the parade!" Doyle was shrill.

"She'll miss a lot more if she really has got appendicitis. What do you say, Joe, can she tag along for the ride?"

"I'll be carrying the coffin in back, and—"

"She can sit up front."

"What if something happens along the way? I'm no doctor."

"Trust me, she'll be fine." Cecilia crossed her fingers. She was 95 percent certain that Bonnie's ailment was either minor or nonexistent.

"Well, all right. But I've got to leave right away, so make sure she's good and ready."

"I will."

"I'll be by the clinic in five minutes to pick her up."

"Thanks, Joe. I owe you one."

"I'll collect someday," he said, and hung up.


Mike was in the parlor with his coffee, waiting for Tom and Jeremy to get out of the shower, when someone knocked on the door. He expected Jason Marsh, but it was little Joe Doyle Junior, whose well-fed figure was greatly exaggerated by a thickly padded winter coat.

"Here." Joe Junior thrust into Mike's face a newsletter, the *Jubilee Days Rag*. Two American eagles in silhouette, clutching olive branch and arrows, flanked the nameplate.

Mike took it and said, "Um, thanks."

"Three dollars."

Mike eyed the kid suspiciously. Nowhere on the publication did it give a price, and it was a grand total of four pages long—a calendar of events and a political ad in support of Frank Tyler for sheriff.

"Who puts this out?"

"The Jubilee Days Committee of the Haven Society. Says so." Joe Junior pointed vaguely at the bottom of the second page. "I'm not stealing or nothing, honest, Mr. Mak."

"Don't you have school today?"

"This is a class project."

"Class project?"

"Passing them out. They stuck me with Stuart Lane."

"Hold on."

He left the door open as he went to the coat closet to retrieve his wallet. The boy came inside, uninvited, sat down on the sofa, put his feet on the coffee table. He took a sip of Mike's coffee and belched.

"Here you go." Mike held out the bills.

Joe Junior's attention snapped from the money to across the room as Tom and Jeremy emerged from the downstairs bathroom. Tom wore a towel wrapped around his waist. Jeremy's was twirled atop his head like a turban; he was otherwise naked.

"I'm ready for my close-up," Jeremy said before noticing there was a nine-year-old boy in the room. "Whoops." He ducked back into the bathroom, pulling the bewildered Tom behind him. The door slammed shut.

"What are they, a couple of homos?" Joe Junior said.

Mike nudged the boy's mud-caked feet off the table. Joe Junior had drained the last of Mike's coffee.

"Come on, kid, take your money and get out."

206

Joe Junior stood and snatched the bills, thrusting out his chin. "I'm not a kid!"

"Don't act like a baby. Go on, you've got work to do."

"Nobody talks to me like that!"

"What are you going to do, tell your dad?" Mike grabbed the boy gently by his coat's hood and directed him toward the door.

"Get your hands off me, you lousy chink!"

"What did you call me?" Mike gave him a final nudge out onto the porch.

Joe Junior spun around and pointed a thick digit. "You'll be sorry, Mr. Mak! I don't care what a big deal your wife is! I hate you, and I hate her! Why don't you go back to China!"

"Hey!" called Jason Marsh from atop his ladder. He was at work on the upstairs bathroom window.

Joe Junior looked up in fright and raced down the porch steps.

Jason quickly descended and ran down the lawn to grab Joe Junior, almost knocking him over. He grabbed the kid by the ear, twisting it harshly, and dragged him back up the porch.

"Apologize to Mr. Mak, Joe," Jason said.

"I don't have to! You're not my dad!"

Jason twisted Joe Junior's ear again, and tears burst from the kid's eyes. "Apologize."

"You don't have to hurt him," Mike said.

Jason let go abruptly.

Joe Junior clutched his ear and began to cry.

"We don't tolerate that kind of talk around here, little Joe," Jason said, though his words seemed more for Mike's ears. "Where did you learn that word you called him?"

"W-what w-word?" Joe said, confused, looking up at Jason with true fear in his eyes.

Jason raised his hand as if about to strike—Mike made ready to reach out and stop him—but it was just a threat.

"You mean *chink*? Timmy Pons told me!"

"Timmy Pons, eh? What did Timmy say?" Jason was stern.

"H-he said Dr. Mak was m-m-married to a ch-chink!"

"Jason, it's okay," Mike said. "Stop it. He's just a kid who doesn't know any better."

"Oh, he knows better, all right." Jason's eyes remained fixed on Joe Junior's, flaming with anger. "He knows better than to open his little mouth and start calling people names, don't you, little Joe?"

"Y-yes, s-sir."

"How would you like it if everyone called you 'fatso,' or 'lard-ass,' or 'fart-face,' or 'piggy'?"

Joe Junior gritted his teeth. "I'd hit 'em."

"What if I start calling you 'piggy' right now? Huh? You going to hit me? Come on, go ahead!"

"I'll tell my dad! He'll put you in the *dog*house!"

Jason looked suddenly cowed, as if there were some kind of meat to this threat. "I'm just trying to teach you a lesson, little Joe."

Every boy's father put him in the doghouse at one time or another, figuratively speaking, but Mike wondered just exactly what Joe Junior meant in this case that made Jason back off.

"And stop calling me 'little'!" Joe added.

"You should learn to respect your elders, no matter what color they are. Isn't that right, Mike?"

Mike felt somewhat dazed by the entire scene. "Uh, sure."

"Can I go now?" Joe Junior's tone was mocking.

"Yeah, you can go, but give me one of those first." Jason grabbed a copy of the *Jubilee Days Rag* out of Joe's coat pocket.

"That's three dollars!"

"I'll pay you later. Go on, get out of here."

Joe Junior seemed to weigh whether he should open his mouth again, decided against it, and scurried off the porch and down the garden path. He yelled over his shoulder, "You guys are going to be sorry! Wait till my dad hears about this!" He tore into a run, as if fearful Jason would come after him.

Jason turned to Mike, laughing nervously. "Don't let it worry you, what little Joe said."

"I'm not worried. He's just a kid."

"He thinks he's a bigshot on account of his dad."

"Are you really going to be in any trouble, you think?"

"Naw, nothing'll come of it. You watch. Joe might want to come and say something to me in front of his kid to show he's all big and tough, and I'll have to stand there and take it."

"What's this about putting you in the doghouse?"

"I don't know what you're talking about." Jason turned around and spat off the side of the porch, staining the snow with a stream of tobacco juice. "If you'll excuse me, Mike, you know I wasn't quite finished caulking when I came to your rescue."

"Oh, sure," Mike said. "Go ahead. Thanks."

"Don't mention it," Jason said, adding, "to anybody."

The sky was not cloudy for the first time in days, and when the sun broke over the Lemhis it actually felt warm; no wind sprang up to drive the temperature down. The snow glistened wetly and melted down the hillsides into Haven's streets, carrying a silty mud that the merchants along Center Street washed into the storm drains with garden hoses. A group of men were hanging red-white-and-blue banners from telephone poles, draping bunting along the second-story windows of storefronts, and tethering strings of pennants from wherever they could find a lofty anchor. It looked more like preparations for July Fourth than for October twelfth. Several posters went up bearing black-and-white photographs of Frank Tyler in close-up, grinning in his cowboy hat, with the message RE-ELECT FRANK TYLER—P.C.S.D. Other signs showed a dated, flatteringly retouched photo of a slimmer Joe Doyle: JOE DOYLE FOR COUNTY CORONER—NOW MORE THAN EVER. A handful of colorful posters bore a grimly accusatory Uncle Sam pointing his finger and saying I WANT YOU TO VOTE—ELECTION DAY IS NOV. 5!

"All this glorious Americana!" Jeremy said. "I for one can't wait!"

"You'll have to get up bright and early," Mike said.

"That's okay—early bird gets the worm." Jeremy nudged Tom.

"Stop." Tom chuckled embarrassedly.

Hank Harrison was coming up the walk in their direction. He saw them, then quickly ducked his head and avoided eye contact.

"Hey, Hank," Mike said. "Hank."

Hank passed on without saying a word.

Mike turned and said to Hank's back, "Have a nice day."

"Haff a nice day," Hank mimicked to himself in a mincing tone, not bothering to turn around. "*Schwulen!*"

"What was that?" Tom spoke up, following Hank Harrison back up the walk and laying a hand on his shoulder.

"Tom, don't," Mike cautioned.

"He's pissed as all hell," Jeremy whispered.

Hank spun around, wrenching away from Tom's grasp, baring his rotten teeth in a snarl. "Get your feelthy hand off me!"

"What did you call us?" Tom demanded.

"Faggots." Hank landed hard on the *g* and *t* sounds.

"No, you didn't, old man. You called us *Schwulen.*"

"Same thing." Hank snorted. "If you will excuse me."

"No, I won't. Not until you apologize."

"Apologize!" Hank grinned broadly, looking all around him, at the clear sky, at the men draping bunting. "He wants me to apologize! My boy, in my day do you know what we did with—"

"What's the trouble, boys?"

Sheriff Tyler was suddenly on the scene, standing in between Mike and Jeremy and placing his arms around their shoulders. Tyler's presence seemed enough to calm Hank down. Mike would have thought it more natural for a peace officer to approach the two quarreling men rather than hang back with the onlookers, but Tyler's approach appeared to work.

"Frank," said Hank. "I'm sorry. Forgive me."

"Hank, these fellows Tom and Jerry—"

"Jeremy," Jeremy corrected.

"Well, they happen to be guests in our humble town— guests of Cecilia and Mike Mak—and I'd personally appreciate it if you'd give them some respect."

"It was all a misunderstanding, Frank," Hank implored.

"He called us 'faggots' in German. *Schwulen*," Tom said.

"You know German, do you?" Tyler let his arms drop and walked up to Tom.

"A little."

"Is this true, Hank? Were you speaking German?"

"I did not realize I was speaking aloud. You know how my hearing is. I could not hear myself talk. It wasn't until this man seized me by the shoulder—" He pointed repeatedly at Tom.

"Did you seize him?" Tyler asked.

"Barely touched him," Tom said.

"I had no idea I had spoken aloud. I thought I was thinking private thoughts to myself. And anyway, is it a crime?"

"Only if it caused a ruckus, Hank. Then I could have hauled you in for disturbing the peace."

"I want an apology," Tom said. "I should be able to walk down the street without being called names."

"Hank?"

"I am sorry," Hank said unconvincingly, refusing to look at Tom. "I did not mean to offend anyone."

"There, you see? No harm done. Hank, you can go."

Hank gave Tyler a feeble, impertinent salute off the top of his head and went on his way.

"I've got to apologize, too," Tyler said. "Hank drinks. He's got a real problem. It ain't pretty. I'm sorry you had to run into something like this in our little town. If you have any more problems during your stay, don't you hesitate to give me a ring up at the courthouse, all rightie?"

Tyler went on up Center, admiring the posters. The men hanging decorations gave him a wavelike salute as he passed, similar to the one Hank had given.

"Four more years!" one of the workers called down to him.

Tyler returned the salute and said, "Carry on!"

Mike could barely believe what Cecilia told him about Bonnie. They were alone together in her office. Through the window that faced Flatiron he could see Tom and Jeremy in the front parking lot before the ambulance, scratching their heads over the various parts of the snowplow attachment yet to be assembled. Mike would have to get back out there in a hurry—they could probably handle it, but he didn't want to stick them with all the work.

"It makes a weird kind of sense," Cecilia said.

"How can it? They sterilized her, for Christ's sake!"

"I'm talking about her and Frank. He wants a big family. They must have broken up because she couldn't bear children."

"Do you think she's stable, mentally?"

"I think so." Cecilia shrugged. "Why?"

212

"Just thinking of the way she threw herself at me down in the mine. Maybe it messed her up psychologically—having the hysterectomy. Or could she already have Huntington's?"

"Probably not," Cecilia said. "She could certainly have personality changes, manic depression, even schizophrenia before there's any physical degeneration—but she's only twenty-nine, and Huntington's usually doesn't strike until the midthirties. As far as I know, she hasn't shown any symptoms. I'm waiting for her to return from Pocatello before I bring it up with her. If she does have a marker for Huntington's—and I still have no idea how Hamilton found this out, if he did—I mean, the gene can be detected, but it's hardly a routine test—the disease will eventually develop, and there won't be anything she can do about it. If she had any children, half would get the gene, and half wouldn't."

"So she may not even know she has the gene?"

"Depends on whether one of her parents had the disease."

"Jesus, that's awful."

"It's a horrible disease."

"Can we do anything to help her?"

"Nothing medically. We can be her friends, though."

Mike's mind was reeling. As he worked on the snowplow attachment, he could not stop thinking about Bonnie. The Nazis had sterilized some people with genetic disorders; others they had sent off to the death camps. They had tried to eliminate all the "bad" genes from the German pool. What they wouldn't give, Mike thought, for the kind of genetic information that was being amassed today.

"Fuck!" Mike had pinched his thumb on the wrench.

"You okay?" Jeremy asked.

"Yeah," Mike said, though it was bleeding.

"Go ask the pretty doctor to give you a Band-Aid."

"I think we're finished. Tom, give it a try, will you?"

Tom was seated at the controls in the cab of the Blazer. "Stand back," he said. Mike and Jeremy backed away.

The plow's electrical motor lurched to life with a low-pitched whine. Then the angled plow itself was lowered to the ground, raised, and lowered again, with great success.

"Did you ever see *Killdozer*?" Jeremy asked.

# Chapter 22

The parade began with a group of eight-year-old girls holding a banner that stretched the full breadth of Center Street:

**JUBILEE DAYS ARE HERE AGAIN!**

A second group followed, bearing

**WELCOME BACK HAVEN'S FAMILIES!**

The girls were all smiles, hair in French braids and of such a similarly blond shade they might have been sisters. They were met with applause, cheers, and the waving of American flags. Behind them came a coterie of baton twirlers—older girls of twelve to eighteen, all wearing miniskirts shorter than Cecilia would have wished on anybody, especially in this weather. The radio had predicted an unseasonable high, but it had not come yet, and even when it did it would hardly feel like Pasadena.

"What is this, *The Village of the Damned?*" Jeremy said.

Heads turned and scowled, and Cecilia cringed. She had

warned him already to try not to offend the locals. The crowd had dressed for the occasion, the men in various styles of cowboy hats, the women in conservative dresses, hair newly done at the beauty parlor. Children were in great abundance. It appeared that far more people had gathered than actually lived in Haven, confirming Cecilia's suspicion that a certain number had driven in to help celebrate Jubilee Days.

The marching band was made up of high-school–aged boys and older men—no girls or women—all dressed in identical uniforms of black cowboy hats, black vests over canary yellow shirts, Wrangler blue jeans, and cowboy boots. The music sounded good for a small-town ensemble—a loud and brassy Sousa march suitable for a July Fourth picnic around a blinding white gazebo.

"'The Thunderer,'" Tom said.

"What?" Mike said.

"The march."

"Tom was drum major of his high-school band," Jeremy said.

"Jeremy was a flag twirler in ours," Cecilia told Mike.

"Rifles, not flags. If you want to see silly, you should have seen Cecilia with her trombone."

"I didn't know you played the trombone," Mike said.

Cecilia felt her face flush, maddeningly.

"It doesn't suit you."

"Geez, you guys've known each other how long and she never told you her deep, dark secret?" said Jeremy.

"What about you, Mike?" Tom asked. "Were you in Band?"

"Oh, no. My mom made me take piano, but I was never in Band. I wish I had been—I could have got out of PE."

"Oh!" Jeremy craned his neck to see over someone's head and removed the lens cap from his Nikon. "A float!"

"Too bad there's no passion play for Jer," Tom said.

"Just call me a Jew for Jesus," Jeremy said.

Havenites turned again to stare. A woman scowled and lowered her eyes. A bearded man put his hands on the shoulders of his young daughter and drew her in closer.

"Oops," Jeremy said. "I guess I'd better shut up." He put his camera to his face and squinted, focusing in on the float.

The girl said something to her father, pointing at Jeremy.

"Shh!" said her father. "Watch the parade." He hefted her up onto his shoulders, and she screamed with delight.

The float came to a halt; the crowd quieted down. The setting was a slope of fake grass and an outcropping of papier-mâché rock. The occupants of the float were a man and a mule, the man dressed in the tattered hat and gray coat of a Confederate officer, hammering at the fake rock with a pickax. The mule was draped with bulging saddlebags hung with tin pans.

"I reckon I'd best be giving up," the man said. "All I've found for months is about one Double Eagle's worth of dust. Yep, this mountain's just about got me beat. One more shot, Nellie—then we're packing it in and heading back to Frisco."

The mule snorted, as if on cue. The crowd laughed.

The man swung his ax once more and examined the rock, tumbling the pebbles and powder between his fingers. His jaw dropped; he fell to his knees and cackled madly. "Jumpin' Jehoshaphat! Will you lookee what we got here! Gold, Nellie! That's right—I said gold, old girl! Jest you look at the size of this dadblamed nugget! By willikers, we're rich!"

"We're rich!" echoed the girl atop her daddy's shoulders.

Cecilia smiled at her and waved, trying to catch her eye. "Hi, there," she whispered. The girl saw but ignored her, turning back to the parade.

The man on the float stood. "Look at this gold!" He dug into the saddlebags and began tossing gold coins into the street. The children scrambled away from their parents and gathered as much of the loot as they could. The bearded man set his daughter down to join the others. When she came back, her cupped hands were overflowing with coins.

"Why, lookee," her daddy said, mimicking the actor. "Becky, you're rich!"

"Can I eat them now?"

"Later," he grumbled, his smile wearing thin.

"I want them now!" Becky stomped her foot.

No response from her father.

"I said I want them now!"

"I said no."

"Hear me now, people of Haven," said the actor, his voice resounding off the storefronts hung with election banners.

"We're a-listening!" shouted a man in the crowd.

Jeremy snapped several pictures of the scene.

"In case you don't recognize me—why, I'm old Henry Jameson Olbrich himself, founder of this here town!"

The crowd clapped politely.

"Thank you, ladies and gents. Yessiree, it was yonder, over at the base of Flatiron, that I went—directed by an Unseen Hand—and discovered the richest vein of gold ever dug up in the eastern Idaho Territory, in the year of our Lord eighteen hundred and sixty-nine. Yessir, that was quite a time, all right. After I laid my claim, other men came here from as far away as Sacramento, some to work in my mine, others to pan placer claims of their own down along the Little Lost. What I had was no placer—no, ma'am—it was the ever-lovin' mother of all mother lodes! That's right—before you knew it, I had fifteen hundred ornery, rascally men working under me, and the town of Haven was born, all rough and tumble–like."

"Gag me." Jeremy said under his breath.

The crowd cheered. A man threw his hat into the air.

"Tell the folks why you called it Haven!" an elderly woman

shouted. It had the feel of a time-honored ritual, as if this scene was enacted every year in this exact way.

"Why, thank you for asking, ma'am. And my, don't she look purty! Haven? I called it that because it was here I finally found peace after the War of Northern Aggression. I was my father's eldest son, and I stood to inherit my family's rich plantation that sprawled across the lush fields of Carolina. But I lost two fingers of my left hand to the Yankees at Chickamauga and later lost the plantation, too, needless to say!"

The crowd hissed as if they meant it.

Jeremy glanced queerly at Cecilia, eyebrow raised, about to open his mouth.

"Don't speak," she said, and he smiled.

"When the war was over, why, my whole family was ruined. I made my way out West, nearly starved to death, lost a couple of toes to frostbite in the winter of 'sixty-seven. But the Lord guided me to this spot, and the hard rock yielded up its riches—to me and my progeny!"

"Yee-haw!" said a man as if shouting "Amen!" at a Baptist revival meeting.

"Yipee-Yi-O-Ti-Yay," Mike whispered.

"That's right, sir! Every ton of quartz mined from my mine yielded two thousand dollars' worth of gold, and by eighteen seventy-three, the year I married Miss Sally Ann Sorenson of Portland, the H. J. Olbrich Gem and Mineral Company had produced in excess of *five million dollars*—more than making up for what I lost to the Yanks! I was growing rich as Carnegie!"

The crowd broke into a frenzy of whistles and applause. Arms reached into the air, hands grasping for something. The man playing Olbrich removed his hat, and more gold coins rained out from underneath. He scooped more out of the saddlebags as well and strafed the crowd before the float started moving again and disappeared down Center, heading for the courthouse grounds.

Mike unwrapped the gold foil of one of the coins and handed the brown disk to Cecilia. "Belgian. Want it?"

She grabbed it before he could change his mind. It was good quality, creamy and smooth. "Mm, yum."

"Who was that asshole?" Jeremy asked.

"Hey, buddy," said the bearded man from the crowd, poking Jeremy firmly with a fat, hirsute finger. "I don't like hearing that kind of language around my daughter."

The girl looked as if she hadn't heard a thing. Her mouth was smeared with chocolate, in defiance of her father.

*Go, girl,* Cecilia thought.

"Hey, don't poke me, man," Jeremy said. "Look, I'm sorry. I'll watch my mouth, okay? Just back off, all right? Jesus!"

The man turned back to the crowd, huffing and puffing as if he wanted to knock somebody's block off. He took one look at his daughter's face and swatted her forcefully on the butt. Tears sprang immediately to the girl's eyes, and her mouth opened wide, but no sound came out.

"I told you no chocolate till later, and I mean it!"

The swat made Cecilia flinch.

"Look, Tom," said Jeremy, "more cowpokes!"

The next float was set in an Old West saloon, with dance-hall girls in silk dresses and petticoats, and Jason and Ted Marsh in boots and chaps and cowhide longcoats with gun belts and ten-gallon hats. They drew their revolvers and shot noisily into the air, making some of the children scream with fright. Puffs of gray smoke came out of the muzzles. Blanks, Cecilia hoped.

"You don't want to mess with those cowpokes," Mike warned.

Hank Harrison was sitting at an upright piano, badly playing rinky-tink music, dressed in a striped shirt with frilly red garters on his arms and a battered bowler on his head, puffing on a fat cigar.

"Yeeee-haw!" shouted Jason and Ted. "Howdy, girls!"

"Howdy, yourself," one said, sounding like Mae West.

The women danced, lifting their skirts up above their knees and kicking their heels in the air.

"Which one's supposed to be Maddie Gahagan?" Mike asked.

Jason and Ted dug deep into their hats to toss out Jolly Rancher candies to the kiddies. The women withdrew lollipops from their bosoms. When the candy was passed out, Jason and Ted began groping at the women, who giggled.

"This is supposed to be family values?" Jeremy wondered.

"I think I'm going to throw up," Cecilia said.

"That's the conservative creed, isn't it?" Mike said. "To return to the good ol' days of greed and guns, when men were men and women were whores."

"Nixon said there was nothing wrong with greed," Tom said.

"I'm sure these people voted for him," Mike said.

"Nixon say anything about whores?" asked Jeremy.

The next float came to a halt before them—a Victorian brass bed draped in shimmering red velvet with tassels. Under the covers was Bonnie Gillette, sitting up against the pillows with bare arms and shoulders, the velvet covers pulled up over her bosom. She was holding a gilded hand-mirror and pinning up her hair, singing to herself,

*"Beautiful dreamer, wake unto me,*
*Starlight and dewdrop are waiting for thee. . . . "*

"Speedy recovery," Cecilia said. "I didn't even know she was back."

"What the hell is this?" Mike said.

"'Beautiful Dreamer,'" Tom said.

"No, I mean *that*." Mike nudged him to look closer.

Bonnie wasn't singing to herself at all; someone lay in bed with her, visible only as a lump in the sheets. The man emerged from under the covers.

The crowd gasped in feigned surprise.

Bonnie giggled. "Oh, Hong Wah, that tickles!"

The man with her wore a Mandarin-style silk cap. His eyes had been made up to resemble broad slits. His skin had been stained an unnatural-looking brownish yellow. He wore an obviously fake, wispy, black mustache, with long hairs sprouting from his chin as a kind of beard. Out from under the cap hung a braided black pigtail. He looked like Boris Karloff in *The Mask of Fu Manchu*.

"What the hell is this?" Mike repeated.

"I don't know," Cecilia said apprehensively.

"Miss-ah Sorry likey Hong Wah?" asked the man in the bed.

"Oh, yes! Sally likey Hong Wah very much!" Bonnie said.

Out of nowhere, a third actor appeared on the float. It was the same man they had seen before, still dressed as Henry Jameson Olbrich in his old Confederate coat. He came onto the stage with pistol drawn, aimed at the lovers on the bed.

The crowd egged him on. "Go get 'em!" someone shouted.

Bonnie screamed theatrically. She dropped the mirror, and her hand flew up to her forehead as if she were about to faint.

"This beats a passion play," Jeremy said, snapping shots.

"Henry!" Bonnie said. "What are you doing here?"

"I live, here, madam, remember?"

"I thought you were gone to Pocatello!"

"The road was washed out."

"Henry, I can explain!"

"Whore of Babylon!"

"My goodness," Jeremy gasped.

Cecilia looked around at all the children smiling with excitement and anticipation. She had the feeling this scene, too, was reenacted each year, and it disturbed her to think so.

"Bitch!" shouted Olbrich, the pistol shaking in his fingers.

"No, Mas-tah Oh-brick, preeze!" said Hong Wah, sitting up to block Sally Ann Olbrich from her husband's aim.

Olbrich fired. The sound made Cecilia jump. Gray smoke puffed out of the barrel.

Hong Wah fell back against the bed, saying, "Miss-ah Sorry!"

"Hong Wah!" Bonnie cried, hugging his body against her.

"I suspected something was afoot!" said Olbrich, still holding out his gun.

"Murderer!" Bonnie spat.

"I ain't through yet, madam."

With that, Olbrich fired three more shots, and Bonnie fell limp against the pillows, clutching at her breast.

"Hong Wah," she cried, and grabbed her dead lover's hand.

"This is what I came home to one evening, ladies and gentlemen," Olbrich said, addressing the parade-goers. "My own bride lying in the lustful embrace of our houseboy and cook! Of course I killed them—I never denied that, not even to the judge. Sheriff Samuel J. Burgdorf actually arrested me on two counts of murder, but when the case came up, Justice Everett T. Calhoun said simply—and I quote—'There is nothing in the law book as I read it that says it is murder to kill a Chinaman, and as for the woman, she was an adultress caught in the act of miscegenation, and I believe that is ample justification for the deeds of the defendant. Case hereby dismissed.'"

The crowd cheered and waved their flags high in the air.

This, apparently, was what they came for—to witness the reenactment of this tawdry bit of Haven history—the founder's murder of his own wife.

It made Cecilia feel dirty.

Olbrich threw more chocolate coins into the crowd, and then the float lurched forward and moved on down the street.

"What was that?" Tom asked. "Some bad Victorian melodrama?"

"The Victorians never saw such a thing," Cecilia said.

"I kind of liked it," Jeremy said. "In a sick way."

"Jer!"

"Racist, sexist *bullshit*, that's what it was," Mike said. His face was a deep, angry red, brows knit together.

"You okay, Mike?" Cecilia put her arm around him.

"No, I am *not*." His hands were shaking. Cecilia touched his chest and felt his heart thumping furiously. "Don't you think that was directed at me?"

"We'll find out," Cecilia said. "At the picnic. We'll ask Bonnie. I need to talk to her anyway."

The parade ended with the marching of the Junior Posse all decked out in their uniforms. The young men all shared a cold, brutish, martial look. Cecilia could not find Lewis Jackson among them. They were followed by a much larger contingent of slightly older men—the Posse itself. Cecilia tried to count them as they marched past—they stood six abreast and there were at least twenty rows. Their expressions were also hard but with a wry, self-confident smirk. The crowd applauded respectfully as they filed past, but the men did nothing to acknowledge it.

Frank Tyler and Joe Doyle came last, sitting together atop the back shelf of an old Chrysler New Yorker convertible driven at a snail's pace by Herb Monroe. A loudspeaker affixed to the hood was piping out Aaron Copland's "Fanfare for the Common Man."

"Bet they don't know Copland was Jewish," Jeremy said.

"It's like all those idiots who thought 'Born in the USA' was some kind of patriotic anthem," Mike said. "Reagan used it to appeal to Young Republicans without even knowing what the lyrics said. Frank Tyler's living in a shining house on a hill—what does he care about the fucking common man?"

The music over, Tyler held the microphone up to his face. Feedback squawked over the speaker before his voice came through.

"Welcome, everybody! You know, it sure is nice to see so many familiar faces whenever Jubilee Days comes rolling around! I just wanted to point out that the election is coming up—"

He was interrupted by a spontaneous chanting of "Four more years! Four more years!" Signs popped up in the crowd plastered across with Tyler's grinning face.

He beamed, soaking up the adoration. "Please, please," he said. "More time for that at the rally! I wanted to welcome everybody and to wish you all a glorious and happy Jubilee Days. Join us down at the park for the noon picnic. Afterward, Dave Clinton's going to open up his beer garden, and if you've still got room after a few pitchers of Haven Bräu, there'll be more food for you there! And tonight, fireworks just after sundown and the Haven Society dance down at the music hall! Joe, do you have any words you'd like to add?"

Doyle took the microphone, hesitated a moment, and said, "Just to say that everybody had better mind themselves and their kids during the festivities. Better to be safe than sorry. Vicky and I would truly hate to come into contact with any of you on any kind of *professional* basis, if you get what I mean!"

The crowd laughed, but Cecilia could sense their discomfort

at Doyle's morbid humor. When he spoke, it had seemed as if
he was staring right at Cecilia. She wondered if he intended it
for them, as a kind of warning or threat to mind their own
business.

"No wonder you guys are so paranoid." Jeremy shuddered,
replacing the lens cap on his camera. "These people are giving
me the willies."

The predicted unseasonable high came during the picnic. Cecilia had to take off her jacket and tie it around her waist. Mike
left his leather jacket on, but he looked too hot in it. Tom and
Jeremy had eaten quickly and were wandering around the
courthouse grounds so Jeremy could take his pictures. The
lawn was a sea of families spread out on checkered cloths, eating piles of food off paper plates. Men in aprons and chefs' hats
were serving up buffalo burgers, hot dogs, and roast chicken
from a central arena of charcoal grills. A line of demure women
served up side dishes of baked beans, casseroles, and potato
salads.

"Do you think they'll be okay?" Cecilia asked.

"Hm?"

"Tom and Jeremy. I'm not sure if it was such a good idea for
them to come."

"You may be right." Mike licked his fingertips and wiped
them on a paper napkin. "But I wouldn't worry about it. They
can take care of themselves. They'll be all right."

"What about you?"

"What *about* me?"

She draped her arms around his shoulders. She could smell
the chicken grease on his lips. "You going to be all right?"

"Yeah." He grabbed her around the waist.

"How do you really feel about staying here for five years?"

"I don't know."

"If you ever want to move back, just say so. I'll call Tim Vandam and tell him it's not working out, see if he can give me an alternative assignment or something."

"Not yet," he said, touching his nose against hers. "Depends on what we find out."

"Find out how?"

"You said you'd ask Bonnie. She's right over there."

"Bonnie!"

"Hi, Maks!" Bonnie kissed Cecilia's cheek and then planted one on Mike's. "What do you think of the picnic? Pretty corny, isn't it?"

"Aw, no—" Mike said disingenuously.

"Yes, it is. Don't argue with me." Bonnie was dressed in her normal duds: cotton shirt and blue jeans, her hair tied in a ponytail in back. She had removed the makeup she had worn to play Olbrich's wife in the parade.

"You look good," Cecilia said. "You feeling okay?"

"Just fine, thanks. I was already feeling better on the drive down to Pocatello. Joe dropped me off first thing at the medical center, and they took a look but ultimately decided I just had really bad gas. It completely went away while the doctors performed their tests. They gave me a clean bill of health, said I had nothing to worry about. Joe swung back around later and brought me on back. I'm so glad! I would have hated to miss Jubilee Days! Nice to see some new faces around here."

"Bonnie, you think you could come in Monday to see me?" Cecilia said. "Just a follow-up."

"Sure, I'll be there first thing. How do you guys like the barbecue?"

"I'm stuffed," Mike said.

"Why do they enact those scenes in front of the children?" Cecilia asked. "Don't they see enough violence on TV?"

"You know, I asked Frank the same thing. He says it's too much of a tradition to change. I don't know how long they've been doing the Jubilee Days parade—I saw the same skits myself as a little girl, and I guess I turned out all right. Though that may be a matter of debate—"

"Skits?" Cecilia said. "You call them skits?"

"No harm done," Bonnie said. "They're historical. People did a lot of rotten things back then. It's the truth, and the truth can't hurt anyone, can it?"

"It hurt me," Mike said. "I thought it was racist."

"Racist!" Bonnie laughed.

"That Chinese character was a total stereotype."

"It's what Hong Wah looked like. We have photographs."

"Where?"

"At the music hall. The Haven Society keeps a library there of Haven history."

"Can I go up there sometime and have a look?"

"I don't know. It's not a public collection. I'd have to ask the Widow. It's her property. She sets the rules."

"Maybe you can answer a question for me. Why did Olbrich dedicate the music hall to his dead wife if he killed her?"

"Search me. Maybe he felt guilty."

"So this 'skit' wasn't done just because of me."

"Why on earth would you think that?"

"I don't know," Mike said. "But I didn't much care for the part about it not being murder to kill a Chinaman. That might put ideas into someone's head—"

"Michael Mak! How could you think such a thing? Why would anyone in Haven want to harm you? Everybody loves you!"

"Is that why someone threw a brick through our window?" Cecilia asked.

"Didn't you hear?" Bonnie said.

"Hear what?"

"Normally, Frank would be up on the courthouse steps about now making one of his tired old speeches, but he's busy inside. He arrested the boy who threw the brick."

"Boy?" Cecilia said. "What boy?"

"Lewis Jackson. And I'm not the least bit surprised."

"Lewis?" Mike said. "That's impossible!"

"It sure is possible," Bonnie said. "Something about that kid's just never been right. He never has quite fit in."

"I still don't believe it. Cee, do you?"

Cecilia hesitated. "I'd have to hear the evidence first."

"Frank's real proud of himself. He told me everything's been going exactly wrong since you two arrived. He's desperate to see that you don't get the wrong idea about us."

"So desperate that he'd go and arrest the wrong person," Mike said.

"Oh, I don't think so," Bonnie said.

"Just what *is* his evidence?"

"The way I hear it, Lewis confessed." Something caught Bonnie's eye; she looked over Mike's shoulder toward the court-house steps. "Why don't you let Frank tell you? He's coming out. I bet he's going to make some kind of statement before he launches into his speech."

Cecilia turned in time to see Tyler step up to the podium.

# Chapter 23

Tyler thumped the head of the mike. "Test, test." A hum came over the loudspeakers. Joe Doyle, standing with Tyler, gave a pronounced nod toward someone in the audience, then stepped up and fiddled with the snaking mike stand. Fathers in the crowd took advantage of the delay to stand up from their picnic cloths and train their camcorders on the dais. Applause spread throughout the crowd until all the picnickers were on their feet.

"Thank you," Tyler said. "Thank you."

Doyle spread his arms to quell the enthusiasm, a sour look on his face.

"Sorry, folks. Can you hear me all right?" Tyler had removed his hat; the stark afternoon sun hit his face full force, reflecting off his broadly gleaming teeth. He had to squint a little, which only added to his generally amiable expression.

"Clear as a bell!" someone shouted back.

"I've got something important to say," Tyler began, looking down sadly at the podium and then up at the clear sky.

"Four more years!" shouted a drunken man near Cecilia.

"No, no." Tyler shook his head. "I'm not here right now about politics. I'm here about Haven. I'm here about us. About our way of life. I'm here right now as your sheriff because in any town—even a town as good as ours—"

A smattering of applause. Tyler paused.

"Even in a town as good as ours, a few bad apples will sometimes come to light. In Haven we believe in the family. We believe in our heritage. But as Jim Hamilton used to point out, even a good tree with sound roots can sprout poisoned fruit."

No one said a word, though some babies cried out; their mothers tried to quiet them down.

"I stand up here today, frankly, ashamed. Those of you who've come back to visit friends and family here in Haven may not be quite aware of some of the troubles we've been going through, but I'm here today to tell you they're going to stop!"

Tyler pounded his fist on the podium, paused, and took a deep breath through his nose. The crowd didn't stir.

"Some of you may have noticed the absence of Dr. Jim Hamilton in this year's parade. Well, I'm happy to report that he's retired to his favorite fishing hole down in Argentina, and he and Susan are alive and well and doing just fine. He'll be celebrating his eighty-eighth birthday around Christmastime, as a matter of fact, and he told me just the other day he's looking forward to the millennium.

"Jim searched far and wide before he decided on a replacement. And what a replacement he found—our lovely Dr. Cecilia Mak. If any of you haven't had the chance to meet her, stop on by her office sometime. I'm sure she'll be glad to see you. Or introduce yourself today at the picnic. I see her standing right over there, in the shade of that tree. Cee, why don't you step out of there and show your face!"

Tyler pointed. All heads in the crowd turned.

Cecilia was surprised and embarrassed, but she came out of the shade so the people could see her. Tyler waved at her.

"Now, the actions of a few idiots could make Cecilia Mak and her husband feel unwelcome. Let me tell you, plenty of other communities would be happy to have her. A woman, with her skills? Hell, she could go back to Seattle if she wanted to. *And she will*, if she continues to be the victim of harassment."

Peg Harrison had made her way over to Cecilia and Mike's spot. Her warm, fleshy hand clutched onto Cecilia's arm.

"You're not thinking of leaving, are you?" Peg's black eyes held an earnest expression that jarred Cecilia for a moment.

"No, Peg," Cecilia said. "I think Frank's just trying to make some kind of point."

"Because if you ever think of *leaving*," Peg said, dropping her voice to a whisper and looking around warily as if she were about to divulge a secret, "come talk to me first, will you?"

"Okay, Peg, I will."

"Promise?"

"I promise."

"Good girl."

Peg tapped her arm kindly and went back to join Hank, as well as four middle-aged couples who appeared to be sons and daughters and their spouses, and a multitude of grandchildren. Cecilia had never seen any of them before; they must be among the out-of-town guests. Peg reached down and hefted up one of the white-blond toddlers, holding her up to watch Tyler's speech. The little granddaughter picked her nose deeply and wiped the results on Peg's collar. Peg beamed at her, but the girl's open-mouthed attention was directed at the stage.

"When Cecilia arrived, we went out of our way to make her and her husband feel welcome. To let them know that they had a real home here in Haven. That it didn't matter who they

were. Though I know we're here during Jubilee Days to celebrate the legacy left to us by our founder, Henry Jameson Olbrich, I can't help but point out that the world has changed a
whole bunch since then. There aren't even any more Olbrichs.
But it appears we've still got some people who think like him,
and I'm here now to tell you that I won't put up with it. If I
catch anyone engaged in any form of harassment of Cee or Mike
Mak, I will arrest them, and they will go to jail."

Cecilia was growing more embarrassed by the minute. She
would have preferred hearing Tyler's words in private—if he
even meant them—not broadcast to the whole town. And she
wasn't sure Tyler was doing the right thing by drawing so
much attention.

"Let me tell you what's happened here. Cecilia has been receiving harassing phone calls at all hours of the morning. A
couple nights ago—just after Lizzie Polk's funeral, may she rest
in peace—someone threw a brick through the Maks' bathroom
window. We set up a trace to see who was calling, and I tracked
down a few other leads. When I confronted my suspect, he
right-off confessed. He's behind me now, inside the courthouse,
locked up in the jail until the juvenile court can decide what to
do with him. As some of you may have heard, it's Lewis Jackson."

Murmurs arose as people turned to one another in disbelief.

"Well, I want everybody to listen up and listen good. I'm
not going to stand for shenanigans of this kind. We will have
order. I'm still the law, and as long as I'm the law, we will have
justice. Otherwise, we'll end up like all these other little burgs
across this great land of ours—whole communities crumbling
from the decline of the family, lack of moral leadership, drug
lords poisoning our children, babies having babies . . ."

Slightly out of breath, Jeremy and Tom rejoined Cecilia and
Mike. Jeremy removed his camera from around his neck and

put it back in his bag. "I got some great shots," he said. "Ran out of film. Got to get more."

"Love your sheriff," Tom said, thumbing toward Tyler.

"I thought he was William Bennett for a moment there," Jeremy said.

"Frank's just Frank," Cecilia said, surprised to hear almost a note of affection in her own voice.

"I think he's trying to impress you, Cee," Mike said.

"Oh?" She had a weird feeling Mike was right.

"Maybe he's just trying to get votes," Tom suggested.

"No one's running against him," Mike pointed out.

"Shut up, you guys," Jeremy said. "I want to listen."

Tyler had just finished enumerating the nation's social ills, hardly any of which appeared to apply to Haven. He bit his bottom lip and looked out over the gathering. The wind tousled his hair.

"I'm sorry this announcement comes the day before Dottie Jackson is to be buried. I have to say that in light of this arrest, I've got no choice but to reopen the Raphael Abramowitz case and hold an inquest to determine what really happened on that September morning. You see, after Lewis's arrest, his grandfather allowed me into his room to look for evidence. What I found was some of the most sickening stuff I've ever seen."

Even the babies had grown quiet. Joe Doyle handed Tyler a glass of water, from which he took a long, slow drink before Doyle retrieved it. Tyler clasped either side of the lectern and breathed in through his teeth.

"Hate literature," Tyler shouted. "That's right, you heard me—pamphlets, newsletters, books, even some writings that Lewis made in his own hand—hate-filled journal entries decorated with swastikas, SS insignia, pictures of Hitler, and all kinds of symbols of death and destruction.

"Clark told me he had no idea Lewis kept a collection of such things or harbored any such feelings of hatred toward anybody. But he also told me he felt personally betrayed. Now, we all know that Clark was among the small group of German refugees my grandfather brought over after the war. I won't be embarrassing Clark if I tell you he fought bravely in the German army against the Reds."

"Are you buying any of this?" Mike whispered to Cecilia.

Cecilia heard a woman weeping off among the crowd.

"Right now I'm asking Cecilia and Mike to give us one more chance. I don't want them to get the wrong impression about us just because of the actions of some misguided kid. Mike didn't have to come here, you know. He gave up a great job in Seattle to follow his wife out here."

"I wish he'd leave me out of this," Mike said.

"That may sound strange to us," Tyler went on, "but like I said, the world's changing. Why shouldn't a woman be allowed to have her own career and ask the man to wash some dishes for a change, huh? Am I right?"

The crowd laughed, a little too hard.

"As if I'm just sitting around being a househusband," Mike seethed. "Waxing the floor and baking cookies."

"You and Hillary," Jeremy said. "At least she will be, back in Arkansas, after the election."

"If there's any other young folk out there who think the way Lewis Jackson does, I want you to come drop by my office sometime for a private talk so I can knock some sense into you.

"I'd like us all to remember some of the last words Lizzie Polk had for me. She reminded us that America was the great melting pot, that we were all of us descended from immigrants. America, Lizzie said, was a haven for the cast-outs. A home for the homeless. A refuge for what she called 'the vast unwashed.' And I think if she's not too busy up in Heaven, she's probably watching us right now and smiling. Yes, I believe she's definitely smiling! Cecilia and Mike, come on up here! Come on!"

Tyler motioned with broad swings of his arms. The crowd turned to face them, applauding wildly and parting for them.

"I guess we have no choice," Mike said under his breath.

People reached out to shake their hands and say, "Please stay. We love you."

Joe Doyle reached out to give Cecilia a hand up. Mike followed behind, staring out warily into the picnickers, shading his eyes from the sun. They stood flanked by Doyle and Tyler, who grasped their hands and held them up high like politicians who have just won their party's endorsement.

"Please, everybody, please," Tyler said. "I wanted them to come up here so we could show them how much we really care, and I guess you've showed them! Cecilia, Mike? Any words?"

Mike shook his head, but he told Cecilia, "Go ahead."

Cecilia took Tyler's spot on the podium and stared out over the sea of faces. "I don't know what to say except thanks."

Cecilia turned the podium over to Tyler. Mike looked more than a little annoyed by the whole affair. Joe Doyle was giving the audience a big grin and Nixonesque victory signs.

"I don't have anything to add," Tyler said. "Except to say that I hope we've all learned the true spirit of Jubilee Days here today. And I hope that after the games, Cecilia, Mike, and their friends from out of town will agree to be our special guests at the beer garden. How about it, huh? All the Haven Bräu you and your friends can drink!"

The games Tyler spoke of were various athletic competitions for the children: softball, touch football, and track and field events. Tom and Jeremy wanted to stay and watch, but Cecilia and Mike needed a break so they could talk, in private.

"We're going home to sack out for about an hour," Mike said.

"Sack out, eh?" Jeremy said with a wink and a nudge. "You're going to skip out on the Haven Olympics?"

"Do you want to meet us at the house later?"

"How about we just meet you at the beer garden?" Tom said. "Jeremy and I saw it when we were walking around."

"Sure," Mike said, "we'll see you there. You guys watch out, okay? Don't buy all this good cheer. This is still hostile territory."

"I hereby promise not to kiss Tom in public," Jeremy said, holding up his hand as if in a Boy Scout pledge. "Come on, Mike, we're not here to provoke anybody. Take it easy."

"All right, all right, I'm sorry. Just be careful."

"Yes, Ma," Jeremy said.

"And don't tell us we're paranoid," Mike added.

"Okay, we won't tell you, will we, Tom?"

# Chapter 24

They collapsed on the sofa in the living room, Cecilia leaning against Mike's chest. The quiet was nice—though they could hear the distant roar of the crowd cheering on the athletes and the occasional peppy march from the band.

"Lewis didn't have anything to do with any of this," Mike said. "I'm sure of it. I'd like to talk to him myself."

"Mike, you're not a lawyer."

"What's that supposed to mean?"

"Can't you admit you were wrong? This all started with you thinking Clark had done the shooting. What if it was Lewis? Don't you think Frank's taking a step in the right direction?"

"Reopening the case? I'll believe that when I see it."

"He can't back down now."

Mike stared at her in disbelief. "How much of that speech did you believe? I didn't buy a word of it. He's into this thing up to his eyeballs and just trying to confuse us."

"What thing, Mike? What has anyone in Haven really done to us? If Lewis is guilty, it would explain a lot."

"It's not him, I'm telling you."

"Why not? Think—all the things that have happened—he let Dottie get so sick no one could help her. And how do we know he didn't sic the dogs on Lizzie?"

"Clark was there. If Lewis has done anything, Clark is just as guilty."

"You can't let go of that, can you?"

Mike folded his arms and seemed almost to pout.

"Think, Cecilia, what was Frank's speech about? Us. We were the only audience that mattered—we and maybe Tom and Jer. He wanted us to question the conclusions we've been reaching. He wants the town to put a clean face out for Tom and Jer so they don't go back to Seattle saying what a creepy town Haven is."

"I just don't know, Mike."

"I'll prove it all to you." He spoke matter-of-factly, as if this would be the easiest thing in the world. "I don't know how, exactly, but I'll find a way. Faith, girl."

"Maybe you're right and Frank's got me all confused."

"That's what he wants. The big mind-fuck. It didn't work on me. I'm onto him. Don't let him fool you."

"What do you mean, onto him?"

"He's connected to this thing. I don't know how."

"A conspiracy?"

"Cee, honey, don't start denying what we've uncovered. The evidence is right there in front of you. What about Bonnie's hysterectomy? You told me yourself Hamilton had sterilized her. Why? Think about it. She was engaged to marry Tyler—"

"That's what she said."

"And it was called off after Hamilton ran some tests on her and found some bad genes. She wasn't a suitable mate, especially for someone who wants tons of children filling up his big house. The Nazis did this kind of thing as a matter of routine."

"Mike, even that doesn't prove anything. I haven't had a

chance to bring it up with Bonnie. It's not just Nazis who would sterilize a woman with a marker for Huntington's. Any doctor might recommend it. Bonnie might have asked him to do it, for her own sake. The fact is, we don't know."

"Cee, will you listen to yourself? You're defending them. Face it. We've stumbled onto something, and now Tyler's feeding us disinformation. He wants us to think he's on our side. You know how loyal he is to his grandmother."

"What has that got to do with this?"

"She's one of them."

"One of who?"

"The Nazis who run the town. Look, hon, I'll show you. All this furniture belongs to the Widow, right? Did you ever look closely at any of it? At the manufacturers' stamps? Our bed was made in Munich, and the black-lacquered bookshelves and the dining room table are all of a set made by the same company in Berlin. The artwork! It's Nazi art, for Christ's sake! That's why it's so banal!"

Mike got up and pulled down the painting that had hung all this time over the mantel and held it in front of Cecilia's face.

"You remember that documentary we saw on PBS? Hitler said modern art was 'decadent' and championed a style like this. Look—a perfect example of Aryan manhood, a hard worker, young, full of vitality. His wife—there to serve him and to bear him children. She's watching over them—that's her sole function, darning the socks, brewing up porridge, having more babies. They have three kids already, but they're a young couple, they'll have more. The kids are all studying and setting perfect examples for the youth of the day. They're all healthy, blond, smiling, perfect little Germans. Perfect little Nazis."

"It's just a bad painting. It could be from anywhere."

"Here." Mike pried loose the nails along the back of the frame. "If you don't believe me, see for yourself."

The artist's signature had been covered by the frame, but now it could be read: *A. Gebhardt—Nürnberg, 1936.*

"You knew this was there?" Cecilia asked.

"I assumed so," Mike said, examining the signature, positively gleeful. "Just a guess."

"Okay, Mike, let's assume the Widow Tyler was married to a Nazi. Does that mean we're in any danger?"

"Some Nazi wives were pretty awful. You ever heard of Ilse Koch, the wife of the commandant at Buchenwald? She asked her husband to have some lampshades made of human skin. One day they rounded up a group of male prisoners and had them strip to the waist. She went down the line picking out ones with interesting tattoos. Her husband had them killed and got the lampshades made for her. She also supposedly used mummified human thumbs as light switches, but I'm not sure I believe that."

"I don't think anyone wants to turn us into lampshades."

"Maybe not, but they might not be too happy if they think we've found out their secret. We could be in real danger."

"Then why, if she's afraid of being found out, did the Widow furnish our house with old German furniture and Nazi art?"

Mike frowned at this. He set the painting down on the coffee table and sat back down on the sofa.

"What if she wants to be found out?" he suggested.

Cecilia challenged him: "Why?"

"Her husband's gone, and Hamilton's gone, and maybe she feels guilty?" He didn't sound like he believed it, though.

"A guilty Nazi?" Cecilia was doubtful. "Maybe you're right, maybe she's trying to warn us. She thinks Hamilton made a mistake bringing me here, and she's trying to let us know why we should leave."

"That's twice you've brought up leaving," Mike said. "I hadn't even thought of it. I think you want to."

"No, I don't. But I'd like to know what's going on."

"It's settled then. I'll see what I can dig up, one way or another. You don't have time for this—you've got your work. I'll
try to look at the library at the music hall. If the Widow won't
let me, maybe I can break in some night and—"

"No." Cecilia was firm. "You can't go breaking in. When
Lizzie and I went out to the Jackson place, we tripped some
silent alarm that brought Tyler right to us."

"Why would such a ratty old house be rigged with an
alarm?"

"I don't know, but if the music hall's so important, they're
bound to have one, too."

"I don't think the Widow's going to let me go in."

"Ask Bonnie to ask her."

"Even if she lets me, how am I to know they aren't hiding all
the important papers? The only other thing I can do is go out
of town—maybe Boise—wherever there's a good library for
Idaho history. I don't know if I should leave you here alone."

"I'll be fine."

"What about Tom and Jeremy?" Mike said. "Shit—we were
supposed to meet them half an hour ago."

"Relax. They'll be there." Cecilia gave Mike a kiss on the
lips. "They've probably had a pitcher of beer already. They're
not going to wait for us. If Jer gets drunk, he'll be the life of
the party."

"That's just what I'm worried about. Come on."


The beer garden at the Little Lost Brewing Company was a
large space enclosed by high walls crudely constructed of cin-
der blocks. The tables and benches were arranged in long rows
but didn't look German at all—they were the same model used
at countless picnic grounds and campsites throughout the National Forest system, hewn of sturdy wood and painted a dark

maroon. Cecilia had never seen so many of them placed end to end like this.

Bonnie, Sadie, and Millie were among the servers bringing out plastic pitchers of beer and setting them down at each table. Most people looked as if they had already had a round. Everyone drank out of clear plastic cups—not a beer stein in sight. Also missing were all the children who had been running around.

Tom and Jeremy had been saving seats for Cecilia and Mike at a table in the middle of the middle row. Jeremy stood up on the bench, beer in hand, and waved them over.

"Hey, it's Cee-Cee and the Mike-inator."

"Oh, God," Mike muttered.

"See?" Cecilia said. "They're fine."

By the time they had squeezed their way through the throng, Tom and Jeremy had tall cups awaiting them, filled to the brim.

"That was more than a quickie," Jeremy said to Mike, winking, as if some kind of macho congratulations.

"Where're all the kids?" Mike asked.

"Oh, they were rounded up in little toy boxcars and taken down to the music hall for a double feature," Tom said.

"*Schindler's List* and *Europa, Europa*," Jeremy said.

Cecilia almost believed him for a moment.

"No, really," he went on, "they're showing *Triumph of the Will* and *Olympiad*. Gott to gitt zem vile zey are *jung*."

"Jer . . ." Cecilia was in no mood.

"No, seriously—" Jeremy began.

Tom cut him off. "Would you believe *Lassie Come Home* and *National Velvet*?"

"Maybe," Cecilia said. "From you."

"I wish I could go," Jeremy said. "A regular Liz Taylor film festival. You still wear that White Diamonds I bought you?"

"I don't think any of these people want to let Jeremy near their children," Tom said.

Jeremy held up his beer. "Here's to family values."

They drank to this.

"By the way, when are you two going to start making babies?"

"Not now," Cecilia said. "Not here."

"Well, I don't mean right here on the fucking picnic table, for goodness sake!"

"Not while we're in Haven. Not until I get my career going—probably once we're back in Seattle."

*Yes, of course. I hadn't considered that. If you were to have a child, where would Haven be?*

"Can I be its godfather?" Jeremy asked.

"Boy, you are drunk," Mike said.

"When's the due date?" Tom asked, as if he hadn't been paying attention.

"I am not having a child," Cecilia said.

As soon as she spoke, she realized that although they had been in Haven for six weeks, she hadn't had her period since they were in Seattle. So it was late—that didn't mean anything—but she wondered, in all the chaos of the move, could she have forgotten to take her pill?

"Cee?" Mike said. "Honey? What's wrong?"

"Nothing," she said.

"Hot flash?" Jeremy said.

*God,* she thought, *I hope not.*

She sipped surreptitiously at her beer all afternoon, but it wasn't until later that Mike asked her why she wasn't drinking.

"All these people in from out of town?" she said. "What if one of the kids gets hurt or something? What are you going to do with a drunken doctor?"

*"Hooray, and up she rises!"* Jeremy hefted his plastic cup.

It was about the only song that hadn't been sung. The beer garden had erupted several times into American folk song, from "Shenendoah" to "Froggy Went A-Courtin'." Mike had said to Cecilia, "Look at them. If this isn't an Octoberfest . . . Shut your ears and you can picture them singing *'Deutschland über Alles'* or the Horst Wessel song." She had had to ask him what the Horst Wessel song was.

"This whole day reminds me of a Nuremberg rally," Mike said.

"What are you talking about?" Jeremy had overheard.

"You've seen *Triumph of the Will.*"

"Actually, I haven't. I couldn't stand to. *The Sorrow and the Pity* is more to my taste."

"I haven't seen it, either," Cecilia admitted.

"I have," Tom said. "But I don't agree with you that these Jubilee Days are anything like a Nuremberg rally. That was a gathering of the party faithful, like a big convention. Everyone was supposed to go home all pumped up about Nazism, brainwashed by the propaganda, mesmerized by the symbolism. I haven't seen anything like that going on here."

"What about Tyler's speech?" Mike said.

"Not a very good speech, but hardly Hitler."

"And all the flags at the parade?"

"It's just the American flag. What's wrong with that?"

"The Nazis didn't see anything wrong with their flag, either," Mike said. "Couldn't you read between the lines of what Tyler was saying? Like he was meaning the exact opposite?"

Tom and Jeremy looked at Mike in bewilderment. Cecilia was more willing to trust in his reasoning.

"Think about it." Mike lowered his voice. Rowdy and noisy as the beer drinkers were, he could still be overheard if he were to get too excited. "Basically, he's pointing us out. He's saying,

245

'There they are. She's a white woman married to an Asian man, and don't forget about their gay friends.'"

"Mike," Jeremy said.

"No, wait. I used to underestimate this guy, but now I think he's not that stupid. None of his speech makes any sense at all unless you look at it my way. He's telling them the opposite of what he really means. It works two ways: It's deliberate obfuscation for *our* benefit and also a kind of coded message to the rest of the crowd. They're in the know, or at least they know *him*, and they know he doesn't mean what he says when he's saying something that doesn't sound a whole lot like him—"

"Mike, stop," Cecilia said. "You've lost me, too, now."

"I give up," he said. "Look, my gut is telling me this. When he brought us up on stage, I felt like a target. Like he was saying, 'Here's the one we have to do something about.' And he didn't leave you guys out of it, either."

Tom and Jeremy looked at each other.

"Mike," Tom said. "No one's been anything but civil to us."

"What about Hank Harrison?" Mike said.

"Well, okay, one."

"Remember what he said? What was it—'In my day, you know what we did with people like you?'"

"He started to say something like that," Tom admitted. "He didn't finish."

"You know what he means. When he was a young Nazi—"

"Mike," Cecilia cautioned. "Keep your voice down!"

"He would have sent you two off to labor camps with pink triangles pinned to your lapels."

"I think we'd better continue this later," Cecilia said, looking around at all the faces, many of them unfamiliar.

"Okay, you're right," Mike said. "Sorry."

"I know," Jeremy said, "let's all stand up and start singing the 'Marseillaise.'"

\*     \*     \*

In the evening, they joined the throng filing into the music hall for the dance. They were stopped at the door by Jason and Ted Marsh in their Posse uniforms.

"Sorry," Jason said, blocking them with his arms outspread.

"Don't tell me," Cecilia said.

"You didn't know this is a Haven Society dance?"

"We're just as much a part of this community as anyone else," Mike said.

"Talk to Frank Tyler," Cecilia said. "I'm sure he'd want us not to miss out. You heard him earlier."

"It's not up to the sheriff, Dr. Mak. The Widow heads the Haven Society, and she's strict about who gets let in."

"Did she say you couldn't let us in, specifically?"

"No, ma'am," Jason said. "But we've got orders not to let in anyone who's not a member."

"He's only following orders," Jeremy whispered to Cecilia.

"How do you know we're not members?" Mike asked.

Jason paused a moment. "How do you mean?"

"How can you tell? I don't see anyone showing you their identity cards—"

"Membership badges," Jason corrected him.

"Whatever."

"I've been running the door here a few years—I think I know who is and who isn't a member. If I ask someone to show their membership badge, and they produce it, they go in. Now I know your friends there aren't members." Jason motioned vaguely at Tom and Jeremy. "Have you and the good doctor got badges?"

"Sorry," Ted said with a wide grin, backing Jason up. "Love to have you, but rules are rules."

Cecilia didn't mind; Jubilee Days had left her exhausted, and the thought that she had missed her period was of more immediate concern than whether anyone in Haven might now be or ever have been a Nazi.

She sighed and took Mike's hand tenderly. "Come on, guys, let's go."

# III
## Harm

# Chapter 25

A cold rain came the day of Dottie's funeral. The temperature was expected to drop and the rain to turn to snow, and no one could predict when the snow might end. That morning, Tom and Jeremy decided it was time to leave, while they had the opportunity. Tom wanted to visit an aunt in Portland before they returned to Seattle; if a big snow delayed their escape from Haven, they might have to forego the sidebar.

Cecilia watched out the front bay window as Mike and Tom, in rain slickers, carried bags out to the car. Jeremy sidled up behind and touched her shoulder.

"Hey, girlfriend," he said.

"Hey."

"Any psychiatrists in Haven?" he asked.

"No. Why?"

The rain was turning the gutters of Stuart Lane into twin creeks. By midnight the roads would be ice.

"I know you're kind of humoring him, letting him go on with his crazy theories—"

"I'm not humoring him, Jer, and he's not crazy."

"That's not what I mean—you know that."

"It's the move," Cecilia said. If Jeremy didn't buy their arguments by now, he wasn't going to. "He'll be okay."

"You're not doing him any good. He should get help, and if he won't ask for it, you might have to find it for him."

Cecilia considered this and said, "Shh. They're coming."

"Bye!" she said, huddled with Mike under the eaves of the porch. Mike had removed his slicker and was dry underneath. Though she was wearing a heavy woolen sweater, she was shivering. He held her tightly against him.

"Have a safe trip!" Mike called out to them.

"We won't!" Jeremy shouted, leaning over Tom to speak out the half-open driver's window.

"When are you guys going to come visit?" Tom's voice melded with the dull rainy roar.

"Never!" Mike said.

Cecilia shrugged. "I don't get any time off!"

"Then we'll have to come back!"

"You're welcome anytime! There's always room!"

Tom gave a final wave. His window whined as he closed it. He backed out of the drive onto Stuart Lane, and then he and Jeremy disappeared in the gray mist as they went down the hill. They would land on Center, which would become the Haven Road once they crossed the bridge over the Little Lost.

Cecilia hated to see them go. It had only been a few days, though they had originally planned on staying a week. Mike thought the town had scared them off. She thought that *he* had, but she wasn't about to say so.

*Jeremy thinks you ought to see a psychiatrist*, she kept thinking, but she couldn't bring herself to say it. He would be insulted and she, embarrassed. He would ask her if she agreed with Jeremy, and she would have no answer. He would tell her he had thought she was on his side.

She *was* on his side. She couldn't help but believe in him.

"Yes?" Mike said.

"Huh?" She jumped.

"You were going to say something."

"No I wasn't."

"Yes you were."

"I was not. I know you like to think you're psychic, Mike, but I wasn't about to say anything, honest."

"That's not true."

"Is so," she said.

"Okay," he said. "My mistake. Sorry." He turned her head to rest against the crook of his neck. He kissed her forehead.

"Are you going to the funeral?" she asked.

"Not this time. Long as you don't mind."

"That's fine. You didn't know her."

"Neither did you."

"I have to go."

"Let's go in," Mike said. "You're freezing."

The black coffin hung suspended over the open grave. The rain bore down upon it in a steady, tinny drone. The drops collected into beads on the nonstick coating and washed over the sides in rivulets. The earth below had become a sodden cushion. The box would sink into place and be packed in with the pile of mud that was crawling with rain-worshiping worms. Tonight the ground would freeze inches deep and send the worms below. It would not likely thaw again until spring, when the mountain wildflowers would come and make Dottie's grave something to smile at.

Today, however, the sky was charcoal gray. The mourners had unfurled black umbrellas. Their hands were gloved, in black leather or woolen knit, clutching umbrellas or wrapped around a spouse. The rain poured over them onto the soggy turf, pooling at their ankles.

They were all waiting again for the Widow Tyler.

The Reverend Mr. Cleveland kept sneezing, his thick glasses falling to the tip of his nose. Lewis Jackson had apparently not been allowed to come. Clark Jackson stood alongside the reverend, his one good eye looking down at the coffin, hands clasped in front of him, protected by Vicky Doyle's umbrella. Joe Doyle and Joe Junior stood to the other side of Cleveland. Marge and Dave Clinton looked tired after playing host to such a large crowd at the beer garden. Hank Harrison stood alone under his umbrella. Peg was notably absent.

Cecilia put a peppermint candy in her mouth to act against the smells of worms and damp earth. She wondered if Peg had been kept away to prevent her bursting into song. Cecilia had expected to see Bonnie here—though she didn't know why she should—perhaps she was needed at the Raven's Roost, given all the extra clientele this weekend.

Finally, the black Mercedes drove silently up, halogen headlights a dirty yellow in the gray mist and rain. Sheriff Tyler brought his grandmother up the path to stand next to the reverend. She wore the same dress and overcoat as before, along with her veil. She brought another bundle of wild violets and tossed them in at the end of the minister's recitation.

Jason and Ted Marsh turned the cranks and lowered the coffin into the breach. The Widow once again knelt at the edge of the hole; this time, her gloved fingers grasped a sodden clod of mud, which she heaped in with a dull splat that died upon the coffin lid. Some of the mud still clung to the fabric of her glove. As she rose precariously to her feet, Joe Doyle removed a handkerchief from his coat pocket and wiped her hand clean.

She paid no attention, either unaware of his service or expecting it.

"Good-bye, Dorothea," the Widow said.

"Hello. This is Tawanda Neebli of the *Post-Intelligencer*. I'm either away from my desk or I'm on the phone. Leave your name and phone number on my voice mail, and I'll get back to you."

"Tawanda? Mike Mak again. It's Sunday, about twelve-fifteen. You're probably not around the office. I'd really like to talk to you when you have a chance. It's important. Maybe a story. I need your help. Call me back as soon as you can." He gave her the number and hung up.

Cecilia had told him she thought the line might have been bugged by Jason Marsh when he came to do the trace—but to hell with it if it was. If anyone in Haven had wanted to eavesdrop, they could have rigged up the entire house long ago, before he and Cecilia moved in. He wouldn't know the first thing to look for; he doubted if today's bugs looked anything like the wire-mesh buttons in the old James Bond movies. He could spend the rest of the afternoon ransacking the house, tearing up floorboards, and climbing up to inspect the chandelier—if he really wanted Cecilia to think he was crazy. Chances were, he wouldn't find a thing, and she would start thinking about finding him a psychiatrist. Tom had told him in confidence, when they were taking bags out to the car, that Jeremy had been talking along these lines and might be suggesting such a thing to Cecilia—"But don't take it too seriously. Jer's an old-fashioned boy, very twentieth century. He thinks everyone should lie on the couch once a week with some old man in a Vandyke. So to speak."

Mike hoped he might elicit Tawanda's help in tracking down information about Haven. Too bad it was Sunday. Tawanda's home phone number was unlisted as a consequence of the threats her articles on right-wing extremism had generated. Mike had gone through several unpacked moving boxes but had been unable to find the address book that had her home phone number.

He looked out the window of his upstairs office, hoping to catch a glimpse of Dottie's service. Although the window normally afforded a fine view of Green Hill, the rain today obscured it. His palm was cold against the pane. His breath misted up the glass. He hoped Cecilia didn't mind his not going.

Downstairs, the doorbell rang.

Mike stepped into his house slippers and went down to answer the door. He undid the chain as he looked through the peephole.

Bonnie Gillette was on the porch, shaking out her umbrella.

Mike opened the door and said, "Hi."

"Hi!" she said, smiling, throwing her arms around him and planting a kiss on his cheek. "Can I come in?"

"Uh, sure."

Mercifully, Bonnie let go of him.

"I didn't know if I'd find anyone home." She stepped past him, through the foyer and deep into the parlor. She peered over the swinging doors, into the kitchen. "Is Cecilia here?"

"No," Mike said. "She's at the funeral. I would have thought you'd be there, too."

"Dottie was no friend of mine. Did you know she only spoke German? All her life, refused even to learn English. I don't speak a word of German, so I couldn't rightly be her friend, could I? She never let us non-Germans get close to her."

Mike had been annoyed at her presence, but now he wondered if he could get anything more useful out of her. Maybe he could keep her here until Cecilia got back; Cecilia had been wanting to talk with Bonnie about her medical history and that of her family. It was not a subject Mike could broach; Bonnie's records were supposed to be confidential. It was not in Cecilia's character to have shared them, and he did not want to get her in trouble in any way that might jeopardize her license.

"Bonnie, I was going to make a pot of tea. Want some?"

"That'd be great. I'm chilled to my gizzard."

"Have a seat on the sofa. Make yourself comfortable."

He went into the kitchen and put the kettle on the stove. He was spooning oolong into the teapot when Bonnie came in.

"What happened to your friends?" she asked.

"Tom and Jeremy? Left this morning. They were worried about the weather and wanted to visit Tom's aunt in Portland."

"Everybody's leaving, all worried about snow."

"The people who came for Jubilee Days," Mike said.

"That's right."

"Who are they?"

"All kinds of people."

"Where from?"

"All over. Some are relatives of Haven families. Some are families that used to live here but moved away because of the sag in the logging industry. And other interested parties." Bonnie shrugged in conclusion.

"Interested in what?" Mike asked.

"I was hoping to see you at the dance," she said.

"We weren't allowed."

"Why not?"

"We're not in the Haven Society."

"Goddammit!" Her face grew apple red. "Who kept you out?"

"The Marsh boys."

"Didn't you show them your invitation?"

"Invitation?" he asked stupidly. "What invitation?"

Bonnie sighed. "I'm secretary of the society, so you can trust my word on this. We sent you guys an invite a week ago. Licked the stamp myself."

"To the dance?"

"Yep, also to join the society. You never got it?"

"Not a thing," Mike said. "You're sure you mailed it?"

"Yep. You think Cecilia could have accidentally thrown it away or anything?"

Mike shook his head. "I'm here every day when Peg brings the mail. I'm always the first to see it. It must have gotten lost."

"It couldn't have been, unless Peg—"

"Hmm?" Mike prompted.

The kettle whistled. Mike poured the water into the teapot.

"Let's go into the living room and let this steep," he said.

"Parlor," she corrected.

"Whatever."

They went out and sat together on the sofa.

"I'll make sure you and Cecilia receive a new invite, but you can go ahead and consider yourselves invited to join the Haven Society. You can come to this Wednesday's meeting at the music hall if you like."

"I'll tell Cee."

"I should have introduced you to the Hintons."

"The who?" Mike pretended to forget the name.

"The family that used to live in this house. They were here for Jubilee Days, but they left this morning like your friends. The dad was a salesman who moved on to a new territory last year, somewhere in California. The Widow saved this place for you guys, even though she knows I'd like to have it. I own my own house, and she won't take it in trade. Nothing like this."

"Don't you know her better than anybody?"

"'Cept Frank."

"The Widow's one of the Germans, isn't she?"

"Sure enough."

"When did she come over?"

"Late forties. She and Dr. Tyler were the first ones. They bought the place up on the hill and started investing in other properties. Long before my time, of course. Dad was only four-teen when they came. The year my grandma died."

"Your grandmother? She must have been pretty young."

"Thirty-eight. She had Huntington's. Is the tea ready?"

Cecilia was determined not to let the Widow Tyler go this time without a word. As the Widow turned to leave and the others stood their ground, Cecilia broke ranks. She stepped around the perimeter, tromping unexpectedly through a puddle, to meet up with the Tylers as they embarked down the path to the Mercedes. She came up on the Widow's free side to avoid any hindrance from Tyler, who was holding the umbrella entirely over his grandmother and letting the rain tumble over his hat and sheepskin coat.

"Hello," Cecilia said, trying to look past the veil. Vaguely, she made out dark eyes and red lips. "I'm Cecilia Mak."

The Widow turned her face sharply away, toward Tyler, then turned back to stare.

"Cecilia." Tyler's voice betrayed a childish, nervous tremolo. "Can you excuse us? This ain't exactly the time for—"

"On the contrary," the Widow said in a smooth, hearty voice. The Widow extended her hand in a kiss-my-ring gesture. Cecilia shook it instead.

"Come on, Gran," Tyler said. "Got to go home."

"Not just yet," the Widow said.

The other mourners had all turned to watch the encounter.

"I'm sorry about Dottie," Cecilia said. "She was an old friend of yours?"

"You could say that," said the Widow. "Now, what is it that you really wish to say?"

Cecilia would not allow herself to be intimidated. She kept a calm, friendly demeanor. "Only that my husband and I have never had the opportunity of thanking you for your generosity. The house, the furniture. Without your assistance, the town could never have afforded to hire me. I wanted to say thanks."

"You could have come up and seen me anytime, my dear."

"I was respecting your privacy."

"As a matter of fact," the Widow went on, as if Cecilia had not said a word, "my grandson and I were just about to invite you and your husband—Michael, is it?—up to our house for tea. Now, obviously, is not a good time. Say, in a few days, perhaps? Let's see, this is Sunday—Frank, what would be a good day for us to have them over. This Thursday? Or should we make it Wednesday, before the society meeting? Wednesday's best, don't you think?"

Tyler seemed at a loss for words. "I don't know, maybe—"

"Wednesday it is." The Widow touched Cecilia's shoulder. "Four o'clock sharp. That's not too early for you, is it, honey? You won't be so busy you can't come up for tea, will you? Check with your hubby and see if it's all right."

"Sounds fine," Cecilia said. "Wednesday at four."

"Good. If you'll pardon me, I must get out of this rain—my rheumatism. Oh, I almost forgot, you're a doctor, of course! Maybe you can do something more for me than Jim Hamilton, that old quack. He was never half the doctor my husband was, I'll tell you—"

"Gran," Tyler said impatiently.

"Why don't you mark me down for an appointment at your clinic for a week from Monday, hmm?"

"You don't have to come down to the clinic," Cecilia said. "I do make house calls."

The Widow dismissed the thought with a wave of her hand. "Oh, I can come see you. You can't bring all of Hamilton's fancy torture devices up to see me, and I don't get out enough as it is. I wouldn't want you to think I was some wicked recluse, hiding up in that house, madly counting up my gold."

"Of course I don't."

"Yes. Of course. Well. You are sweet." Without lifting the veil, she planted a kiss on Cecilia's cheek. She smelled overpoweringly of rosewater. "I can hardly wait to meet your husband. I've heard so much about him. Franklin?"

"Cee." Tyler smiled at her and tipped his hat, allowing a trickle of water to spill over the brim. Cecilia sensed a reproof for initiating contact with his nutty grandmother.

"Thanks," Cecilia said to them. "Take care." She stood there, midway between the mourners and the black sedan, as Tyler opened the passenger door for her and helped her in.

Marge Clinton came up and stood behind Cecilia. "Well!"

"Well what?"

"Nothing," Marge said, "except that's the most words I've seen the old bitch share with anyone in years."

Mike handed Bonnie a steaming mug as he settled again into his warm spot on the sofa. "Careful, it's hot."

"Smells nice." She took it with both hands and leaned back against the pillows. "Mmm."

"My mom sent it to me," Mike said, then changed the subject as briskly as she had done earlier. "Stop me if I'm prying, but your grandmother died of Huntington's? Isn't that genetic?"

"That's right." Bonnie was cool and clinical. "It's a dominant trait, which means there's a fifty-fifty chance of it being passed down to your offspring."

"Did your father have it?"

"I'll never know," she said. "Huntington's usually rears up between the ages of thirty-five and fifty. My dad died in an accident when he was forty. Same accident that killed Frank's father. My dad was driving the car. As far as anyone knows, he hadn't developed any signs of the disease. I never saw any."

"You think you're in the clear?"

Bonnie took in a sharp breath, crossed her fingers in front of her, smiled nervously (self-consciously?), and said, "Your guess is as good as mine. I'm being optimistic. I figure I've got only about a twenty-five percent chance of ever getting it, just because my dad's risk is still unknown."

"I hope you're right."

"I think it worried Frank a little, though," she admitted. "That's the only reason he broke off our engagement, far as I can tell. He still loves me, I know. He just didn't think I could ever give him the kind of family he wants."

"I'm sorry."

"Oh, Mike." Bonnie fell against his shoulder and wrapped her arms around him. She held him tightly and began to cry.

He patted her on the back and said, "You'll be all right, Bonnie. Don't worry about a thing."

Perhaps she had no idea that Hamilton had run a genetic test, but she hadn't gone so far as to tell him she had been given a hysterectomy. Mike wondered if she really had no idea Hamilton had performed the operation as a means of sterilizing her. Whatever she knew or didn't know, hers was not a happy situation.

"Bonnie," Mike whispered, stroking her hair. "Everything's going to be okay." His kindly instincts took over, and he turned and planted a kiss on her ear.

"Mike, I think I love you."

He looked nervously toward the front door. All he needed was Cecilia to come walking in.

"Don't push me away this time," she said.

"Bonnie, shh." The moment was growing increasingly awkward, and Mike didn't know exactly what to do.

"I've never met a man like you." Her arms explored his back, reaching up to embrace his shoulders. She was wearing some kind of subtle scent. Cecilia was bound to smell it on him. No matter what happened, he would be providing dumb explanations.

"Bonnie, please." He tried gently to extricate himself, but she clung onto him more tightly. "Let go."

"Mike, don't."

"Let go."

He wondered, though, if he could use her to help him gain access to the Haven library at the Olbrich Music Hall.

She kissed him on the lips, and he thought, *Oh, shit.*

# Chapter 26

Cecilia slipped coming up the garden path but managed to catch herself, thrusting the open umbrella up in one hand while her leg went flying. She was glad no one was watching to laugh at her Chaplinesque maneuver. She almost lost the plastic grocery bag on her other arm, containing a slice of cake for Mike she had pilfered from Dottie's wake. The observance had been held at the Old Haven Church, and she had been surprised and a little disappointed to find the interior no different from any other church. The floor was carpeted in indoor-outdoor of a dirty blond shade that was stuck here and there with blackened gobs of old chewing gum and betrayed several water stains owing to the reputedly leaky roof. The goodies had been spread out along folding card tables upon the altar that were tastefully draped in starched white linen. The Reverend Mr. Cleveland had stood in the middle directing traffic like a restaurant captain. Cecilia had leaned against a hardwood beam and spoken mostly with Marge and Dave Clinton, who wanted to know what the Widow had said to her. Since she was unsure just what the politics were, Cecilia steered conversation onto their local success with Haven Bräu. They were flattered that she liked it. Marge hoped Cecilia wasn't too disheartened by Lewis Jackson's "shenanigans." Dave eventually came around to asking what was on his mind: whether Mike enjoyed ice fishing.

Cecilia was careful going up the porch steps. The rain had become a misty drizzle that was falling everywhere and glazing surfaces in a thin sheet of ice. She closed the umbrella and shook it out. Another umbrella, she noticed, was standing outside the front door, laid up against the siding to drip dry. She stood hers alongside it and opened the door to go in.

"Mike?"

"Hi, Cecilia." It was Bonnie Gillette, coming into the foyer from the parlor, pulling her sweater down over the waist of her jeans. Her hair was tangled and disheveled, her face looking raw and red as if she had been crying.

"Hi," Cecilia said. "Where's Mike?"

"In there," Bonnie said.

Cecilia could only see half of the parlor from here, and she couldn't see Mike. She experienced a sudden, shocking image in her mind's eye: streaks of blood smeared all over the wainscoting, Mike lying bloodied and dismembered on the floor, a woodsman's ax resting up against his head.

"I'm in here," Mike said, though she still couldn't see him.

She wondered why he hadn't spoken up before.

"I was just going," Bonnie said, biting her bottom lip. She jockeyed around Cecilia to the front door.

"Bonnie, wait," Cecilia said. "We still on for tomorrow?"

"I'm sorry?"

"You were going to come in for a follow-up, remember?"

"Oh, sure. I haven't forgot. I'll call you first. Bye."

Bonnie slammed the door solidly as she left.

"Mike?"

Cecilia found him on the floor of the parlor on his knees, mopping up something on the rug with a paper napkin.

"She knocked her tea over," he said.

"You had her over for tea?"

"It's not what you think."

"What's not what I think?" she said, and thought, *My God, am I an idiot?*

Mike put the soggy napkin into an empty mug and grabbed the handles of both mugs together in one hand with a *clink*.

"How was the funeral?" he asked, not looking at her.

"Did she kiss you?"

"What?" His free hand sprung up to his face, as if he could cover the lipstick and she would never notice. "She tried."

"No wonder you didn't want to go to Dottie's funeral."

"Cee." His voice became deep and serious. He flashed her an incongruously charming smile. "I told you it's not what you think. I need to take these to the kitchen."

"Wait," she said. She took the mugs from his hands. She was close enough to smell him, but what she smelled was Bonnie.

"She tried to kiss me," Mike said. "She was wearing some fragrance. I've probably got it all over me."

"All over?"

"She was crying, and like an idiot I tried to comfort her, and she got carried away again. I finally pushed her away."

"What do you mean finally? How long did you let her get carried away?"

"It was just for a second. It was a shock when she kissed me. I didn't want to hurt her feelings, but I had to push her away. Her leg went flying and knocked over her tea. She was up and apologizing just before you came in. That was it."

She went off to the kitchen with the mugs. Mike followed.

"Cee, don't make me feel guilty for something I didn't do. I've never had any interest in Bonnie or anyone else."

She considered springing it on him: *I'm pregnant.* But she wasn't at all positive that she was. Mike would be overjoyed, and that was the real problem. As a political position, he supported a woman's right to choose, but when it came down to Cecilia's bearing his child, his true manly colors would shine through and he would be unlikely to want to leave the choice entirely up to her. He would want to share the news with his parents, and if he did, she would be backed into a corner. It was an even bigger issue than whether Mike might have dallied with Bonnie, and it would be cheap to use it as a trump card.

She filled the sink with sudsy dishwater and scrubbed out the mugs. Mike came up behind and wrapped his arms around her.

"Don't forget what Paul Newman said about Joanne Woodward," he said, kissing the nape of her neck. "Why go out for hamburger when you've got steak at home?"

"What if the hamburger comes to you, and the steak comes home to find you belching?"

"Cee, come on, honey. You know I'd never hurt you."


"It's not worth trying to have a look at the library here. I want to make a trip to Boise. They're bound to have plenty of information there. I'll spend a day and a night and come back."

"Sounds okay," Cecilia said.

After a long silence, Mike said, "Do you think you could come with me?"

"I have to work." She put a piece of baked potato in her mouth.

"Will they really miss you? Just two days?"

"I can't just go, Mike, and we can't afford to hire a temp. You go ahead. I'll be fine. Nothing's going to happen to me."

"I'm going tomorrow."

"That's fine."

"I'll be back Tuesday night," he said. "I promise."

267

"You don't need to promise me anything," she said. "If you need another day or two, go right on ahead."

"Are you saying you won't miss me?"

"Of course not." She stopped herself from going much farther. Too much sympathy and she would be giving in and helping him relieve his guilt, if he had any. She had to try to let him stew, let him believe she wasn't going to let him off. "Be back before Wednesday. The Widow's invited us to tea."

"You're kidding," he said. "Wednesday?"

"What's wrong? You have something else scheduled?"

"No, Wednesday's fine. It's just strange. Bonnie also gave us an invitation."

She glanced up at him coldly.

"To the Haven Society," Mike said. "Wednesday night, regular meeting, regular place. She claims we were sent an invitation in the mail. She seems to think Peg lost it somehow. We were supposed to be allowed into the dance, too. So she claims."

"Then you don't have to go to Boise. You could wait until next week, when you're a member, and go use their library at the music hall. Right?"

Mike shook his head. "I don't trust them to let me see everything, and who knows if their collection is even any good? I have to head for neutral territory."

"How do you know they're neutral?"

"How do you mean?"

"For all you know, Boise could be in on it, too."

Mike seemed hurt by this, and Cecilia could understand why. She had gone too far. He thought she was making fun of him, that she no longer believed him. She wanted to let him know it wasn't true, but she was damned if she was going to apologize tonight over anything.

"What time are you leaving?" she asked, and began clearing the table.

# Chapter 27

The promised snow had not yet come. The temperature had fallen overnight to twenty degrees, and the air was crisp and dry.

Mike had not used the Camaro's heater in some time; on his way down the Haven Road the warm air came out dusty and stale. He sneezed; his chapped lips opened up and he tasted blood.

Halfway to Elliott, on rounding a curve, he saw in the dull light of morning a pair of coal-black skid marks that led straight off the road and over into the ravine.

There was no traffic, so Mike stopped the car on the shoulder hugging the hillside. He got out, leaving the car to idle at a low, noisy rumble. It was six o'clock in the morning and damnably cold. His breath came out as short puffs of mist.

Mike looked over the edge of the road, but there was nothing to see. The skid marks must not have been that fresh after all. The scrub below was so patchy and the terrain so rough that it was hard to tell if any vehicle had gone tumbling down. None of the bushes showed evidence of having been burned;

there had certainly been no explosion. Hubcaps, fenders, and bits and pieces of any wreckage would have been strewn about, but he saw none. The Little Lost River continued tumbling along halfway up the sides of the dusky boulders along the bed.

Mike knelt down on the pavement and examined the marks more closely. He had not driven this far down since the move; for all he knew, the skids could have been here all along, vestiges of an ancient accident—Clem Kadiddlehopper in a '58 Ford. He was unable to detect any smell of burned rubber or anything other than the cold mountain air.

Tom and Jeremy weren't supposed to be back to Seattle for a few days yet. Mike wondered if Cecilia had the name and phone number of Tom's aunt in Portland. If anything had happened to them here, the accident had been neatly cleaned up.

The gas station at Elliott was closed. No cars were out front. The lights were out. No one was in. The town itself was dead.

Mike did not need gas. He had intended to ask the old man some questions: what he meant by what he had said to Cecilia, what he knew or thought he knew about Haven.

"Hello?" He rapped again on the window, with no luck.

Glancing around, he had the feeling no one in Elliott was awake. If he had more time, he might try to find the gas man and wake him up, apologizing but claiming that his car had run out of gas and that it was something of an emergency.

He had a five-hour drive ahead of him to Boise, though, and decided it would not be worth the time and trouble. Going up and knocking on people's doors, he might even find himself in a hostile situation like that of the Japanese student in Louisiana a few years back who had come to the wrong house looking for a party and ended up being shot dead by the crazed homeowner. Mike would never forget that the shooter had been *acquitted*. What was it Henry Jameson Olbrich had been told by the judge in his case? *"There is nothing in the law book as I read it that says it is murder to kill a Chinaman. . . ."* American jurisprudence had apparently changed little since then.

He could see it now—the old man sneaking up on him with a shotgun, shooting him or having him arrested, claiming to have caught him in the act of breaking in. Self-defense, Your Honor. What local jury would convict an old, wounded ex-Marine and World War II vet of murdering a young Asian-American male in Elliott, Idaho? At least Elliott was in Custer County, not Prospect, so the case would not be tried in Haven.

Mike got back into his car and pulled out onto US 93, turning up the heater. He checked his rearview mirror, but no one was there. No one awake in Elliott, no one on the road behind. The pavement was dry and clear. He had it all to himself. He put the Stone Temple Pilots in the CD player and cranked the volume way up, blasting over his speakers. There was no better way of listening to music than by yourself in your car on a long highway drive.

He passed Greylock Mountain and inched through the towns of Sunbeam and Stanley, then on past Castle Peak and Galena Summit, heading steadily downhill most of the while. The farther he got from Haven, the better the Camaro performed. For the last six weeks, it had been sitting for the most part, but what a car like this with a big V-8 needed was some occasional quality time with its owner out on the open road. Mike stopped in Ketchum to get some coffee, and when he turned the ignition key back on, the engine responded with a healthier start-up than it had given since Seattle. He wondered whether he had readjusted the carburetor properly enough for Haven or if it was still in need of some fine-tuning. Ketchum was at a lower elevation, and it seemed to be just right.

Sun Valley was just a few miles up a side road, which meant some of the best skiing in the world was his for the taking not more than two hours from Haven. It would be a shame, in a way, if circumstances forced them to reconsider Cecilia's job— though Mike would feel guilty spending a lot of time this winter skiing in Sun Valley while Cecilia worked, if he wasn't writing the novel as he had promised both her and himself. She was not likely to tolerate this laziness for long. She might not see it as sponging at first, but if he didn't start writing something soon, she was bound to bring it up.

Mike wondered just what good he was to her anymore. He was sure that her career was the most important thing in her life, and perhaps that was as it should be. He had the unpleasant feeling that if things didn't work out in their marriage and he had to leave her, she would get along just fine without him.

He would be the one to suffer. His job had been less than fulfilling, and he didn't know if he had the talent or the stamina actually to write a novel or any kind of book. The most important thing to him right now was Cecilia. Maybe that was why he was having such difficulty getting started.

He was still stung by last night's conversation and by Cecilia's suspicions. She had never disbelieved him like this before, and he wondered what he would have to do to prove himself. He understood how it must have looked when she walked in, but the fact was nothing had happened. She wouldn't take him at his word; she had lost faith in him. He wondered, though, if the change was because of Bonnie or something else. Maybe she agreed with Jeremy that he was simply crazy.

Mike was somewhat jealous himself of the time Cecilia spent professionally with Tyler, and he might have reacted similarly if he had discovered her on the sofa with the sheriff. If she was willing to suspect him of sleeping with Bonnie, he could just as easily imagine her with the sheriff. Even in all their recent discussions, she seemed ready to come to Tyler's defense, despite the fact that his own grandmother was the most prominent of Haven's Germans and probably the widow of a Nazi.

Frank Tyler wasn't her type. Mike knew that. Even if she wanted to seek an affair with another man, she would not go rushing into the arms of someone who reminded her of her asshole brothers or her asshole father. He would be stupid, though, to take that for granted. He had to regain her confidence.

One way would be if he could find enough information in Boise to back up his theories. He had to succeed and show her that he was no paranoiac.

After Ketchum, Mike began to notice a dark sedan in his rearview mirror. It maintained a discreet distance—far enough back that he was unable to determine make or model. When he slowed down or sped up slightly, the other followed suit. He tested this several times, and in each case the distance between his vehicle and the other remained constant. He was never able to get a good look at it. Other cars would pass it and fill the space momentarily, then leave the space, revealing the dark sedan still hanging back there, tailing, apparently.

The speed limit in Idaho had been raised back to the good old days of sixty-five; Mike pressed his foot to the floor now and sped up to seventy-five, then eighty, before he managed to see the sedan fall back in the distance. He maintained this speed, watching out for squad cars of the Idaho Highway Patrol, until he reached the junction with US 20. Once he turned onto the new highway, he could no longer see the sedan behind. He hoped he had lost it.

US 20 ran fairly straight most of the way, and Mike decided to take his chances and keep up his high speed. He had to slow down, however, to go through Fairfield, Corral, and Hill City.

Whenever he did, the dark sedan would sneak back into his rearview at the farthest visible point behind.

In the forty-five miles from Hill City to Mountain Home, Mike occasionally went as fast as ninety. He was sure he was going to be stopped by a trooper, but his luck held. Though he saw no sign of the car, he was sure it was there. Near Mountain Home, US 20 merged into I-84, which would take him in to Boise. If he could manage to weave in and out of enough traffic, he might shake the sedan completely. By now it wouldn't take a genius, though, to figure out he was headed for Boise.

Mike made it all the way into the city without seeing the car again, which made him feel somewhat safer, but he was not going to let down his guard. If someone was suspicious enough to want to keep tabs on him, maybe they were ready to do worse. He was not sure he was fully prepared to defend himself, but he could keep his eyes open and get help in a flash if he needed it. This was the state capital, a city of over a hundred thousand people, and they had police, the FBI, the ATF, and everything else.

By the time he turned off I-84 onto the Business Loop that took him down Broadway Avenue, it was just before lunchtime. He was pleased with himself for the good time he had made. He hoped he might actually have enough time to find what he needed and head back to Haven tonight, but this would depend on how late the library was open and how successful he was in his search. He supposed the world would not come to an end if he had to stay the night at a motel, but it would be the first night in years that he had been away from Cecilia, and he doubted he would get any sleep from all the worry. There had been many a night during Cecilia's residency at University Medical Center when she had worked a thirty-hour shift and left him to sleep alone, but he had rested easy in the knowledge of where she was and what she was doing.

The downtown seemed deserted, but maybe this was one of those places where no one walked, where they hopped into their cars to drive a couple of blocks. Mike's dad would call that attitude "typically First World"; back in Laramie, he walked to the university in winter and rode his bicycle in the summer and fall. Mike could picture the spot on the bike rack outside the entomology lab where his dad always locked up his Schwinn ten-speed. It wasn't as if his parents never used their cars, it was only that his dad felt proud of his daily routine. He had conserved energy before it was necessary, before Jimmy Carter appeared on the TV set to ask everyone to turn down the thermostat and put on a sweater. While growing up, Mike had been embarrassed by his dad's bicycling, thinking it made him look too typically Chinese, which he had thought a bad thing. Mike never, of course, said so to his father's face. Now that he was older, he saw nothing wrong with riding a bike or looking too Chinese.

He drove around the capitol building and then down Capital Boulevard before coming to the Boise Public Library. The American flag and Idaho state flag were fluttering atop the pole, both of them cheap, frayed nylon. Not a single car was in the parking lot. He had noticed only a few people walking along the street. Something strange was going on.

He parked his car in the closest nonhandicap space and went up to the entrance, noting the CLOSED sign on the glass door and wondering why. He finally realized before it was confirmed to him by the words on the small, hand-lettered sign taped to the inside of the glass, just above the door handle:

**WE WILL BE CLOSED**

**MONDAY, OCT. 14**

**IN OBSERVANCE OF COLUMBUS DAY**

**PLEASE RETURN ALL LIBRARY MATERIALS**

**TO THE BOOK DROP—THANK YOU!**

# Chapter 28

Cecilia knocked on the Harrisons' front door for five minutes before Hank answered.

"You want something?" Hank asked through the screen door, scratching the back of his head. He looked down at the black doctor's bag Cecilia clutched in her hand. "Who called you?"

"Nobody." She noted the burgundy of his nose and the whiskey of his breath. "May I come in?"

"What for?"

"I'd like to see Peg."

"She doesn't need any doctor."

"Where is she?"

"Resting. It's her day off. Federal holiday. No mail."

"Oh, of course." She hadn't realized until then. It could only be Columbus Day. "I'd still like to see her."

"About what?"

"I think that's between me and Peg," Cecilia said, as if she had an actual reason for coming. "If she wants to share it with you, that's her prerogative."

"Well, okay." Hank raised a wary eyebrow and opened the screen door. "Come in, then."

"Thanks a bunch, Hank."

Peg's absence from Dottie's funeral had put the thought in Cecilia's head that Peg might be ill. If Hank was anything like Clark Jackson, he wasn't likely to call for help. When Cecilia had gone home today for lunch and saw that no mail had been delivered, she had thought only of Peg, not of Christopher Columbus. After lunch, her usual house-call time, she decided to come on up uninvited, like Dr. Bellows, and have a look. She had plenty of excuse: Peg's age and obesity predisposed her to all kinds of health problems, and it was only logical for a doctor to want to check up on such a patient.

"You know," Hank said, leading Cecilia through the spare but immaculate living room, "she has been feeling a little under the weather. Touch of asthma, I expect. Always comes around this time of year, whenever the barometer takes a swing."

"That can be very serious," Cecilia said, not too forcefully. Hank was not the kind of man who liked a woman telling him he didn't know something. "Why didn't you call?"

"Jim Hamilton gave her an inhaler."

Her instincts had been correct, then. She was going to have to be more aggressive in her approach to her patients. They were stubborn western folk who didn't cotton to doctoring. Jim Hamilton had apparently met them halfway, but she would not.

Hank rapped lightly on the bedroom door. "Peg o' My Heart? Hon, Dr. Mak's here, wants to have a look at you."

He opened the door and they went in. Peg was lying on the bed in the master bedroom, watching *Another World*.

"Oh, Hank!" Peg's eyes were watery, her flesh pale. "How nice of you to give her a ring! What a surprise!"

"It's nothing," Hank mumbled, the rest of his face turning as purplish as his nose.

"Hi, Peg," Cecilia said warmly.

Hank continued to stand in the doorway, glowering.

"Hank, do you think you could leave us alone?" Cecilia said. "It'll only be a few minutes."

He shrugged, said "All-righty," and went back down the hall.

Cecilia closed the door.

"Wasn't that nice of him?"

"You should have called me yourself," Cecilia admonished.

"I know, I—" Peg began coughing from deep within her lungs, a wheezing, painful sound, and reached for the inhaler on the nightstand.

Cecilia touched her hand lightly and prevented her from using the device. She was suspicious of Hank's unprofessional diagnosis, not to mention anything Hamilton had had a hand in. Even if Peg had a history of asthma, a wheezing cough could mean a lot of things. Gently, she took the inhaler from Peg's fingers. Sure enough, the prescription, for aerosolized isoetharine, had been written by James K. Hamilton, M.D., on 02-11-96, and had been refilled once. She replaced it on the nightstand.

Peg coughed again and looked questioningly at Cecilia.

"I'm sorry, Peg. Can you hang on and let me have a look at you first? Then you can use your inhaler."

Peg nodded trustingly. She caught her breath and said, "Sure, Cecilia, go ahead. The damned thing doesn't seem to be doing me any good, anyhow."

Peg was running a fever of 102.4°F, which pointed toward a likely bacterial infection, and the symptoms indicated pneumonia or at least bronchitis. Cecilia took Peg down to the clinic for chest X rays, which showed a mild pneumonia of the left lung. Pending lab work that would try to pinpoint the exact bacterium, Cecilia prescribed a week's course of ciprofloxacin, a broad-spectrum antibiotic that would work on most organisms. It was an expensive medication, so Cecilia handed Peg seven small packets of free samples from the pharmaceutical manufacturer, which contained two pills each and would constitute a complete prescription. If a bacterium was isolated in the meantime, Cecilia could alter the regimen to be specific for the organism. Though Peg's condition did not appear serious, pneumonia at her age could become complicated, and Cecilia would have to check on her frequently over the next week to make sure her condition improved. If it worsened, Peg would have to go to Pocatello.

Cecilia drove Peg back up the hill to the Harrisons' house, just off Pemberton Lane, on Longstreet Lane.

"You're going to be fine," Cecilia said.

"I'm glad you came."

"You're lucky. You should have called."

"Isn't it enough that Hank called?"

As they neared the house, Cecilia saw Hank sitting on the front stoop, smoking a cigarette.

"Hank didn't call," Cecilia said. She had considered allowing Peg her illusions, but it was important that she know.

Peg looked disappointed but not surprised. "Then how did you know to come?"

"I was hoping you'd sing at Dottie's funeral, but you weren't there. You have a lovely voice, really. I'll bet you're classically trained."

Peg blushed, looking healthier than she had all day. She clutched Cecilia's hand. Her eyes lit up. Tears rolled down her plump cheeks.

"Can you keep a secret?"

"Patient-doctor privilege," Cecilia said reassuringly.

"I sang at Bayreuth," she said, "and at the Munich National Theatre, and at the Dresden State Opera. There were recordings. I used to be Herta von Möllendorff—not so well known as Elisabeth Schwarzkopf, but I once sang for Wagner's daughter, and for Richard Strauss, and even for the—the—"

Abruptly, she let go of Cecilia's hand.

"For the what?" Cecilia prompted.

They were stopped in the driveway. Hank was coming toward them to help his wife out of the truck.

"For Hitler?" Cecilia asked.

Peg nodded eagerly, taking the bait.

"Don't be ashamed." Cecilia hoped she did not sound too false. "That must have been quite an honor."

"Oh, I cannot tell you!" Peg beamed in remembrance, wiping away her tears. "Thank you, Cecilia. For saving me, I mean."

Hank knocked on Peg's window, staring at them both queerly.

"Everything all right?"

"Yes, Hank," Peg said, stepping down from the cab without his help. "The doctor says I'll be fine. *Just* fine. And she knows what she's doing, this girl. We're so lucky to have her."

Hank waved at Cecilia, slammed the door, and turned back to look at her again as she backed out of the drive.

Bonnie's appointment time came and went, with no sign of Bonnie. Cecilia called the Raven's Roost. Sadie said that Bonnie wasn't coming in today. Cecilia asked why, but Sadie didn't know. She tried Bonnie's home number but got no answer. She tried paying a call on her house, but the lights were out and no one appeared to be home. The doors were locked. Bonnie's Ford

Bronco, with its own snowplow attachment, was still parked in the driveway.

Cecilia sleepwalked through the rest of her day, unable to shake the encounter with Peg from her mind. She could hardly wait for Mike to get back so she could tell him.

When she came home and remembered there was no mail, she realized the library in Boise was bound to be closed for the holiday. She wondered if Mike had realized this before he left. He couldn't have known, or he would have put off the trip for another day. He was going to be disappointed. He would probably spend the night, and she wouldn't see him until tomorrow.

At least he would be calling, and then she could tell him about Peg's other life. Jeremy was an opera buff; she wondered if he had ever heard of a Herta von Möllendorff. They would be at Tom's aunt's house now for the next few days, though, and she did not know the number or the aunt's name.

Then again, she shouldn't share it with anyone over the phone line. If it was really bugged, she would be giving away Peg's secret. It might get Peg into trouble. The only other Haven Germans who had given any clue to their past had been Lizzie and Dottie. Raphael Abramowitz may have known something as well, and his was only the first of three "accidental" deaths associated with the Jacksons that could as easily have been murders: Abramowitz could have been shot on purpose, the rottweilers could have been sicced on Lizzie, and Dottie certainly seemed to have been left to die in the sickroom.

If "they" found out Peg had said anything, Peg might be next. All "they" had to do was keep her from her ciprofloxacin. Hank hadn't wanted to call in the first place. Maybe he knew she had pneumonia and was allowing her to die. Maybe singing in German in front of Cecilia and Mike had been enough of an error.

If so, why had Hank gone ahead and opened the door? It was still his house, and he had every right to refuse her entry.

She threw the ambulance keys in the bowl in the foyer.

She had a headache.

The red light of the answering machine made her hope that Mike had called. She pressed the Play button and at first didn't recognize the voice.

"Mike? Tawanda. It's one-twenty, Monday the fourteenth. I'm returning your call. Your story wouldn't be horning in on my territory, would it? Which reminds me, I was wrong when I told you all of the Idaho ones were centered around Coeur d'Alene. There's one calling itself the Idaho Militia that's head-quartered closer to you guys, someplace called Blackfoot, about halfway between Pocatello and Idaho Falls. Not all that close but still your neck of the woods. I see on the map that between Haven and Blackfoot is something called the Idaho National Engineering Lab of the U.S. Department of Energy—atomic re-search stuff. I don't know if this is your story, but I'd be a little scared having one of these citizens' militias operating anywhere near there. Those Oklahoma City bombers had ties to these militia groups, and they all hate the federal government, which I guess would include the DOE. After Oklahoma City, think of what these nuts might want to try if they could get their hands on some plutonium. You can learn how to make an A-bomb on the Internet, you know that? What if some guy in one of these militias is a disgruntled nuclear engineer who's got access to this facility? I'm not trying to get you wigged out here, I just wanted to throw some ideas at you and see if I'm in the ball-park. Sounds like something's up, and I'd really like to know what. Call me back as soon as you can. Bye."

Cecilia saved the message. She doubted whether Mike had

been thinking anything along these lines. Whatever was going on in Haven, she doubted it had anything to do with any militia or plans to use an A-bomb in an act of domestic terrorism. That was about as likely as Jeremy's pert suggestion that they were keeping Hitler's head on ice.

Cecilia went to the parlor and sank into the sofa.

She found herself staring at the art on the wall. Of course it was Nazi art. That was obvious. The date, signature, and naïve style were not the only clues, however. Though it showed no swastikas, uniforms, or other paraphernalia, it represented the crux of Nazi philosophy. It was set in the family's living room, which was, in a word, exactly what Hitler wanted to give the Germans: *Lebensraum*—living space. That he wanted it at the expense of those already on it was what had led to the great horrors. The painting pared life down to what the Nazis believed was essential: heroic working husband, submissive wife, perfect Aryan children, and many more children on the way. What was nonessential had no place in this painting.

The doorbell rang, startling her.

She sprang to her feet, went to the door, and looked through the peephole.

It was Sheriff Tyler, hat in hand, face up close and greatly distorted by the fish-eye lens. His radio mike squawked on his epaulet.

She undid the chain and invited him in.

# Chapter 29

Before coming to Boise, Mike had had the idea that the library might have telephone directories of other cities—including New York, from which he could photocopy the phone numbers of all the Abramowitzes. Now, because of the holiday, he would have to wait, though it would have been the perfect use of his time, alone all evening in his room at the Motel 6. He could try directory assistance, but he would have to know first names to ask for phone numbers, and even if he did he would end up making hundreds of calls and getting nowhere.

He set up his laptop computer so he could take some notes and organize his thoughts. He slid a Green Day CD into the CD-ROM drive to give him some music while he worked, and it was only then that he realized what a fool he was being. There was software on the market from more than one company that had nearly all the U.S. residential phone listings packed onto a single CD-ROM disk. He could probably find it somewhere in Boise for less than a hundred dollars, and he had plastic with him.

He went back out and found that it was snowing. He had

deliberately parked the Camaro several stalls down from his motel room, and on his way to it he spotted a black Mercedes 500SEL sedan not unlike the one owned by the Widow Tyler. Snow was beginning to collect on the highly polished surface. The car was clean and shiny and did not look as if it had made the same trip as the mud-speckled Camaro. If this car had followed him all the way from Boise, the driver had had it washed. It bore Idaho plates, but many cars in the lot did as well. Mike rubbed off the snow that had collected on the side windows and took a peek inside, but there was nothing that might provide a clue. He had only seen the Widow's car from a distance and had no way of knowing if this was it. Certainly the Widow wouldn't be driving it, and her son the sheriff couldn't just up and leave for the day to keep tabs on Mike. It wasn't the only Mercedes 500SEL in the world, either.

All the same, when he got to his own car, he raised the hood and took a glance around the engine, then lay down on the snowy ground and looked all around the chassis, in case there was a bomb. He didn't see anything, though he wasn't sure he would have known what to spot. He wouldn't be the first journalist to die of a car bomb while in hot pursuit of a conspiracy.

There was a moment when he turned the key in the ignition that his heart seemed to stop—but once the engine came to life and he heard no *kaboom*, he took a deep breath and was fine.

He told himself he was being an idiot.

He found what he was looking for at Wal-Mart. By then it was dark, and on his drive back to the motel he couldn't tell if the headlights following him belonged to a Mercedes. The headlights made a turn onto a side street only a couple blocks before he reached the motel.

Back in his room, he put the CD-ROM disk in the drive and executed the setup program. Once it was up and running, he could search names and phone numbers of just about anyone. If he had had a fax/modem attachment for the laptop, as well as a headset with microphone, he could have made all his calls from his computer by scrolling down through the list. Instead, he planted the motel phone to the right of the laptop and began to punch out each number by hand.

He went through all the Abramowitzes in Brooklyn. If someone came on the line, he said he was looking for the family of a Raphael Abramowitz. They told him he had the wrong number. He saved those listings for which no one had picked up, so he could try back later. Brooklyn took him close to an hour.

After Brooklyn, he wondered if he should try Queens but decided on Manhattan instead. Far down the list, when he came to Saul J. Abramowitz, he struck pay dirt.

"Who is this?" said a man's voice.

"Sir, my name is Michael Mak. I'm a reporter, formerly with the Seattle *Post-Intelligencer*, and—"

"How do I know that?"

"I could fax you my credentials—"

"I don't have a fax machine. Who gave you this number?"

"I looked it up, sir."

"Why are you calling?"

"Could I ask if you're related to Raphael?"

"I have a son by that name. Haven't heard from him in over a year. Why?"

"It's very important. I know you must be going through a trying time right now, but please don't hang up on me."

"What trying time? What are you talking about?"

"About Raphael."

"Why, what's happened?"

"You don't know about Idaho?"

"Hey, I don't know Idaho from Iowa. What's going on? Has something happened to my son?"

"I'm sorry, I thought you knew. Didn't the coroner call you?"

"Coroner? Who did you say you were?"

"I'm a reporter. My name is Michael Mak. I live in Haven, Idaho. You never received any call from anyone in Haven, about a month ago? Not the sheriff or the coroner?"

"Are you telling me my son is dead?"

"I'm sorry, sir. I was told you had the body shipped back already for the funeral."

"I never spoke to nobody. And I haven't heard from Raphael in nearly a year. Is this some kind of prank?"

"No, sir, it's no prank. I was there. I saw the body."

"My God," said Saul Abramowitz, as if to himself. "If this is a joke . . . but what would Raphael be doing in Idaho?"

"I was hoping you could answer that for me, sir," Mike said.

"I'm afraid I can't answer any more questions until I learn what happened to my boy. I want the name of that sheriff."

"It's Frank Tyler, of the Prospect County Sheriff's Department." Mike gave him the phone number. "I can tell you what happened, though. It was a hunting accident."

"Hunting accident? Raphael doesn't hunt."

"It was a couple of hunters from Haven. They were out in the woods, and Raphael was shot by mistake."

"I don't get it. What was he thinking of? What would he be doing in Idaho? The last I heard, he was in Los Angeles."

"Sir, I'm going to ask you another question, and it may sound strange, but I'm hoping you'll give me a straight answer."

Mike took the silence as tacit assent.

"Mr. Abramowitz," Mike proceeded, "did your son have any interest in Nazis?"

"Did he have an interest?"

"I mean, in tracking them down. Ones who may have escaped."

Again there was only silence.

"Mr. Abramowitz?" Mike prompted. "Are you there?"

"I'm sorry," Saul Abramowitz said. Then he hung up.

Mike tried calling him back but was met with a busy signal. He imagined Saul Abramowitz was trying to reach Tyler.

He called Cecilia, but the line kept ringing and the answering machine never kicked in. She must have turned the machine off by accident. Even so, he wondered why she wasn't there. She could be out of the house on an emergency, of course. Perhaps she had simply turned the ringer off—but that wasn't like her, especially if she was expecting him to call. He had to know she was all right. She didn't know where he was staying—or even that he *was* staying. She ought to be able to figure it out, as long as she was aware of the holiday.

Mike kept trying to reach Saul Abramowitz for the rest of the night, into what would be the wee hours of the morning in New York, but the busy signal never went away.

He tried Cecilia as well many more times, until it was late, but she never answered. He would have to call her first thing in the morning and check in. He hoped she wasn't still mad at him.

Before going to bed, he peered out the window and saw that the Mercedes had returned to the lot, dusted with more snow.

# Chapter 30

When Cecilia returned from the kitchen with a glass of water for Tyler, she found him sitting on the sofa in the parlor, before Maddie Gahagan's fireplace, beneath the Nazi art. He had set his cowboy hat on the black-lacquered coffee table that had been manufactured by one S. Wolff of Berlin. Cecilia wondered whether S. Wolff had been a Jew and if some of the Widow's furniture might not have been looted from apartments of the dispossessed.

"Here," she said.

"Thanks, I'm parched, this air's so dry." He downed half the glass in one gulp. "You got a coaster?"

"Coaster? No, sorry."

"Wouldn't want to hurt the table."

She tore a subscription card out of a magazine for him.

"I just wanted to come over personally to tell you," Tyler said. "Lewis Jackson's been released into his grandfather's custody until the final hearing."

"When's that?" Cecilia looked into Tyler's steely blue eyes.

His features were of a similar cast to those of the husband in the painting.

"I'd give it about two weeks. I wouldn't worry about him doing anything. I just wanted you to be aware of the situation. He's supposed to be under a kind of house arrest, but Clark probably can't watch him all day. Herb and I are going to be patrolling out there more regular to keep an eye out. We've got this electronic bracelet on Lewis's ankle that'll signal to us if he leaves the house. We're also going to patrol your place to make sure nobody tries anything funny."

"Thanks."

"Is Mike, um, working?" Tyler's eyes indicated the ceiling.

"He's not here."

"Well, be sure to let him know what I told you. If you have any trouble, call us right away, okay? I only hope Lewis hasn't been sharing any of this hate literature with any of his friends. I don't want there to be any reprisals."

"I thought Lewis didn't have any friends."

"You never know. It wouldn't take more than a couple of like-minded teens. They might try something against you. Hell, they might go after me for punishing Lewis."

"Frank, could you show me the booklets and things you found in Lewis's room? I'd be very interested."

"Afraid I can't. It's all bagged and tagged. I couldn't show you until after the trial. Sorry."

"You didn't make photocopies of anything?"

"Didn't think of it."

She found this hard to believe. "What did they say?"

"A lot of stuff."

"Like?"

"You don't want to know."

"Don't think you're protecting me from anything."

"They were filled with all kinds of things against all kinds of

290

people. You know, the usual about the power of the media and the Jew World Order, and how we're giving away handouts to the immigrants, and the Japanese are buying up America, and the Chinese have got an army of a hundred million preparing to invade the U.S. All kinds of paranoid conspiracy theories."

"Don't you think it would have been useful for your case against Lewis to make copies of this?"

"I didn't think much about that, seeing how he confessed."

"What did he say?"

"Sorry, I can't divulge that until the hearing."

"Are you letting him have a lawyer?"

"Funny, somehow I wouldn't think you'd be concerned about that, after what he did to you and Mike."

"How do you know he's not covering up for somebody else?"

Tyler shook his head pityingly and said, "Trust me, Cee."

"Don't call me that."

"Pardon?"

"I don't like being called Cee except by Mike."

"You said yourself, Mike isn't here." Tyler leaned forward, lacing his fingers together and smiling implacably.

"That makes no difference."

"It makes a difference to me. You see, I'm not so sure I approve of a young husband leaving his beautiful wife all alone in a town where people have recently attacked their house."

"He's coming back tonight."

"Oh, really?"

"He could be back any minute."

"I don't think so."

"Why not? He didn't tell you where he was going."

"No, and he didn't tell me what he was doing, either, but that doesn't mean I don't know."

"How could you?"

"I'm not sheriff for nothing, Cee. I'm sorry—*Cecilia*. Is that better? A lot of my job is detective work, and in this case it hasn't taken a whole lot of detecting to know what's going on."

"What are you talking about?"

"Sadie told me you were asking after Bonnie, is that right?"

"Yes."

"She missed an appointment with you, didn't she?"

"How do you know that?"

"Janice Fremont told me. Sadie didn't want to tell you where Bonnie was, but I feel it's almost my duty. She went to Boise, and she's not planning on coming back till tomorrow."

It was a surprise, but she tried not to let it show.

"What has that got to do with Mike?" she asked.

"Didn't he go to Boise, too?"

"I don't have to tell you where he went."

"No, that's right, you don't have to tell me. But I happen to know it's true. Bonnie told Sadie she was going there to meet up with Mike. I'm not sure how much more of this denial I can take from you."

"It's not denial, Frank." She wanted to laugh in his face, but something kept gnawing at her that it might be true.

"The wife is always the last to know. The whole town knows about the incident up at the Olbrich mine. They both denied anything happened, but isn't that what you'd expect them to do, especially if they're still carrying on?"

"I'm tired, Frank. Can we continue this some other time?"

"Cecilia." His hand came forward to touch her thigh.

She jerked away from him. "Frank, I don't believe a word of it. Bonnie's living in a dream world. She thinks she can have Mike, but he doesn't want anything to do with her. She may think she's meeting up with him in Boise, but I think Mike would be surprised to hear it."

Tyler's grin became one of satisfaction. Cecilia realized her mistake: She had just confirmed to him where Mike had gone and that he was far, far away from her.

"It's never good to be the bearer of bad news. Now you're going to blame me for what your husband's gone off and done."

"Mike hasn't done a thing."

Tyler looked at his watch. "Maybe not yet. The night is still young. Listen, you going to be okay tonight? You want me and Herb to patrol up here every now and then and make sure you're safe?"

"I can take care of myself until Mike gets back."

"Don't wait up for him. I don't think it'll be tonight." Tyler grabbed his hat from the coffee table and stood. "Well."

Cecilia showed him to the door. "I know you think you're doing me a favor, Frank. You just don't know Mike."

"I know Bonnie, though," Tyler said with a sigh as he put on his hat. "She's had just about every man she could ever get in Haven, and she's used to getting what she wants."

"Funny, she said sort of the same thing about you."

"Warning you against me?" He shook his head as if Cecilia had got him all wrong. "See, now, she's just turning my own words against me. She knows this is how I've characterized her, and this is her little way of getting back at me. I'm not like what she may have told you. Honest injun."

"How do I know whom to believe?"

"Well, for one thing, if what Bonnie said was true, I wouldn't be leaving you here all alone tonight, I'd be carrying you up that staircase to that lovely yellow bedroom."

"That's what you think," she said, and closed the door.

# Chapter 31

Still half asleep, Mike picked up the phone when it rang.

"Cecilia?"

But it was his wake-up call, at seven in the morning, and no one was there. He hung up, then rang her up himself.

"Hello?" It was her voice, for real, at last.

"Hi, Cee, it's me."

"You stayed over."

"I tried calling you—"

"I'm sorry, it's my fault. I accidentally turned off the answering machine."

"Uh-huh."

"I didn't realize till this morning. All the ringers on the phones were off. Did you do that?"

"No."

"The answering machine, too. Tawanda left you a message yesterday. I must have accidentally shut it off."

"Tawanda called? What did she say?"

"Hang on, I'll go down and play it for you."

Mike waited, wondering who had gone into their house and

turned off all the phones. They could have sneaked in and done it while Cecilia was at work.

"Here it is," Cecilia said.

All he heard was tape hiss.

"Cee, there's nothing there. Hello?"

There was a series of beeps.

"Mike, I don't know what happened."

"You're sure you didn't touch the Erase button?" He hated the way he sounded: the know-it-all husband.

"Positive. I was saving it for you."

"Maybe it starts later on the tape."

"No," she said after a bit. "There's nothing on it. I don't get it, unless Frank Tyler—"

"What was he doing there?"

"Nothing. He just came by."

"What for?"

"Lewis Jackson was released to Clark's custody."

"And?"

"That was it. He wanted to let us know."

"Did you leave him alone at some point?"

"I got him a glass of water. Why would he erase the tape— unless he knew what was on it?"

Mike kicked himself for being so stupid. It was early in the morning yet, but that was no excuse. What on earth were they doing talking like this over the phone lines? The only way Frank Tyler could know what was on the tape was if someone had listened in and told him. Mike wanted to know what Tawanda had said, but he couldn't ask Cecilia, not anymore. He could call Tawanda himself.

"Cee—"

"Mike, he had to have—" She broke off. It was early for her, too, but she must have realized this confirmed her suspicions.

"You know," she said, "I must have turned the ringers off myself and just forgotten about it."

"I'm sure that's the answer."

"I must have hit the Erase button while I was rewinding the tape," Cecilia said. "Silly me!"

"That's okay, honeybunch," Mike said—a name he never called her. He felt as if he were speaking in code. "I'm sure it wasn't anything important." He scribbled a note to himself to call Tawanda ASAP.

"I didn't make any sense of it. She was talking nonsense, anyway, but you know her."

"Oh, yeah. How's ol' Frank?"

"Oh, he's fine."

"That's good."

"How's Boise?"

"Fine, fine."

"You haven't run into Bonnie, have you?"

"No, why?"

"Frank thought she'd gone to Boise herself yesterday. Isn't that a coincidence?"

"Yeah, sure is." Mike carried the phone over to the window and parted the curtain. The Mercedes was gone. "Say, have you heard from Tom and Jeremy?"

"They wouldn't have gotten through with the ringers off."

"Suppose not. Do you have the number of Tom's aunt?"

"No, I don't. Why, what's the—should I—"

"Oh, I just wanted to ask Tom something about my back. I guess it can wait till they get back to Seattle. I'm getting worried, though . . . about my back. Hurts like hell."

"I understand, honey. Wish I was there. Coming back soon?"

"Yeah, I'll be leaving around—"

"I don't need to know when, okay? Just surprise me."

"Uh, okay. I don't think there's anything more we can say. I've already found a lot of neat stuff for my novel."

"I'm glad."

"I'll fill you in when I get back. I miss you."

"I love you," she said.

"You, too, precious." He made kissy noises and hung up.

"What kind of information do you have on old Idaho mining towns?"

"Depends on which one. Idaho City? Silver City? Nampa? Bellevue? Pierce?" The reference librarian was a bald, mustached man no older than forty, though he looked older because of sunken eyes and cheeks and translucent, marbled skin. He wore a shirt that was two sizes too big and a tie that hung slightly askew. Mike wondered if he was ill. He looked like people he knew back in Seattle who were in the late stages of AIDS.

"Haven," Mike said.

"Oh, Haven!" The librarian stood up from his desk, fingers shaking as he reached for a stubby wooden pencil. "I bet you're interested in the Haven Massacre."

Mike gave him a blank stare.

"Don't be offended. I thought since you're Asian—God, I'm really putting my foot in my mouth now! I shouldn't jump to such conclusions. Randolph Carter, assistant librarian."

"Mike Mak." It was like shaking the hand of a skeleton. "It's okay. I've never heard of the Haven Massacre. Is that what they called the mining accident?"

"I don't know anything about any accident. We have a great little booklet on the massacre, with photos of the Chinese cemetery. Here, I'll help you find it."

The librarian took him to the special collection on Idaho history and was able to pluck out the booklet after a brief scan of the shelves: *When the Little Lost Ran Red: The True Story of the Haven Massacre*, by Sister Mary Francis Burger. It was a slim paperbound chapbook privately printed by an Idaho Catholic organization twenty years ago, on the event's centennary. On the inside front cover was the red-white-and-blue stylized star that had been the official logo of the nation's bicentennial.

"This can't be checked out, by the way," Randolph said. "It's our only copy, and that title is no longer in print."

"I'll read it here."

"If you need any more help, just give a whistle." Randolph Carter smiled and returned to his desk.

Mike took a seat at an empty carrel far at the back of the nonfiction section. He flipped through the book for photographs but found only one, of Haven's founder, Henry Jameson Olbrich, looking sternly off to one side as his fist firmly clutched the lapel of his Confederate officer's uniform.

---

On a trip to Portland in 1873—according to Sister Mary Francis Burger—Col. Henry Jameson Olbrich decided it was high time he picked himself out a wife. Construction had recently been completed on his mansion, and he needed a woman to run the house and, more important, provide him with heirs. He had dreams of filling all his rooms with children. He spent some time in Portland and met all the best families. The night he first laid eyes on Miss Sally Ann Sorenson at a social gala, he deduced from her fine, Nordic features that their offspring would be equally handsome. He courted her during his stay and presented her with a diamond engagement ring. She accepted the proposal, and her father eagerly gave his consent. Some weeks before the ceremony, Colonel Olbrich took his prospective bride to a phrenologist, who attested to the nobility of her features and the strength of her moral character, as determined by the shape of her skull. They were soon married, and he brought her back home to Haven.

By 1876, Haven's population had reached its all-time peak: 5,500, mostly unmarried men, about half of whom were Chinese. The few women were largely employed as "hurdy-gurdy girls," and some of those were Chinese as well. All Chinese laborers were required to pay the territorial government a tax of $4.00 a month for the right to work—miners and prostitutes alike. Haven was a violent place: Less than 10 percent of all deaths were of natural causes. In addition to the church on Green Hill, the only other religious structure of any kind was a joss house across the river in Chinatown, the lower floor of which was taken up by a temple, the upper floor by a gambling den. Log cabins and clapboard homes sprawled all over the hills, connected by a web of muddy roads.

In the three years since Sally Olbrich's arrival, the town had grown, but the Olbrich household had not, other than the addition of maids and a Chinese houseboy and cook, a Hong Wah. The doctor told Colonel Olbrich that his wife was barren and there was nothing to be done about it. But to Olbrich, a wife who bore him no children was no wife at all.

It was in June of that year that Olbrich planned to accompany a large shipment of his gold to Pocatello. It was not his custom to do so, but he had further business to attend to in that city. He informed his wife that he would be gone for at least three weeks. The forty-mile journey by ox team to Challis alone would take five days. At Challis, the men would transfer the gold to horse-drawn coaches for the speedier trip down the mountain road to Pocatello. The townspeople gathered around the Wells Fargo office to witness Olbrich's departure and, as a result, witnessed an incident that was to prove significant.

Sally Olbrich was standing on the boardwalk laughing at the colonel and the teamsters as they wrestled to fix the yoke that had come loose from the oxen. In her small, white-gloved hand she held a parasol crafted of thin bamboo and brightly colored paper that depicted a wide-nostriled, fire-breathing dragon. Her face was cast in shadow, but everyone heard her laugh.

The men needed help or they would never get out of Haven. The strongboxes were loaded with precious bullion fresh from Olbrich's kilns; Henry was eager to get it all safely on board a Snake River steamer to Portland, and thence to San Francisco.

"Hong Wah!" Sally called, and tilted back her parasol, looking up and down the boardwalk for their houseboy.

Hong Wah emerged from the Wells Fargo office behind her, carrying the last of Henry's bags. He wore splendid snakeskin boots, black pants and vest over a freshly laundered shirt, straight tie, round collar, and silken Mandarin cap, his raven-black hair tightly braided into a pigtail in back. Despite the heat and dust, his smooth, dusky skin had not broken a sweat.

"Yes, Miss Sally?" Hong Wah said.

"You can help the colonel fix the team, can't you?"

"Of course, Miss Sally." Hong Wah smiled broadly.

Colonel Olbrich dodged a sudden jerk of the oxen's horns and his brown derby flew headlong into a murky puddle. He swore a manly streak and went to retrieve his hat. By now the townsfolk were beginning softly to snicker, emboldened by Sally Olbrich.

Hong Wah let out a short, disgusted laugh and shook his head at Henry's ineptitude. Setting down the bags, he descended the steps onto the muddy, rutted street. The oxen groaned and planted their hooves deeper into the earth, setting their legs in a wider stance. Hong Wah grabbed the first ox by the horns and spoke to it loudly in Chinese, shaking a scolding finger at it.

"They no want to go, Master Olbrich," Hong Wah said.

"Do you think I don't know that?" Colonel Olbrich spat a stream of tobacco juice in consternation, his face flushing redder than his already deep sunburn. He went back to scraping clumps of dark mud from his hat.

Hong Wah shrugged, grabbed the ox by the ear, and whispered something to it. He spoke to the other animals as well, and within a few minutes the huge creatures miraculously deigned to allow the teamsters to finish securing the yoke. The beasts fell into a more relaxed stance and looked around chewing their cud as if wondering what these stupid men were waiting for.

"They ready now, master." Hong Wah smiled at the colonel.

Olbrich ignored the houseboy but went up to speak to his wife. He remained standing in the street, however, at a level a good head shorter than her.

"Woman, explain yourself!" Olbrich said, blustering. "How dare you laugh at me before all these Christian folk!"

"Stop acting like a fool, Henry. I meant you no harm."

"What ever possessed you to send our boy out there? You made small of me in front of the town!"

"Henry, keep your voice down."

"How dare you!" His face was shaking and sweating like a steam boiler ready to burst. "How dare you!"

"Henry—"

"Where in hell did you get that . . . that thing!" He pointed at the parasol, finger shaking. "Answer me, woman!"

The townspeople quieted to a hush. For weeks, Sally Olbrich had been seen around with this Chinese parasol, and rumor had it that it had been a token of love given by the Olbrichs' houseboy.

"I bought it at Hinky Jack's Mercantile across the river," Sally Olbrich said. "If it is any business of yours."

The colonel's lower lip trembled, and his beard stood out

from his cheeks like a ridge of hackles. With his open palm, he slapped his wife across the cheek.

"Damn your obstinance!" he said. "One of these days, my dear, I swear I am going to find you lying dead in Chink Alley at the hands of some coolie!"

Sally covered her face with her free hand and sobbed openly.

Colonel Olbrich wrenched the parasol from her grasp, closed it, and cracked it in half across his knee, throwing the shredded paper and busted bamboo into the mud and dung of Center Street.

"You are a monster," Sally was heard to say.

Olbrich grinned as if this were a compliment. He stomped across the remains of the parasol and climbed aboard the buggy that would be following behind the ox team and his precious gold. He carried his own pistol on a belt; the teamsters were armed as well, the driver with a large-bore shotgun.

"Keep shy of them savages!" someone called to them.

"We'll get them before they get us," Olbrich said.

The crowd along Center waved to him, which he returned with a lax, royal air. The bull-whacker cracked his blacksnake over the oxen's heads and shouted, "Gee-ahh!" The animals moved slowly, but Sally Olbrich continued to stand there until the colonel's jaunty buggy vanished from view.

The clouds to the west were gathering into thunderheads.

Hong Wah helped Sally Olbrich up into the buckboard. The crowd did not disperse until they had witnessed the two ride off together on up the steep trail to the Olbrichs' lonely, twin-gabled mansion. Rumors arose about more than the parasol.

Nobody knew what might have gone on between Sally Olbrich and Hong Wah. The day after Colonel Olbrich's departure, the maid and other help were unexpectedly given the night off—a fact that quickly became known all over town. As the maid herself put it, Sally had "asked Hong Wah to stay the night to protect her," though it was known the houseboy always slept in a cheap room he shared with another Chinese on the other side of the river and had never before stayed at the Olbrich house.

It was said that Sally was no better than the whores at Maddie Gahagan's, a place her husband was known to frequent. Further rumor was that Sally had not come from one of Portland's better families at all but that Colonel Olbrich had met her in a Portland brothel and married her with his eye on reforming her. A general consensus arose that he had failed in that regard.

When Colonel Olbrich, his wagon and buggy, his teamsters, and his shipment of gold returned to Haven the night after their departure, no one gave a thought to warning Sally. Though the colonel claimed that the road to Challis had been washed out by recent storms, some in the town conjectured that the entire trip had been a ruse designed to entrap the wayward wife.

Olbrich testified in court that he had come back from the ill-fated trip and entered his own bedroom to find, in the dim glow of an oil lamp, his houseboy on top of his wife, "engaged in carnal acts upon her prone figure." The red velvet cover had fallen to Hong Wah's waist, "revealing his naked yellow back in the lustful clutch of my wife's grasping fingers," as he told the presiding territorial judge, the Hon. Everett T. Calhoun.

Colonel Olbrich shot first Hong Wah, then his wife—which acts he freely admitted, asserting that both killings had been his God-given right.

Justice Calhoun agreed and acquitted Colonel Olbrich of all charges. Here in this booklet, as set down by Sister Mary Francis Burger, were the exact words Mike had heard spoken in the Jubilee Days parade: "There is nothing in the law book as I read it that says it is murder to kill a Chinaman, and as for the woman, she was an adultress caught in the act of miscegenation, and I believe that is ample justification for the deeds of the defendant. Case hereby dismissed."

Colonel Olbrich was freed from the courtroom to the roar of a cheering crowd. From that moment on, he presented a slightly different picture of events, insisting that his wife had been drugged with opium—an unwilling victim—and that Hong Wah had been attacking her at the moment he came into the bedroom. Seeing Olbrich's gun cocked and ready to fire, Hong Wah had used the pale body of the drugged Sally as a human shield that had, alas, taken the first bullet. Around Haven, it was assumed that Colonel Olbrich had chosen not to take this position in court out of its sheer preposterousness. But they were willing to go along with him in casting his wife as the victim of a tragedy whose fault was Hong Wah's.

Olbrich had signed contracts with most of his Chinese laborers that they would work a minimum of ten years for a wage of four dollars a day. Most of them still had more than five years to go. At the time he had signed them up, it had been a great benefit; he had needed the labor, and he simply could not find enough white men willing to come to Idaho to do the work.

In the space of a few years, that had rapidly changed. White prospectors who had moved to Haven by the hundreds and whose placer claims along the Little Lost had not panned out were eager to work at the Olbrich Lode Mine for the lucrative white man's wage of six dollars a day, but no positions were available. As other mines in the territory failed, those men also came to Haven seeking jobs. The Chinese, however, had proved tenacious—hard workers who sent most of their earnings home to family in China and had no intention of leaving until their contracts with Olbrich expired.

Although it cost him less to pay the Chinese, Colonel Olbrich no longer wanted any part of them, proclaiming them to be "thieves and devils." He met with Sheriff Burgdorf, who "owed" him for arresting him on two counts of murder (this despite all the hard cash that had freely flowed from Olbrich's pocket into his since his appointment). Olbrich brought along with him a sack of gold Double Eagles, which he set heavily on the desk. He informed Burgdorf that this was the payroll for a certain enterprise he had in mind that would provide a solution to "the Chinese problem." He ordered Burgdorf to deputize every white man he could and thereby form a posse that could go across the river into Chinatown and burn the place to the ground. Colonel Olbrich dug into his sack, withdrew a handful of Double Eagles, and poured them into Burgdorf's cupped hands.

The enterprise went off fairly easily. The excuse given was the recent murder of a white hooker who, unlike those at Maddie Gahagan's, was said to have accepted Chinese customers. In what passed for a spontaneous fit of righteous anger, white men from all over Haven gathered together with torches and firearms and crossed the wooden bridge into Chinatown, which in size was equal to Haven proper. What followed was not only the burning of the Chinese people's homes but wanton rape and murder, until by the end of the enterprise less than a hundred Chinese remained to bury their dead. Women and children had not been spared. Months later, when the survivors' work at the separate cemetery was completed, the last of Haven's Chinese packed up and left.

Colonel Olbrich hired over a thousand white laborers to take the place of those he had "lost," giving first preference to those who had recently been deputized by Sheriff Burgdorf.

A year after the Haven Massacre, to the date, Olbrich's wooden mansion burned to the ground in what was widely suspected as an act of arson. It was rumored that the survivors had not returned to China but had found work in Leesburg, and it was speculated that a few of them had returned to exact revenge.

Colonel Olbrich was unhurt, however; he was not home at the time but in the arms of a girl named Lavinia in the plushest room at Maddie Gahagan's.

The people who lay buried in the Chinese cemetery had not died as a result of any explosion or cave-in; they had been slaughtered in cold blood.

That meant Bonnie was a liar.

Mike was surprised that such a tragic and tawdry tale should have been the purview of the plump, bespectacled nun whose photo graced the back cover. It was hard for him to understand why she would have any interest in writing about such an obscure chapter of the Chinese experience.

He returned the booklet to Randolph Carter.

"Fascinating," he said.

"Isn't it?" The librarian looked at the author photo and smiled in memory. "Sister Mary Francis. You know, she was my English teacher at Saint Joseph's."

"Is she still alive?" Mike asked. Although the book had been printed in 1976, the author photo looked as if it had been taken ten years earlier, and in it she appeared about sixty. She was either ninety or dead by now.

"She'll probably outlive me," Randolph Carter said with a laugh. "She was sweet. We were never very nice to her, though. Called her the Hindenburger."

"Is she very fat?"

Carter shrugged. "To us she was. She's also got a German accent. With a name like Burger . . . well, kids are kids."

Mike looked at his watch: eleven-fifteen already.

"What time do you close?"

"Late. Nine o'clock."

"Do you know where I could find her?"

"Sister Mary Francis? I see her in here sometimes. I don't know where she lives, but she still does volunteer work at Saint Alphonsus."

"What's that, a hospital?"

"You're not from Boise?"

"No."

"Whenever I'm there—which is all the time, these days"— Carter rolled his eyes—"she always stops by to say hello. She's looking a little frail, but she's still here. Like me."

Mike wanted to get away before Randolph Carter felt compelled to tell his life story. Though he sympathized, he did not have the time today to hear the tale.

"Where do I find this Saint Alphonsus?"

Carter pulled out a map and pointed it out. "Emerald and Curtis, just off I-184. If she's not there, the sisters might be able to tell you where to find her. You writing a paper?"

"A novel, maybe." The all-purpose excuse.

"About Haven?"

"Do you have any idea why she was interested in this?"

"I think she was from there, or something."

"You're kidding."

"I'm not sure. Seems to me. I can't trust my memory these days, though."

"Thanks. I'll be back." Mike shook his hand.

"I'll be here." Carter knocked on his wooden desktop.

Sister Mary Francis Burger was at the children's wing of St. Alphonsus, reading a story to the patients. Mike waited outside until it was over and approached her as she came out. She was small and considerably thinner than in the photo, her face lined like a carved apple left to dry in the sun.

"Sister Mary Francis?" He extended his hand.

"Yes?" She shook his hand firmly and looked up at him through thick-lensed eyeglasses, squinting and showing her dentures.

"My name's Mike Mak. I'm a reporter with the Seattle *Post-Intelligencer*. Could you spare a few minutes to talk with me?"

"Depends on what you want." She glanced at her watch.

"It's about Haven."

"Haven?" She looked at Mike as if this were the last thing she had expected. She smiled and held her arm out for him to take. "Let's go down to the cafeteria. I'm starving."

At the cafeteria, they piled up a single tray with food. Mike expected that since Sister Mary Francis was a volunteer, she might have free food privileges, but when they got to the register, she deserted him to go find a suitable table, and he got stuck with the bill. She chose seats at the far end of the dining hall, away from other people.

"Give me the tray," she said. "I like having the tray to eat off of in case I make a mess."

Mike unloaded his dishes and passed the rest over to her. She ate without another word.

"I read your book," Mike said.

"Which one?"

"*When the Little Lost Ran Red.*"

"So you want to know about the Haven Massacre, then?"

"Why did you write it?"

"Mike, is it?—when I first saw you I thought maybe you were the grandson of an old friend. But I guess that's impossible. He died before he ever had any children. Must have been, oh, sixty years on."

"A Chinese man?"

"That's right, I did mission work in China in the thirties."

"Do you mind if I ask your age?"

308

"My age? Heavens! I was born in July of ought-five. I guess that makes me ninety-one, doesn't it?"

"What about this man you knew? Who was he?"

"Just someone who used to attend our services. I think he had a special fondness for me, but who knows? That was in Nanjing. He was killed when the Japanese came."

"You were there?"

"Not something I really like to talk about. I thought you were here about Haven."

"I was down at the library this morning. Randolph Carter told me I might find you here."

"Poor boy. Has AIDS, you know. I remember when he was yea high to a beanpole. Now he's up here getting transfusions."

"He thought you came from Haven."

Sister Mary Francis Burger nodded her head vigorously, her cheeks bulging with food. "I was born there, way back when. That's why I wrote about the massacre. There were old folks who remembered it well, told me all about it. No one outside seemed to know. Eventually I got around to that book. Doesn't do it justice, though. Afraid I'm not much of a scholar. A lot of what I came up with is just anecdotes. But you got your evidence, the old Chinese cemetery. You seen it?"

"I live there," Mike said. "Haven, I mean."

"Never thought I'd live to see the day there'd be another Chinese in Haven!"

"When was the last time you were there?"

"Nineteen twenty-three. That's when I went off to convent. My folks were the last Catholics in Haven, and I was their only child. A year after the Depression struck, their house was burned down, with them in it."

"They were killed?"

"That's right. I was already in Nanjing by then. The news

309

didn't reach me for months. I never went back to Haven. Never wanted to."

"Did they catch whoever did it?"

"Oh, they had no idea, officially, but I suspect the Posse."

"The Posse. How did that get started?"

"The massacre. All those men who participated—it was like a point of honor—they thought they were cleaning up the town. When I think how it must have been . . . all I can think of is Nanjing. . . . Those men were never undeputized. They formed a kind of masonic lodge, and from what I'm given to understand, they've been responsible for all kinds of mayhem. Once they got rid of the Chinese, they went after other folks. Not everyone in Haven was like them. Lots of regular citizens tried to bring them to justice, but they started getting themselves shot dead on the street. Some of them shut up, and the rest hightailed it out of town. That's how Olbrich tightened his grip."

"So much for democracy. What ever happened to Olbrich?"

"Which one? The First or the Second?"

"The first."

"Oh, Colonel Olbrich died long before my day."

"What about the son?"

"Had him by his second wife. Junior was still running things when I came around, and he was even ornerier than his father, what I hear. When some of the miners tried to organize—nineteen thirteen, I think it was—he sent the Posse in to bust it up. Those brutes hit the men with clubs. Some of those miners' heads were split wide open. My pa witnessed the whole thing. The mine was going boom and bust, but it never seemed to hurt the Olbrichs much. They made a mint during the Great War. The mine went belly-up around the time I left, but Junior didn't seem to give a care. He'd taken his inheritance and spun it into a scad more dough. Anyway, he had other interests."

"Such as?"

"Eugenics. They called it the 'science' of eugenics. Ha. Junior had a newspaper—the *Haven American*—that grew stranger and stranger. He reprinted a lot of Henry Ford's anti-Jewish editorials from the *Dearborn Independent*."

"Henry Ford?"

"Oh, he was a great anti-Semite! I guess they don't tell you that, do they! Junior hobnobbed with Ford and a load of other industrialists. Lots of them were caught up in this whole eugenics bug. They poured millions into research grants. There were books published all the time. Some of them seemed very scientific, all about the effects of heredity on a person's intelligence and how it was immoral to allow the feebleminded to be born. Today you've got *The Bell Curve*. Same thing, really, just a new set of clothes. The idea was to let only those of social worth have babies and the hell with the rest—just sterilize them. Hell, these fresh-mouth Republicans are talking today about forcing welfare mothers onto Norplant. Newtzies, that's what I call 'em. You live long enough, you see everything come back into fashion."

"Even fascism?"

"You'd be stupid not to think so. The eugenicists were trying to scare everyone into thinking the nonwhites were going to take over America. Ford's paper reprinted the *Protocols of the Learned Elders of Zion*. Wasn't anything innocent about it. These were out-and-out racist tracts. Some of these American books actually influenced the Nazis."

"How do you know this?"

"I read a lot of books. The leader of the Hitler Youth told his jailers at Nuremberg that he became a committed Nazi in the twenties after reading a collection of Henry Ford's anti-

Semitic pieces. His mother was an American, and his great-grandfather was a Union officer who was wounded at Bull Run. Eugenics was what the Nazis were all about, and some of the most important works were written by Americans. All the American eugenicists—including amateurs like Henry Olbrich the Second—got quite excited about what was happening in Germany. All the theories they'd been writing about for years were being put in place, and they began flocking over to witness it firsthand. There was a very foolish one, Lothrop Stoddard, who wrote one of the most influencial racist books, *The Rising Tide of Color*, in nineteen twenty. He was able to use this as an entrée to get an interview with Hitler after the war broke in Poland. Hitler told him he had read his book and was a great admirer. Stoddard quickly dashed off an apology for Nazism called *Into the Darkness*. It came out in nineteen forty, though I didn't read it till some years later. One passage I'll never forget. He reported that in Germany in 'thirty-nine, the Jewish problem is a 'passing phenomenon, already settled in principle and soon to be settled in fact by the physical elimination of the Jews themselves from the Third Reich.'"

"Jesus," Mike said. "I guess no one read the book."

"Or else no one cared," said Sister Mary Francis. "Hitler stated all his plans in *Mein Kampf*, which was out in English in the thirties."

"And Henry Olbrich's son went over there, too, to see the Nazis for himself?"

"I'm told that he did, yes, though I don't think he ever wrote anything we could look at. He probably would have met with German industrialists, who all stood squarely behind the Nazis. I'm told Olbrich the Second went to Germany several times up until 'forty-one. He attended the convention of the American Nazi Party at Madison Square Garden."

"He was a Nazi, then?"

"You tell me. He was mixed up with the America First Committee and the German-American Bund, lobbied Congress to try and keep America from joining the war. A lot of the money for these organizations flowed in from Germany, but most of it came from rich Americans like him."

"So what do you know about the Haven Nazis?"

"What Haven Nazis?" she asked, blinking.

"The ones who moved there in the fifties."

"Oh, you mean the Germans? The ones who were in *Life*?"

"You didn't know they were Nazis?"

"How could they be? They never would have been let in."

"I'm not so sure," Mike said. "You seem up on this stuff. Don't you know about the—I don't know what to call it, the underground railroad?"

"You don't mean that old story about the Vatican?"

"That's exactly what I mean. Weren't there powerful men in the Church who helped Nazis forge South American passports and citizenship papers?"

"South American passports, not American passports."

"How do you know it didn't happen?"

"I couldn't possibly believe that any Catholic—"

"If it happened elsewhere, why not here? My guess is, if a Nazi had enough money, he could go anywhere he wanted."

"I don't want to talk to you anymore," said Sister Mary Francis. She stood up, shoving the tray across the table at Mike. "I have important duties to attend to."

Mike caught up with her at the end of the table, holding her gently by the shoulder. "Wait. I'm sorry if I offended you."

"You didn't offend me." She dropped her voice to a whisper.

313

"It's not safe to talk about such things. I'm an old woman, and they can come get me if they want. But you?"

"Who are they? Who are you afraid of?"

"Let go of me," she said, wrenching her shoulder free. "I've got more dying children to read to."

He let her go.

# Chapter 32

Driving down from Peg Harrison's at two-thirty, Cecilia could hardly see the road in front of her. The snow this time was a wet sort that gathered into large clumps before hitting the ground. A good twelve inches had fallen since noon. In a few hours, Haven would be a skier's nirvana.

Peg had looked about the same as yesterday. Her fever was lower, though it had gone up and down over the course of the day, according to the log she had been keeping at Cecilia's request. Both Peg and Hank swore she had been taking the ciprofloxacin, and Cecilia had no reason to doubt them. She hoped it was true.

The ambulance's defroster was working overtime and had still only cleared the lower third of the windshield. She wiped the rest in front of her with her coat sleeve. Her headlights illuminated little but the snow before her. The sun had been all but blotted out, the day become an eerie gray.

A pair of headlights was turning from Pemberton onto Longstreet, heading right toward her. She veered sharply to the right, the other truck went to the left. They both came to a stop. The other backed up until the driver's window was parallel with hers. She rolled her window down. A shelf of snow fell into her lap and began to melt.

Immediately, she saw the familiar gold star, black eagle, and P.C.S.D.

She felt her stomach turn.

"Cecilia!" yelled Tyler out his window. "You all right?"

"I'm fine, Frank. I saw you."

"You were on the wrong side of the road."

"Sorry."

"I'm not criticizing. Just a warning—you'd better be careful. With all this, just take her easy, all right? We're right in the heart of the big storm, and it doesn't look like it's going away. I've got some rounds to make—lots of folks I check on when the storms hit. You might be better off back at your office for the rest of the day."

"I'll consider it."

"Whatever. Bonnie called. She's heading back from Boise. I tried to tell her to wait it out, but she wouldn't listen to me. Said she can't afford to stay away from her business that long."

"How long?"

"Three, four days to wait for the roads to clear. 'Least, that's been my experience. When's Mike supposed to come back?"

"Tonight." She had not wanted to let Tyler know, but now it was too late.

"You'd better call, ask him to wait. He probably won't even make it to Elliott before they make him turn around. What does he drive, a Camaro? Those things are for shit in the snow."

"I know."

"Call him."

"I will. Thanks." She began to roll up her window.

"Wait, Cecilia—"

She stopped, in case he had anything important.

"If you need me for anything, say, in the middle of the night, just call, and I'll be there."

"I assume you mean a medical emergency."

"I sure do." He winked. "I'm in need of some urgent care."

"I'll be the judge of that."

"That means you'll have to examine me."

"Janice Fremont will be happy to do that for you."

"It wouldn't be the first time. I mean it, Cecilia. I'm at your beck and call. How many men have said that to you?"

"Wouldn't you like to know?"

"Don't you want to know what you're missing?"

"Frank, how can I make it more clear to you? I'm really not interested. Give it a rest, will you?"

"Cecilia, wait—"

She rolled up her window and drove on. Tyler's taillights vanished in the snowy expanse in her rearview.

She hoped she had some Alka-Seltzer at the clinic. Her stomach was tied in a knot. Bile was rising in her throat.

At the corner of Pemberton and Center, she felt strong abdominal cramps and had to stop the truck. She opened the door and vomited over the side, into the deep snow.

Back at the clinic, she stared at herself in the rest-room mirror and noticed the bags under her eyes and how her face drooped. She tried smiling, but it looked false. Just over a month in Haven, and already she needed a vacation.

She was happy about one thing: Her period was back. She was relieved, though it worried her that her menses had come so late. She had not been exercising or dieting strenuously. The stress of the move and all that had happened must have thrown her hormones out of whack. High stress could result in an estrogen deficiency that could have disrupted her ovulation. If such was the case, she had nothing to worry about as long as she could get her life back to normal. On the other hand, amenorrhea in a healthy woman of her age was not something to be taken lightly. She could not run her own tests and make her own diagnosis. She would have to make an appointment with a gynecologist in Pocatello as soon as she could free up a day from her schedule.

She was eager to tell Mike all about it. She was a little worried, though, that he might react badly to the fact that she had kept it a secret. Anyway, she saw no reason to worry him unnecessarily about her ovaries until she saw the gynecologist. After all their talk of Bonnie's hysterectomy, she could see him getting even more wigged out over what was probably nothing.

Janice Fremont knocked on the door.

"Dr. Mak? Are you all right?"

"Yes, Janice, thank you."

"The waiting room's empty, and I'm all caught up on my paperwork."

"Okay." Cecilia felt dazed. She wasn't ready to come out.

"Everybody's canceled their appointments. It's coming down something fierce. My husband says we're supposed to get three or four feet by the time it's over."

"Why don't you go on home, then, Janice?"

"Oh!" said Fremont. "What a nice idea! Thank you!"

"See you tomorrow, Janice."

"Yes, Dr. Mak. See you tomorrow."

Cecilia heard her pad softly down the hall.

Some minutes later, when Cecilia came out, the waiting room was dark, the front shades drawn. Only the hall lights and the lights in her office were on. She wondered if Fremont had bothered to lock the door. She went to the cabinet and found some Alka-Seltzer, dropped the fizzy tablets into a glass.

From her desk, she called the Motel 6 in Boise, but they told her Michael Mak had checked out that morning. She asked if by any chance a Bonnie Gillette was staying there. They were sorry; Ms. Gillette had checked out shortly after Mr. Mak.

She turned out the lights and stared out the window but could see little of Haven. Flatiron had been rendered completely invisible. Her breath on the glass fogged it all up.

With her finger, she wrote some words on the glass: *Come home Mike.* She thought for a moment, then added *Now.*

# Chapter 33

Randolph Carter was away from his desk, which was just as well. Mike didn't want to answer any questions about whether he found the nun and how she was doing. He had little time for chitchat. He had to find out whatever else he could and head back home. Then he and Cecilia would have to sit down and have a long talk about leaving Haven. Five-year contract or no, she would have to see that they had an alternative—even if he had to be an old-fashioned jerk of a husband about it.

In the reference stacks, Mike scanned through bound copies of *The Reader's Guide to Periodical Literature* from the early fifties, but he came up with nothing when he looked under the subject heading "Immigration." When he tried "Emigration," he struck gold with an article entitled "Freedom Seekers: Refugees of the Iron Curtain Find Ports and Happy Havens," from a 1951 issue of *Life* magazine.

The library had old issues of *Life* on microfilm but few microfilm readers; he had to wait fifteen minutes for an elderly woman to finish with one she was using for genealogical research. Once Mike got the film spooled up, it did not take long for him to find the issue, which had a black-and-white photo of Sen. Joseph R. McCarthy plastered on the cover. The article was deep inside, a somewhat fluffy piece with photos only of the women, including a much younger Elizabeth Polk in cat's-eye glasses and a curly, triangular hairdo. The caption gave very little information:

"Elizabeth Polk, mother of six, hails from the ancient German city of Leipzig. 'We want a fresh start,' she says unabashedly. 'I love everything about America—your grocery stores, your washing machines, your Arthur Godfrey!' "

The piece was about many different groups of refugees who had managed to get out of various Eastern bloc countries to settle in America. Only a few paragraphs mentioned the group of East German families who were planning to move to Idaho:

Wary of what might be termed the "Katzenjammer" sentiment, this bunch has gone so far as to take on such famous American names as Monroe, Harrison, Polk, and Fremont.

"My wife was against it," says Nathaniel Monroe, "until I suggested she call herself Marilyn." She decided, however, on Joyce. Their children—formerly Horst, Brunhilde, Heinrich, Franz, and Magda—are now Billy, Connie, Richard, Frank, and Marsha.

The Harrisons, a dapper, well-groomed couple with seven well-fed children in tow, offered an explanation. "It is not an attempt at deceiving anyone," says Henry Harrison. "It is because of our deep respect for the traditions of your country—some of which happen to be German, by the way."

"That's right," says wife Peggy. "Your national anthem was set to the melody of an old German beer-drinking song. Back then half of the people here spoke only German."

"And without the help of General von Steuben," Henry instructs us, "you would still be paying taxes to the King of England."

With the generous support of Franklin Tyler, an Idaho physician and philanthropist, this group is helping resettle Haven, an old, nearly abandoned mining town high up in the mountains of west-central Idaho. Why Idaho?

"From the photos Dr. Tyler has sent us," says Ralph Polk in between long drags on a Dunhill, "it looks to me very much like Bavaria, for which I keep a very special place in my heart."

The article gave no clue as to their original identities. It seemed conspicuous that no mention was made of what any of them might have done during the war. It was only six years after Germany's unconditional surrender, and these were couples in their early thirties who had probably each contributed to the war effort in some way—yet all *Life* cared about was the fact that they were fleeing the reds for a home in the land of the free and the home of the brave. If they did indeed have links to the Nazi Party, they had ample reason for fleeing Stalin.

Mike checked the library's microfilm index, but they did not have the *Haven American* on microfilm. He found Randolph Carter back at the reference desk and asked if the university library might have it.

"Oh, we've got it," said Carter, wiping his sweaty forehead with a handkerchief. "They're in bound volumes, though. I'll show you. Say, did you find Sister Mary Francis?"

"No."

"Shame. I think you two would have hit it off. She has a

thing for Chinese guys. Sorry—hope I'm not offending you again. Here we are."

Carter opened up the door to a room of glass-cased bookshelves containing leather-bound folios. A wide round table sat in the middle, with four leather chairs around it.

"This is our morgue, if you will," Carter said. "We've got old newspapers here from small towns all over the state—most of them from the nineteenth century, though I think the *Haven American* runs up until the sixties."

"Do you mind if I have a look around?" Mike asked.

"Be my guest. I'll leave you alone." Carter backed out of the room, pulling the door closed behind him.

Mike checked the knob to make sure he hadn't been locked in.

He scanned the spines of the bound *Haven American*s, which ran through 1948. He took down the 1948 volume and opened it up on the table. He sank into a chair and began flipping the pages.

The *Haven American* was a daily that ran a total of eight pages an issue. The pages were yellow and brittle, and Mike turned them with care. Henry Jameson Olbrich, Jr., was listed as publisher and executive editor. The editor was an Orville Gillette—who also wrote most of the stories. The editorials were violently anti-Communist. Some of the news was foreign, some national, but most was of local social events and personalities. Under other circumstances, Mike might have taken some time to browse through the most innocuous of items. Instead, he searched assiduously for any mention of Dr. Franklin Tyler.

In the coverage of the Jubilee Days of October 1948, the name never came up, and Mike was beginning to believe that Tyler must have arrived sometime later. Finally, in the month of December, he found what he had been hoping for:

## HAVEN WELCOMES NEW DOCTORS

### *HJO Reunited with Daughter, Son-in-Law*

## By Orville Gillette

Haven, Id., Dec. 9—On this auspicious evening, not only did Haven gain two new doctors but our most noted citizen, Henry Jameson Olbrich, Jr., gained a "new" son-in-law and was reunited with his most prized possession, his beautiful daughter, Anna.

The doctors are two Englishmen, Franklin R. Tyler and James K. Hamilton, originally of Manchester but lately of Buenos Aires. The girl some of us remember as Anna Olbrich met the dashing Dr. Tyler in Europe during a prewar tour with her illustrious father. Some ten years ago, HJO saw them married in Berlin and returned home alone whilst the happy couple sailed the *Normandie* to Rio de Janeiro for a sunny honeymoon.

So why has it been so long since we've seen our Anna, and why has HJO held his cards so close to his vest all these years? It all has to do with the outbreak of the war and the position Dr. Tyler took alongside his buddy from medical school, Dr. Hamilton, in Buenos Aires.

"These matters are still somewhat hush-hush, as Frank and Jim would say," boasts HJO, "but I would hint that they played a certain role in intelligence during the war."

The Tylers will be moving into the Olbrich mansion. Dr. Hamilton and his beautiful wife, Susan, will be taking up residence temporarily in the old Gahagan house until the snows melt next May, when they plan to have a house of their own built up on Olbrich's Ridge.

For details of the welcoming celebration, see my piece in column 2. Photos to come in the Sunday edition.

Mike turned to the *Haven Sunday American*, unsure what to expect. Orville Gillette evidently thought the event important enough for a spread over the entire back page. The celebrants were all eating cake and drinking champagne. Henry Jameson Olbrich, Jr., looked to be nearly seventy years of age, with fat, jolly cheeks, hair parted in the middle, a waxed mustache, and a pince-nez that reflected the glare of a bursting flashbulb. The photogravure images made the subjects' faces stand out in high contrast and a good amount of detail, which was what made the shot of Dr. Franklin Tyler and his wife so inexplicable.

It should have been no great surprise, perhaps, that the doctor looked so much like his grandson and namesake.

The great shock came when Mike looked at Anna Tyler, *née* Olbrich, and mistook her at once for Cecilia.

# Chapter 34

Cecilia was sitting in the dark of the parlor when the phone rang. She had it in her lap and picked up the receiver at once.

"Mike?" she said.

"Hi, Cee. How'd you know it was me?"

"I didn't. I just wanted it to be."

"Are you all right?"

"I'm fine. Why?"

"Nothing. I tried the clinic, but all I got was your recording. You came home early?"

"It's the storm."

"Storm? What storm?"

"Mike, where are you?"

"Still in Boise. I was just leaving."

"Maybe you shouldn't."

"I have to, I—"

"Mike, I'm looking at the snow now outside our window. You should see it for yourself. The Haven Road will be closed before you can make it home."

"I have to try."

"Mike, please, it's too dangerous. Stay in Boise until the roads open up. It might be a few days."

"I have to see you."

"I'll be fine, Mike. I can take care of myself."

"Cee, you don't understand. I found out something very important that I have to tell you."

"Research for your novel?"

"Exactly."

"It can't be so urgent that you have to take any risks. Can't you just sit it out?"

"No, Cee, I can't."

"Don't let your machismo kick in, Mike. I'll be fine."

"Cee, I'll tell you what. I'll drive as far as I can. If I have to turn around, I'll put up at the nearest town. I'll probably make it at least to Challis. If they've salted the roads, maybe I can make it on through to Haven."

"They won't have salted the roads. It wouldn't do any good. It's too dangerous. Don't do anything foolish on my account."

"It's on our account," he said. "Honey, I love you."

"I love you, too, Mike."

"See you in a few hours."

"Wait . . . Mike!"

He had hung up, or the phone line had otherwise become disconnected. A few clicks, a burst of silence, then the droning of the dial tone. She replaced the receiver and waited several minutes for the phone to ring again. Eventually, she got up and moved it back to its place on the side table.

Cecilia had gone ten pages into reading a novel before she realized she had no idea what she had just read. She flipped through the few broadcast channels but saw only afternoon talk shows—nothing she wanted to watch. The wind bore against the house, making loud creaks and popping noises that made her flinch. Her nerves were on edge. She looked at her finger-tips and discovered she had bitten the nails all the way down; she thought she had licked that habit during college.

This was useless. It had been only an hour since Mike had called. Even if he made it home tonight, it would not be for a few more hours. She thought of going upstairs to the computer and loading up one of Mike's old arcade games like Asteroids or Centipede, but this would probably keep her entertained about as long as the novel. The bathroom needed cleaning, and she considered it—for about two seconds.

She went into the kitchen instead and pulled down one of Mike's cookbooks. She was starving, anyway, and she needed something to keep her mind off worrying about Mike. This was not a night to go out to the Raven's Roost, nor could she count on one of Mike's own home-cooked specialties.

She looked first in the freezer. There were some frozen burritos she could pop in the mike, but what she needed tonight was to really cook something. On the stove. In the oven. Something that would take time and trouble. If it came out less than perfect, Mike would not be around to shake his head at her lack of domesticity. He always liked to remind her she couldn't even chop lettuce. It had turned into a reverse macho thing with him, his showing off how well he could cook just to prove what a thoughtful modern husband he was.

The refrigerator had no meat, but there were some reasonably fresh vegetables and a pint of milk. She found some yellow onions and a large sack of Idaho potatoes in the pantry. She looked through the cookbook and landed on cream of potato soup. The recipe did not look difficult, and she thought she had everything except the sprig of parsley, but that was just a garnish, and who gave a damn? She went to work on Mike's huge cutting board, chopping onions, peeling carrots, slicing celery. When it came to the potatoes, she decided not to bother

328

with peeling; she liked the skin, and peeling was too much bother. She used bouillon rather than the called-for soup stock—Mike would have been horrified—dumping in some extra dried parsley for good measure. She was about to put in the celery and onions when the phone rang again and she put everything down.

As she reached for the kitchen phone she realized this was the first time she had ever used it.

"Mike?" she said. *I've changed my mind,* she wanted to say. *I'm being stupid. Come home.*

"Uh, Cecilia?" Her father's voice, gruff and bewildered.

"Dad?" Utterly betraying her surprise.

"Well, hello, girl! What's the matter? Mike not there?"

"No, he's out."

"Out! In the storm?"

"How do you know about the storm?"

"That's why I called. I was watching the live Doppler radar on the five o'clock news. All over your part of Idaho it's lit up bright red."

"I never knew you were so concerned."

"These mountains storms . . ." He drifted off. "Mike isn't out in this, is he?"

"Dad, since when did you care about Mike?"

"He is, isn't he? And you're worried sick. I could hear it in your voice. For a moment, you sounded just like your mother when I'd be calling late in bad weather—"

"Dad—"

"She always thought I'd be flying off a cliff somewhere, like I couldn't handle my own car!"

"Dad, what do you want?"

"Just to see how you're doing. Is that a crime?"

"No, I'm just surprised." She held herself back. If she kept talking, she would venture into things she did not wish to discuss. He had a way of making her blood boil, and that was the last thing she needed this evening.

"Can't a father be concerned for his daughter?"

"Since when? You wouldn't even come to the wedding."

"I told you I had a business trip I couldn't get out of. If you want to keep on misconstruing—"

"The father of the bride usually pays for the wedding."

"Oh, it's about money, is it? I'll send you the money."

"Keep your damned money. I'm just saying it's unnatural for a father not to even want to come."

"Unnatural? You want to talk to me about unnatural?"

"Dad, I have to go."

"Oh, no, you don't. Hold on a minute, girl."

"I'm expecting a call."

"From Mike?" It sounded as if he was gritting his teeth.

"And my pot's about to boil over."

"Don't tell me you're in the kitchen! I'll be damned!"

"Campbell's soup." She refused to give him the pleasure. "Got to go. It's been real, Dad. Bye."

"Damn it, Cecilia!" he pleaded, too late.

She was hanging up.

# Chapter 35

On his way out of Boise, Mike stopped by Hap's Gun Shop far out on Broadway Avenue. It was the last thing in his life he thought he would ever do, but now here he was, looking over the selection of pistols Hap himself had taken out of the case for his perusal.

"What you lookin' for, exactly?" Foul-smelling cigar smoke drifted out of Hap's mouth. He tapped the end of his stogie against the ashtray that sat by the cash register, an odd-shaped clay thing, colorfully glazed, that must have been made by some kid in grade school.

"Protection," Mike said.

"Which one strikes your fancy?"

"Which one's the most powerful?"

"Well, now, there's power and then there's power. If you're looking for protection, you'll want something's goin' to stop that intruder dead in his tracks. A twenty-two or a thirty-eight's just goin' to make him mad, and he may not give you a second chance. I wouldn't sell you anything less than a three-fifty-seven Magnum or one of these nine-millimeter jobbers."

"This is a Magnum, right?" Mike hefted a silvery revolver, surprised at how good it felt hugging his palm. The price tag dangled from the trigger: $864.95.

"You got that right, friend. That there's your Colt Python, three-fifty-seven, double-action, four-inch barrel, combat stock. She's a real beaut, ain't she?"

Mike snapped open the chamber and looked through the holes up to the light. "Only six shots?"

"Well, that's the thing with a Magnum. You lookin' for more sustained firepower?"

"I don't know. Price is a little steep, anyway."

"I'll give you ten percent off." Hap saw right away that Mike would not be enticed, and he didn't miss a beat. " 'Course, she's kind of a high-end weapon. You might want to consider the Llama Comanche III or the Smith and Wesson twenty-nine. That's a forty-four Magnum, the Smith and Wesson."

"Blow your head clean off," Mike said.

"You got that right. 'Course, she only holds six rounds. You look to me like a nine-millimeter man. Take a gander at these puppies. All in your price range. You got your Glock twenty-three, holds thirteen rounds—your Browning BDM, holds fifteen—your Beretta 92F Centurion, holds fifteen—your Auto-Ordnance Thompson, holds nine—"

"What about this one?" Mike picked up an attractive silvery gun with a sturdy black stock.

"The Ruger P-eighty-nine, holds fifteen. Go on, give her a look over. Real nice little gun. Knock out a whole swarm of burglars."

The tag bore a price of $410.

"I like this one," Mike said. "I'll take it."

"How many?" Hap said jovially.

"Just the one. And a couple boxes of ammo."

"I'll show you what I got. You know what you want?"

"Yeah," Mike said. "Hollow-points."

"Heh, you really are goin' to do a job on that intruder!"

"There's no waiting period on the gun, is there? I need it today."

Hap spat on the floor behind the counter. "Waiting period? You fuckin' kidding me? Just show me your driver's license and you and me's in business. This goin' to be cash or charge?"

Mike rolled down his window for the highway patrol officer.

"May I see your driver's license please, sir?" Her voice was husky and professional, her mouth a firm, grim line in coral. He saw his own face in the mirrored lenses of her sunglasses.

"Uh, sure." Mike pulled the card from his wallet.

"And your registration, please."

Mike reached over to the glove compartment and tried to remove his papers without her catching a glimpse of the gun.

"Do you know why I stopped you today, sir?"

"Going too fast?" He tried a smile.

"That's right, sir. My radar clocked you doing ninety-seven in a sixty-five zone. Sound about right to you?"

"Ninety-seven? Huh!"

"Be back in a minute." She took his license and registration and went back to her patrol car.

He looked at his watch. Jesus—he still wasn't making as good time as he had hoped. It was late afternoon, and he still had a couple of hours ahead of him. The radio had reported a heavy snowstorm in the mountains. He hoped he could make it.

He checked his rearview and saw the officer speaking over her hand mike, smiling and laughing with the dispatcher.

*Come* on, *get on with it!*

He grabbed the folded papers from his back pocket—the last pieces of information he had managed to obtain from the library. It was all he would need to convince Cecilia. The first page was a photocopy of the photograph from the *Haven Sunday American* showing the young Widow Tyler and her husband. That in itself might not be enough; Cecilia could argue that the resemblance was coincidental, or she could look at it and still be in total denial. The second page was another photograph he had copied from a book. It was a group shot of great clarity, in the style of a class picture, that showed a handful of physicians in full SS dress uniform, all of the rank of captain or higher, who had conducted sadistic medical "experiments" on primarily Jewish victims at Dachau.

"Sir?" The officer cleared her throat.

Mike tucked the pages back into his pocket hastily. "Yes?"

"If you'd like to accompany me back to my squad, I can show you the reading on my unit."

Mike looked again at his watch, second hand ticking away.

"Only take a minute," she said.

"Can you just give me my ticket?"

"Haven't written it up yet. Come back with me, and we can take care of it in my squad."

He wanted to say that he was in a hurry but held his tongue.

There wasn't much space in the front seat of her cruiser; his knee pressed against her shotgun locked in its rack, aimed at the ceiling. He noted that he had indeed been clocked at ninety-seven—not that there had been any doubt.

"Nice car you got there," she said.

"Thanks," he muttered, fidgeting.

"Glasspacks and everything, huh? I guess you'd describe that as high-performance? And you're, what, twenty-nine, I guess, says here. How much you pay in insurance?"

"I get a nonsmokers' discount."

"You have any idea how many points you just racked up?"

"Don't tell me."

"You ever think of selling it, you call me first, okay?" She handed him her business card, with the logo of the Idaho Highway Patrol. "That's my work number. Now, if you'll just sign here."

She passed him her clipboard, and he scribbled his signature on the citation madly, like a doctor.

As she handed him his copy, he glanced up and saw a black Mercedes go whizzing by, probably faster than he had been going. A dark-haired woman was at the wheel. He was sure it was Bonnie—Cecilia had said she had gone to Boise, too.

"You'd better go after that one," Mike said.

"Too late. My radar's still locked on yours."

"You can see she's speeding."

"I'm not starting a high-speed pursuit over a speeder, Mr. Mak. You make sure I never see you again, or you'll get into some serious debt to your insurance company."

"I'll take that under advisement," he said, and got the hell out of her squad, slamming the door with a *chunk*.

He got back in his car and drove on cautiously. The patrol car followed him for several miles before finding a new speeder and revving on past. The officer waved at him as she flew by.

He kept to a more prudent speed, hovering around seventy-five. Once he turned onto State Highway 75, he had to be even more mindful, since troopers might be hiding behind any old tree. From here on it was all uphill. It was growing dark, and he would soon meet snow.

He had hoped to see the Mercedes stopped by the side of the road along with some flashing red and blue lights, but no such luck. Bonnie would be back in Haven before he would. He wondered why she had been spying on him—for herself or for the Widow?

Up into the Sawtooths, past Ketchum, he ran into black ice and wisps of snow making ghostly treks across the road. His tires had plenty of tread, at least, even if the Camaro was short on traction.

"Come on, baby, hold together," he said aloud, aping Han Solo's words to the *Millennium Falcon*. He had seen *Star Wars* nine times the summer of its release, when he was ten. For years afterward, he had recited long stretches of dialogue as if it were Shakespeare, to the great annoyance of his family.

As the black ice became a layer of snow and the wet flakes came flying into the path of his windshield wipers, he turned off the radio and tried to maintain his sanity by seeing how far he could remember the *Star Wars* screenplay.

"R2D2, where are you?" he asked aloud. That was as far as he got. He broke up with laughter.

Another highway patrol officer stopped him five miles out of Challis, only it wasn't for speeding. The road was thick with snow, at least five inches deep. The wind drove the flakes blindingly across the path of Mike's headlights. For the last thirty miles, ever since it had grown dark, he had noticed that he was the only car on the road. Anyone would be a fool to try driving in this weather, at least without four-wheel drive, snow tires, and chains.

The cruiser was parked in the oncoming of the two lanes, yellow caution lights swirling on top. A wooden sawhorse barricade blocked Mike's lane, and on top of it a large orange diamond-shaped sign:

ROAD

CLOSED

To the right of the barricade was the reinforced guardrail, and beyond the guardrail a steep drop-off to the raging Salmon River.

The officer, standing in the road in a knit cap and heavy winter coat, flagged Mike down. He was a potbellied older man with a gray mustache, five o'clock shadow, and a deep scowl.

Mike rolled down his window. "Can you let me through?"

"You'll have to turn around." The officer leaned inside, his stale breath reeking of cigarette smoke.

"When did you close the road?"

"About half an hour ago. The snow's too deep. Conditions are treacherous. Believe me, you wouldn't want to risk it."

"How long until it opens up again?"

"Depends on how long it takes for the plows to get through."

"I've got to get to Haven."

"That's out of the question. You just head on back to Challis now."

"It's an emergency."

"Is that a fact?" No niceties with this officer.

"It's my wife, she's in—"

"Don't tell me she's going to have a baby."

"You'll have to let me through, you see it's—"

"If she's in Haven, she'll still be there when they open up the roads. It might be a few days, though."

"I can't wait that long. It's urgent."

"Look, buddy, the state crews will come up and plow the highway, but they'll have to keep plowing it to keep it open, and that's going to keep them busy. The Haven Road never opens up so fast. It's a low priority, not a through way."

"What am I supposed to do?"

"Go back to Challis and get yourself a motel room for a few

days, that's what I'd do. You get there, you give your old lady a call and tell her you're safe."

"It's not that simple. Can't you let me take my chances?"

"You haven't been listening. No go, *comprende?*"

"All right, all right. Tell me one thing, though. Did a black Mercedes go through here before you closed the road?"

"Would that be your wife?"

"No."

"Didn't think so."

What was that supposed to mean?

"Yeah, she was the last one, about an hour ago. I had half a mind to turn her around, too, but I hadn't got word yet to go ahead and close it up."

"Thanks," Mike said gravely. "Thanks a lot."

He rolled up the window, threw the transmission in reverse, and backed up as if making ready to turn around.

The officer hitched up his pants and lit a cigarette, preparing for another long stretch of shit duty.

Mike was tempted to take his advice. For all he knew, Cecilia was in no immediate danger. On the other hand, maybe the road wasn't so bad. Bonnie could have tipped the officer some of the Widow's cash so he'd close the road early. She could have specifically asked him to keep Mike out. Mike couldn't afford to take that chance.

He could get through. He wouldn't even have to ram the barricade, merely nudge it aside. He doubted the officer would bother going after him; it would mean abandoning his post.

Mike threw the transmission back into Drive and crept ahead.

The officer stepped forward as if hoping to be of further assistance.

Mike pressed the accelerator just fast enough to keep the officer from jumping in front of him.

"Hey!" the officer said as Mike flew past.

Ignoring him, Mike aimed for the left prop of the barricade and went on through, knocking the sawhorse over into the snow.

"Hey, come back here!"

Mike clicked his headlights onto bright and plunged ahead, looking in his rearview to see the officer waving his arms ineffectually. The officer made no move to get into his squad.

"*Sayonara*, sucker," Mike said.

As he rounded the next bend, the yellow swirling lights disappeared into the darkness behind him. Mike used the reflectors along the side of the road as a guide. He could only see about thirty feet ahead. He felt his wheels lose traction at times, but the going wasn't that difficult. As long as he watched out for any giant drifts, he just might make it.

The Haven Road was rougher. Piles of snow had fallen from the rocks overhead. Mike hoped the rumble of his glasspacks would not start an avalanche. He would be buried for days, perhaps longer, with no food and only melted snow to drink. At each drift, he was able to eke out just enough space to get through. Hell, if the Mercedes could make it, so could he. Any telltale tracks, though, were long since covered up.

He was driven on by the thought of the photograph he had found in the book. Among the posed group of Nazi doctors—if they could be called doctors—was a handsome blond officer who was obviously the same man who was in the photo from the *Haven Sunday American*, the Widow's husband, whose name, according to the caption, was really Capt. Ernst von Meissner. Mike might have questioned the certainty of this—after all, how many handsome blond officers had there been in the SS?—if it weren't for the man standing next to him with his arm flung chummily around von Meissner's shoulders.

This man, somewhat taller and with darker hair, only attracted Mike's attention because of his name: Capt. Albert Gebhardt.

Mike had stared at the faces in the photograph for another ten minutes before finally recalling where he had seen that name before, scrawled in the bottom right corner of the painting that hung over the mantel back home.

Home—that was a laugh. He and Cecilia had been tricked. He felt dirty just for having lived in the house, slept in the bed, shelved his books on the bookcases, eaten at the table.

The thought of being away from Cecilia even for another three days made him deeply anxious. Once he got back, they would be stuck until the road opened, but if they played it cool, they might still get out without anyone getting onto them. Cecilia would have to abandon her clinic, but that hardly mattered anymore. They could find another damned doctor.

He would not let them have her.

As soon as they got out, Mike would contact the FBI, the State Department, the Simon Wiesenthal Center—anyone who would listen—and let them know that Dr. James K. Hamilton, presently of San Carlos de Bariloche, Argentina, was really Albert Gebhardt, whose various atrocities against Jewish prisoners were recounted in hideous detail in the very book from which Mike had copied the picture. There was no doubt of it in his mind. The book mentioned that the "doctor-butchers" Gebhardt and von Meissner had been friends since their school days in Leipzig; Mike could recall Cecilia saying that Hamilton had worked alongside Dr. Tyler since medical school. As far as he was concerned, he had all the facts. He looked forward to the day he would see Sam Donaldson go to Argentina and confront Hamilton-Gebhardt before the eyes of the world.

He would point out to Cecilia her resemblance to the

Widow. There was a reason why Hamilton had chosen Cecilia, out of all the doctors in the Rural Physicians Program.

Somewhere in all of this Mike could smell her father.

Painful as it was, she would have to be told.

As he neared Haven, he was dodging larger drifts and proceeding at only fifteen miles an hour. When he reached the bridge over the Little Lost, he could not even see the lights of the town for all the blowing snow.

A drift had collected on the bridge. Mike accelerated on his approach and blasted through it, dumping mounds of snow on the hood and into the path of the wipers.

"All right," he said. "Almost there."

From here on in, Center Street had been plowed, though a few inches of new snow lay along the path. It must have been one of the locals with a truck and a plow attachment.

As he crept along Center, he saw not a soul on the street. It was as eerily quiet as on that first night.

The lights were on at the Haven Clinic, including Cecilia's office window, though her blinds were pulled down. He saw no sign of the ambulance.

Heart pounding fiercely, Mike pulled up and parked in front and got out of the car.

It was then he heard the truck coming around the corner.

Slamming the door, Mike went around the back of the Camaro, heading for the clinic entrance.

The truck came around from Stuart Lane, plow raised high. As it turned, the headlights blinded him, and he threw his arm up in front of his eyes. The truck wasn't heading out into Center Street but straight into the clinic parking lot, coming directly at him, upshifting noisily and picking up speed.

"Hey! Stop!" he shouted, but the driver didn't see him.

He made a dash for the clinic door but slipped and fell into the snow. Scrambling to his feet, he knew it was too late. He had enough time to see the corner of the plow coming at his head.

After that, all he felt was the cold, then nothing at all.

# Chapter 36

After carefully stabilizing the head, Cecilia made a shallow two-centimeter vertical incision just below the Adam's apple to expose the membrane of the cricothyroid. With a gloved finger, she palpated the membrane to ensure she was in the right spot, then proceeded with a one-centimeter horizontal incision into the trachea. Janice Fremont inserted the Trosseau dilator and gently widened the incision while Cecilia inserted the tracheal hook to pull up the membrane and help her properly insert the tracheostomy tube that would keep Mike's airway patent.

The extent of his neck injury was unknown, and he was suffering from severe maxillofacial trauma; she could hardly recognize the bloated, purple features. His head seemed to have grown twice in size. She had to perform all possible measures to maintain adequate respiration. Fremont had kept him breathing on a hand-held respirator out in the parking lot until Cecilia arrived on the scene. It was lucky for Mike that Fremont had been at the clinic; Cecilia had no idea why she had returned so late, in this weather, when she had earlier wanted to go home, but she was grateful for her assistance and was not about to ask. Without Fremont's initial efforts, Mike might have been difficult to revive at all, even if he had been discovered five minutes after the hit-and-run.

Cecilia removed her bloody gloves, dropped them in the waste bin, and reached for the telephone. The Medflight number in Boise was encoded as a speed dial. She set the phone on speaker, listened for the dial tone, pressed the button, and waited.

Two interminable rings later: "Medflight."

"Yes, this is Dr. Cecilia Mak calling from Haven, up in the Little Lost Range."

"Gotcha."

"We've got an emergency. I need a helicopter right away."

"What's the nature of the emergency?"

"A severe blunt trauma case."

"Head wound?"

"Head wound, chest injury."

"Cervical spine?"

"I assume so, but I can't tell. No time for X rays." She spoke loudly to be heard over the speaker phone; she was busy re-scrubbing her hands. Fremont dried them for her and slipped a new pair of gloves over her splayed fingers. "We're trying to stabilize him, but he's got internal injuries I can't assess short of surgery, and I'm no surgeon. I'm not equipped to do much more than I'm doing. Please hurry."

"I'm not sure we can get the chopper up there. You're right in the middle of the storm."

"You think I don't know that?"

"The pilot might refuse."

"I know," she said resignedly. It would make no difference whether she told them the victim was her husband. She did not want to sound hysterical.

"Give me your number. I'll call you right back."

"Can you keep me on the line?"

"Okay, can do."

"It's urgent. He can be saved if you can get here."

"I'll be right back, Dr. Mak. You just sit tight now."

Cecilia kept the phone on speaker and instructed Fremont to place a 14 French catheter in the right antecubital vein. She performed the same procedure in the left. They infused the tubes with crystalloid solution that would help restore Mike's circulation. He had been very lucky: Despite the severe bruising and the bleeding wounds, his vasculature seemed largely intact. He was, however, in severe shock that was immediately life threatening, and he desperately needed fluid replacement.

The extent of his chest injuries led Cecilia to suspect a hemopneumothorax of the right lung; the blood would have to be drained. She made an incision between the fourth and fifth ribs at the midaxillary line, creating a short subcutaneous tunnel through which she sharply divided the fascia and intercostal muscle. Using a Kelly clamp, she perforated the pleura. She inserted her finger all the way to the first knuckle to confirm that she had penetrated into the thoracic cavity. Fremont was ready with a large-bore thoracostomy tube, which Cecilia fed posteriorly, several inches into the cavity, toward the pleural apex. Cecilia secured the tube with heavy-duty polyethylene sutures while Fremont attached the other end to the collection apparatus.

Mike seemed barely to stabilize. They had helped him over the first hurdle, at least, but without care from a Level One trauma center, he might not make it. Cecilia did not even want to entertain the possibility. He *had* to make it.

Together, they began tending to Mike's multiple bleeding wounds. The fluid-replacement therapy would do little good if they could not halt the bleeding. Transfusion would likely be unnecessary as long as Medflight arrived in time.

"I'm here, Mike," she said in his ear. "Help's coming."

He was completely unconscious. She doubted whether he could hear her.

"Please try to hang on. I need you back."

Fremont glanced up with an uncharacteristically sympathetic look, then returned to her coldly efficient work.

Cecilia grabbed a sterile needle and sutures, took a deep breath, and joined her in the stitching.

Several minutes had passed; the dispatcher had not returned.

"How's he doing?" Sheriff Tyler asked.

"He's alive," Cecilia said, "but he belongs in ICU. Stand clear, Frank. I don't want you contaminating anything. I've called Medflight, but they couldn't give me a firm answer. They're balking because of the storm. If they see an opening on the radar, they'll take it—but they'd better come soon."

"I've arrested Bonnie," Tyler said.

"You what?"

"Booked her for hit-and-run, severe vehicular injury. She says it was an accident."

"Then why'd she run?"

"She can't say. She's up at the jail, at least for now."

"I thought she was out of town."

"She got back a couple hours ago and started helping us plow the streets. Says she came around the corner, couldn't see him because of the snow. She braked, couldn't stop in time. Says she's sorry. If Mike doesn't make it, it'll be vehicular homicide."

"Mike's going to make it," Cecilia said determinedly. "I'll see to that."

"I'm sure he will. He's lucky to have a wife like you. What if Medflight can't make it?"

"I'll do whatever it takes."

"By the way, I'm going to need Mike's personal effects—anything he had on him when he was struck. Clothes, whatever."

"What for?"

"Evidence. I'm sorry, Cee. Procedure."

She didn't give a damn anymore about correcting him.

"Here." She handed over to Tyler the plastic garbage bag into which she and Fremont had placed the bloody clothing after cutting it off Mike's body. "Do I get this back?"

"Once we're through with it."

"His wallet's probably in there."

"We'll take care of it. I'm just going to dry everything out, bag everything, and seal it up. It'll all be yours."

"If you'll excuse me," she said, staring hard at him, severely annoyed. "I don't have a lot of time to chat."

"I'm sorry, Cee, truly I am. I hope he makes it."

"He will."

"You know, I believe you?" he said, as if this were something amazing. "You're a regular miracle worker."

"No miracles, Frank. Just science."

"There anything I can do?"

"Just go," she said. "Please."

"Since you put it so nicely . . ." He tipped his hat and left, taking the garbage bag with him. The door swung closed.

"Bonnie," Fremont said, shaking her head. "I'll be damned."

Cecilia checked the electrocardiogram readout, examined a bit of the tape: not great, but improving. She was doing everything right. How long he could last like this was another question. She was concerned about possible spinal fractures, but at this stage they could not risk moving him into the X-ray room.

She didn't believe it had been an accident, but she couldn't allow herself to become distracted by that now.

"Hello, Dr. Mak? Are you there?" It was the phone.

"This is Dr. Mak."

"Medflight here. You're in luck."

"Oh, God, thanks. A break in the storm?"

"Somewhat. We've also got a daredevil pilot tonight. They're already airborne, heading your way."

"How long?"

"Hard to say, given the conditions. Give 'em half an hour. Only place they can land is your courthouse square, looks like, so you'd better be able to get the patient down there. They're not going to want to stay on the ground too long."

"We'll be there. Thank you."

"My pleasure."

Half an hour, she thought. It was far too long. She mulled it over in her mind: half an hour here, perhaps as long getting back, then to the hospital emergency department, the radiology suite, the operating room, the intensive care unit . . .

"Hang on, Mike," she said, touching his head. "You've got to hang on. We're almost there. Stay with me here, honey."

She tried to keep the tears at bay. Had to remain professional, could not let Fremont see her cry. Had to be strong, for Mike. She would have time to let loose later.

"Sorry, Mike," she said. "I'm so sorry."

"It's not your fault," Fremont said.

*Oh, yes it is,* she thought. *It sure as goddamned hell is.*

The transfer to the ambulance was tricky. Mike's condition was worsening. Fremont drove the truck while Cecilia rode along in back, keeping him going on a hand-held respirator fixed to the tracheostomy tube. They had to jerry-rig the IV fluids, hanging the bags of crystalloid from hooks in the ceiling of the Blazer. The dome light was dim. She could hardly even see.

Despite the plowed streets, the ride was jarring.

Cecilia listened for sounds of a helicopter, but all she heard was the wind's fierce howl.

Fremont parked at the courthouse square and climbed in back.

"Half an hour," Cecilia said. "They should be here."

"How's he doing?"

"Just hanging on."

Fremont took over the respirator while Cecilia placed the stethoscope against his chest and listened for heart sounds. They were becoming more erratic.

Suddenly, the snow began to swirl all around them, and the sounds of the helicopter came, faint at first.

"They're here," Fremont said.

The sound grew much louder as the craft descended.

The Medflight trauma team was of great help with the transfer. A large crowd of Havenites, attracted by the spectacle, gathered around to watch as Mike was carefully loaded onto the helicopter.

"Take me with you," Cecilia said as they were about to slide the door closed.

"Too risky!" one of them shouted above the rotor's whine. It was gaining in pitch, gearing up for takeoff. "In this storm, at this altitude—we're overloaded as it is!"

"I want to be with him!" she said.

"Trust me, he's in good hands! We've got everything he needs!"

"I'm not just his doctor, I'm his wife!"

"Sorry, no can do! No time to argue! We've got to get your husband back to Boise!"

Cecilia wanted simply to leap into the craft and force them to take her. But if it would risk the safety of the craft—and risk Mike's life—it would be better that she restrain herself.

"Promise you'll take good care of him!" she said at last.

"Promise," the man said. "Okay, we're out of here! Now go on, stand clear!" He slid the door shut, and the rotor's whine grew higher and stronger.

Tyler came up from behind her, throwing an arm around her and tugging her back with him away from the chopper, back toward her ambulance. They turned to watch it take off into the sky. The Havenites held onto their hats.

As the lights of the helicopter vanished over the mountains and the snow finally settled, she could see the stars above. The storm was clearing—or else they were in its eye.

"He'll be fine," Tyler said. "They've got good doctors there at Saint Luke's."

She began crying convulsively, and the shame of doing it in front of Tyler made her cry all the more. She did not want to appear weak in front of him—or in front of any man but Mike.

"There, there," Tyler said. "Let it all out."

She wanted him to get the hell away from her.

If Mike died in Boise, she would never forgive herself for not forcing herself aboard. Now it was too late.

# IV
## Haven

# Chapter 37

Cecilia sashed the bedroom curtain to the yellow wallpaper and stared out at the snow that continued to fall. It came down quietly now like flakes in a snowglobe. The sky was brighter than yesterday, a blanket of white cloud that had arrived in the blizzard's wake. Haven below her was as white as the sky, the peaked roofs piled with cake frosting. Dark woodsmoke chugged out of the chimneys. Haven was staying home today, perhaps for the next few. Although it was the last thing in the world she wanted to do, she would have to go in to work and make more afternoon rounds than usual. It was Wednesday, she realized, and as on any morning, Mike should still be asleep in bed. The bed lay empty, though, covers rudely rumpled from her restless sleep.

She had remained in contact with St. Luke's in Boise throughout the night, worrying every minute. The attending surgeon, Dr. Saronica, had reported no spinal fractures, but they had performed emergency surgery to repair internal damages and had drained excessive fluid from his brain. At last report early this morning, they had put him in intensive care and listed him in critical condition. He had not yet regained consciousness. They were cautious about his prognosis and made no promises about his chances for recovery. Even if he pulled through the crisis, complications could arise, not the least of which was the possibility of permanent brain damage.

Cecilia was afraid to call back so soon. Only a few hours had passed, and his condition could not have changed much.

She showered and dressed and, lacking any appetite, forwent breakfast. The ambulance stood high in the driveway. She started the engine to let it warm up while she brushed off the mounds of snow that had gathered overnight and scraped the cystalline ice off the windows. She hardly felt the cold.

Volunteers—all men from the Posse—had kept busy plowing the streets during the night in their trucks. Cecilia wondered why Bonnie had been out plowing when only men were doing it—and why she had felt so inclined just after returning from a long trip. She supposed Tyler would have her Ford Bronco down at the courthouse.

As she pulled up into the clinic parking lot, she recognized the sleek shape of Mike's Camaro, entirely covered in snow. The door to the clinic was locked; Fremont had not yet reported in. No one was waiting to be let inside. She could not let the Camaro sit out there all day wrapped in a snowy shroud. She took her brush and scraper from the ambulance and went to work on it.

As she got down to scraping the windows, she looked inside, wondering if Mike had left anything on the seats. She noticed the pink copy of a citation crumpled in the passenger seat, nothing else. She unlocked the door and got in.

She examined the speeding ticket, which bore Mike's sloppy signature at the bottom along with the officer's. It gave off the sharp chemical smell of NCR paper. He had been stopped for going ninety-seven miles an hour in a sixty-five zone. She folded it in fourths and placed it in her pocket.

She saw nothing else in the interior but Mike's CD cases and a McDonald's bag on the floor that contained two blue Filet-O-Fish wrappers and a frozen bit of unfinished soda at the base of a cup. Mike's keys were not in the car; they must have been on him when he was hit, now in one of Tyler's evidence bags.

She wondered what else Mike might have had on him, in his wallet or stuffed in a pocket. She should have looked before Tyler had come, but in the urgency of the situation the thought had never crossed her mind. Even if it had, she would not have been able to afford the time. They had merely cut his clothes away and dropped them into a bag, and that was the last she had seen them. Tyler had promised she would get his stuff back, but chances were he would go through it first. If Mike had taken any notes in Boise, she could kiss them good-bye.

She pressed the glove compartment latch and found it locked. Strange, since Mike never bothered to secure it. She opened it with the trunk key.

The auto registration lay on top where Mike must have replaced it after showing it to the officer. Underneath, she saw a large silver-and-black pistol and some boxes of ammunition, along with a bill of sale from Hap's Gun Shop, made out to Michael Mak, of Haven, for the purchase of a Ruger P89 nine-millimeter handgun and a few dozen rounds of CCI 180-grain hollow-point bullets. He had used his American Express card at 3:45 P.M. and signed with a flourish, as if in a great hurry.

The ease with which this transaction had apparently come off would have angered Mike no end—at least the Mike she knew. He had always been passionate, even eloquent, about the need to tightly regulate nonsporting firearms, of which a nine-millimeter loaded with hollow-points was a prime example. Nobody used such a thing for deer hunting. Mike had to have been sufficiently afraid to feel the need for protection.

Cecilia glanced up quickly, half expecting to see Tyler peering in through the window while she examined the gun, but no one was there. She saw no one at all on the nearby streets. They were all sleeping in, as she wished she could have.

Hastily, she put the gun inside her coat. She searched the glove compartment for anything else he might have left but found only the usual road maps and the Chevrolet owner's manual.

She got out and locked the door, went around to the other side and made sure it was locked. From the trunk she removed Mike's overnight bag, which she hoped might contain something of interest.

She opened up the clinic and went straight back to her office, setting the overnight bag on the floor behind her desk. All she found inside were the few clothes he had brought along, his toiletries, his laptop computer, and his address book. She would look through the files on the laptop later. For now, she leafed through the address book, noting a Post-it note alongside Tawanda Neebli's phone number. She also found a hastily scrawled phone number for a Saul J. Abramowitz of New York City.

"Cecilia?" came Fremont's voice from down the hall.

Cecilia stashed the address book in her desk and got up.

"Any word?" Fremont asked as she came into the room.

"He's going to be all right," Cecilia said, knowing it was wishful thinking. "He's in ICU, condition still critical. I can't thank you enough for all your help, Janice."

"Just doing my job."

Cecilia wished Fremont's icy exterior would melt for once.

"What made you come back to the clinic last night?" she asked. "If you hadn't been here—"

"Something nagging me, that's all. Paperwork, something I'd left half finished. I would have fretted about it all night."

Cecilia didn't believe her, though she didn't know why or what difference it made.

"Why didn't you go with them?" Fremont asked casually.

"I tried. They wouldn't take me."

"If there's anything I can do . . ."

"I'll let you know. Thanks, Janice."

Fremont smiled uncomfortably and went back down the hall.

Cecilia closed her office door and went back to set up Mike's laptop. She found a residential address disk in the CD-ROM drive. She searched through his word-processor files but found none dated more recently than last week. Perhaps he had felt wary about entrusting his thoughts to the computer. He may not have brought anything back except what was in his head.

Her experiences in the emergency department at University Medical Center had taught her more than any textbook about how fragile human beings could be. She had treated bicyclists who had not been wearing helmets and had been struck by cars, splitting their heads open. Some had died, some had slipped into a permanent coma. Mike's head injury was less severe than that. He had no fractured vertebrae and his spine had not been severed. It was within the realm of possibility that he would be restored to her.

She opened up his address book and found his parents' phone number in Laramie. She dreaded making the call, but it had to be done.

When she picked up the receiver, she was met with no dial tone, only white noise.

She opened her door. "Janice, what's with the phones?"

"Storm knocked them out. They've been down all morning."

Cecilia sat at her desk and began making a list of numbers she would have to call once the lines were restored:

*St. Luke's*

*Mike's parents*

*Jeremy (?)*

*Tawanda Neebli*

*Saul J. Abramowitz*

357

# Chapter 38

She tried to keep herself busy to ward off a funk. Being unable to use the phone was making her antsy about Mike. Several of her scheduled appointments showed up, and she saw to them. She wondered whether Mike had actually spoken with Saul J. Abramowitz—Raphael's brother? father?—and what they had talked about.

She was able to go out for her rounds early. When she arrived at the Harrisons', it was 11:00 A.M. Hank was outside in red plaid hunting coat and cap, working on his walk with a snowblower that spewed chunks of the stuff in a tall arc into the middle of Longstreet Lane.

"Hi, Hank. Mind if I go in and see Peg?"

"Go right on in. Door's open." He had a smile for her. "Sorry about your husband."

"He's going to be all right." She crossed her fingers within her coat pocket.

Peg was in the back bedroom tucked snugly under several blankets, looking toasty warm in a room that was already overheated, watching *All My Children*. Her face brightened.

"How are you feeling today?"

"I was up half the night coughing. Feeling a bit better now, though. I'm drinking my fluids." Peg nodded toward the Coca-Cola bottle at her bedside. "I feel just awful about Mike. Such a tragic thing to happen to such a nice young man."

"Let's have a listen." Cecilia got out her stethoscope and had Peg sit up and lean forward so she could get at her back. "Take a deep breath, and out." There was still some wheezing and a faint rattle. Peg might be getting better, but slowly.

"That Bonnie," Peg said. "She's got a mind of her own."

"Why do you say that?"

"Don't know why she'd go and do something like that."

"It was an accident." Cecilia was wary of venting her suspicions. "Didn't they tell you that?"

"Lots of accidents been happening around here, case you hadn't noticed." Peg glanced warily toward the window. Hank's snowblower continued to roar dully in the background.

"You're talking about Lizzie?"

"Poor Lizzie, yes. I never trusted Clark's pets, mind you, but I've delivered their mail every day, bringing packages up to the doorstep with those dogs carrying on—never once have I seen them break out of that pen. If I had, I would have told Clark to come down to the post office and pick up his own mail."

"Why didn't you tell me this before?"

"Not worth bringing up, I figured. What's done is done, and I can't prove anything. All I know is, I've lost my Lizzie. Herb Monroe gave those dogs what was coming to them, if you ask me—with both barrels. And there was that Jew."

"Raphael Abramowitz?"

"Was that his name? Never heard of anything like that happening in these woods. Maybe Frank gave you the impression these things happen all the time."

"Not exactly." Cecilia shined her penlight in Peg's eyes. "Peg, I have the feeling there's a lot you're not telling me."

"Oh, no. You think they'd trust me with anything?"

"Just tell me if any of this has anything to do with Mike."

Peg's mouth snapped shut like a sprung mousetrap.

"It wasn't an accident, was it?"

"I told you, I wouldn't know. You'd have to ask Bonnie—not that she'll tell you. That girl's been the cause of more trouble . . ."

"Such as?"

"That scene she made when Frank called off the wedding! You should have seen it! Out there in front of everybody, smack dab in the middle of Center Street. They had to hold her back to keep her from clawing Frank's face! She was screaming like a bobcat. I thought they were going to cart her off to the nuthouse. Jim Hamilton gave her a shot and took her down to the clinic. She didn't show herself for a week, but after that she was something like her old self again, all cheerful and pleasant. They gave her one more chance, and she seems to have been just fine since then. But we all know what she's capable of. Craziness does sort of run in her family."

"Who gave her one more chance?"

"Well, Anna, for one."

"Anna?"

"The Widow Tyler. She always did cotton to Bonnie. Must have seen some of the same spunk in her. Otherwise, I think we would have seen the last of Bonnie some time ago."

"What do you mean, she would have had to move away?"

"Had to move away—that's a nice way of putting it. I've seen a lot of people have to move away in my time."

"Are you talking about Haven or Germany?"

"Why, Haven, of course. I'm not to talk about Germany."

"You let slip about Bayreuth, in case you don't recall."

"That's just between us, need I remind you." Peg gave a wheezy sigh. "No one remembers Herta von Möllendorff anymore."

"You might be surprised." Cecilia attempted to appeal to her vanity. "You've probably been reissued on CD. I bet there are some opera buffs out there collecting your work. Like my friend Jeremy. I'm sure he would have loved to meet you."

"Do you think so?" Peg's eyes widened appreciably. "How I would love to hear those old recordings again. I couldn't take any with me, of course, when we left—"

Peg stopped short, her eyes leaving Cecilia and settling on the doorway.

The sound of the snowblower could no longer be heard.

"Peg, you been makin' up stories again?" Hank asked, stepping into the room. "She's got an overactive imagination, Cecilia. Just because she's the postmistress she thinks she's a woman of the world."

"They're very entertaining stories," Cecilia said wryly.

"She tell you I was set to inherit a baronage in Bavaria?"

"Hank!" Peg said, shocked.

"Tell me, Doctor, do I look like an aristocrat to you? Does she look like a diva? You think anyone would actually pay to hear her sing? I have to hear it all the time. Wagner, Strauss, Beethoven—she never lets up. Give me Tex Ritter."

"Hank!"

"I've been given a reprieve, now that she's laid up."

"Excuse me," Cecilia said, feeling uncomfortable. "I'd better be going. Hank, you see she takes her meds, will you?"

"Have been, and I'll continue to do so."

"I'll come again tomorrow, Peg, and you can tell me some more of your stories."

"It will be a pleasure," Peg said grandly. "Forgive me for not getting up. The Baron von Möllendorff will show you out."

Hank offered Peg a deepening scowl.

Cecilia closed up her bag and could not help but smile, though it was all somehow sad.

"I'd like to see Bonnie."

Herb Monroe took in a deep breath and said, "I'll have to check with the boss." He reached for the radio on his desk and keyed the mike. "Frank, you out there?"

"What is it now, Herb?" came the squawky voice.

"I've got the doc here, wants to talk to Bonnie."

"Is she there? Put her on."

"He wants to talk to you." Monroe handed her the mike.

"Frank, it's Cecilia. I just want to see her for a minute."

"I got no problem with that. You're not going in with a grudge, are you?"

"No, Frank, I just want to talk. I also want to see how she's doing. She missed an appointment with me the other day, and it's important I see her. So it's half official, anyway."

"Like I said, no problem."

"Frank, is anyone doing anything about the phones?"

"We had some downed lines. The Marsh boys are working on it. They say it'll be back up in no time. Now, you tell Herb to let you in. Bye."

"He says to let me in," Cecilia said.

Monroe rolled his eyes and grabbed the key ring. "I don't think it's such a good idea, but who ever asks me?"

Monroe pulled up a chair for her outside Bonnie's cell so they could speak through the bars. "Give a call when you're done. Otherwise, you got ten minutes before I come back to get you." He disappeared down the hall, locking the outside jail door.

Bonnie's long hair was tangled, her clothes unkempt. Purplish rings encircled her eyes.

"Hi, Bonnie." Cecilia felt intense anger on seeing her, but she tried to keep herself under control.

"Cecilia, I don't know what to say except I'm sorry. Please tell me Mike's going to be all right."

"It's too early to say," Cecilia said. "The phone lines are down and I can't get through to find out."

"It was an accident, I swear," Bonnie insisted, coming closer to stand at the bars.

"So everyone keeps telling me."

"I'm in a fix now. I shouldn't have run."

"I didn't come here to start blaming you. I wanted to see how you're holding up. You were supposed to come see me on Monday, remember? Frank told me you went to Boise."

"Business," Bonnie said, looking away. "I went to see a guy about some fixtures for my place."

"Did you know Mike was there?"

"He was? I had no idea. But I don't think I should start answering a bunch of questions like that without a lawyer."

"Fair enough. I'd like to ask you some other things, if you'll let me."

"Go ahead. I got nothing better to do."

"Your medical file at the clinic is incomplete. I was hoping you could fill me in."

"Incomplete? How would you know?"

"It's obvious there's some pages missing. I don't know if it was Hamilton or Fremont or who, but somebody tampered with it before I arrived."

"I wouldn't know anything about that."

"I'm not saying you do. I suspect it was Hamilton. He didn't want me to know the real reason for your hysterectomy."

"I told you, cervical dysplasia. He had no choice."

"Are you sure?"

"I've never doubted it. Should I have?"

"You're sure it had nothing to do with your parents?"

Bonnie eyed her suspiciously. "Why would it?"

"They're both dead, am I right?"

"Yeah, so?"

"At a relatively young age, too. Would you like to tell me how they died?"

"I don't see why this is relevant."

"It's relevant if they died of Huntington's."

"Just because they had it doesn't mean I'm going to." Bonnie was defensive.

"But there's a very good chance. Fifty-fifty. You must be aware of that."

"It's not something I like to dwell on. I'll take my chances."

Cecilia glanced at her watch. She only had seven more minutes. She had to get right to the point, blunt as it was.

"Do you mean to tell me that Jim Hamilton never discussed genetic testing with you?"

"Testing? No. I wouldn't have wanted to, anyway. If I've got the gene, I wouldn't want to know. He never brought it up."

"Did he ever run other tests on you, blood tests and such?"

"Of course. Just routine stuff—cholesterol, blood sugar. He did more tests when Frank and I were going to get married."

"He took more blood than he normally would, say, for a checkup?"

"Yeah, as a matter of fact, he did."

"Bonnie, I have something very important to tell you. The test results are missing, but there's a notation in Hamilton's hand that he did run a genetic test on you for Huntington's."

"He what?"

"Without your consent, clearly. It's unethical. Unconscionable."

"What else?"

"I thought you didn't want to know the results."

"You've gone this far. You may as well tell me. It's not as if I've never entertained the possibility. Are you telling me I've got the gene?"

"I wouldn't go so far as to confirm that without seeing the actual results."

"How dare he!" Bonnie clenched and released her fists.

"You know that if the disease does develop, there's little I can do for you. There was no treatment in your parents' day, and there's none now."

"Yes, I know. I never had cervical dysplasia?"

"Maybe you did, maybe you didn't. I have no idea. The records are too sketchy. But from what I know about Hamilton, that was just an excuse to perform the operation."

"What do you think you know about Jim Hamilton?"

"I'm not positive, but I suspect he was a Nazi."

Bonnie laughed. "They said you were smart."

"You knew?"

"Of course I knew. Everyone does."

"Your family didn't come over from Germany, did they?"

"No. They were old Haven stock, like I told you."

"And they knew who the Germans were?"

"Of course."

"Why did they let them in?"

"Let them in? They invited them!"

"How much are you willing to tell me?"

"Depends on what you want to know."

"Is this going to get you into trouble?"

"I'm in enough trouble. Go ahead. You've got about three more minutes, by my watch."

Cecilia glanced down the hall. Monroe was nowhere in sight.

"Clark Jackson shot Raphael Abramowitz, didn't he?"

"That's right, from what I hear."

"It wasn't Lewis, then. Why was he shot?"

"Why do you think?"

"Because he was a Jew."

"He was a Jewish spy. He was going after Hamilton, and he had guns with him. So maybe you could say it was self-defense."

"Hamilton's not his real name. Who is he, really?"

"Someone the Jews would like to get their hands on and cart back to Israel for a show trial."

"A war criminal?"

"What's a war crime?" Bonnie countered. "Wars happen and people die. What difference does it make how they died? Are the Allied fliers who bombed Dresden war criminals? What about Harry Truman? He dropped a couple of A-bombs on women and children."

"What about the six million Jews the Nazis exterminated?"

"Don't start throwing those numbers at me! They didn't give a hang about the Jews any more than we gave a hang about the Vietnamese. Two million Vietnamese, there's a number for you. How many innocent children did we dump napalm on? Do you think anyone in America gives a hang about them? You bring those Vietnam vets before a war-crimes tribunal before you start talking to me about Jim Hamilton."

"Why do you want to defend him? After what he did to you?"

"If I've got the gene, I guess it was for my own good."

"He sterilized you without your consent. He's not a doctor, he's a sadist."

"Your words, not mine."

"So what's his real name?"

"Albert Gebhardt."

"And you're saying Raphael Abramowitz figured out his true identity? That's why he was stopped?"

"That's right. You want to know where the body's buried?"

"Whose—Abramowitz's? I thought Joe Doyle had him shipped back to New York."

"Ha! Not on your life. You heard about when me and Mike went up to the Olbrich Lode Mine and ran into Doyle and Monroe? Our timing was just a little off, or Mike would have seen Doyle taking Abramowitz's body out of the back of Monroe's truck."

"They dumped it in the flooded mine shaft," Cecilia said, feeling the color drain from her face.

"That's where they always dump them," Bonnie said. "That's where they dumped your friends."

"My friends?"

"I've told you too much already, I may as well let you in on it. On their way out of Haven, your friends met with a little accident. Their car went off the road and down the ravine."

"Tom and Jeremy? Why? What did they do to hurt anybody?"

"I don't know. I think someone got pissed off that they were taking pictures."

"I can't believe it. Are you telling me the truth?"

Bonnie nodded. "Sorry, Cecilia. You go dredge that mine shaft and you'll see I'm not kidding. Oh, time's up. Here comes Herb."

"You girls finished?" Monroe called, stomping down the hall in his boots, jangling his keys.

Bonnie looked anxiously toward him. "Yeah, we're done."

"Thanks," Cecilia said.

"It's been a pleasure, Cecilia. Nice knowing you."

Bonnie stuck her hand out through the bars.

Cecilia shook it firmly. "Are you going to be all right?"

"Of course I am." Bonnie smiled placidly. "Herb treats me nice, don't you, Herb?"

Monroe grunted. "Come on, Doc. Girl talk's over."

# Chapter 39

She stopped by the house and took the painting down. She jim-mied it out of the frame to see the signature again: *A. Geb-hardt—Nürnberg, 1936.* Mike was right; she wished she could tell him.

She wished she had never allowed Tom and Jeremy to come. Now it was her fault that they were dead—if Bonnie was to be believed. Mike had been concerned about them when he called from Boise. He must have seen some evidence of the accident on his way out of town.

She knew now she had to get out as soon as the roads opened. Haven was too dangerous a place for any outsider.

She tried the phone again, but it was still dead. She won-dered whether Jason and Ted were really trying to restore ser-vice or if that was just another lie. For all she knew, they might have knocked it out on purpose to prevent her from reaching the outside.

The Jackson place was quiet; they had not yet replaced the dogs. The automobile graveyard was hidden beneath huge drifts like burial mounds. As Cecilia had hoped, Clark's pickup was not in the driveway. She went up the path and knocked on the door.

"Lewis, open up. It's Cecilia Mak. I want to talk to you."

The bolt was thrown back, the chain undone, and Lewis opened the door. He looked gaunt and unhealthy, as if he had not been eating properly or getting enough sleep.

"Come in, hurry!" he said.

She stepped in, and he slammed the door shut behind her.

"Am I glad to see you!"

"Are you all right?"

"Do I look all right? Please, sit down."

They went into the living room, and Lewis shut off the TV. As he sat on the sofa, his pants leg rose up enough for her to see the blank ankle bracelet with the flashing red LED.

"That's your monitoring device?"

"If I leave the house, they'll know. They might as well have put me in leg cuffs. You've got to help me."

"I'll do what I can. You'll have to answer some questions for me first."

"I heard what happened. Is Mike all right?"

"I think he'll make it, but there's no guarantee."

"Cecilia, you have to get out of here and take me with you. You think that was an accident, what happened to Mike?"

"No, I don't. He knew too much, is that it?"

"Something like that."

"And that puts me in danger, too."

"They don't want to harm you, but if I were you, I'd get out while you can."

"How soon will the roads reopen?"

"Depends on how long they want to keep the state plows away. Maybe you can ask for a helicopter again."

"And take you with me."

"If you don't, I don't know what'll happen to me. Maybe another accident. They don't want me anymore. I don't fit in, and they know I never will. They want to get rid of me like they got rid of everyone else who ever disagreed with them. I'm just a scapegoat. I didn't have anything to do with throwing that brick through your window."

"Who was it, then. Your grandpa?"

"I heard it was the Marsh brothers."

"What about Raphael Abramowitz? That was Clark, wasn't it?"

"That's right. I had nothing to do with it."

"You were there. Why didn't you stop him?"

"You think I could have done anything?"

"Why should I trust you?"

"Please, you have to! You're my only hope! You don't know how happy I was when you and Mike came to Haven. I've been wanting to get out for a long time. But I'm afraid."

"Of what?"

"Afraid they'll find me. I need to get into a witness protection program or something. You have no idea."

"I'm beginning to. They're all Nazis, aren't they? The families from Germany? Including your grandpa?"

Lewis nodded. "I used to think of killing myself. I've got no future here. I'm of no use to them, and whatever's not useful they destroy. They killed my parents. Officially, another accident. They were driven off the Haven Road, into the river."

"Can you prove this?"

"There's no doubt in my mind. They wanted to leave Haven for good, and somehow somebody found out. I don't think they ever thought of going until I started getting older, and they were thinking of me more than themselves. My grandpa's always told me it was my fault, and I used to believe him. I don't blame myself anymore. But it makes me hate them. They've tried to 'reeducate' me, and I've pretended to go along, but they can tell. I'm gay—maybe you figured that out. I wouldn't be telling you all this if I didn't trust you."

"Bonnie told me Tom and Jeremy were run off the road, just like your parents."

"They haven't told me anything, but it wouldn't surprise me. Now you know why we have to get out. Anyone they see as a threat isn't going to be sticking around much longer."

"It's going to be hard," Cecilia said. If she got the chance to leave Haven, she would bring him along. "I'll think of something. Are you in any imminent danger?"

"I don't know. I think so."

"No wonder you look so haggard."

"Not very becoming, is it?" He laughed sadly.

"Are there any other people in Haven who can help?"

Lewis shook his head. "I wouldn't trust anyone. The people here, they're almost like a religious cult. Most of them didn't even come over from Germany, but they're all believers."

"Do they have a choice?"

"It's hard to be brave. Easier to follow orders and not ask questions. Look at me. I've never done anything to fight them."

"Maybe you're ready now."

"There's nothing we can do except go and hope that they never find us. I'm scared, Cecilia."

"I know. Me too. Tell me about Lizzie Polk."

Lewis hid his face in his hands and began to cry. "I should have stopped them. Grandpa took my whistle away from me and let them loose. I had no idea what he was going to do. He said he was acting on orders. Oh, poor Lizzie!"

"Is it because she talked to me?"

"I guess so. You were finding out too many things before they were ready for you to know."

"You mean they were going to tell us eventually?"

"Not Mike. They never wanted him to know anything. They were going to wait until they could get him out of the way."

"Why didn't you tell us?"

"I was too afraid. It doesn't make any difference anymore. Mike almost died, and it's my fault, and I'm next on the list."

"What do they want with me?"

"It's because you're perfect."

"Hardly."

"I mean genetically."

"How would they know?"

"Beats me. That's what I heard. Hamilton was telling people you were a perfect match."

"Perfect match for what?"

"For Tyler. You're supposed to have his children."

Cecilia tried to think if there was any way Hamilton could have obtained a sample of her blood, but it was impossible. The only thing she could think of was the last time she had given blood at the American Red Cross, but that was over a year ago, back in Seattle, and it was inconceivable that any of it could have found its way to Hamilton. There had to be another answer.

"No chance of that. I've still got Mike, and they can't force me to have anyone's children."

"Do you see why you've got to get out?"

"It isn't going to be easy, Lewis."

"I'm willing to try if you are."

"Now that sounds very brave. I'll work on it. You just sit tight for now. Don't do anything foolish. We may have to wait for the roads to open."

"What about a helicopter?"

"It's not that simple. If they land and see that it's not an emergency, they won't take us. They didn't have room for me when Mike came, anyway. And they're not going to believe any story about Nazis."

"You'd better go before Grandpa gets back."

"Okay." Cecilia stood and gave him a hug. "You be good. Stay on Grandpa's good side. Get some rest. Eat something."

"What are you going to do?"

"The only thing I can do. Play along. I'm supposed to have tea up at the Tyler place today."

"Be careful," he said, opening the door and looking out. There was no sign of Clark's pickup. "They'll try to trick you."

"We'll see who tricks whom."

# Chapter 40

The sun came out after lunch, and the temperature rose enough for the snow to begin melting. Outside her office window, the snow was heaped all around, in drifts left by the wind and in gigantic, dirty piles where the trucks with plows had pushed it. Along the walks, where the snow had been cleared, running water trickled, shimmering in the sunlight. Flatiron was caked in white, looking more than ever like the Bavarian Alps.

The phones were still out, and all Cecilia could think of was Mike. She should have forced her way onto the helicopter, should have been there for him.

At a quarter to two, the phone rang. Fremont answered it in a split second.

"Yes," Fremont said, solemn. "Yes, I'll get her. Cecilia! It's for you. Saint Luke's in Boise."

She picked it up. "Dr. Mak here."

"Hello." The man cleared his throat. "Dr. Mak?"

"Speaking."

"This is Dr. Higgins calling from Saint Luke's."

"How is my husband?" she asked, trying to recall if she had ever spoken to a Dr. Higgins there. She had never heard of him.

"I'm afraid I have some bad news."

"Wait," she said. "Who did you say you were?"

"Dr. Higgins," he repeated.

"What happened to Dr. Saronica?"

"I'm the ranking physician on duty, Mrs. Mak."

"It's Dr. Mak," she said testily. "Dr. Saronica was Mike's attending surgeon."

"Dr. Saronica works a different shift," Higgins said, though he seemed to have trouble pronouncing the name. "Really, Dr. Mak, you're making this more difficult. We've been trying to reach you for some time."

"Yes, I'm sorry. Our phones have been down."

"I'm afraid your husband didn't pull through."

"Excuse me?"

"Michael Mak is your husband, is he not? We tried everything we could, but in the end there was nothing more we could do. I'm sorry, Dr. Mak. Truly I am."

Cecilia had no response. She didn't believe him. He did not have the manner of a physician conveying bad news. It was a trick.

"If you'd like me to have Dr. Saronica call you, I'd be more than happy to page him."

"Yes," she said. "Please do. Please have him call me."

"Would you like to make any arrangements at this time?"

"Arrangements?"

"For the body."

All she could think was that she didn't want Joe Doyle's grubby hands on him. Mike's parents would want to handle this, wouldn't they? Jesus Christ.

"Who do I talk to about that?"

"You can talk to me."

"I can't discuss it right now. Tell me the name of the morgue attendant, and I'll contact them myself."

"I'm afraid I don't have that name handy."

"Have you got the number of the hospital morgue? Or maybe you could transfer me."

"Well, I can try to transfer you, but I'm always cutting people off when I do this. Hang on."

She heard a series of clicks, and a moment later the dial tone returned.

"Goddammit!" she said, slamming the phone down.

"Cecilia, are you all right?" Fremont came rushing in.

"Sorry, Janice, I want to be left alone for a minute."

Fremont, cowed, closed the door silently.

Cecilia thumbed Mike's address book for his parents' phone number and was halfway through the number before she hung up.

She did not trust that the phone call was genuine. Mike could not possibly be dead. If he were, she would know it deep inside. The supposed Dr. Higgins's manner had been highly unprofessional, and why hadn't it been Dr. Saronica?

The dial tone was still there. She phoned the reception desk at St. Luke's.

"Could I speak to Dr. Saronica, please?"

"One moment," said the singsong voice.

While she hung there listening to a Muzak version of "Do You Know the Way to San Jose?" she was sure that it was all a part of the scheme. They had messed with the phones and called her themselves, probably from right here in Haven. It was all a ruse. They wanted to beat her down.

"Hello?" came a woman's voice.

"Is this Dr. Saronica's office?"

"This is his answering service. He's not available at the moment. Would you like to leave a message for the doctor?"

Cecilia left her name and phone number and had the message flagged as urgent. "How soon do you think he'll call back?"

"I'm afraid I can't answer that, ma'am," said the voice.

"Thanks. Bye."

She wondered if she had really gotten through to Boise at all or if this call had ended up somewhere in Haven, with fake Muzak and all the trimmings.

While she still had the dial tone, she had to hurry and make her other calls. She filed through her desk to find the list she had come up with yesterday.

*Mike's parents*—no, not yet. She couldn't talk to them without knowing his condition.

*Jeremy (?)* It was worth a try. Mike's hints seemed to suggest he thought something had happened to them, but what if Bonnie was lying? She was hardly trustworthy. Cecilia managed to get through, but it was their answering machine that picked up. "Hello. This is the party to whom you are speaking. We can't come to the phone right now. Tom's all tied up, and I'm not kidding. Leave a message after the muffled scream. *Ciao.*"

"Jeremy, it's Cecilia. It's Wednesday, a little after two. If you're back or checking your messages, please call me back as soon as you get this. Something's happened to Mike, and I've been worried about you guys. I have to talk. It's urgent."

When she hung up, she still had the dial tone.

*Saul J. Abramowitz.* Hastily, she punched the number and waited for the rings to be picked up. If Dr. Saronica or Jeremy called back, they would appear on line two and she could still talk to them.

"Hello, you've reached the Abramowitz household. Ruth and I can't take your call right now. Please leave a message, and we'll get back to you. Thank you."

After the beep, Cecilia left her name and number and said, "You don't know me, Mr. Abramowitz, but I think you spoke to my husband. It's urgent that I get in touch with you. Please call me back as soon as you get this message. You can call collect. It has to do with a Raphael Abramowitz, who may be a relation of yours. It's very important."

At this point, she was cut off by another beep, and the line went dead. She hoped it was only the Abramowitzes' machine.

*Tawanda Neebli.*

"Neebli," she answered.

"Tawanda? Cecilia Mak."

"Cecilia? Hey, girl, how's married life?"

"Could be better. Mike's in the hospital."

"You taking good care of him?"

"Not here, he's in Boise. He was in an accident."

"Is he all right?"

"Hard to say." Cecilia hedged her bets. "He's in critical condition, last they told me."

"Hey, I'm sorry. Tell me where I can send some flowers."

"It's Saint Luke's, in Boise. I gave him your message the other day. Did he ever get back to you?"

"Yes, he did. I've got something for him."

"Can you give it to me?"

"Sure, Cee. Let me find it here. It's somewhere under this pile of crap. Here we go. Henry Jameson Olbrich. This is some good stuff. You want me to fax it to you?"

"Yeah, but can you read it to me first?"

"It's pages of stuff, but I can give you the gist."

"Please."

"You'll have to thank Mike for me. This was a great tip. This guy Olbrich, I looked him up."

"Haven's founder."

"Not that one. This is the son. Olbrich the Second. Died in nineteen forty-eight. Seems he was heavily involved in the German-American Bund."

"Sort of a pro-Nazi group?"

"Sort of! Looks like he helped bankroll them, at least for a while. There was going to be a congressional investigation, but as far as I can tell it got hushed up and never materialized. Before we got in the war, he made speeches and lobbied Congress to try to keep us out. Real 'America First' stuff. He also went to Germany as late as nineteen forty and praised the way the Nazis were running the country."

"Where'd you find this?"

"He wrote a book. Looks like it was cobbled together from his speeches. *The Real Germany*. Goes on and on about how the Nazis rebuilt everything and revitalized the economy, how Hitler had restored the Germans' dignity after Versailles, all the usual apologies. Really a remarkable book. Sick but remarkable."

"Mike put you onto this?"

"He just gave me the name. Is he doing a piece on this?"

"I don't know. If you find anything you want to use, I'd say publish it."

"I'll check with Mike first," Tawanda said.

"Mike might be on the mend for a while. Tawanda, I'd better tell you what's going on here. There was a group of Germans who immigrated to Haven in the fifties, and one of them was an Albert Gebhardt, you got that?"

"Albert Gebhardt? Is that a *P* or a *B* in Gebhardt?"

"*B* as in boy. Apparently some sort of war criminal. I think he was living here under the name of James Hamilton. He was the doctor I replaced. He just retired to Argentina. A town called San Carlos de Bariloche. You got that?"

Cecilia looked down. The light for line two was flashing.

"Got it, but Cecilia—"

"Tawanda? Can I put you on hold a minute? I have another call."

"I'll wait," Tawanda said.

Cecilia pressed the button. "Dr. Mak," she said, praying it was Dr. Saronica.

"Dr. Mak. Saul Abramowitz. I'm at work. My wife told me you called our home."

"Yes, Mr. Abramowitz, thanks for calling back, I wanted—"

"I've been trying to get through to someone in Haven for days now. Ever since your husband called, we haven't had a wink of sleep. Is this some kind of prank? What the hell is this about Raphael? Your husband told me he's dead."

"You mean no one ever spoke to you? The coroner was supposed to—"

"I've been trying the coroner's office, the sheriff's office, your office, everybody. I called the state police, and they said it wasn't their business. Will somebody please tell me what the hell this is about?"

"Mr. Abramowitz, I'm sorry. We had a storm here, and the phones have been out. Was Raphael your son?"

"Raphael *is* my son. What was he doing in Idaho? Your husband said something about a hunting accident."

"There was nothing we could do. He was shot in the chest."

"When did this happen?"

"About a month ago. The coroner told me he had spoken with the family and shipped the body back to New York."

"That's news to me. Listen, until I see my son's body, I'm not believing anything, all right? I haven't spoken to Raphael for a year, and I didn't have any idea why he would be in Idaho. But your husband asked me something very peculiar. He asked me if Raphael had been interested in tracking down Nazis."

"Yes?"

"The truth is, it was something of an obsession for him. Not hard to see why, but what I mean is, he carried it to an extreme. We always thought it was a little unhealthy. He saw Nazis everywhere, and he was sure they were out to get him. Ever since he was fifteen. It distracted him from everything else. He dropped out of college. He was always clipping things from newspapers—I'd look at them, and they meant nothing. He'd say the president was a Nazi or that the pope was a Nazi. He was always a little unbalanced. The last I heard, he had gone to the Simon Wiesenthal Center in Los Angeles and offered his services. They turned him down. They didn't really take him seriously, and they thought he had a violent personality. Someone from the center called me and suggested I get him some professional help. By then, I'd lost track of him, and I haven't heard from him since. Now I get this call from your husband, and—"

"Mr. Abramowitz," Cecilia said, calmly, "does the name Gebhardt mean anything to you?"

"Which one? Karl or Albert?"

"Albert, I guess. All I have is the initial *A*. He was a doctor, if that helps any."

"They were both doctors."

"Nazis?"

"Of course. Karl Gebhardt was Himmler's personal physician. Albert Gebhardt is better known as the Devil of Dachau."

"Mr. Abramowitz? I suggest you contact the FBI about what happened to your son."

"Hello? Are you still there?"

"I'm still here, Mr. Abramowitz."

"I can't hear you. Is anyone there? Hello?"

"I can hear you just fine. Mr. Abramowitz?"

"Hello? Tell me this is just a joke! Dr. Mak? Hello? Is anybody there? Hello!"

The line suddenly fell dead. Both lights on Cecilia's phone went completely out. She tried pressing line one, but it was dead. Tawanda was gone, too. More important, Dr. Saronica had not yet called back. Now he would never get through.

Cecilia's window of opportunity had closed.

# Chapter 41

Cecilia tried to imagine how any doctor could ever look at a patient as anything less than human. The knowledge of who Jim Hamilton was and what he had done made every examining room feel like a torture chamber. When she held an instrument in her hands, she could not help but think of how it could be misused. She wondered if any of the Nazi doctors had been women.

Having no more appointments, Cecilia decided to pay another visit at the courthouse. Tyler was out and about. Herb Monroe was seated at his desk, scanning the radio, which seemed to emit only static.

"I've come for my husband's personal effects," Cecilia said. "Joe Doyle says they're no longer of any evidentiary value since Bonnie's confessed, and he doesn't see any reason why I can't have them signed over."

"Is that right?" Monroe said. "I'll have to radio Frank. Why don't you have a seat?"

Monroe got up, forgoing his own radio, and went back to the privacy of Tyler's enclosed office.

"Okay," Monroe said, jangling his keys. "Follow me."

They went down a hallway, to a door with the words PROPERTY ROOM painted in an arc across the frosted glass. He unlocked the bolt and the knob and went in, flicking on the lights. He had Cecilia stand at the chest-high counter while he went in back among the rows upon rows of shelves. She wondered exactly why this room contained so much unclaimed property. Perhaps it had something to do with all the bodies in the flooded mine shaft.

Monroe returned a few minutes later with several brown paper bags that were stapled and taped shut, marked EVIDENCE. He set them in a row along the counter and passed Cecilia a sheet on a clipboard.

"You just sign here," he said, indicating.

"Are you sure this is everything?"

"That's it. Need any help carrying all these out to your truck?"

"Yes, Herb, that would be nice," she said with a forced smile. "Thank you."

"My pleasure. Any word of your husband?"

She spread newspaper over the table in the breakfast nook and methodically opened the paper bags to remove Mike's effects. The sight of all the blood made her sick. It had dried an oxidized, rusty color all over his shirt, underwear, socks, jeans, and the lining of his leather jacket. A manila envelope contained his wallet, with driver's license, cash, credit cards, and Cecilia's photo; it did not appear to have been rifled through, but perhaps Tyler had been careful. His car keys and pocket change were in another envelope. There was nothing else.

Cecilia stared at the items, thinking there must be something she was missing. Perhaps Tyler had taken it.

She checked the pockets of his jacket and found an unopened pocket pack of Kleenex.

She went through the rest of the pockets. Reaching into the back pocket of his jeans, she was surprised to find some pieces of paper, folded into fourths.

Tyler could not have overlooked them, or could he?

The white pages were spotted with blood and stuck together. She opened them carefully.

The first was a photocopy of an old newspaper photo of Dr. Franklin Tyler and his wife, Anna. Anna had to be the young Widow. She was beautiful, a blond goddess.

The second page was something quite different: a group shot of several uniformed Nazis. The caption identified them as SS doctors and recited some of their crimes. One of them was Capt. Albert Gebhardt, and he stood alongside a Capt. Ernst von Meissner. At once she saw the resemblance between von Meissner and Doctor Tyler; she already knew who Gebhardt was and recognized something of Jim Hamilton's manner in the face.

She went back to the photo of Dr. Tyler and his wife. She continued to stare at it for some time, wondering why it bothered her so.

# Chapter 42

Since Maddie Gahagan's vanity was out of commission, Cecilia checked herself before the mirror over the pedestal sink.

At the vanity table, she removed the clip from Mike's nine-millimeter and methodically filled it with hollow-point bullets from the box. She slid the clip firmly home into the grip and pulled back the hammer to ensure a round was at the ready. She unlocked the safety catch and placed the pistol in her purse.

She was ready for tea.

As she crossed the bridge over the Little Lost, she saw that it was running. It had not frozen during the storm but had only washed the snow down. The snow had accumulated only along the banks. The black boulders and smooth stones glistened wetly.

The local volunteer crews had plowed the Haven Road only as far as the turnoff to the Tylers'. Beyond that was a wall of snow that sloped up to meet the angle of the hill. The remaining forty miles of the Haven Road would be a job beyond the capacity of the townies' small trucks. It would not likely melt away, either, until the return of spring. Whatever evidence there might be of Tom and Jeremy's accident was buried for the duration.

Cecilia turned onto the Tylers' private drive, a narrow, paved road with hairpin switchbacks that zigzagged steeply up the hill. The town lay far below, the whitewashed steeple of the Old Haven Church in the distance. Flatiron stood against the sky.

The house stood at the back of a vast, snowy clearing. Snow draped the gables and eaves. Huge drifts pushed against the walls of granite flagstone. Pole lamps resembling ancient gaslights stood along the snowblown walk.

Cecilia parked the ambulance next to Tyler's sheriff's truck and stepped out. To the side of the house stood a separate, three-car garage. The Widow's Mercedes would be there, shielded from the elements.

"Cecilia!"

Tyler came down from the front stoop to meet her, offering his arm. It was the first time she had seen him out of uniform. He was wearing a dark jacket, white shirt, narrow black tie, and noxious aftershave.

"Watch the ice," he said. It had been scattered with rock salt, turning some soft, the rest to watery brine.

"Thanks." She took his arm. "I'm not used to pumps."

"That makes two of us." He blushed at his non sequitur. "I mean, I feel awkward out of my boots."

"Herb minding the store?"

"I sure hope so. Up we go." He helped her onto the stoop.

Tyler opened the great wooden doors and motioned her in.

"Let me take your coat."

She allowed it to slip from her shoulders into his arms. He reached for her purse, but she pulled back.

"I'd rather hang on to it, if you don't mind."

Tyler shrugged, turning to hang her coat in the closet. He shook his head to himself.

Cecilia followed the Persian rug a few steps to stand under the chandelier in the foyer. The rug stretched far down the hall, branching off to ascend a grand, curved staircase. Perched upon wooden pedestals on either side of the stairs were two snub-nosed creatures that looked like a cross between a lion and a pug. The woodwork was darkly stained and finely detailed. The wallpaper was an off-white with an intricate, pale green botanical print.

"Gran'll be down in a minute," Tyler said, leading her into the large living space. "Have a seat."

Cecilia knew nothing of antiques, but the room seemed filled with fine pieces, from the overstuffed sofas and chairs to the tables and bookcases, the bronze figurines and gilded bric-a-brac. The painting above the fireplace, she was certain, was of the dead Dr. Tyler: a white-haired gentleman with dark mustache and sallow face, done in a bland, almost naïve style. She wandered over to it and checked out the signature: *J. Hamilton, Haven, '79.*

"Dear old granddad?" she asked.

"Sourpuss, isn't he?"

"Can't say I like Hamilton's style," she said.

"I wouldn't call him passionate."

She found an old wind-up gramophone in the corner by the bookcases and opened the lid. An old 78 lay on the turntable: Bing Crosby. She leafed through the heavy platters in their brittle brown-paper sheaths, glancing at the artists: "Paul Whiteman and His Orchestra," "Arturo Toscanini and the NBC Orchestra," "Rudy Vallee and His Connecticut Yankees," Enrico Caruso, "Guy Lombardo and His Royal Canadians," Elisabeth Schwarzkopf, Herta von Möllendorff . . .

"I'm not sure if that thing still works," said Tyler. "Come on, have a seat. Relax."

She took a comfortable-looking chair, and he sat opposite on the edge of the plush sofa.

"Sorry, my nerves are rattled."

"No word on Mike?"

"Phones are still out."

"Jason and Ted thought they'd fixed the problem, but there must be another line down outside of town somewhere. They're doing what they can."

"What about the roads?"

"Highway department says they can't start until Monday."

She didn't believe it for a second. "That's a long time. Does this happen all the time?"

"Only the major storms. Couple times a year, that's all. Try to get your mind off it, Cecilia. There's nothing you can do. Mike's in good hands. I mean, isn't he?"

Cecilia heard the steady creaking of the stairs and looked up to see a woman in a black gown descending.

"Does she need any help?" Cecilia asked.

Tyler laughed. "Oh, no, she's fit as a fiddle."

The pale arm barely seemed to clutch the railing, the sharp fingers gracing it lightly with each step. The gown was slit as far as the knee, revealing slim legs clad in dark hose.

"Our guest has arrived?" came the Widow's voice.

"She's right here." Tyler stood and approached the stairs.

Cecilia followed. "Hello, Mrs. Tyler."

"Please call me Anna." Her face was smiling and radiant, skin stretched taut over her cheekbones, silvery hair neatly curled and somewhat short. It was the first Cecilia had seen her without a veil, and she was surprised at the relative youthfulness of her features. Perhaps Jim Hamilton knew a talented plastic surgeon.

The Widow reached out with both arms and embraced Cecilia.

"My poor Cecilia. I'm so sorry about this tragedy."

"It's not a tragedy yet," said Tyler, taking the words out of Cecilia's mouth. "We haven't had word on Mike. She never got any phone call. He could still pull through."

The Widow threw Tyler a glance. "I'm sure he will." She released Cecilia, though now she grasped her hands. "You look beautiful, my girl."

"I don't feel it."

There was something about the Widow's face, something in the crystal-blue eyes, something strange and at once familiar.

"Frank can take your purse. Frank—"

"He offered. I'd rather keep it."

"Don't be silly."

"Gran," Tyler said.

"Oh, very well. I cannot tell you how I've been looking forward to this!"

The tea was served them by what the Widow referred to as "the girls from the village." Along with the tea came a chocolate torte and a strudel. Cecilia had taken a slice of the torte but had not touched it.

"Is anything wrong, my dear? You're not eating."

"I don't have much appetite." Cecilia took the excuse to lay down her fork and nudge the plate forward.

"Would you care for more tea?" the Widow offered in a singsong, laughing sort of voice. It was a finishing-school voice of a sort that had fallen out of fashion after the war. Cecilia had only heard it in certain Hollywood movies of the 1930s.

"Thanks," Cecilia said.

"I must say it's grand," said the Widow, "to have such youth and beauty in this musty old house again."

"You've got Frank, haven't you?"

Tyler blushed, squirming in his seat. He looked like he wanted to tear off his tie and get some air.

"He is young and beautiful, isn't he? But so seldom *here*. I've never seen him looking so smart. Doesn't that jacket hang nicely on him?"

"Gran," Tyler said.

"Don't be embarrassed. In my day, women weren't allowed to admire a man openly. I think I like the way the world has changed. Are you feeling outnumbered, darling?"

Tyler squirmed but kept his mouth shut.

"What happened to the rest of the family?" Cecilia asked, hoping to extricate Tyler from this. "If I'm not prying."

"Flew the coop. Haven was too small for them. They had other things to do, out in the world. I suppose I'm too old and have too many memories. . . . We like it here just fine, don't we, Frank? Though the house is too big. I wouldn't mind a half-dozen great-grandkids running around at my feet!"

"I'm not crazy about kids," Cecilia said.

"I was like you once," the Widow said, undaunted. "Though I was a tad younger. I had my man and wanted nothing else. But even the most devoted husband can't give a woman everything. You aren't complete until you've had children."

"But no matter what you do, you don't have any control over how they're going to turn out."

"When did you and Mike marry, just a few months ago? You must realize the *intensity* of a new marriage is bound to wear off. Mike has other interests, and you have your work. In a couple of years, you'll come around. Frank's grandfather had his research, and then came the war. Terribly disruptive. Still, we managed to squeeze in the time for children. I don't know what I would have done without them—gone quietly mad, I suspect. After the war, my husband had more time for all of us, as a family. There's nothing quite like a family of your own. You'll see, in time."

The young women came in with a fresh pot of tea.

"Some couples would rather devote their lives to each other," Cecilia said.

"Every married couple has a responsibility to the future."

"I'd say they have a greater responsibility *not* to have any children. We're approaching what, six billion people?" Cecilia glanced at Tyler as if deferring to his knowledge.

Tyler shrugged.

"A bleeding heart can be an admirable trait," the Widow said. "But the fact is, none of the right people are having children. If they do get pregnant, they go off and get an abortion. Do you realize how the birth rate in this country has declined? All the children are being born in Asia, Africa, the Middle East. What do you think's going to happen as those places get even more crowded? They're all going to want to come here!"

Tyler looked from his grandmother to Cecilia, like a spectator at a tennis match. He gulped down his tea and poured himself another cup.

"It can't be stopped," Cecilia said. "I think we should do all we can to welcome them and harness their talents."

"What about our jobs?" Tyler asked. "Look at what's happened in Germany, all those Turks."

"The Turks were there twenty years ago because Germany imported them. They needed the labor. Suddenly you've got all these East German unemployed. What are you going to do, kick the Turks out? It's their home now."

"Cecilia, you're being unrealistic," the Widow said.

"Not everybody wants to come to America. No one wants to leave their homeland unless they have to. Look at you."

"Me?" the Widow asked. "What about me?"

"You had to leave Germany, didn't you?"

"It was hardly my homeland. I was born right here, in this house. I'm as American as you."

"I thought . . . didn't you come here with your husband?"

"Yes, and my husband was German, as I gather you've figured out. We stayed for a while there, then came here. My maiden name was Olbrich. Henry Jameson Olbrich was my grandfather. How else do you think I came by this property?"

"I thought . . . didn't you come here after the war?"

"That's right."

"You married Dr. Tyler before the war, in Germany?"

"Also correct."

"Only his name was Ernst von Meissner, wasn't it?"

The three of them fell silent as the young women came in from the kitchen with additional slices of torte and strudel.

"Ah!" the Widow said. "Cecilia, perhaps you would care for strudel rather than the torte?"

"I'm not hungry."

"Suit yourself. I believe I'll have another slice of torte, and Frank I'm sure will have one more of the strudel. I had it made specially."

Once the servers had returned to the kitchen, Cecilia went on: "Jim Hamilton was really Albert Gebhardt. He and your husband were captains together in the SS."

"Yes, my dear," the Widow sighed. "That is quite right. What of it?"

# Chapter 43

"What proof do you have—do they have—that my husband, an honorable man, committed any of these so-called crimes against humanity? Are you willing to believe everything you read? I thought you were of a keener intelligence, Cecilia."

"You're not going to deny the Holocaust."

"What is there to deny? Many people died on both sides, so what's so special about these Jews? Germany was being strangled and had not the resources to feed its prisoners."

"They didn't die of famine, Anna; they were exterminated. Your husband conducted medical experiments. . . ."

The Widow pounded her fist against the table. The dinnerware clinked.

"It's a fact, Anna."

"Because one person said so? If you were a prisoner, held against your will, do you think you would tell the truth about your captors? How much credibility do any of these witnesses have? Do you think a Jew would ever have a kind word for a Nazi?"

"Jim Hamilton was the Devil of Dachau."

"He was—is—one of the kindest, gentlest men I've ever known, and no butcher."

"Then why did he run?"

"To escape persecution. No different from the Pilgrims and the Puritans. He came to America so he could be free."

"By way of Argentina," Cecilia said. "It wasn't hard for a Nazi to get an Argentinian passport. Once there, he and all the rest of you got new identities, fully documented, and emigrated a few years later to America. How am I doing so far?"

"You skipped a few steps, but that's largely accurate."

"You and your husband came first. You were the ones with the money. You had the Olbrich fortune behind you, and maybe von Meissner had some money of his own. You smuggled it out somehow, or you had it all in Swiss bank accounts. The others came over later. I suspect they paid you. The Baron von Möllendorff, for example. Hank Harrison doesn't look like he's got much left. And I doubt Herta was a pauper, either. Now she delivers your mail. I wonder how she likes it."

"You can ask her, obviously. Herta could have spent the war singing for the Met in New York—they extended an invitation—but I'm afraid she was quite devoted to the cause. You should have heard her sing in *Parsifal* in Berlin. Really gave it her all. Hitler was quite overcome and invited her up to the Berghof for a command performance for him and his staff. You should ask her about it. Fascinating story."

"Why are you all hiding out here in Haven?"

"Jim Hamilton and my husband were the only ones 'hiding out,' as you put it. They were the only ones who stood accused of anything, and if we'd blown their cover they would have been carted off to Israel like poor Eichmann. All we ever wanted was a new life that we could live out in peace, without being badgered about memories of something that happened fifty years ago and was quite beyond our control."

"You were all a part of it."

"All of us? Even Frank here?"

Tyler smiled.

"You and the other old ones, the real Nazis."

"So you're quite certain we were all Nazis? Well, I won't deny it."

The Widow drew in a deep breath. She rang the bell, and the servers came in and cleared the tea set and dessert plates.

The Widow and Tyler embarked on a bottle of brandy, and they offered some to Cecilia, but she declined. The air in the front room was stifling, and her skin was prickly all over. She wanted to get out but could not leave until she had learned all the Widow was willing to tell her.

"Why was Raphael Abramowitz killed?" she asked from the comfort of the sofa, staring up at the portrait of Dr. Tyler. "And Lizzie and Dottie. And my friends."

"What friends?" the Widow said. She sat at the other end of the sofa from Cecilia, nursing her snifter. In the brighter light of the living room, her pale face was aglow. "I don't have any idea what you're talking about."

"Me neither," Tyler said, slouched in an overstuffed armchair, downing brandy in large gulps. "What's this about your friends? I thought they went home."

"I thought so, too. I think they met with one of your accidents. I think you killed them."

"Me?"

"Maybe the Marshes, maybe Herb Monroe, maybe someone else. I know something happened to them. Why don't you tell me? I thought you didn't want any secrets between us."

"Why would anyone want to harm them?" the Widow said.

"I don't know. Because Jeremy's Jewish? Because they're

gay? I don't think so. I think it's because Jeremy was taking pictures of all those people at Jubilee Days."

"That's absurd."

"What do you think I might find if I were to go scuba diving in the flooded mine shaft up at the Olbrich Lode Mine?"

Tyler's face flushed the color of a rich burgundy.

"You must have something you're trying to protect."

"Such as?"

"I doubt you've saved Hitler's brain or anything like that."

The Widow laughed. "If we had, I assure you it would be quite useless with that gaping bullet wound ripping through it. The coward's way out—but then Hitler was a great bungler. No one *I* know is trying to clone the Führer like some Jurassic dinosaur. It wouldn't do anyone a bit of good if they did. Adolf Hitler was quite the worst thing that ever happened to National Socialism, if you ask me."

"Don't get her started on Hitler." Tyler stared into his glass.

"Hitler ruined Germany. He built up the thousand-year Reich and then tore it down with his bare hands. If he hadn't shot himself, he would have been strung up by his balls like Mussolini—by the German people. He betrayed us. He betrayed the party. I don't believe I shall ever forgive him."

"Herta thinks Gran's too harsh," Tyler said.

"Well, it's true *I* never got invited to the Berghof, but I don't believe it would have altered my estimation of the man. He didn't know when to stop and consolidate our gains. He surrounded himself with all those yes-men—first Hess, then Bormann. Ugh! Anyone who knew him at the end will tell you he never knew when to shut up. But of course, Herta adored the attention."

"He had all her recordings," Tyler put in. "Big fan."

"It was the big blond wig," the Widow said. "He made her wear one, you know, at the Berghof."

"You're jealous," Cecilia said.

Tyler snorted, pouring himself more brandy.

"Oh, I already hated him by then. It was clear for a long time we would never win the war. He could have held on to Austria, Czechoslovakia, Alsace-Lorraine, and waited a few more years for Poland. No one would have done a thing. If he'd kept off France and aimed for Russia, you wouldn't have heard a peep out of Britain, and America would have only bothered with the Japanese. The Third Reich would still be standing today, and we would have had none of this intervening nonsense."

"You mean the Cold War?" Cecilia said.

"Naturally. Fifty years from the invasion of Poland for Germany to be put right again. Fifty years down the toilet. We're having to start from scratch."

"Start what?"

"Ah!" The Widow sipped her drink, smiling warmly at Tyler. "See, Frank, she's not interested in Herta's adventures. She wants to get right down to cases. That's our girl."

Tyler nodded wearily, eyes half-closed.

"When I first met Hamilton," Cecilia said, "he kept crowing about the new millennium."

"Yes, the millennium," the Widow said. "It's practically here. Nothing I do or say is going to change that."

"It seemed to hold some special significance for him."

"It's going to be quite a different world, that's for certain. What the cold war kept at bay is springing back, and there's no longer any resistance. Look at what happened in Yugoslavia. Biggest land grab since the war, more concentration camps, wholesale slaughter of the Muslims. Ethnic cleansing. *Völkermord*. No one lifted a finger against Serbia. Serbia! Are you going to tell me that the combined power of NATO couldn't have crushed them? Of course they could have, but they didn't want to! Nobody gave a damn any more than they did when Chamberlain signed over the Sudetenland. The Serbians *knew*. They knew they could get away with whatever they liked, because no one in the world had the will to fight them. Hitler had the same foresight when he engineered Munich."

"So nationalism is back and there's nothing to keep it in check?"

"Absolutely. Europe is uniting at the same time they're jettisoning their socialist policies. Newt Gingrich is doing a superb job undoing the New Deal. Something has to take its place."

"You really think America's headed in that direction?"

"The liberals are done for. They're throwing in the towel. The world is changing, and one must embrace it to survive. The next century won't have much room for rebels."

"I can't stop believing what I believe."

"Which is what? House the homeless? Save the animals? Maintain the welfare state? Give handouts to immigrants? Sounds like communism to me, Cecilia. We've seen what that does to people. They have no incentive to work, no incentive to live. The State gives them just enough to get along, and they become slaves with no will of their own. Is that what you want?"

"I'm no Communist," Cecilia said. "Still, the Russians were better off under Gorbachev."

"Things are changing there, too," the Widow said. "Our way."

"You like Zhirinovsky?"

"He's a little flaky. There are others."

"You like seeing Russian synagogues burn?"

"This was another fault of Hitler's. He became too distracted with the Jewish problem. It was a small part of the overall plan, and they could have been dealt with in time. If he had moved more slowly and concentrated on the east, he could have held on to all that territory. Afterward would have been the time to deal with the Jews. It was unwise to try to do everything at once."

"You really are sorry it didn't come to pass, aren't you?"

"It was a glorious time. It's too late to save Germany now. It's not too late for America."

"You want the neo-Nazis to take over?"

"Oh, no, not the way you're thinking. To you, a neo-Nazi is some cartoon character in a uniform with a swastika armband, marching around saying, 'Sieg heil!' and giving the salute. You imagine some armed insurrection, a putsch. No such thing could possibly happen here, and you know it. What you don't realize is that we've already practically taken over. You can't see it, that's all. Stealth tactics, that's the key. People sympathetic to the cause are being elected all over America: school boards, state legislatures, the Congress, everywhere."

"Closet Nazis?"

"I'd say we have only a few of those. The rest—and their numbers are great—aren't likely to think of themselves as Nazis but as American patriots. We all stand for the same thing. That's what's so exciting! We have all these disparate groups coming together—the Christian Coalition, the conservatives in Congress, the citizen militias, the anti-abortion activists, the anti-immigrationists, the states rights movement, the Pat Buchanan crowd, Rush Limbaugh's listeners—together, they make up a widespread nationalist movement. The fact that there's no overall name for it is irrelevant."

"Fascism," Cecilia said.

"You can cry wolf all you want. Not a soul will listen. They're laying the groundwork, creating a new national consciousness, making it safe for a new kind of leader to step on the scene and show America its destiny."

"You have someone in mind?"

"Politicians are whores; if you pay them enough money, they'll do whatever you like. It would have been imprudent of us to place all our eggs in one basket, so we've had to spread the wealth among a number of lackeys."

"Why won't they just take the money and run?"

"Power and fear. Power is not only corruptive, it's addictive. And we can threaten to take their power away. If that doesn't work, there's always fear. What happened to Huey Long and John F. Kennedy can always happen again, especially to a politician who tries to stray from the agreed-on course."

"I'm sure of that, after all the murders I've seen here. And attempted murder, in the case of my husband."

"Now just a damn minute," Tyler said.

The Widow sat up and held up her hand, silencing him. "We had nothing to do with Mike's accident."

"It was no accident," Cecilia said. "You know that."

"Whatever it was, Bonnie acted quite on her own, I assure you. We warned her against doing anything about Mike."

"Why would anything have to be done about him?"

"We had hoped that we could reason with him, as we are with you. We don't mean you any harm. We want you on our side."

"How much are you willing to offer?" she said cynically.

"It's not really a matter of money, though of course you could live quite well if you chose. I think you'd need more reason than that, though."

"Fear?"

"Please, Cecilia, don't be vulgar. I mean to change your thinking. You have to think of your own survival. The smart person will desert the weak and go over to the strong. The smartest generals throughout history have done this. Alcibiades, Josephus—"

"How are you going to convince me? All I see is a big house and a town full of misguided people, some of whom may have once been Nazis. How am I supposed to believe your wealth is enough to buy any influence? I don't even know how much you have—or how little. What if this new millennium is all in your head?"

The Widow shrugged. "That is a risk you'll have to take."

"What if I choose to die with my convictions?"

"That's a very abstract notion. You don't know what it's like to have to choose. Let's say you were a homosexual man in Berlin in nineteen thirty-three. You're picked up by the Gestapo and they ask you to name other homosexuals. Would you give them the names or take the risk of remaining silent and facing the consequences?"

"I wouldn't give them the names of my friends."

"That's what you say now. You've never faced such a moment. I'd be inclined to believe that you would give in. We all would. Wouldn't you, Frank?"

"I wouldn't have been a faggot in Nazi Germany," Tyler said.

"I chose a disagreeable example. The same would have been true whether you were a homosexual or a socialist or a Jew—you couldn't tell them all by looking at them, and there were plenty of Jews who turned in other Jews, I assure you."

"There were plenty who didn't," Cecilia said. "Why even bother with me at all? I don't have anything to offer. I don't have a congressional seat or money or special expertise. I'm just a country doctor."

"You're one of us."

"No, I'm not. I hate everything you stand for."

"You're a part of the family, our own flesh and blood."

Cecilia didn't know what to say to this.

"She's your grandmother, for Christ's sake," Tyler said,

401

standing up from his chair, clutching the neck of the brandy bottle. "You were born down there at your own goddamned clinic."

Cecilia said, "No, that's not possible."

"Take a good look," the Widow said, raising her chin. "Don't you see the resemblance? I realize there's many years between us, but—"

"Hamilton delivered you," Tyler went on, pacing the rug. "Ask Janice Fremont. She was there. You and I were born just a couple of months apart. My dad and your dad were brothers. We're first cousins."

"It's not true. I was born in Seattle."

"Who told you that?" Tyler said.

"My father."

"He's *her* son." Tyler pointed the brandy bottle toward the Widow. "My uncle. He was just a kid when they all came over. Your dad was a little younger than mine. Your family name is von Meissner, got it? Your mother was from Haven, too. She was a Hugenberg, wasn't she, Gran?"

"Yes, that's correct. Erna Hugenberg." The Widow grabbed the bottle from his hand and set it on the coffee table.

"My mother was Betty Jones, and she was no Nazi."

"Quite right, she wasn't," the Widow said. "She had a disagreement with your father over your upbringing. I warned him against marrying her. I saw something rebellious in her nature."

"You killed her."

"I did nothing of the sort. She died of cancer. You know that. Not that it did us any good. Your father did the best he could with you, but the harder he tried the more you turned away. Natural, I suppose. The minister's daughter always turns out to be the wild one, doesn't she? So the Nazi's daughter grows up to have a career of her own and marry outside of her race! Well, it's never too late to change things."

"It can't be true."

"I'm afraid it is. I'm sorry if I'm not the grandmother you'd hoped for. I am what I am, and I love you anyway."

Then this was all her father's fault. He had arranged for her to come to Haven. "What did you do, bribe the Rural Physicians Program? You paid Tim Vandam, didn't you? You bought him off."

"Your father was all too happy to find a way to get you here at last. It was always in the cards, but I'm afraid we finally got you—ten years later than originally planned."

"Planned?"

"You were supposed to come here when you were nineteen," Tyler said. "*We* were supposed to get married. *We* should have had five kids by now!"

"Marry my first cousin?"

"It would have been perfect," the Widow said. "I know, you're thinking about inbreeding and birth defects, but Hamilton assured me that's not always the case and that you two were a perfect match. He's had your blood studied at his genetics institute down in San Carlos de Bariloche."

"I never gave him any blood."

"He took it when you were an infant, before you left Haven. He's been studying you for years, mapping out your genetic code, comparing it with Frank's. The two of you together would produce the most astounding offspring. *Übermenschen.*"

"I won't have any part of it." Cecilia got up to leave, clutching her purse close against her belly. The gun shifted heavily inside.

"No one's going to make you do anything." The Widow rose. "All I ask is that you take some time to think everything over. The choice you make will determine your future. I would take it very seriously."

"I'm going."

"As you wish. Frank will show you to your car."

Tyler moved to take her arm, but Cecilia backed away.

"I can show myself."

She turned and walked into the foyer, grabbing her coat from the closet and heading out the front door. No one followed her. She resisted the temptation to look over her shoulder. She did not want them thinking she was afraid.

*If they want to shoot me, now's their chance, while my back is turned.*

She managed not to slip on the ice as she hurried out to the ambulance. As she climbed into her seat, she saw Tyler and the Widow standing at the front door. She started the engine and waited for it to warm up and for the defroster to work.

While she was waiting, Tyler came alone down the walk. She opened her purse and palmed the pistol. Tyler rapped his knuckles against her window.

She rolled it down. "What do you want?"

"Just to tell you to drive safely, cousin. Give me a kiss?"

"Go to hell."

# Chapter 44

Halfway down the hill road, her radio beeped an alert. She picked up the mike and said, "Mak here. What is it?"

"Cecilia? It's Janice. Where've you been?"

"It doesn't matter. What's going on?"

"They need you at the jail. It's an emergency. Something's happened to Bonnie. You'd better hurry."

"Where were you?" Monroe said.

She ignored him and knelt to examine Bonnie. The belt had been removed from around her neck, but the markings remained. She had no pulse, and her skin was already cool to the touch. Her features were blue from the cutoff of oxygen.

Cecilia thought of Martin and Eva under the blue spruce.

"She was still alive when I pulled her down," Monroe said. "I tried CPR on her, but it was no use."

"How did this happen?" Cecilia said.

"She used her own belt. Hung it from the light fixture and stepped off the bed. I heard something and came running in and pulled her down."

"Why'd you let her have her belt?"

"How was I to know what she was going to do?" Monroe said.

Tyler came into the jail, still wearing his civilian clothes and reeking of alcohol.

"Frank, I'm sorry," Monroe said.

"I guess I should have seen it coming," Tyler said, kneeling down. "She's been acting funny recently. Frankly, Cecilia, I'm not so sure it really was an accident. Her hitting Mike, I mean."

"Why would she do it?" Cecilia asked.

"I think she wanted to hurt him. Maybe he rejected her back in Boise, who knows?"

"I don't think they ever met in Boise, Frank."

"That's your prerogative," he said condescendingly. "We'll have to ask Mike, I guess, when he comes out of it. I guess you haven't had any word, what with the phones."

"No, I haven't. Look, I've got to fill out a death certificate, and can you guys get on the radio and get Joe Doyle over here? Jesus Christ."

Cecilia didn't know what to think. Bonnie might have actually killed herself, despondent either over what she had done to Mike or over the fact that she had the Huntington's gene. More likely, Monroe had done it to her. A tidy way of wrapping up a case and dispensing with someone who had outlived her usefulness.

God, I'm getting cynical. Mike would be proud of me.

Cecilia closed Bonnie's eyelids, feeling sorry and sick to her stomach.

*I'm the cause of all of this. It's all about me.*

"How's your grandmother going to take it?" she asked Tyler.

"Take what?"

"She and Bonnie were close, weren't they?"

406

"Oh, yeah. I'm sure she'll take it hard. Real hard." He shook his head. "Why don't I go call Joe Doyle—radio him. Be right back."

"Aw, gross!" said Joe Junior. "Dad, check out her face!"

Cecilia had been working on the death certificate. Monroe and Tyler had already excused themselves, going back out on the street since they no longer had any prisoner to guard. She was taken unawares by the arrival of Joe Doyle, Vicky, and the boy.

"Joe, get the kid out of here," Cecilia said.

"She peed her pants, too!"

"Come on, Cecilia," Doyle said. "He's going to inherit the business someday. Might as well get him started."

"Joe, I mean it."

"It's not like it's my first one! I've seen tons of dead people."

"Joe Junior!" Vicky admonished. "Hush!"

Doyle laughed nervously. "It's all right, Cecilia. If he promises to be quiet . . ."

"Get him out." She was firm.

"You can't make me! You're not such a big deal."

Cecilia stood and stared the kid down. "I'm bigger than you. If you're going to inherit your dad's business, maybe he should teach you some respect for the dead. Do you know who that is over there? That's Bonnie, who used to feed you buffalo steak and apple pie and plenty of it, I'll bet. She was a real person, and she suffered horribly."

"Cecilia," Vicky said, "this isn't your business to—"

"I wouldn't wish what happened to her on anybody," she continued, unabated, trying to put the fear of God in the boy. "You take another look at her. Take a good, hard look, and think of all the nice things she ever did for you, Joe Junior. This isn't some cartoon."

"Cartoons are for babies."

"And you're acting like one."

"Am not! Dad, tell her to shut up!"

Cecilia snapped her attention to Doyle as if daring him to say something. He opened his mouth, but nothing came out.

" 'Shut up' is not a nice way to talk. Maybe you've never been taught respect for anyone, living or dead. When was the last time you dad gave you a good spanking?"

"Cecilia, that's enough!" Vicky placed her hands on the boy's shoulders. Joe Junior smiled smugly. "You're scaring him."

"I'm finished. I'm sorry. You're right, it's not my business how you raise your kid."

"Are you quite finished?" Vicky said.

Doyle continued to stand there, speechless.

"Yes, I'm finished. I'm finished writing out Bonnie's death certificate, and I'm finished with little brats, and I'm finished with spineless parents who couldn't care less if their kid grew up to be a little Hitler!"

"What's wrong with—" Joe Junior began.

Vicky quickly clamped a hand over his mouth. It looked like Joe Junior was biting her fingers, but she kept them there, smiling valiantly as tears sprang to her eyes.

"Good night, folks."

As she left the jail area, she overhead Doyle say, "Must be the stress," and Vicky, "Why didn't you do something?"

That was a good question. Doyle was one of the people in Haven whom others seemed to fear, yet he had stood there with his knees knocking as she ripped into his boy.

# Chapter 45

She walked toward the flames, her gauzy gown flowing behind her in the back draft, the hot wind singeing her flesh. A winged man rose from out of the coals, naked but for a pair of knee-high jackboots. His spiked tail swung madly around her, cracking like a whip. The boots fell deep in the ash as he came for her. His engorged penis jutted straight out, balls swinging between well-muscled thighs. A forked tongue shot out of the shaft, and as it grew nearer she saw the reptilian eyes on either side of the head. The shaft reared back like a cobra and struck between her legs. The teeth pierced her, and she felt the sting of venom. She cried out. The demon wrapped her in his membranous wings, enveloping her in a cocoon as he thrust deep inside her. He clamped his mouth against hers and breathed fire into her lungs. His yellow eyes stared deeply into hers, his chest heaving against her breasts as he drew out her last breath.

She had nodded off shortly after coming home. Her head felt as if someone had driven nails into it—all that tea, she assumed. She had only napped for half an hour, and she did not feel rested. She downed a glass of Alka-Seltzer at the bathroom sink. She looked awful, unhealthily so. She had to get out of Haven fast, before she turned into a witch.

She was not surprised to find the phone lines were still down. She was certain it was deliberate. The call from "Dr. Higgins" had certainly been a trick. They had not expected her to disbelieve it. They had wanted her to come to tea in a terrible funk, so she would be at her most vulnerable and might think she had no alternative but to go along with them. She had to believe Mike was still alive; for his sake she had to get out.

She knew how she would escape. The rocky bed of the Little Lost River would be the route. As long as the ambulance could navigate those rough forty miles, she could make it to Elliott and the highway and from there to Boise. It would not be easy, but it was the only way. The whole town would be gathering at the music hall at eight for the Haven Society. They expected her to attend, but it would take them a while to figure out what she had done. She would have a head start, the ghost of a chance.

She waited until seven-thirty before heading out to the Jackson place. Clark would likely be there; he wasn't going to go off to the meeting and leave Lewis unguarded while Tyler and Monroe were indisposed. She would be ready for him, though.

She drove up into their driveway, alongside Clark's pickup. She slung her doctor's bag over her shoulder as she went up the walk. Opening the bag, she reached inside, grasped the grip of the gun, and slipped her finger past the trigger guard.

She rang the doorbell.

"Who is it?" Clark Jackson bellowed.

"Dr. Mak," she said.

"You? What do you want?"

"I've come to check on Lewis, if that's all right."

She was afraid he wouldn't open up, but at last she heard the clink of the chain lock being undone, the *chunk* of the dead bolt being thrown back. She hoped she would be catching him by surprise, that he wouldn't be meeting her with a shotgun.

Clark opened the door, his shirt half undone, a tall beer in one hand. "Lewis is just fine. Did Frank Tyler give you permission to come see him?"

"Here's my permission." She brought up the gun with both hands, aiming it at his face. "I'm coming in."

Clark's beer slipped from his fingers and spilled foam all over the carpet. A cat sidled over and started licking it up.

"Hands away from your sides," she said. "Easy."

The corner of his mouth twitched as he obeyed her. "You're getting yourself into a heap of trouble, missy. I'd put that gun away, if I was you."

As he backed up, she stepped inside, kicking the door shut behind her. "If I were you, I'd keep my mouth shut. I'm aiming at your good eye."

"You're a doctor—you can't shoot nobody."

"Don't tempt me. Where's Lewis?"

"In the basement. I'll call him." He waited for her nod. "Lewis! Get up here!"

"Coming," Lewis called. She heard him plod slowly up the stairs. He stumbled over a cat as he came into the room, and his mouth fell open. "Cecilia! Thank God!"

"You little bastard," Clark said.

"You be quiet," Cecilia said. "I'm loaded with hollow-points."

"Shoot him," Lewis said.

"Only if he doesn't cooperate. We've got to get him out of the way for a while. What do you suggest?"

"Take him to the basement and tie him up," Lewis said excitedly. "We've got stuff down there that'll hold him."

"Good. You heard him, Clark. Down to the basement. You first, and I'll follow. Lewis, get behind me."

Clark muttered under his breath, leading the way down the hall and the rickety wooden stairs. Cecilia kept the gun trained on the back of his head. She wasn't sure she could really shoot him, but if he tried to surprise her it would probably happen.

Once he reached the bottom of the stairs, she had him stand in the middle of the room. The basement was cluttered—half workshop, half storage, a rack of guns against the far wall.

"Go for the guns and you'll be sorry," she said.

"I'm not doing shit," Clark said. "Not that it's going to do you any good. The two of you'll never get out of town."

"We'll see. Lewis, you got something to bind his wrists?"

"How's this?" Lewis grabbed a couple of heavy-duty dog leashes, snapping them taut. "They're good leather."

"Great. Did they teach you knots in the Junior Posse? I'll cover him while you truss him up."

"Hell, Lewis can't make a knot to save himself."

"You want to bet? Put your wrists behind you, old man." Lewis pulled the end of the leash through the loop-handle, cinching it like a noose around his grandfather's wrists. He wrapped the leash several times around the wrists and around the space between, tying it off with a series of knots that looked more than sufficient.

"Jesus, you're cutting off my circulation."

"That's the idea," Lewis said with glee.

"Come on, we haven't got a lot of time," Cecilia said. "What are we going to do, string him from a beam?"

"I got something better," Lewis said. "Jasper's cage."

"You little fuck!" Clark said.

"Shut up. On your knees, Gramps." Lewis kicked lightly at

the back of Clark's shins, and he fell onto his knees. "Now on the floor."

"Gently," Cecilia said, nervous.

Grumbling, Lewis helped Clark forward onto his stomach, his face against the gritty floor. He grabbed the second leash and secured Clark's ankles as he had done the wrists, then strung the end of the leash through his wrists, hog-tying him.

"You're going to break my bones," Clark said. "Jesus!"

"Tell me why you shot Raphael Abramowitz," Cecilia said.

"Orders."

"Whose orders?"

"Hamilton. Jim Hamilton. He said this Jew was coming after him, told us to go find him. Lewis was there, he can tell you."

"Lewis already told me."

"You're going to trust this little fuck?"

"What did you do with the body, Clark?"

"Doyle took it. He dumped it in the mine shaft."

"What about my friends from Seattle?"

"The Marsh boys ran them off the road. Now they're up there, too, in the shaft."

"I say we shut him up," Lewis said, tearing off an arm's length of duct tape.

"Okay, go ahead," Cecilia said.

Clark didn't manage to get out another word before Lewis slapped one end of the tape over his mouth and wrapped the rest three times around the back of his head.

"Okay," Cecilia said, dropping the gun back into her bag. "Where's this cage?"

"Under the stairs. We always kept the dogs down here in the cold weather, and it was safer to keep them in their cages. Jasper's has a bigger opening. I think he'll fit."

Lewis dragged the cage out and swung open the door. The blanket inside was dusty and covered with small black hairs.

"Looks a little small," Cecilia said. "It'll have to do."

Clark made muffled sounds of protest.

"If it's good enough for Jasper, it's good enough for you," Lewis said. "Cecilia, you're going to have to help me here. He's pretty heavy."

She grabbed one end, Lewis the other.

"Headfirst," she said.

It was a tight squeeze, but they got him in, pushing until his knees were barely inside. His head was pressed up against the back wall. He made a lot of noise. Lewis slammed the door shut and slipped the latch.

"You got a padlock?"

"Right here," Lewis said, rifling through a set of plastic drawers atop the worktable. "Rusty old thing, but it ought to work. Don't know if there's a key."

"Doesn't matter," Cecilia said. "They'll find him soon enough, and I'm sure they'll get him out somehow. Don't think they'll be too happy with him, though."

Lewis closed the padlock around the door. Cecilia gave it a yank. It held firm.

"Now," she said, "what are we going to do about your ankle bracelet?"

"I don't know. If we cut it off, they'll know."

Cecilia looked at her watch: 7:50. "We'll have to. Don't want them tracking us. But we'll have to wait until the meeting starts. Tyler and Monroe both go to the meetings, don't they?"

Lewis nodded.

"They won't know till they get back to the courthouse."

"I don't know. I guess so."

"We'll have to risk it. Let's go upstairs so we can keep a lookout until it's time."

Lewis followed her up and turned out the lights.

414

*   *   *

At eight o'clock sharp, they cut off the ankle bracelet with a pair of bolt cutters. It started beeping madly.

"Let's go," Cecilia said.

"Did they open the road?" Lewis asked as they headed down Davis.

"Nope."

"Then how are we getting out?"

"We're taking the riverbed. No snow there. I saw it."

"They'll come after us."

"It'll take them a while to catch on."

"We should torch the place."

"Excuse me?"

"The music hall. While they're all inside. Set it on fire and take care of everybody."

"Lewis, we can't do that."

"How else are you going to stop them?"

"I'm just trying to get out. We're going to Boise to meet up with Mike. Then we go to the FBI."

"How's Mike doing?"

"I don't know."

"Even if we make it to Boise, they'll come after us. They'll track us down. We've got to take care of them."

"By burning a thousand people alive?"

"They deserve it."

"No one deserves it. There's a better way."

"How else are we going to be safe?"

"We'll have to take our chances. I can't have a thousand lives on my conscience. I don't want to kill anybody."

"I wish they were all dead. They killed my parents."

"Not all of them. Look, it's not a point we're going to argue. We're not torching the music hall. We'll leave them to the

FBI. They'll send people out here and put an end to the whole show."

"What proof are you going to give them? All we've got is some crazy story they're never going to believe."

"You've got a point. But what could we possibly give them?"

"There must be stuff up at the Tyler house," Lewis said.

"We haven't got time to go look."

"If we don't give the FBI something, we won't have any protection. The Widow will send someone after us."

They were at the bridge. Not a soul was in sight. The music hall was far behind, hidden behind the twists and turns of Center Street. No one would see them. They could go down along the riverbank now and get away.

Lewis was probably right, though: It wouldn't do them much good. And the FBI would need hard evidence.

"Okay, we go up to the house."

# Chapter 46

The house and grounds were dark, lighted only by the glow of moonlight and the reflecting snow. Cecilia pulled up before the walk and threw the transmission into Park. They sat for a moment with the engine rumbling.

"What are we waiting for?" Lewis asked, his hand ready at the door latch.

"I think I'd better go in myself."

"You want me out here as a lookout?"

"No. If they come back up the hill, we'd both be trapped. Do you know how to drive?"

"Sure, no problem. I've got my license."

"Good. Now listen to me. Once I'm inside, you take the ambulance back down. When you get to the bottom, turn off your lights so no one sees you. Go off the road and drive down into the riverbed. Park under the bridge. If they come back, chances are no one will see you. You sit there and wait for me."

"You're going to come back down the hill?"

"It's the only way. If I hear them coming back, I'll sneak out the back of the house and get down as fast as I can. Wait for me. If someone spots you, you're on your own. You can get out of Haven and don't have to worry about me."

"I'll wait for you as long as it takes," he said.

"Don't be stupid."

"Just don't take too long, huh? If you can't find anything quick, just forget about it, all right?"

"Okay," she said. They shook on it. "I'd better hurry."

"Be careful. Remember who you're dealing with."

"Yeah, my own grandmother and my first cousin. If I get caught, I've got a better chance of getting out of it than you."

She was in a good pair of hiking boots, which made the icy walk less treacherous than it had been in pumps. The front door was locked, and she was not about to try picking it. She had brought the heavy steel-encased flashlight from the ambulance's tool kit. Turning away, she brought it down hard and smashed the front picture window. A gust of wind shrieked inside with the shards of glass, as if she had crashed through an airlock. She knocked out the remaining pieces that clung to the window frame like shark's teeth and vaulted delicately over the sill. No alarm sounded. If there was a silent alarm, she would still have a little time to look around before anyone showed.

She turned back to Lewis and gave him a thumbs-up. He gave her a quick wave and drove off.

Cecilia trained the flashlight on her surroundings. She was in the large living room, the dead Dr. Tyler, her grandfather, glowering at her from above. She could take nothing like that or the Herta von Möllendorff recordings. She needed physical evidence that would prove beyond doubt. Such things would be in a private place—the Widow's bedroom or a secret library or storage room, probably somewhere in the basement.

The Widow's bedroom would not be in the basement,

though, and she wanted to check that first. She went through to the foyer and bounded up the grand staircase.

The upstairs hall was lined with scarlet wallpaper on which were hung oil paintings and charcoal drawings far more accomplished than anything she had seen by Hamilton.

She began by opening doors along the south side of the house; the Widow would want a room that overlooked the town. Cecilia scanned each room briefly with the flashlight, but none appeared to reflect the character of any particular person, and she assumed them to be guest rooms. Each had masterful works of art on the walls. At the third room, she spotted one that looked somewhat familiar and went in to check it out.

It was a shadowy painting of a man somewhere between middle and old age, with bulbous nose, ruddy cheeks, weary eyes, and a thick, scraggly beard, clothed in dark seventeenth-century garb. She had seen self-portraits of Rembrandt before and recognized the face, though she had never seen this painting or any photograph of it. She could find no signature, and the frame bore no plate of identification—but the work itself was unmistakable. She doubted it had actually been purchased by the Tylers; it had probably been a gift of Hermann Göring or something, pilfered from some European museum during the war.

She had already wasted a good couple of minutes staring; she left the room and continued down the hall.

What she took to be the Widow's bedroom she found at the far end. Much larger than the others, it was really a small suite, with a front sitting room, the bedroom lying beyond through an open set of French doors. The drawers of the desk were locked, and on top everything was neatly ordered—phone, pad of paper, pens, letter opener, lamp—nothing of particular interest. The end tables around the antechamber were occupied by statuettes and gilded lamps. The furniture was well-kept Old World chintz—perhaps of value but not to Cecilia's taste.

She went into the bed chamber and opened the walk-in closet. The racks were hung with fine dresses and gowns, the shelves stacked high with hat boxes. It would take her too long to go through the boxes, and she was likely to find only hats. Most of the floorspace was taken up by shoes, though the Widow was no Imelda Marcos. Cecilia had no time for the closet.

She made a quick scan of the room, about ready to give up and go downstairs, when she spotted something. The top of the dark-stained dresser was lined with framed photographs, including the Widow's wedding photo and others that included the smiling face of the young Dr. Tyler–von Meissner. In the youthful Widow, Cecilia could not help now but notice the resemblance to herself. The thought would never have crossed her mind if she had never been told. She supposed Mike must have seen it at once in the newspaper photo. No wonder he had wanted to rush back.

She gathered up the wedding photo and two others of the doctor and slipped them inside her roomy coat pocket. The face clearly matched that of the SS doctor in the group photo. This was good, solid evidence, even if illegally obtained.

Still, it might not be proof enough. She had to go downstairs and look through the basement.

She imagined her father as a child, running through these halls, sliding down the bannister of the grand staircase—unless the house was so well ordered that such things were not allowed. Joe Junior came to mind. She wondered how many brothers and sisters there might have been, now moved away to all parts of the country to raise their own children the way her father had raised her brothers, inaugurating them into secret societies and trying to beat old-fashioned values into them. She wondered now for the first time exactly what went on at the lodge to which her brothers belonged. How many such lodges existed around the country, with how many members? They would be much more dangerous than an openly hateful group like the Klan. One probably met them on the street every day.

The staircase into the basement was tucked under the grand staircase, and the door was firmly locked. It was made of wood but constructed of thin panels, and it looked old. She planted a firm kick on the panel nearest the lock, and the wood splintered. One more kick and her hiking boot went through. She reached through the hole and opened the door from the inside.

The stairs were old and creaked under her feet. At the bottom, she found herself in another long hallway. The basement looked as if it had been finished in the fifties or sixties: walls lined with cheap, fake-wood paneling in need of dusting. The doors here were simple and nondescript. Behind one she found the boiler room and behind another, a bathroom with shower.

The third door opened onto something of an arsenal. A rack extending the length of one wall was filled with shotguns and semiautomatic assault rifles, all locked behind a couple of iron bars with huge padlocks. The steel shelving along another wall was packed with wooden crates with open tops. Inside some she found hand grenades. Others housed sticks of dynamite. Small cardboard boxes nearby were full of dynamite caps. Several tin cans the size of large coffee cans were marked simply X-379—CAUTION. The rest of the room was taken up by twelve gigantic plastic drums. She pried the lid off of one and shined her flashlight over the contents, some kind of bluish green crystals. Though it was unmarked, she took this to be ammonium nitrate, the volatile fertilizer that had been mixed with gasoline to make the Oklahoma City bomb.

Behind the fourth door was a kind of huge pantry filled with canned goods, boxes of powdered milk, boxes of crackers—

421

enough to feed a lot of people for a long, long time, if not very well.

The fifth door led to a large room lined with black filing cabinets along one wall. The opposite wall was lined with computers, a high-volume photocopier, a couple of fax machines. The back wall contained bookshelves full of tall bound volumes. It would take days to go through all the filing cabinets, and she had no time. The drawers were labeled with arcane catalog numbers of some kind, giving no hint as to what was shut up inside. She tried a few of the drawers and found them all locked. No amount of kicking was likely to open them, and she could never pick the locks. But she could tell the FBI about them—as well as the arsenal—should they want to think about drafting a search warrant. The ATF could get involved, too; they could have another Waco on their hands if all of Haven wanted to shut themselves up in the Tyler house.

She went to the bound volumes and began leafing through them. The first shelf was full of old issues of a newspaper called *The Haven American*, which apparently ceased publication in 1971, since none came after. Glancing at the editorials, she noticed the paranoid political leanings of a John Bircher. None of this would mean anything to the FBI; it was nothing that might not have been printed in any other backwards small town of the time.

On the second shelf, she hit pay dirt. They were scrapbooks of a sort—family albums, really—genealogical records of the families that had come over from Germany. The spines were labeled VON MÖLLENDORFF, GEBHARDT, VON MEISSNER, HALDER, JÄGER, MOLTKE, RATTENHUBER, DÖNITZ, SAUCKEL, VON HASE, LINDEMANN. . . .

She took the VON MEISSNER book to the computer table. She knew she was taking this with her, but she had to sneak a glance at what was inside. It opened up in the middle to a set of photographs, some in black-and-white, others in faded color. She recognized a copy of one of her own familiar baby pictures, taken in a studio, with pleated drapes behind. The caption, penned in neat black script, stated *Cecilia Elizabeth von Meissner (Jones), age nine mos.*

A few pages later, she saw a picture of herself a little older, with pink ribbons in her blond hair, playing with alphabet blocks in a crib with a baby boy in a crew cut. The caption here was *Cecilia and Frank III at play, September, 1968.*

At the front of the book was an elaborate family tree with photos above the names of those from the last century. The family's noble German ancestry was traced back to the 1500s, leading up to the photos of grandly dressed aristocrats and decorated military officers with huge Prussian mustaches and closely cropped beards. Ernst von Meissner (looking smart in his full-dress SS uniform with medical insignia and swastika armband) had married Anna Olbrich (this photo looked even more like Cecilia), who had borne him seven sons and two daughters. Page after page was devoted to the offspring. Turning to her father's page, she recognized a shot she had seen before of him as a young man. It was shocking to see the one of her mother, looking so plain and yet beautiful. All the "Jones" children were listed, with representative photographs taken during the grade-school years. Each of her brothers was there, looking altogether innocent—and there she was in that photo from third grade that she had always hated, her hair in French braids, her face covered in freckles, her smile prominently missing a tooth. This had been the year of her mother's death, though she could no longer remember if the photo had been taken before or after.

This book was coming with her.

On the third shelf were bound copies of a newsletter called *The Black Eagle.* The first issues, from the early sixties, were

done on a typewriter and mimeographed. The content was genuine, hate-filled Nazi propaganda, not unlike examples
Tawanda Neebli had reproduced in her series of articles in the
*Post-Intelligencer*. Had the FBI never run across any of this? Had
they never bothered to come on up here and check out the organization?

The more recent issues had a professionally printed look, in
full color, which had allowed them to improve on the original
masthead. Now, on either side of the Germanic lettering *The
Black Eagle* were two representations of their logo: a black silhouette of the classic American eagle clutching olive branch
and arrows, superimposed over a red-white-and-blue shield.

She had seen the logo before, long ago. All at once it came
back to her—what had really happened that day when her father had found her with what she had always remembered as a
big black bird bleeding all over the linoleum.

Her father had gone out to get cigarettes, and her brothers
were off at baseball practice or something, and she had been
left home all alone. She was drawn to her father's downstairs office, the door to which he always kept locked, and found it
open.

She entered the smoky room, crinkling up her nose at the
smell, and began looking at the books that were low enough
for her to reach. But they were all books for grown-ups, with
big words she couldn't read and no pictures. She tried putting
them back, and other books fell from the shelves, falling on her
toes.

She climbed onto his chair and opened the desk drawer. It
was cluttered, but she saw a lot of pennies thrown in. She
picked a few and held them tightly in her fist, thinking she
could buy candy with them. The drawer had been easy to pull
out, but she had difficulty closing it. She had to put all her

weight against it, and her finger got pinched in the drawer when she finally got it shut.

She was about to leave when her eyes landed on her father's bowling bag. This was the bag he brought out with him every Wednesday night, when she and her brothers were left with the baby-sitter. He had shown her his bowling ball before, and she wanted to see it again.

She opened up the bag, but it was dark inside and she couldn't see much. She tipped it over, and the bowling ball came rolling out. She reached in and grabbed his bowling shoes, which were in two different colors and looked funny. As she pulled out the second shoe, something else fell out, clinking onto the floor. It was a big, shiny ring.

She put the pennies in her other fist, picked up the ring, and placed it over two of her fingers. On top, it had a funny shape painted red, white, and blue, and over that was the black shape of a bird holding stuff in its claws.

"Fe, fi, fo, fum!" boomed her father's voice behind her.

She stood up suddenly, startled. "I'm sorry, Daddy, I . . ."

"Just what the hell do you think you're doing, young lady?"

"I . . . I didn't mean to, honest!"

"Put that thing down!"

He grabbed her by the wrist, wrenching her arm and pulling the ring from her fingers.

"Ow, Daddy, that hurts!"

"This is going to hurt even worse!"

Still holding onto her arm, he closed the door and pressed the button to lock it. He pulled his chair away from the desk, picked her up, and threw her across his lap.

"No, Daddy, please!"

"You're not getting out of this one."

He lifted up her skirt, pulled down her panties, and began spanking her bare bottom.

"Ow, Daddy, stop!"

"Oh, no."

"I'll never do it again, Daddy!"

"You bet you won't."

It hurt worse than anything, and pretty soon she was crying. He kept hurting her, and suddenly she began to pee.

"Jesus Christ!" he said.

"I'm sorry, Daddy!" she said through her tears.

The spanking stopped, but she felt his fingers slide down her bottom, to where she had just been peeing.

"Daddy, I'm sorry, please."

She felt a sudden, horrible pain as he stuck his finger inside her. She screamed, and he put his hand over her mouth.

"There, Daddy's not going to hurt you."

But it did hurt, and she kept screaming through his fingers, and he didn't stop, not for a long, long time.

When it was over, he let her go, and as she was pulling up her panties she noticed the red drops of blood on the floor.

"Here she is," someone said.

Cecilia turned around with a start, clutching the von Meissner book against her chest.

The fluorescent lights flickered to life. Frank Tyler entered the room in full uniform. After him came the Widow, Herb Monroe, and Joe Doyle.

"If I'd known you were so interested," the Widow said, "I would have kept the basement door unlocked."

Cecilia looked around the room, but it had no windows. Though she had the gun tucked inside her coat, she could not get it out in time to ward them off; both Tyler and Monroe had their sidearms on their belts.

"I thought you had more sense," Tyler said. "What's gotten into you? We've been straight with you. You don't have to go spying on us. We would have let you down here if you wanted."

"You forget how independent she is," the Widow said.

"Let me go," Cecilia said. She still couldn't shake the thought of her father stumbling in on her, and all that had come after. "I . . . I just had to know for sure. I had to see proof. That's all I came for, honest."

"You don't take me at my word? Your own grandmother?"

"Come on, Cecilia," Joe  Doyle said, "what ever made you want to spoil things, huh? Can't you be a team player?"

"I rather think she doesn't much care for our team," the Widow said. "Give her time, though. She'll come around. She doesn't have any alternative."

"Are you threatening me?" Cecilia said. "You'd want to hurt your own granddaughter?"

"No, no, you misunderstand me, my dear. I'm only talking about the choice you will make. We can allow you a great deal of time to decide."

The best thing to do was remain quiet, she decided. If she tried fighting them now, she would have no chance of escape.

"Take her upstairs," Tyler said, directing Monroe.

Monroe grabbed her arm gently and reached for the book.

"No, that's all right," the Widow said. "Let her have it. I want her to read it and get a better sense of her heritage. It's hard to turn one's back on one's destiny."

"Come on, Doctor," Monroe said, and led her out of the room and back up the stairs.

# Chapter 47

"What's your family name, Herb?" Cecilia asked. "I mean your real name. Halder? Moltke? Sauckel?"

"Lindemann," he confessed. At the top of the stairs, he turned to whisper in her ear: "You'd really better join us, you know. If you know what's good for you. I don't think they'll let you do anything else."

"Confidentially, I'm thinking about it," she whispered back. "I'm just trying to get the best bargaining position. That old bitch isn't going to live forever, but I don't want to be ruled by Frank."

"You want to take her place?"

"Maybe. I'd certainly look well on anyone who helped me."

"You're talking to the wrong guy."

"If you say so, Herb. You know, you're really much better looking that Frank."

"You think so?"

"Of course. You've got great buns."

Monroe's face turned bright red. He took her into the living room and sat her down on the sofa before the fireplace.

"What's taking them so long?" Cecilia said.

"Must be checking to see what else you were looking at."

Cecilia listened carefully but couldn't hear the sound of any-one coming up. The stairs were noisy, and she would know if they were coming. They were probably in a little confab, de-ciding just what exactly to do with her.

"I took some things from the Widow's bedroom," she said.

"Where'd you put them?"

"In here." She touched her coat.

"Better hand them over now."

She reached inside, touching the gun, then hesitated. Mon-roe's hand went instinctively to the butt of his sidearm.

"Don't worry," she said. "It's just some photographs."

Slowly, she pulled out one of the smaller pictures of her grandfather and set it on the coffee table. Monroe relaxed, and his hand moved away from his gun. He reached for the photo.

"I've got more," she said.

She pulled out the pistol, aiming it right at his head. "Shh. Don't make a sound. Hands."

Monroe put up his hands, a smirk crossing his face.

"You wouldn't," he said.

"I said don't make a sound."

She stood up slowly, keeping the gun trained on him with one hand while she held onto the von Meissner family album in the other. She could hear the others coming up the stairs.

"We'll have the Marsh boys remove her things up to the house," the Widow was saying.

Cecilia backed slowly out of the living room, into the foyer. Monroe slipped out of her sights as she neared the front door. She opened it and ran out.

"Herb, you idiot!" the Widow said. "Where is she?"

Cecilia went running down the front walk. Two sheriff's

trucks with the black eagle logo of the PCSD and the Widow's black Mercedes were parked out front.

"She pulled a gun on me!" Monroe was shouting.

"I'll get her!" Tyler said.

The Widow laughed. "Where can she go?"

Cecilia hoped Lewis was still waiting for her. If not, she would have to try to get out of Haven on foot by way of the Little Lost.

She ran around the first bend, out of sight of the house, and cut through the trees. The snow was high, but the recent warm weather had made it crusty, and her feet only sank a few inches. The woods were dark; she had left her flashlight behind in the computer room. All she had to see by was the little moonlight that filtered down through the treetops.

She heard the trucks starting up.

Her path took her straight down the hill, crossing the winding road. It wouldn't be long before they caught up with her. The steepness of the hill gave her momentum, and she ran as fast as she could through the maze of trees. As long as she followed the hill down, she would meet the riverbed.

"Cecilia!" It was Tyler's voice over the loudspeaker on his truck, coming from uphill. "Cecilia, stop! Come on out! We're not going to hurt you!"

*We're just going to eat you,* she thought.

"You can't go anywhere! We'll find you sooner or later! Give yourself up and no harm will come to you!"

She crossed the road again, hearing the trucks not far behind her. They couldn't see her yet.

"Gran wants you back! Cecilia, please!"

As she ran through the next patch of forest, she saw a glimmer of light from their headlights as they passed the bend behind her.

"Come on out! You can't outrun us!"

When she emerged onto the road again, the ambulance was there, heading up the hill. It came to an abrupt halt.

"Come on!" Lewis shouted from the window. "Hurry!"

She climbed in the driver's side and took over the wheel, handing Lewis the book and the gun.

"What are you doing here?" she asked, turning the truck around. The road was narrow, and she had to go halfway, back into Reverse, and then forward again before they were going downhill again.

"You were up there too long, and I heard them calling for you. Come on, go!"

She slammed on the accelerator just as the trucks were coming around the bend behind them.

"I thought you'd had it," he said. "When they came over that bridge—"

She had to slow a little to make the next turn. With the snow still on the road, they could easily skid off into the trees, four-wheel drive or no.

"I waited, though. I was just about to take off when I heard them calling."

"Thanks," she said, glancing in the rearview mirror and seeing headlights gaining on them.

After the next bend, the private drive joined the Haven Road, and she turned toward the bridge.

"Here goes," she said, taking a deep breath. She slowed to a crawl and headed over the rim of the riverbed. The angle was steep, but the truck handled it.

"They're going to follow us," Lewis said.

"I know," she said, clicking the headlights onto bright. "You got your seat belt fastened?"

\*　　　\*　　　\*

The riverbed was just narrow enough for them to navigate. It followed a shallow angle downhill, winding gently through the deepening ravine, bounded on all sides by snow.

Cecilia tried to avoid the larger boulders that might send them flying into the air. They had a good head start on the trucks behind them. It must have taken them a moment to decide whether it was prudent to follow. Now they were far behind, perhaps less eager about this route than Cecilia and Lewis.

"Jesus!" Lewis said, giddy with excitement. "You're either going to get us out of here, or you're going to get us killed!"

A gun blasted behind them.

"They're way back there," Cecilia said, trying to reassure herself, if not Lewis. "All they can see is our taillights."

The undercarriage scraped the top of a boulder.

"Careful," Lewis said.

"I'm trying."

Her fingers tensed against the wheel. Her heart was pounding like mad. Lewis looked over the back of the seat.

"They're gaining on us," he said.

Cecilia pressed down on the accelerator.

The ride was jarring, but she was keeping to the levelest spots possible. She had to slow to climb past a particularly large boulder, but Tyler and Monroe would have to do so, too, when they got here.

"More headlights," Lewis said.

"Must have radioed for help. How many?"

"At least three—no, four. Two of them way back there."

"You think they found your grandpa?"

"I don't care."

"Turn on my radio. See if you can find their channel."

The radio came on full of static. Lewis searched it until they picked up Tyler's voice.

"Careful, just aim for the tires," he was saying.

"Faster," Lewis said.

"I can't," Cecilia said.

They turned down a sharp bend in the riverbed, and it felt as if the truck might roll over.

Ahead of them in the headlights, the riverbed appeared to come to a stop, with only blackness beyond.

Cecilia slammed on the brakes.

"Stop!" Lewis cried out. "The waterfall!"

The wheels locked, and the ambulance skidded across the icy rocks, stopping just short of the edge.

"Goddammit!" Cecilia said.

She grabbed Lewis by his coat and dragged him out of the driver's side with her. They jumped to the rocks and scrambled up the side of the hill, through the snow, hiding behind a thick tree.

"You got the gun?" She glanced over the precipice beyond the ambulance, but it was too dark to see bottom.

Lewis handed it to her. "I can't shoot for shit."

The headlights were coming around. She aimed in their direction, firing a round at the first truck's tires.

She wasn't sure whether she had hit it, but for whatever reason the truck failed to slow down. It slammed hard into the back of the ambulance. The ambulance was sent over the rim, plunging nose-first into the void. The sheriff's truck only came to a stop after its front tires had landed over the edge. It rested there for a moment, hanging partway over.

It was Tyler at the wheel. He was trying to open his door, but it was stuck, jammed shut by the impact. Joe Doyle, beside him, managed to scramble out the passenger door, onto the rocks, but Tyler was still trying to get out his way. His eyes met Cecilia's, and he froze for a moment.

The second truck, Monroe's, slammed into Tyler's. With

Tyler hanging half out the window, his truck went sailing over the cliff end over end.

Cecilia heard his scream all the way to the bottom, where his truck fell hard against the ambulance.

Monroe's truck didn't go over. The others behind managed to come to a stop. Monroe got out wielding a shotgun. Joe Doyle, on the other side of the riverbed, had a handgun. Jason and Ted Marsh got out of the other two trucks with rifles.

"Stay back," Cecilia said to Lewis.

She stepped out from behind the tree, aiming at Monroe.

"Anyone fires, Herb's going to die," she shouted. "I've got him in my sights."

"Now that doesn't sound very friendly, Cecilia," Joe Doyle called. "Put your gun down and come with us."

"No way, Joe. You put yours down, all of you. I won't have any problem killing Herb here. I'm serious."

Monroe dropped his gun; the others kept theirs aimed.

"You'd kill an unarmed man?" Monroe said.

"I sure would, and I'm going to in about three seconds if you don't call them off."

"Boys?" Monroe's voice was a tremolo.

*They can't shoot me,* Cecilia was thinking. *I'm the Widow's granddaughter, heir to the throne. One of them shoots me, they'll have to take the consequences, from* her.

"Do I have to shoot first before you'll listen?" Cecilia said.

Doyle and the Marshes kept their guns trained on her.

"You just get back in your trucks and go back to town."

"You got Lewis Jackson with you?" Jason Marsh called.

Cecilia wasn't going to answer.

"We found Clark in their basement. He's dead."

"We didn't kill him," Cecilia said.

"Yes you did," Jason said, keeping his rifle aimed straight

for her. "You gagged him pretty good with that tape. He must have got sick to his stomach. He threw up and choked on it."

*Jesus,* she thought.

"We're bringing the two of you in."

"Herb's going to get it in the head in a few seconds if you don't all hop in your trucks and go back."

"I don't think you'll do it," Jason said.

"Don't tempt me."

"For Christ's sake!" Monroe shouted. "Do what she says!"

"If you let us go, no one's going to know how it happened," Cecilia said. "You can tell the Widow we just got away."

"What about Frank?" Jason said.

"It wasn't our fault."

"She's right," Monroe said. "We just tell the Widow we ran across the ambulance, and it was empty. Tyler slammed into it and went over the edge. She won't know any better!"

"*You* ran into *us,*" Doyle said. "You pushed him over!"

"It was an accident! Come on, guys!"

Cecilia had a pang of uncertainty—perhaps they were willing to sacrifice Monroe.

"I've got fourteen rounds in here," Cecilia said. "It's a semi-automatic. Once I've done Herb I might take out any one of you before you can get me. And if you get me, you'd have hell to pay from the Widow."

Everyone was silent for a moment, breath coming out as mist.

"Okay," Jason said, lowering his rifle. Ted Marsh followed suit. "Joe, put your gun down. Put it *down,* Joe."

Reluctantly, Doyle lowered his pistol.

"Leave your guns on the ground. You've got plenty more back home."

They threw their guns off into the snowdrifts.

"Good boys. Now get in your trucks and go back."

Joe Doyle limped back to Jason Marsh's truck. Monroe got in with Ted Marsh. Cecilia kept the gun trained on them until they had turned around and disappeared behind the last bend in the riverbed. She listened until the sound died out in the distance.

"Jesus," Lewis said. "Do you think that's true?"

"About Clark?"

Cecilia put the safety on and put the gun back in her coat. "I don't know. Somehow I doubt it."

Lewis shook her hand. "Thanks for helping me."

"Don't thank me yet," she said. "We still have to walk all the way down to Elliott. I don't know how many miles we got left, and I don't know about you, but I'm freezing my ass off."


They climbed carefully down the side of the ravine to where the two trucks lay smashed one atop the other. Tyler's upper body was hanging out the window of his overturned truck. The weight of the truck had crushed the rest of him.

"Cecilia," he said. Blood oozed from his mouth and down the side of his head. One of his eyes was swollen shut, but the other stared at her fixedly.

"Frank?"

"I can't move. For Christ's sake, help me!"

"It's too late, Frank," she said, staring up at him.

"Then shoot me."

"I can't."

"Go on. Shoot me in the head. Execution style."

"Sorry, Frank."

He began to laugh, then coughed miserably on the blood. "You and I . . ."

"You and I what, Frank?"

"Were made for each other. Gebhardt . . . experiment . . . made for each other."

436

"Frank?"

He made no more sound. She climbed up on top of the wreckage, grabbed his arm, and felt for a pulse that didn't come.

"Is he dead?" Lewis asked.

"Yes, he's dead."

"Good. What was he talking about?"

"I don't want to know."

Cecilia climbed back down. She smelled gasoline and was worried about an explosion. She saw, however, that the ambulance had not been entirely crushed and that one could crawl inside.

"What are you doing?" Lewis said.

"Looking for the book."

She climbed carefully into the wreckage of the front seat and saw it lying right there amid the broken glass and shards of plastic. She grabbed it and made a hasty retreat, backing far away from the wreckage.

"I thought it might explode," Lewis said.

"Yeah, me, too."

"Let's torch it." He held up a packet of matches.

"No. Frank's dead, and we don't want to start a forest fire. Just leave it."

"Okay," he said, dejected.

"Come on, kid. It's a long walk down to the highway."

# Chapter 48

It was several hours later before they heard the dull roar of the
Salmon River telling them they were nearing Elliott. The book
grew heavier by the mile, and they took turns carrying it. They
spoke little and tried to keep up a good pace, looking over their
shoulders every now and then to see if anyone was following.
They saw no one.

At the confluence of the tiny Little Lost and the big Salmon,
they climbed up the steep ravine but kept sliding back in the
snow. Cecilia's legs felt like rubber; it was the most difficult
part of the trek, but eventually they made it up.

She never thought she would be so happy to see the glow of
the plastic sign: ERNIE'S SELF-SERVE GAS & FLY STORE. The fluorescent lights above the pumps were alight as well, and the
lights of the store were on. The rest of Elliott was dark.

"We made it," she said, gasping for breath as Lewis struggled to make the last few steps up the ridge.

"Are they open?" Lewis was winded, too, leaning forward
and resting his hands on his knees.

"Looks like." She glanced at her digital watch: 3:37 A.M.

A truck whizzed past along US 93, buffeting them with a cold gust of wind in its wake.

Cecilia put her arm around Lewis's shoulders, and together they walked, bedraggled, up the stoop and into the shop.

The old man was behind the counter, listening to some late-night talk-radio program, cleaning his fingernails with the blade of his pocketknife. He glanced up at them, out the window, and back at them. He frowned, puzzled.

"Where in tarnation did you come from?"

"Our car broke down up the road," Cecilia said.

"Don't look like you been walkin' on the road. Don't I know you from somewheres? You, boy, ain't you from around here?"

"No, sir," Lewis said, looking away, grabbing a bag of tortilla chips and staring at it.

"Can we just warm up for a bit?" Cecilia said.

"Go right on ahead. You want some coffee?"

"Love some."

"Cream and sugar?" The old man chuckled.

"Skim milk," she said.

"Don't have no skim milk. Half 'n' half."

"That'll be fine."

"I'll have some, too," Lewis said.

"You two brother and sister or somethin'?"

"No," Cecilia said, watching him pour the coffee sloppily.

"Damn," he muttered as it spilled over his fingers. "That's hot coffee."

"That's what I want."

"You take it black, son?"

"Hmm?" Lewis kept his face turned away. "Half 'n' half."

"I reckoned as much. I'll just pour a little for myself here. Nice and black, that's how I like it."

"You stay open all night?" Cecilia asked.

"Have to. Only gas station for miles. Do good business. Here you go. Cream for the lady, and cream for the lad."

Cecilia grabbed both cups and handed one to Lewis.

"Buck fifty."

"Run me a tab," she said. "I think we'll get some food."

"All righty."

She burned her lips on the coffee, decided to nurse it a while. Lewis was off on the other side of the store.

"What's that you got there, little lady?"

"A book."

"I have a look?"

"No."

"Aw, come on."

She ignored him, looking at the stacks of snack food. He turned back to his radio show.

She found Lewis among the frozen foods, eyeing burritos.

"You got a mike?" Cecilia called.

"A what?" the man said.

"Microwave."

"Yeah, I got one."

"Looks good," Cecilia said to Lewis. "I want some, too."

He grabbed a couple of mild ones, and she grabbed a couple of hot. They brought them up to the counter and ripped open the ends. "We'll have these. Just stick them in there on high for ten minutes."

"I know what to do with them," the man grumbled.

A caller on the radio was venting himself to the host:

*"I'll tell you straight, I used to be a liberal. I mean, I even voted for Carter. Embarrassed to admit it."*

*"What were you smoking?"* the host asked.

*"But I'm telling you, this country's going to hell in a handbasket. I'm tired of seeing these immigrants come in and work for peanuts. I mean, I was a computer programmer, and my company laid us all off.*

440

*Were they going out of business? Oh, no, they replaced us! They brought in these Indians—"*

"You mean India Indians—"

"That's right! They were willing to work for half my salary, so me and all the rest, we got the boot. Two weeks' notice, and we had to train our own replacements!"

"Now that's just not fair."

"You bet it's not! I been out of work for two years now, and I got a wife and two kids. What am I supposed to do? I'm being discriminated against! I'm a middle-aged white male, you think anyone's going to hire me? All they want is women and blacks and foreigners. I tell you, I can't find work, and I got a master's degree and twenty years' experience!"

"So, tell me, how are you voting on November fifth?"

"Conservative all the way. They're the only ones who're going to fight for me. The liberals would rather protect some dumb owl. We got to get rid of these quotas and laws that give special privileges to minorities, and—"

"I hear you, I hear you—"

"I'm better qualified than any woman, and I deserve to get paid what I was getting before. This girl at the unemployment—she put me in a job training program. You know what they tried to train me for? Tap dancing! I kid you not!"

"Caller, I think you're pulling my leg."

"What do they expect me to do, tap dance on the street corner and beg for change? I was making fifty grand doing what I was doing. Where am I going to find another job like that? You bet I'm voting conservative. Time to turn this country around. Too many special interests. We got to bring our values back."

"I'm with you, caller. . . ."

"Here you go," the old man said, handing them the burritos on paper plates, with plastic forks and knives and paper napkins.

He had taken the burritos out of the wrappers so they looked alike.

"Which are the mild?" Cecilia asked.

"Those two."

"Here, Lewis." She handed them to him.

"Lewis! Why, I should have known!" the man crowed. "You're that Jackson boy from up at Haven."

"No, sir," Lewis said.

"Yes, you are. And you, I know who you are, you're that new city girl up there, that doctor, ain't you?"

"You must have me confused with someone else," she said, slicing into her food.

"No I don't. Where's that husband of yours?"

She didn't fall for the bait.

"You couldn't have come down from Haven, though."

"I told you, we had car trouble. I don't even know where Haven is."

"It's up that road a piece, there. You can't see it, 'cause it's under all that snow. But I know who you are, you can't fool me. You were headed back up there, weren't you?"

"I don't know what you're talking about."

"You took a little trip out of town, is that it? You and this boy, while hubby sleeps away all alone in his bed. Robbing the cradle, are you?"

"You have us confused. We were on our way to Twin Falls."

"Twin Falls, eh? Whatever you say, missy, whatever you say." He gave her a wink. "You need a lift back to your car?"

"No, thanks. It's dead."

"My boy Hollis can take you back down the road. I'll ring him up, raise him out of bed. He'll do it for ten dollars."

"I said, no thanks. Our car threw a rod. You can have it for scrap if you want, up the road about five miles. We're going to hitch from here. You got some paper and a fat marking pen?"

"I can sell you some."

"Fine."

The old man turned up the radio.

*"Go ahead, caller, you're on the air. . . ."*

*"Yeah, I just want to say I agree one hundred percent with that last caller. I'm sick and tired of all these—"*

# Chapter 49

It was nine o'clock Thursday morning, the seventeenth of October, when they reached Boise. A trucker had seen their sign and picked them up in front of the gas station. He allowed them to climb into the cramped quarters in the back of his cab, and they fell right asleep, huddled together for warmth. When they got to the city, Cecilia asked him if he could drop them off at a car rental agency; he managed to spot one on his way down Broadway Avenue and dropped them off on the agency's doorstep.

They rented a Ford Taurus on Cecilia's American Express and searched the complimentary Boise street map for the location of St. Luke's Regional Medical Center.

Cecilia leaned forward into the tall reception counter and felt the butt of the gun press against her stomach. She had stuck the barrel down her pants; it was hidden by her coat, but it was not terribly comfortable. She was glad it had not set off any alarm when they entered the hospital.

"Can I help you?" asked the perky reception clerk.

"Yes, we're here to see my husband. His name's Michael Mak. He was flown in and put in ICU a couple of days ago. I don't know his condition. I was snowed in and couldn't make it down."

"Calm down, Ms. Mak. I'll check. Just one moment." The clerk typed on her computer keyboard. "I don't see anything."

Cecilia grabbed Lewis's hand and squeezed tightly, glancing around the reception area. The place was quiet, most of the seats empty. She had never seen a hospital look so barren.

"Dr. Saronica was his attending surgeon, if that's any help," Cecilia added. "I'd like to speak with him, if he's on duty."

"Bill Saronica's in surgery at the moment. I'm sure he can talk to you later."

"There was another I spoke with—a Dr. Higgins?"

"Higgins? Unless I'm mistaken . . ." The nurse leafed through a roster on her clipboard. "No, we don't have a Dr. Higgins."

"That's what I thought." Her hopes rose. Dr. Higgins and his phone call had been phonies after all. Chances were good that Mike was still alive.

"Why don't you two just have a seat and relax? I've buzzed the ICU nurse, and she'll be right with you."

"I want to know what's happened to my husband."

"I know, and I'm trying to get that for you. Please."

Lewis had already sat down in one of the vinyl chairs and was leafing absently through the current issue of *Time*. It featured on its cover a close-up shot of the conservative presidential candidate and asked, THE RIGHT MAN FOR AMERICA?

"Dr. Mak?"

Cecilia stood up. A husky nurse greeted her and Lewis.

"I'm Nurse Benson, from intensive care?"

"My husband—how is he?"

445

"Stable. We gave him a free upgrade this morning. He's doing fairly well. Come and I'll take you to him."

Cecilia and Lewis followed her down the hall.

"We were hoping you'd make it," Nurse Benson said. "I've heard so much about you."

"I'm surprised he's up and talking."

"I'm sorry, I didn't mean from your husband, I meant from your father."

"My father? What's he doing here?"

"He's been here since yesterday. He was here all night, in fact. I told him to go find a nice motel room and crash, but he wouldn't budge. When your husband's condition was upgraded, I finally persuaded him to go take a break. He went out to find some breakfast fifteen minutes ago. You just missed him."

"Is he coming back?"

"Said he was."

"Was anyone with him? My brothers or anybody?"

"No, he's alone."

"Has he been acting strange?"

"Well, he seems under a lot of stress," Nurse Benson said. "One of the male nurses told me he stumbled onto your father at the bathroom sinks, weeping."

"That doesn't sound like him," Cecilia said. "I've never seen him cry."

"Well, he's very concerned about his son-in-law, obviously."

"Are you sure we're talking about the right guy? A tad shorter than me? Husky build? Salt-and-pepper beard?"

Nurse Benson nodded. "It's also been frustrating for him that we can't let him in to see Mike. Not immediate family."

Cecilia was glad they hadn't allowed him in. She was suspicious about why he had come all the way here from Seattle in the first place. The only way he could know about Mike was if someone in Haven had contacted him. He could have been sent here on a mission, could be up to no good. She wondered if he was really coming back after his breakfast. In a way, she hoped he was not; she had been telling herself she never wanted to see him again.

They reached the entrance to the ICU and the sign that told them no unauthorized personnel were allowed beyond this point.

"Your friend's going to have to wait out here," Nurse Benson said, indicating the chairs in the ICU waiting room.

"I don't get to see Mike, either?" Lewis said.

"Afraid not," Cecilia said, and she gave his hand another squeeze. "But I'll tell him you came. He'll be glad. When my father shows up, you ask one of the nurses to get me, all right?"

She scrubbed her arms and face clean, and Nurse Benson gave her a clean smock and pants to put on.

Mike was in a large, dim room with other noncritical cases. He lay there flat, breathing with the assistance of a mechanical ventilator, a nasogastric feeding tube up one nostril and taped to his upper lip. The cuts to his face were stitched and healing. His head was no longer bloated out of all proportion. His hair was closely cropped. His eyes were shut, and he appeared unconscious.

Cecilia pulled back the sheet and saw fresh bandages over much of his torso. His arms were heavily bandaged, his left leg in a full plaster cast.

She stroked his head. "I'm here, Mike."

"He's on pain medication," Benson said behind her.

"You're going to be all right," Cecilia told him.

"His major nerves aren't damaged, but his ribs were damaged and his lungs aren't fully functional just yet. That's the

447

only reason for the ventilator. Dr. Saronica says he has a good chance of a full recovery, with time and some physical therapy."

"And there's no doctor here named Higgins?"

"No. Why?"

"Nothing," Cecilia said. "Just somebody's idea of a joke."

"Well, I'll leave you two alone. If you need anything, press the yellow button next to the bed." Benson left the room.

Cecilia sat in a hard plastic chair, holding Mike's hand and stroking his head. He didn't stir.

"Mike, I'm so sorry," she said. "My fault."

She found herself leaning against the cool metal sidebar, unable to keep her eyes open. She tried to fight it, but her eyelids persisted in closing, and her mind was going blank. The in-and-out pumping noise of the ventilator droned in her head. She fell gently against the bar and nodded off.

When she awoke, Mike was squeezing her hand. She opened her eyes to find his barely open, one of them red from burst blood vessels. He blinked at her—deliberately, it seemed. He would be unable to speak until he was unhooked from the ventilator.

"Mike," she said.

He made a soft grunting noise. The ventilator mask obscured the entire lower portion of his face, but the muscles of his upper face rose slightly, as though he were smiling.

"Lewis and I made it out," she said.

She tried to tell him all that had happened since Bonnie had struck him, but she didn't make it very far before he lapsed back into unconsciousness.

Some time later, Nurse Benson came in, saying, "Your father's back. Lewis said you wanted to know."

"Thanks." Cecilia felt a pang of guilt as she extracted her

448

hand from Mike's grasp. She did not want to leave him again. She would much prefer staying here, anyway, to going to see her father, but it was imperative that she find out what the hell he was doing here.

Lewis was asleep, lying across three vinyl seats. Cecilia's father was pacing the hall, and when she appeared from the ICU, she was met with the sight of his back as he headed away from her. He turned to head back and came to a sudden stop when he saw her.

"Cecilia," he said. He came closer, tentatively.

She made no effort to meet him. "Why did you come?"

"We have to talk." It wasn't his usual, gruff voice. It seemed somehow timid and frightened.

"So talk."

"Somewhere private."

"I don't want to be alone with you." Cecilia was terse.

"Outside, then? Nothing's going to happen to you. I'm not here to hurt you. I've hurt you enough already. Please."

She followed him to the nearest outdoor exit, keeping a safe distance behind. Once outside, she made sure he came no closer than fifteen feet. They were on a sidewalk at the edge of one of the parking lots. It was out in the open, and there were people about, getting in and out of cars. They could also be seen from many windows of the hospital. She felt a little safe.

"Why are you so interested in Mike all of a sudden?"

"I have to ask you to forgive me," her father said.

"I guess Haven's phones are working after all. Who called you? Who told you about Mike?"

"They wanted me to come down and make sure he didn't pull through. I thought I was going to, but by the time I got here, things had changed for me. I couldn't go through with it."

449

"I don't believe that. I don't believe you really care. You just know you'd never get away with it."

"I don't want him to die, Cecilia. I never meant for any of this to happen. I was in over my head. How could I say no to them? To *her*?"

"The Widow? I know she's my grandmother. I know everything. I even know what you did to me when I was a girl."

"I don't know what you're talking about." He sounded as if he had been taken off guard.

"Maybe you blocked it out, too. You don't remember that day when I found your Black Eagle ring, and you caught me down there in your office? You don't remember what you did to me with your finger?"

"Stop it," he said. "Cecilia, I need your help. I'm in big trouble. I couldn't go through with it. I couldn't kill Mike. They put the burden on me. It was decided by a vote. I had to come down here and do it. They said I made too many mistakes with you, that I'd let you grow up out of control so that you were beyond their reach. They wanted to beat you down any way they could until you were theirs. They didn't expect you to call Medflight. Mike wasn't supposed to make it. Then they'd have you. They made me come down here to finish it. But I can't."

"I still don't buy this change of heart, Dad. You've lied to me your whole life. How am I supposed to believe you now?"

"Cecilia, listen. I've always thought you went beyond my control, through no fault of my own. I thought I'd done the best I could with you. But on the way down here, I got to thinking, maybe that was what I wanted of you all along. Maybe somewhere deep down, I wanted you to be able to break free and escape like I've always wanted to do. I never had the guts. I was always too worried they would come after me. Now it's too late. I've fucked up. I'm in deep shit. You've got to help me."

"Dad," she said, "I don't think I can ever forgive you, but the first thing you can do is come with me and Lewis down to the FBI office. I want you to tell them everything you know about Haven, about the Black Eagles, anything else you know."

"I can't," he said.

"Maybe they can offer you some kind of protection. This has to come to an end. Maybe you wouldn't help them with Mike, but think of all the other murders they've committed. I bet it's a lot more than I know about. Bonnie Gillette told me where the bodies are buried. You give the FBI reason enough to obtain a warrant to search the old Olbrich mine shaft, you'd be doing the world a lot of good. Those involved need to be prosecuted. You can be a material witness, probably."

"Okay, I will. What other choice do I have? Once they know I failed, they'll be asking me to pay. I could even end up in the mine shaft myself. So could you, and Lewis."

"Maybe I should call the FBI now and have them meet us here. I want them to hear your story, and I want them guarding Mike. If the Widow knows you failed, she could send somebody else to do it, couldn't she?"

He nodded. "Go call. I'll talk to them. I want you safe, and I want you happy. I want Mike to stay alive. Maybe someday you'll be able to stop hating me."

She didn't want to break the news to him that it was much, much too late for that. She needed his cooperation. But she could never forgive him. He had lied and schemed and allowed too much to happen for far too long. She could never feel sorry for him; he was no victim of anyone but himself. She doubted whether he'd had a complete change of heart; she was certain he was still the same old Dad, still bigoted and wrongheaded. The sooner he was put in the FBI's protective custody, the better.

Their war was at an abrupt end, with him in full retreat.

Strange, though, that she had never really hated him until now.

"Come on," she said, feeling as if she were the parent and he the child, "let's go back inside."

# Chapter 50

*From the Seattle* Post-Intelligencer, *October 24, 1996 (page A1):*

### THREE FEDERAL LAWMEN
### KILLED IN IDAHO STANDOFF

HAVEN, Id., Oct. 23 (AP)—Three federal law-enforcement agents were shot and killed here as the standoff with a group of alleged white supremacists continued into its second day.

The agents—two from the Federal Bureau of Investigation and one from the Bureau of Alcohol, Tobacco, and Firearms—were part of an abortive raid attempt on the house in which members of the group have barricaded themselves. The group—some of whose members are wanted on federal murder and conspiracy charges—is believed to be armed with illegal semi-automatic rifles in addition to explosives.

Special Agent Fred T. Fletcher of the F.B.I., who coordinated the raid attempt, said his agents would regroup.

"If no progress is made in negotiations," he said, looking grim, "we'll have to try again." He added that tear gas remained a possibility, though it is unknown whether any

*(continued on A23)*

*From the Seattle* Post-Intelligencer, *November 17, 1996 (page A5):*

### GERMANY SEEKS TO EXTRADITE
### EX-NAZI FROM ARGENTINA

BONN, Nov. 16 (Reuters)—The Germany Ministry of Justice said today that it would seek extradition of the alleged Nazi was criminal Albert Gebhardt from Argentina so he can stand trial for war crimes.

Mr. Gebhardt, who was a doctor with the rank of captain in the Nazi German SS, had until recently been a resident of the U.S., living under the assumed name of James K. Hamilton in the remote town of Haven, Idaho, according to a senior official of the Federal Bureau of Investigation. The connection, if any, between Mr. Gebhardt and Haven's neo-Nazi organization, the Black Eagles, is "being thoroughly investigated," the official said.

"It is unknown how Mr. Gebhardt originally gained entry into this country," the F.B.I. official said, declining further comment on the case.

### The "Devil of Dachau"

Mr. Gebhardt, who is believed to be in his late eighties, left the U.S. in September, settling in the Andean resort of San Carlos de Bariloche, where he has for many years kept a genetic research clinic, according to reports by ABC News.

An investigative team from ABC News, led by reporter Sam Donaldson, tracked Mr. Gebhardt to his Argentine home last week, surprising him on the street. Mr. Gebhardt freely admitted his identity but denied having committed any war crimes, saying he was only following orders and had no other choice.

He deferred any further questions to his attorneys. He is currently under house arrest in Bariloche, a move ordered as a "preventive measure" by federal judge Manuel Rojas, though no charges have been brought against him.

Mr. Gebhardt is accused of having performed so-called medical experiments on Jewish and other victims interned at the Dachau concentration camp during World War Two. He has been directly implicated in the deaths of several hundred prisoners there. His reputation among survivors of the camp earned him the title the "Devil of Dachau."

The notorious Nazi medical experiments were conducted by "fewer than two hundred murderous quacks," William L. Shirer wrote in *The Rise and Fall of the Third Reich*. Among these so-called experiments were shutting prisoners in airlocks and withdrawing the oxygen, subjecting them to gross extremes of atmospheric pressure, dumping them naked in ice water, shooting them with poisoned bullets, poisoning them with mustard gas, inflicting gas gangrene wounds on them, using them as donors for bone-grafting trials, and seeing how long they could live on a diet of salt water. Women were sterilized and men castrated. Subjects of the experiments included Jews, Slavs, gypsies, homosexuals, and others.

Several leaders of German Jewish organizations applauded the government's move at a news conference today and remained "cautiously hopeful that the Argentinian courts will approve the extradition," according to their spokesman. The Jewish leaders said they were requesting that Mr. Gebhardt's trial be televised live on German television.